Beguiled

The Tribulation Conspiracy

Beguiled

The Tribulation Conspiracy

JOANNE F. LYONS

Published by One Pearl Publishing

The characters in this book are purely fictitious. Any similarities to any one individual or actual organization are coincidental. Events have been compiled from several different well-known historic events to assist in the relativity of the topic. Although Space Ship One and White Knight actually exist, as does Virgin Galactic and the Spaceport in New Mexico, the flights and abilities depicted within this story are fictional as well as all other events.

ISBN-10: 1468039202
ISBN-13: 978-1468039207

One Pearl Publishing
"Publishing Pearls of Wisdom"
1700 Pierce Street, Suite 704
Hollywood, Fl 33020

A portion of the proceeds from the sale of each book is donated to divorce recovery ministries, helping the victims of shattered hearts to heal.

Distribution/Orders Amazon - http://www.amazon.com/

DEDICATION

This book is dedicated to the ninety-nine percent in America. I pray that we make it through these tough economic times and come out better on the other side.

Other Titles by Joanne F. Lyons

Non-Fiction

Healing after Divorce…It's About Time!
(Previously published under the title)
It's About Time! It's ALL About Time…time, love, and tenderness.

Healing after Divorce…It's About Time! Facilitator's Guide

Fiction

The Tower Apartments Series
The Tower Apartments: Andrew's Fury
The Tower Apartments: Drug Cartel

The Aging with Grace Series
Aging with Grace: The Formative Years
Aging with Grace: Growing Up in the Shadow of Camelot

Beguiled: The Tribulation Conspiracy

The Seventh Trilogy
Book One: The Seventh Portal
Book Two: The Seventh Gate
Book Three: The Seventh Gatekeeper

ACKNOWLEDGMENTS

I thank my parents for instilling in me a respect for education, and for enforcing schoolwork before play and television. I thank my high school friend for passing on her parents' higher standard: earn a college degree. I thank my parents for being flexible enough to pay for my undergraduate degree, even though it wasn't in their original plans for my life. Education and a thirty-two year career in education allowed me to retire while I was still healthy and energetic. Retirement has given me the time to be creative and to write non-fiction works, as well as several different genres of novels; and my chosen career has given me a steady pension so that I could do so. I thank my husband for his encouragement and for listening to many drafts. I thank God for orchestrating my life and placing these persons on my path and journey. And even though mentioned last, He is first and foremost of my acknowledgements. Without Him there would be nothing.

CHAPTER 1

Members of GUILE usually inherited their positions. In a few cases, they were carefully appointed when no heirs existed. All were considered good business men and women; they were ruthless. It was said that they made pacts with the Devil.

GUILE economists predicted the world economy was slowly failing. They wanted a global monetary system, like the Euro, and felt it would turn things in favor of the crony capitalistic GUILE members. But it just wasn't happening fast enough. They had to shake America up a bit; then everything else would fit into place.

The plan was in the works; it would happen soon. The blame would go to a militant group named Al-Qaeda. GUILE had carefully groomed them to be the scapegoat.

Global **U**nion of **I**nternational **L**eaders of **E**conomy was a perfect name for the group. The dictionary defined 'guile' as insidious cunning in attaining a goal; crafty or artful deception; and duplicity. All of these definitely described the members of GUILE and their behind-the-scenes scheming. Their manipulating management truly beguiled the world.

Spring
New York City

"Yes, Mr. Iran; we have taken all the demographic information and created a perfect profile for the kind of men you're interested in targeting. When the program our IT department wrote is run, it will identify your prospects by name, address, phone numbers, and even email addresses," the young advertising marketer reported.

"Great. Email the model to my office. We'll get back to you if we experience any problems with the program." He snapped his phone shut, ending the call.

Mr. Iran wasn't the boss of GUILE. Of course, Mr. Iran wasn't his real name either; it was only his code name. He wasn't from Iran and had never spoken Farsi a day of his life. He hadn't ever set foot in Iran and he wasn't a Muslim. He was just one cog in a large gear that made up the GUILE organization.

"Jeff, I'm expecting an important email with a demographic program attachment. Be on the lookout for it today," he said, walking past his executive assistant's desk.

"Yes, Mr. Jones." Jeff stopped typing on the keyboard and glanced his way. Giving the boss his full attention with eye contact was important. Jeff didn't know of his involvement with GUILE.

"I'm going to my tailors and out to lunch. I expect to be back in time for the meeting in the conference room at three." Jack Jones continued down the plush-carpeted hallway in his Bally moccasins made of goatskin.

Moments later, Jack was on the ground level. The special elevator was non-stop from his penthouse offices. His footsteps were soundless as his kid glove soles touched the green marble floor of the lobby. The security guard caught the movement from the corner of his eye. He tipped his hat as Jack passed by.

The assistant had called ahead. The limousine was waiting for Jack at the curb. The chauffeur stood beside the open back door.

Jack passed by the doorman and went straight to the car.

The driver, with his usual plastic smile, greeted Jack as he entered the backseat of the black sedan, "Good morning, sir. Where to?"

"To my tailors, Fred."

"Yes, sir," the chauffeur answered. He swiftly closed the door and took the front seat.

The downtown city traffic was backed up as usual. The ten-block distance took half an hour to complete, but it didn't matter to Jack. It was a beautiful spring day and he had lots to consider.

Back in the office, Jeff downloaded the new program. It required a password and Mr. Jones hadn't given him that information. He saved the .exe program on his computer and placed a copy on Mr. Jones' desk computer, as well. He was typing the agenda for the afternoon meeting when the phone rang.

"Hello, Mr. Jones' office. This is Jeff, his assistant. How can I help you?"

Calls never came directly into the office, but through the switchboard. This one hadn't been forwarded to Jeff's desk. It was on a direct-line level for the CEOs.

"Hi, Jeff. This is Bradley Lewis of Lewis Enterprises. May I speak to Mr. Jones?"

"I'm sorry sir. He isn't in the office at the moment. May I take a message?"

"Please tell him I called. He knows where to reach me."

"Okay, Mr. Lewis. Have a nice day," Jeff said, making a notation of the call and time before returning to his task of typing the agenda.

Uptown, the tailor greeted Jack with excitement in his voice, "Good morning Mr. Jones. Your suit is ready for the first fitting. We're glad you made the time to come in. Would you like some cappuccino before we start?" His clients usually didn't have time to come in for all of the fittings, but without the sessions the garment never fit the way the tailor wanted. At least, Mr. Jones appreciated his craft and made an effort to show up.

"Yes, thank you, I would," Jack answered, taking a seat on the black leather sofa.

The tailor hurried to the back room to retrieve the jacket, while the assistant brought a freshly brewed cappuccino to Jack.

"Thank you," Jack said, accepting the demitasse cup from the young woman. When he finished, he set it on the side table and walked to the fitting room.

The tailor was waiting with the new suit jacket. Jack slipped his arms into the sleeve holes. The tailor positioned the front, smoothing out any wrinkled areas. He made a few chalk marks on the dark worsted wool fabric to indicate pocket placement and button position.

"The sleeves will be in place in two days; please find time to come back for the next fitting, Mr. Jones."

"Okay, I'll make a note of that. I would like you to make me a special tuxedo jacket for an affair I'll be attending in a month. I'd like a shawl collar of satin. Could you show me some fabrics while I'm here?" Jack asked as the tailor removed the jacket under construction.

"Splendid," the tailor said, handing the coat to his assistant. He helped Jack into the jacket that he'd worn in. The tailor said, "Come with me," and led Jack into the fabric room.

The tailor pulled several bolts of fabric from the high shelves and displayed each on the cutting table. Jack ran his hand across the satins, selecting one of deep purple brocade for the collar.

"Would you like a cummerbund or waistcoat to match?" The tailor asked with a smile. He knew Jack Jones had a creative flair; he always tried to encourage it.

"Yes. Make me the vest this time," Jack said decisively as his phone vibrated in his pocket. He ignored the call and selected a fine black wool fabric for the coat and slacks.

Jack felt it extremely rude to interrupt one business transaction to handle another. Both tended to suffer. He knew the call could wait. It didn't require him to say, 'I'll call you back.' He just would.

Stepping back into the limo, he instructed the driver to take him to his regular restaurant for lunch. He glanced at the number on the phone display. He had time to return the call on the way. The sound-proof glass was closed as usual, affording him the privacy he needed.

"Yes, Mr. Egypt, we have the new demographic program. I'll run the models this evening and get back to you with the information in the morning." Jack closed the phone as the car pulled to the curb.

Jack stepped out of the car, dismissing the driver to get his own lunch.

The maitre d' was expecting him. "Good afternoon, Mr. Jones. I have your table waiting," he said, leading Jack to his usual seat.

Jack ate lunch there almost every day. It was a standing reservation. His friend, Claudia Lei, always joined him for lunch, if she had the time. He seldom ate dinner out, unless there was a benefit occasion and absolutely unavoidable. He preferred a meal prepared by his personal chef.

"Hi, Jack. Sorry I'm running a little late," Claudia said. The maitre d' pushed in her chair and laid the napkin in her lap. Her long raven black hair was striking against the pink silk dress she was wearing.

"I just got here myself," Jack replied. He requested the waiter to bring them each a glass of champagne. He always had a glass before lunch if Claudia was there.

"I stopped at the tailors this morning and selected the tux fabric for the benefit later this month. Have you selected your fabric with your seamstress yet?"

"No, that's on my list. I know she'll need several weeks to get it made and fitted properly."

The waiter came with their glasses of Bollinger. They toasted with the queen's champagne to the beautiful weather and friendship. They were wed to their companies. They knew they always would be from the moment they graduated from Cambridge twenty years earlier. They had met in England when getting doctorates in Business Administration and Finance.

Jack took a sip and closed his menu. "I chose a gorgeous purple brocade fabric for my collar and vest today. I thought it'd go grand with a similar hue for your gown. You always look so good in lavender, especially silk chiffon."

"Oh Jack, you're so incorrigible," Claudia said, shaking her head as she ordered her lunch selection, "I'll have the Stuffed Portabella with cream sauce."

"And you sir?"

"I'll have a cup of Crab Bisque, followed by the Chicken Marsala."

During lunch they made plans for the benefit, fine tuning the guest list. Everything seemed set. Claudia's assistant would handle the rest of the arrangements. As the time got closer, Jack knew Claudia would consult him on the matter again.

After lunch, they returned to their careers. Jack arrived at the office in time to freshen up for the three o'clock meeting. He splashed a little cold water on his face and blotted it with the warm terrycloth towel that hung on the heated rack in his private restroom. He extracted a fresh rolled cloth with stainless steel tongs from the steamer compartment beside the mirror. He thoroughly wiped his hands, leaving them feeling silky smooth. Nothing was as luxurious as steamed washcloths. He tossed the used cloth into the basket beside the door as he exited the room.

Jeff had placed the folder Jack needed for the meeting on the corner of his desk. Jack opened it. He reviewed the agenda, spreadsheets of data, and the names of the project directors that he'd be meeting with shortly.

The desk phone rang. Jack lifted it from the cradle and glanced through the floor-to-ceiling glass at the clear blue sky outside. He couldn't wait for this project to be completed and move on to the next.

"Mr. Jones, I don't wish to bother you, sir, but it's time for the meeting," Jeff kindly reminded him.

"I'll be right there," Jack assured his assistant. He walked briskly from his office to the conference room with his executive assistant in tow. Around the large table sat six directors, project folders in front of them, ready to answer every question Mr. Jones could possibly ask.

"Directors," Jack greeted, "We're due to go to production on this project in three weeks. Please tell me that all is going as planned." Jack looked each director in the eyes.

The Director General spoke first, "Yes, sir. It looks like all is on schedule. The product, sales promotions, advertising materials, and news releases are set and ready to go to market."

That was exactly what Jack Jones wanted to hear. The bottom-line statement was followed by each and every director presenting a report on their portion of the project.

When the meeting ended, Jack walked briskly back to his office. "Jeff, did the email with the attachment come through without a problem?" He wanted to move on to the next item on his plate.

The assistant placed his laptop on his desk. He walked around to take his customary seat as he answered, "Yes, it did, sir. I saved a copy on your desk computer. Would you like me to run any models for you? I can print out spreadsheets," Jeff offered, trying to anticipate his boss' needs.

"No, Jeff. I'll work with them later. If I need any printouts, I'll let you know." Jack didn't want to be bothered while he worked, so he said as an afterthought, "Jeff, when you've finished typing up the minutes to this afternoon's meeting, please distribute them to the six directors who attended today. I won't need to review them." He went into his office and closed the door.

"Yes, sir," Jeff replied, opening his file of notes on the desktop. He wanted to finish while everything was still fresh in his head. If he was lucky, he could have them distributed before leaving the office at five. He had plans for the evening.

Jack reviewed the new files on his computer. He found the one Jeff had saved. He burned a copy of the .exe program onto a disk so that he could work with it later at home.

CHAPTER 2

Manhattan

"I've prepared a marvelous dinner for you this evening, Mr. Jones. What time will you be dining and where would you like me to serve you?" Chef Jean asked.

Jack often changed his dinner locations, depending on the weather and his mood. Sometimes he ate at the large dining room table, even though there were no guests. Other times, he had dinner on the patio overlooking the city skyline. On many occasions, after releasing the cook from his duties of the day, he took it on a tray to his office.

"Since the time's changed, and it's such a beautiful day, I think I'd like to have it on the patio, Jean."

Chef Jean kissed his fingertips with a smack. "Splendid; excellent choice! Would seven o'clock be a good time, not too dark, not too light?"

"Yes, seven would be good," Jack agreed, already distracted by that night's task. He planned to run the demographic program which was written to search the globe over for young men between the ages of twenty-one and thirty, who were Muslim and dissatisfied with the current state of affairs in the world. This was the new profile for the type of men that GUILE wanted to hire to achieve their next goal.

Jack stepped out of his suit clothes. He slipped into the shower. He bathed twice a day: once in the morning, to make him alert for the workday; and once in the evening, to wash that world away again. He led two lives; he liked keeping them separate and compartmentalized. The shower was a psychological tool and expression.

The steam built up in the large glassed-in shower. The tiles beneath his feet became warm. He washed his hair with a high-end L'Oreal shampoo, breathing in the pleasant scent of the lather. His stylist recommended five years ago for Jack to gradually start dying his hair, keeping his youthful look and covering the gray. Who wanted to look old at forty-five? She assured him that this shampoo would preserve the color, leaving his hair soft and manageable. And it did.

He turned off the water and grabbed his heated towel. Wrapping it around him, he headed to the large walk-in closet/dressing room. Tossing the towel on a Romanesque stool, he dressed in casual clothes for dinner before heading to the patio.

"Tonight, sir, I have decanted a marvelous red wine to compliment the lamb that you'll be having for dinner," Chef Jean told his employer of five years.

Jack poured the wine. After swirling it in the large glass, he breathed in the aroma of plum and blackberries. "Excellent choice, Jean," Jack agreed, walking to the railing to look out over the city. "*Things will only get better*," he predicted before returning to his seat at the glass table.

Chef Jean presented the lamb entrée with two side dishes on a cart, which he had wheeled onto the patio tile while Jack was enjoying his first glass of wine.

"Will there be anything else, sir?"

"No, I'll be fine. You may go. I'll see you tomorrow," Jack said with a wink, lifting the cover from the serving dish. The steam and aroma wafted out, promising his taste buds that they were in for a treat.

"Very well; good night, sir," Jean said, before quickly departing the apartment. He pulled the locked door behind him and pushed the button for the elevator. It serviced the two penthouse apartments. He had never seen the owner, or any staff for the other apartment. Glancing around the vestibule as he waited, he noticed the fresh bouquet of flowers on the small console. Jean was about to take a whiff when the elevator doors swished open. Wasting no time, he stepped in.

Jack ate his meal while listening to instrumental music that soothed his inner being. It relaxed, refreshed, and in an odd way, energized him. He used his dinner hour to reflect on cultural achievements like music, fine art, architecture, and literature. He pictured it in his mind's eye, reviewing the historical data related to what he saw, as if he were watching a documentary. Jack found this activity to always make the perfect transition for him between his two lives.

He stood up from the table and took one last look over the city. The lights against the dark sky made it look like a different place as well. Jack had work to do. Walking out the front door, he locked down the elevator with his key and crossed the vestibule to the adjacent apartment—his office. He stepped into his kind of nightlife.

The apartment was sparsely decorated. Some would call it 'austere' and others might label it 'ostentatious use of space.' Either way, Jack liked its efficiency and purpose. It was his space and his alone.

He inserted the new disk into the computer and ran the .exe program, after entering his password: Iran. He selected the demographic data and hit Enter. The computer began calculating and finding the men they would use.

Walking over to the large stainless steel refrigerator, he removed a bottle of Evian. He drank down half the bottle in practically one gulp. He noted the time on the clock. It was eight-thirty. He referred to the other time-zone clocks that hung next to it.

"*Great! It's not too early*," Jack thought.

He placed his call. "Good morning, Mr. Turkey. I'll soon have a print out of the names we're interested in. I'll forward an encrypted contact sheet later today."

"Thank you. It's been a pleasure doing business with you," Mr. Turkey answered, pushing the end-call button and returning to his morning paper.

Jack closed his phone and finished his water. He tossed the plastic bottle into the half-full recycled bin.

Turkey

The sun was about to rise. A small group of young men bowed in prayer in the rear of the mosque. They had all, at one time, belonged to the International Islamic Youth League. It was a peaceable organization bonding Muslim men together. But like twenty-year old men all over the world, testosterone reigned over their angry hearts.

The prayers ended. They stood and rolled their small rugs.

"Arai, let's get some hot tea," Gani suggested.

The five men agreed and walked down the dirt road to the marketplace. They sat at a roughly hewn wooden table and ordered the tea.

"I was thinking we need a name for our group. You can't get anyone to recognize us without a name," Arai said.

"That's true," Mustafa agreed while he passed the hot cups of tea around the table.

"What can it be?" Gani asked.

"It should explain or define who we are and what we want," Arai answered.

They all nodded their heads in agreement.

"I'm not a morning person. I can't think right now. Don't ask me to come up with a good name," Derin admitted.

"Me, either," Ediz seconded Derin's statement and rubbed his eyes. They had both been out the night before until very late.

Mustafa suggested, "Why not use Muslim, or Islam, or Islamic, in the name?"

"Okay, what would go with it?" Arai asked, trying to encourage the brainstorming to continue.

Gani asked, "Do we want it to spell a word that has meaning, or just use words together in a sentence meaning something?"

"I think it can be both, or either," Mustafa answered.

They thoughtfully nodded in agreement again.

"I think we may have to work on it. It's not easy to find a name of significance," Arai conceded.

"I think it should include the nation of Islam, not just one country and one city," Ediz said, finally adding his two lira's worth.

"Maybe it could be World Islamic League?" Derin excitedly suggested, happy that he could think of something.

"I'm rather sure that exists already. Mustafa, go over and check the Internet to see if I'm right," Arai ordered.

Arai tended to always be the leader. He was the first to be disinterested with the youth league, and had broken his ties. Over time, he encouraged each of his other friends to leave as well. Besides, they had all expressed views in the past of wanting Muslims to take action; so why didn't they?

"You're right. It's taken," Mustafa confirmed, taking his last sip of tea and setting the cup on the table.

"There have to be other groups like us in every city in the Islamic countries. We need to unite. We can make a difference. And it doesn't have to always involve killing. Of course, that doesn't bother me, if it involves the infidel," Arai stated, slamming down his cup to make the point.

Those holding cups slammed them to the table in unity. They all stood; it was time for work. They had to part ways.

As they went their different directions, they were totally unaware that their names had made the computer generated list in Jack's office.

New York City

The program finished its search. The list consisted of young men who were, for the most part, more militant than the average Muslim. Dissatisfied men who wanted the one world religion to be Islam was one of the common factors in the data base. These men wanted to be the ones to make it happen now; they were eager to do anything for the nation of Islam.

GUILE was more than eager to use them for their own purposes.

Jack had a very long list of names, addresses, emails, and contact phone numbers for what seemed to be, almost every male in the Middle East and North Africa. He spent the next hour organizing lists from every major Muslim nation. After printing each, he bound them into binders and prepared corresponding computer disks of the information as well.

He selected the first three groups for action, matching them with three of his colleagues. Jack had contacted Mr. Iraq earlier. He had two more to call regarding their assigned group of men to recruit into the project.

He checked the clocks, then dialed the first.

"Hello, Mr. Pakistan. I know it's been a long night. I wanted to catch you before you go to bed for the morning."

"Thanks for considering our time difference. It's 4 a.m. as you noted; the night gamblers are retiring as we speak. What can I do for you, or rather I should ask, what have you done for me?"

"Both! I have your list prepared and will be sending it off to you shortly. You know what to do when it arrives."

"Yes, exactly. Good night." Mr. Pakistan closed his phone and walked to the front of the casino.

Jack selected another number on his phone. It rang.

"Good evening," Mr. Afghanistan greeted.

"I have your list ready. I'll be sending it to you tomorrow. Have a good sleep," Jack said, ending the call.

He had a few more ends to tidy up before finishing the assignment for the night. But first, he needed more water. He took some from the fridge; and as before, he drank half of the bottle before returning to the desk.

"*I'm glad the program worked. Well worth the million dollars we paid for it,*" Jack thought, as he returned to the task at hand.

He packaged each binder with its corresponding disk into three special courier packets for delivery. He double-checked each address label before placing them into a large shipping box. He removed the original program disk from his computer and placed it into the safe.

"*Can't be too careful; this is a priceless program,*" he thought, as he turned the tumbler.

Jack thought back on GUILE's Y2K project as he shut down the computer. The monitor blinked off. The city lights made an eerie moonlike glow on the marble floor. There were no shadows, but there was enough light to plainly see the door. Gathering up the box, he made his exit. He unlocked the elevator and pushed the button for its return. He smelled the fresh flowers while he waited the few seconds for the door to open.

It was the time of the evening when the security guard made his customary rounds to secure the building and check all the exits. Jack had studied his routine for many years. Even so, Jack didn't assume anything. He had checked his surveillance monitor of the lobby before leaving the penthouse office.

Jack walked through the lobby unseen. He entered the garage across the street, where he kept an old, but inconspicuous, car for doing his private work. He pulled out of the garage and turned toward the nightlife district.

Once there, Jack blended in with other vehicles and taxis, virtually going unnoticed. It took another hour to make all of his courier package drops. Afterward, he returned home and called it a night, thinking it one well spent.

CHAPTER 3

Spring
Monte Carlo, Monaco

Mr. Pakistan, a.k.a. Andre Grimaldi, closed his phone and walked to the front of the casino. As he did, he made one last sweep through the establishment. Most of the tables were empty. It was time to call it a night.

Just like Jack, Andre had never stepped foot in Pakistan; and he didn't speak Urdu, but his contact did.

"I'll see you this evening. Call if anything important comes up," Andre said to the assistant manager, who had just arrived.

"Yes, sir, have a good sleep," he said, answering the owner of the most famous casino in the world as he opened the door for him.

Andre walked into the moist pre-dawn air and on toward the portico where his limousine was waiting. Instantly he was whisked away from the sounds of slot machines, roulette wheels, and excited winners and poor losers, to his stately villa for a good day's sleep. He pulled on the edge of his bow tie; it fell untied against his shirt. Exchanging formality for freedom, he unbuttoned and loosened his collar.

Looking out over the Mediterranean as the car drove higher up the hillside, he placed a call. "I'll have a list for you by this evening or tomorrow morning at the latest."

"Excellent, Mr. Pakistan," his contact answered before the phone went dead.

In a few more minutes Andre reached his destination—the Grimaldi Villa. The two-story massive structure of stone and concrete sat perched on the edge of the cliff, keeping watch over the Cote d'Azur below. The chauffeur opened the back door and Andre stepped out onto the pea gravel driveway.

"Will there be anything else, Mr. Grimaldi?" The chauffeur respectfully asked.

"No, you may go," Andre answered as shifting pebbles crunched beneath each step he made approaching the front door. The mansion had been in his family for centuries. Once he was inside, the driver moved the car to the garage.

Andre ascended the granite stairs, passing large tapestries hanging on the walls. It had the appearance of a castle. It was his castle, even if technically it was a villa.

He turned at the top of the stairs and looked out over the foyer. A large Italian Carrara marble statue stood below. *"My great-great-grandfather certainly knew art when he made that purchase on one of his trips to Florence."*

The house was steeped in history. Andre soaked in his home environment filled with all the ghosts of his family line. Sometimes it seemed as if it didn't belong to him. When he was here, he slept through the days. Almost all of his waking hours were spent at the casino. It was an around-the-clock business which never slept.

He entered his large suite and opened the French doors to the veranda. He could hear the birds beginning their sweet songs to the early morning light. A faint breeze wafted the scent of wild flowers growing in the hedges below. It promised to be another beautiful day on the Mediterranean. Too bad he wouldn't see it.

Andre turned, leaving that world behind, and went inside. He filled the tub as he got out of his tuxedo. The soothing warm water relaxed his tense muscles as he slipped into its depths.

A few minutes later he heard his maid bring in a tray of fresh croissants and the morning paper. She took out his dirty clothes and shut the door again, giving him his privacy. He rarely saw the woman.

Andre lathered up with a large sea sponge and rinsed away the night. Popping the stopper like another champagne cork, he stepped out of the now draining tepid water. While wrapping himself in a thick terry robe, he slipped his feet into a pair of leather sandals. He tied the sash while walking across the room to the breakfast tray.

Andre glanced at the headlines and wondered how it would affect him. He picked up the crispy pastry, took a bite, and washed it down with some fresh-squeezed orange juice. He took the paper to the bed to read all the details.

The large Louis XIV bed had been turned back by Francesca when she had brought the tray. Andre fluffed the pillows and climbed under the covers. He read all the international news before turning to the most local events. Tossing the news aside, he pulled down his silk mask and drifted off to sleep.

At three, Andre awoke to the sound of a vehicle pulling into the drive.

The sound of the gravel alerted him and that's the way he liked it, no surprises. As he walked outside, he saw the courier's van leaving. He pulled on his red silk robe and descended the stairs.

"Mr. Grimaldi, a package just arrived for you. It's by the door. I was going to bring it up to your study, but I didn't want to bother you," the cook said, drying her hands on a towel.

"No problem, Francesca. The van woke me. I'll do it." Andre carried the box up the stairs.

"Do you want anything to eat before going to the casino, sir?" Francesca asked as he ascended past the tapestries.

"I'll have an espresso and biscotti," he answered as he reached the top landing.

Andre placed the box in the study. He removed the reinforced packing tape. Inside, he found the binder of names. Placing the notebook and disk beside his keyboard, he sat in the leather armchair. He leaned over and turned on his computer just as Francesca appeared at the door. She set the tray on the coffee table in front of the sofa without a word and picked up the empty box. She quietly retreated back downstairs.

While he waited for the computer to boot up, he dunked his biscotti into the hot coffee and took a bite. Once online, he checked his email. There was one from his sister.

Hope all is well with you. I'll be arriving in June for my usual summer visit. I'm bringing a few friends along as well. Hope you don't mind.

We won't bother you much, only one night at the casino. Since you sleep all day, we'll be quiet as church mice.

There's nothing like the Riviera in the summer. See you the afternoon of the twenty-first about the time you awaken.

Love,

Michelle

"That's Michelle," Andre said aloud, shaking his head. He could always count on her popping in once each year during the summer months. He hoped it wouldn't be for long.

He saw from the rest of the emails that there was nothing else that he needed to address immediately.

He answered Michelle's email with a short message.

See you when you get here. Who are the new friends and where did you meet them this time?

Andre

He was accustomed to his sister being a jet-setter and picking up the strangest friends. Some were famous and some just wanted notoriety, or to rub elbows with the rich. He shook his head and returned to the important GUILE business at hand.

Andre reviewed the list of names and made note of their backgrounds. Ten of the young men were already on board. He'd need to select replacements for future operations.

He placed his call, "Okay, I have some new names. It's urgent that you instruct the guys that they will go to the States and start ESOL training. That'll take some time. Set them up with the necessary paperwork, plane tickets, and money to get started."

"Yes, I understand."

"I'll send you the list of new contacts for backup."

"Got it," the voice said as the call ended.

Pakistan

The connecting operative delivered the assignment to depart and contacted America for support. "Hello. Several young men will be arriving soon. They'll need a place to stay."

"Sure, I'll work on relocating them. Let me know when they're arriving so someone can pick them up at the airport."

"Expect it to be in two weeks. I'll send you the particulars."

"May Allah be praised," the Imam answered.

California

This wasn't the first time the Imam had been contacted to find a place to house young men just arriving in the country. He always was willing to support his fellow Muslim brothers, even if they weren't from his home country.

The next day after morning prayers, the Imam spoke with everyone leaving the mosque.

"I'm expecting some young men in the next few weeks from your country of Pakistan. Can you pick them up from the airport? They speak little or no English; you can help them in this foreign land."

"Certainly, Imam," the middle-aged man answered.

Speaking to another man several back in line, the Imam asked, "Do you know of a place for some young men to stay? They're from your country. They'll be arriving in a few weeks and don't have any family here."

"I'll look," Ahmed replied. The last place he had arranged, the landlord didn't like so many men in one studio room. He needed to find another complex, or see if he could arrange a one-bedroom unit this time.

Pakistan

The operative told his friend to pass the word that a mission had been given to them. The news traveled quickly through several persons; eventually it reached the selected young men. They were standing ready to serve Allah in jihad.

No one knew the mission originated with GUILE.

Plane tickets were handed to Abdul, Mohammad, Sabur, Naji, and Ahmad. "Here are your tickets. I'm sorry you must go. Go with Allah."

Abdul opened his envelope. Glancing at the destination, he asked Mohammad, "Are you going to Italy? I thought we were going to America."

"Mine says I'm going to France," Mohammad answered, with a shrug of his shoulders.

Sabur noted his flight was different as well. "Maybe we're not meant to stay together. It's probably better that way. We don't want to look suspicious."

Naji agreed, "You're right. We must trust Allah; he knows the plan." He slapped Ahmad on his back. They gave each other strong hugs of good bye.

The next day, Ahmad was boarding his plane when he saw Mohammad walking up to a nearby gate. Ahmad nodded his good bye as he handed the attendant the ticket. He hated leaving his country, but this was for a noble cause. He continued onto the tarmac and anxiously climbed the stairs. He had never been in a plane before.

Mohammad watched as Ahmad's plane taxied and took off. He wondered if they'd ever see each other again.

Sabur's plane left Pakistan late. He felt like turning back, but Abdul was at a neighboring gate. Sabur didn't want to bring disgrace on himself. He prayed for strength, especially during takeoff, and watched until his beloved homeland disappeared from view.

Mohammad landed in France. Upon exiting his plane, he was handed a ticket by a stranger who only said, "Go there, now!"

Mohammad went in the direction that the man had indicated. At the luggage carrousel, he was met by a man who acted as if he knew him. "Mohammad, welcome to France. I have been expecting you. Come with me."

Mohammad followed. They drove to a place to stay for the night. There was very little conversation between them. Mohammad was returned to the airport the next day for another flight.

It was the same for Ahmad, who had left first and landed in a different country. Everything was well planned, and hard to follow on purpose.

California

Naji arrived in the United States first. He was given a ride to the local Islamic Center, where he spent the night. The following day, another man from the center took him to a small apartment that was stocked with food.

"When others arrive, you'll need to share. I'll help you get adjusted to America," the strange man told him.

"Thank you," Naji said as the man departed in a hurry.

When it was near sunset, Naji pulled out his prayer mat, placed it facing west, and began his evening prayers. No one had returned to take him to the center.

Within a few days, two of his friends arrived. They paid the man who was caring for them. The cash had been provided with the plane tickets for the mission.

In turn, the man secured things that required a bank account and identification. By the end of the week, there were six men in the one-bedroom apartment. It was getting cramped, but it felt like home to them.

The man who had supplied the apartment enrolled them in ESOL classes. They needed to learn to speak English fluently.

CHAPTER 4

GUILE had infiltrated all the major governments. They knew about every top secret, secret, and not-so-secret agency. It had taken years for them to gather the information that they needed to control the world.

One of these agencies in the United States was the secret American Weather Agency (AWA); it had been put into commission under the Truman administration after the first atomic bombs were dropped.

The night in 1945 that the first atomic bomb was tested at the Trinity site in New Mexico, a pilot was flying a transport at ten-thousand feet to the West Coast. He reported that it brightly lit up his cockpit, and looked like the sun rising in the south.

Besides the obvious deaths caused by the two atomic bombs dropped on Japan, there were many who died from exposure to radiation and fallout. This caused the American powers-that-be to want more data. From then on, the study constantly collected and monitored the effects of radioactivity on the atmosphere and the environment.

The White House directed these blasts to be observed from the air and to have high atmospheric samples taken. The government tested nuclear bombs at White Sands Proving Grounds for many years following, justifying the commissioning of the AWA.

They hired the best scientists and meteorologists in the world. Dr. Albert Fredric defected to the United States as soon as Hitler had become the Chancellor of Germany in 1933. He was the perfect appointment for the first director of the AWA, working closely with the White House. The agency set up a governmental office in Washington, D.C. and laboratory offices in New Mexico. Many directors had been named since.

Thousands of tests were performed during the Cold War, and most were above ground. Above-ground nuclear tests ceased due to the findings on the adverse effects of nuclear fallout in the Earth's atmosphere. This served to validate the extreme importance of the agency and why they kept it secret.

Yet, even though the government was warned, U.S. citizens, as well as the Marshallese Islanders, were still affected as a result of the nuclear weapons program. Some were rightly compensated a little over a billion dollars for their exposure.

Finally in 1993, the United States redefined the AWA studies. Subjects like global-warming, and others directly related to weather, namely hurricanes and tornadoes, were assigned. Once Vice-President Al Gore became aware of all the generated reports, he urgently pleaded for citizens to take immediate action on global-warming.

AWA was given the task of finding a way to divert hurricanes from American soil, especially those as intense as Hurricane Andrew in 1992. AWA first needed conclusive data to project and predict intensification; and secondly, they needed a lab in the upper atmosphere. Sending planes into the eyes of hurricanes and tropical storms was too primitive. There had to be a better solution.

NOAA had satellites that the hurricane center used to monitor and track all storm activity. Why couldn't AWA have a satellite of its own?

Summer 2001
New Mexico

The American Weather Agency petitioned Congress to put a weather lab into space to help the centers on the ground. Both the Senate and the House agreed to the funding in the summer of 2001. There was one stipulation: the offices in New Mexico had to close.

"Yeah, you're right Director Haynes; the staff was upset over the announcement of the closing. Our meteorologists have been scurrying all morning, contacting TV networks to see if any will hire them," the gray-haired assistant director said.

"I know I've said it before, but I'm really sorry. We had no idea when we first started writing this proposal that it'd take two years to get all the bugs worked out. I had to meet with many different politicians to get the verbiage right so that it'd get approved.

"And since we're under a Republican administration, of course, they want to downsize government," Haynes said, straightening his yellow tie and picking a speck of lint off of his navy pin-striped suit. "We were hoping to get this passed and signed under Clinton's last term," the young AWA Director apologized.

"No one's saying we're blaming you. We're just all disappointed. We've gotten very used to our life here in the high desert far away from the politicians and politics," Ted admitted, looking out over the flat basin of

Socorro, which sat at an elevation of seven thousand feet.

Ted swiveled his government-issued metal office chair back around. It creaked as he propped his legs on the desk. "We've had our eyes glued to the computer monitors too long, I guess," he said, scratching his head and adding, "I don't know how you really deal with that Beltway climate in more ways than one, if you get my drift?" Ted smiled at his own joke.

At the mention of the climate, the director swiveled his plush leather chair and glanced out to see the hazy, hot humidity of a summer day near the Capitol. "Speaking of that, you're close to retiring. Are you coming into our office in D.C. for your last year?" Haynes asked, knowing Ted didn't fit in there.

"I'm not sure about that," Ted answered, buying some more time.

"We can keep you going, or we can transfer you to Houston and Cape Kennedy for the next few years on the WSL project," he offered, as his secretary laid a folder containing letters on his desk.

She whispered, "For your signature, Mr. Haynes."

He nodded his head and watched her walk away before continuing, "If you chose the Lab, then you'll have to promise to stay on until it's in orbit." He paused, as he supported the phone between his ear and shoulder in order to sign the letters.

Ted knew Haynes hadn't finished. He was waiting for the incentive portion of the proposal.

Haynes continued signing and pitching. "You can even retire and stay on as contract, whichever is financially best for you," the director said, giving him several options.

Director Haynes wanted Ted French to stay on staff. If he didn't, Haynes might have to go to NASA himself to supervise the project. Worse yet with all the budget cuts, he might have to fly back and forth, since his office was in D.C.

Ted's salary in the long run might be cheaper for the agency. Besides, Haynes liked his brownstone in Georgetown; he didn't want to leave all the socializing, hobnobbing, and prestige to spend much time in Florida or Houston.

"That sounds like a nice offer. I wasn't looking forward to moving my family to the Washington area, only to be moving away again in one year. It'd hardly be worth it, and my wife agreed.

"To be honest, I've been searching for another federal government job that I could pick up here in New Mexico just to avoid it. But your offer is one that I'll have to think about. How long before you need an answer?" French asked.

"Everyone's supposed to be gone from your facility by the end of the year. You'll have until then to tell me something definite. Then if you choose to stay with AWA, you can have two more months to make the transition."

"Okay, sounds fair. I'll get back to you as soon as I've decided. Thanks for calling," Ted said as he stood, wanting the call to end. He had better things to do than stay on the phone with his egotistical boss. Besides, it was almost time to go home.

"Bye," Haynes said.

The New Mexico office had always worked on East Coast Time. It was almost six in Washington, but only four in Socorro. Before shutting down his computer, Ted wanted another look at the NOAA satellite information.

He wiped the sweat from his hands on his jeans before selecting the image of Tropical Storm Barry. The storm had made a definite turn during the day and wasn't going to amount to a hurricane before reaching the Florida Panhandle.

"Did anyone contact the Naval Aviation Station in Pensacola today?" Ted yelled to anyone on his staff that might hear and answer. The New Mexico office was quite a bit less formal compared to working near the Capitol inside the Beltway.

"Yeah, we gave them a heads-up an hour ago," Ted's secretary answered back. She stuck her head in the doorway and said, "See you tomorrow morning, Ted."

"Thanks Betsy. Has everyone else gone?"

"Yeah, I'm the last. You can lock up," she said, waving as she headed for the main entrance.

Ted ran a few more scenarios on the computer before he was satisfied that the storm wasn't going to become Bad Barry. He shut down his IBM, flipped off the lights, and locked down the panic bar on the front door.

Ted drove slowly down the long dirt road, causing small dust clouds to form behind him. Even though they had the customary fifteen minutes of summer rain at noon, everything looked dry again, except for the one puddle at the end of the road. The locals called this time of year the 'Monsoon Season', but they didn't have a clue as to what a real monsoon would be like. Ted turned onto Route 60 and headed toward home.

Stopping by the post office on the way, he picked up the mail. He glanced at the bills, separating them from the junk mail, then tossed the trash in the bin.

Ted pulled into the driveway of his modest little house in Magdalena. Teddy's old Civic was at the curb. Ted parked under the carport and stepped into the house.

"Hi, Dad."

"Hello, Son. I got your tuition bill today. I'm sure glad you'll be graduating soon. I wouldn't want that bill once I'm retired."

"Well, at least I didn't cost you anything extra for two majors. I got two times the education for the price of one," Teddy said proudly.

Teddy attended the New Mexico Institute of Mining and Technology. He double majored in Earth and Environmental Sciences, and Mechanical Engineering. He was intelligent and a good student. He had taken seven courses a semester, as well as summer classes all three years, and was graduating in the spring.

Ted roughed up his son's hair, like he did when he was young. "You're a good kid, Teddy."

"Do you know what time Mom will be home?" Teddy asked, smoothing his hair back in place.

"It's her day at the library, so I guess she'll be home soon. Public school doesn't start until next week," Ted answered. "Why?"

"I'm going golfing later. I was wondering if she'd have dinner ready before I left. Otherwise, I should go pick up something on the way and leave sooner than I planned."

"Well, let's see if we can tell by what's in the fridge," Ted said, opening the refrigerator door.

Teddy set the table as he usually did, in hopes that he didn't have to spend his allowance on fast food in Socorro. He was saving his money to pay for his master's degree.

"It looks like she's planning to have barbecue chicken, macaroni salad, and probably a hot vegetable. We can get it going if you go start the grill," Ted suggested, knowing the chicken would take a while to cook.

"Sure thing, Dad."

Teddy uncovered the grill and ignited the gas flame, while Ted rummaged through the drawer until he found the tongs. Taking the tray of marinated chicken breasts to the deck, Ted placed them one by one on the bottom rack.

"Hey, Teddy, look in the bottom of the fridge; maybe Mom's thinking corn on the cob."

Teddy opened the bin. There were three ears already shucked inside. He placed them on the counter and pulled out the large pot. Filling it with water, he placed it on the burner just as his mother came in the house.

"What are you up to?"

"I have a game of golf later with some of the guys. Dad and I thought we'd help you start dinner, so I can eat at home before I go."

"That's sounds nice," Freda said, heading to the bedroom to change out of her dress and into a pair of shorts.

Ted came into the kitchen just in time to see her go into the hallway. He followed quietly. He sneaked up and startled her. "Boo!"

Freda screamed. "Ted, you almost made me wet my pants," she yelled, running toward the bathroom. "I've been holding it for the last hour, and I've got to go," she chided as she quickly sat down on the toilet.

Ted lay on the bed, waiting for her return.

"What do you know about possible job prospects? Did you hear anything today?" Freda asked loudly as she washing her hands.

"Director Haynes called today."

"Oh, yeah?" Freda stood in the doorway, drying her hands on the hand towel. "Tell me about it,"

"I'll tell both of you over dinner, but all I'll say is that things might be looking up." Ted gave a chuckle at the double meaning and left to check on the chicken.

Freda didn't waste any time changing into shorts. When she arrived in the kitchen, the water was boiling. She plopped the ears of corn in and set the timer on the back of the stove. After placing the pasta salad on the table, Freda riffled through the drawer to find the corn skewers. She was taking out the butter dish when the guys came inside with the platter of cooked chicken.

Ted set the plate on the tile counter, tossing the grill tongs in the sink. Freda covered the chicken with foil to keep it warm and moist, and added a meat fork to the table. The timer buzzed. Freda removed one ear and tested a kernel for tenderness. Satisfied, she turned the gas off and added the other two ears to the serving plate as Ted poured the iced tea in the glasses. Freda brought the chicken and corn to the table and took her seat.

"Okay, tell us the news," Freda said, placing skewers into her ear of corn.

"The Director called from Washington today," Ted announced, taking the last chicken breast.

That statement got Teddy's attention. He knew the office in New Mexico was closing and wondered how it'd affect him. He'd be going away the next year for his graduate degree, but everything had its consequences.

"So what's happening, Dad?"

"We have three options. We can move to the Washington metropolitan area for one year; and then relocate anywhere afterward when I retire. I don't want to stay any longer than that in D.C.'s fish tank," Ted said, taking a bite of corn. Wiping his face with his napkin he continued, "The second option is to take another federal government job that's located somewhere here and not move at all."

"Do you know of one yet?" Freda asked, stabbing a piece of macaroni with her fork.

"No, not really, but it's still an option," Ted answered, cutting another piece of chicken.

"There aren't too many government facilities here, Dad."

"There's the Very Large Array, but I don't think I'd qualify for anything there. There are agencies in Albuquerque; but that'd be an hour's drive both ways. Most places won't hire me, knowing I'm retiring in a year's time." Ted paused for emphasis, as if he was thinking as he chewed the chicken.

"So what's the third option? It must be better," Freda said, removing the skewers from her bare corncob. She was anxious to know what the director had offered that they hadn't already figured out.

Ted set his napkin on the table. "Okay. Here it goes; last option, I think it's the most exciting."

Teddy and Freda were poised, waiting.

"They offered me a job to oversee the joint project with NASA and AWA for the Weather Space Lab. It'll take two, possibly three, years to complete. We'd move to Houston. I may sometimes have to go to Florida, but that's not clear yet."

"Whoa! You weren't kidding when you said things were looking up." Freda beamed. "How soon?"

"I have to close down this facility at year's end. Then they'll give me a couple of months to relocate. I can go ahead at the end of March and set everything up for us. You can pack up here, closing out the school year. I'll fly back for Teddy's graduation in May, and we'll arrange for the movers to take the stuff to Houston in June."

"I like option three," Freda said.

"Me, too," Teddy agreed.

"Then its set," Ted said with a sigh of relief. It was the choice he wanted as well.

CHAPTER 5

August, 2001
New York City

Jack's business wasn't doing as well as it had in the past. Things had to change. He didn't want to, but there was no way around it; he needed to let employees go and rent less expensive office space.

GUILE had influenced the right politicians during the Reagan years. The taxing on the rich had been lowered substantially, literally getting Jack off the ground floor to the penthouse level. Now twenty years later, some of his businesses were foundering and about to go under.

He had taken measures several years before to outsource the manufacturing to third-world countries, laying-off many American workers in the process. One by one, he removed the 'Made in U.S.A.' stamp from his products. Buyers hadn't seemed to notice; it had become the norm in American industry.

When were things going to improve? GUILE wasn't moving fast enough for him. They had invented creative investments like derivatives, but Jack just wasn't sure about where this was all going to end up.

He placed a call.

"Be patient, Mr. Iran. Things will work out soon. To put your mind at ease, I'll send you the plan. You just need to hang in there one more month," the head of GUILE assured him.

"I'll keep an eye out for it," Jack said expectantly. Nervously rubbing the back of his neck, he stared out of the World Trade Center office window at the Hudson River below.

He opened a file on his computer and reviewed available office space. He wanted another penthouse, one not so high up and cheaper, way cheaper. He had become accustomed to a fine way of life and wanted to maintain his personal spending. The business may suffer, but he wouldn't. GUILE had promised it wouldn't be long, but his stock had been falling for quite some time. Discouraged, he turned off the computer, calling it a day.

Upon arriving home, he found the special courier envelope had been delivered. After dinner, he dismissed his chef. Once Jean was gone, Jack locked the elevator in place and retired to his office across the vestibule.

He took out a bottle of water and drank half in his one-gulp fashion. Jack carried the package and water to the vintage Eames lounge chair. Placing his bottle on the side table, he eased back in the chair and opened the envelope.

Pulling out the pages, he began to read.

> Don't go to work on September 11th. All your worries will end. Call in sick, take a cruise, but don't be anywhere around that location. The operatives have been trained and several locations have been selected as a target. Yours is one.
>
> Also, don't plan any flights that day, or probably two weeks to follow.
>
> More than that is too much to know.
>
> Shred this page. Don't mark your calendar or say anything suspicious. Most of GUILE doesn't know this much and shouldn't.

Jack read it over several times, committing it to memory. "*911, the emergency number, that shouldn't be hard to remember,*" he thought as he placed the message into the shredder.

He called Claudia Lei. There was no answer. He closed the phone without leaving a message. Jack finished the water and took a long shot at the recycled bin, missing. As he walked over to pick up the plastic bottle, his phone rang.

"Hello?"

"What did you want, Mr. Iran?" Claudia asked, using his code name. Jack never called this line; it was obvious to her that it was GUILE business.

"Ms. Saudi Arabia, glad you called back. Would you like to take a cruise? We never take off. And I was thinking that the Mediterranean would be lovely at the beginning of September."

"Sounds great, but I've booked a fall fashion show. I'll be in Paris. Maybe we could go afterward. Want to be my escort at the show?"

"It depends. When is your show?" Jack asked.

"It's September 13th. I have loads to do yet. Half the dresses aren't even finished. I have so much to do before then. But after that, I'll be free to relax and will deserve a break," Claudia admitted.

"Well, I can't leave then. It must be sooner. Maybe we could go before your show?"

The seamstress held up a sketch of a dress.

"Oh my God, no; that'll never work," Claudia said, shaking her head rapidly.

"I'm sorry?" Jack answered, surprised. He had never heard her be so adamant. She was such a cool cucumber.

"Oh, not you; I was talking to the seamstress. Look, I've got to go, as you can tell I'm working late. I'll meet you for lunch tomorrow."

§

The next day Claudia rushed in and sat down, out of breath.

Jack tried again. "Bring us a glass of champagne," Jack addressed the waiter, then turned toward her; "Claudia, take deep breaths; slow down."

"As I told you last night, there's so much to do, and so little time to do it. Since I said I was coming today, I didn't want to disappoint you," Claudia said, flinging her straight hair over her shoulder. It had fallen on her menu and was blocking the Chef's Pick of the Day.

"Too bad the cruise plan didn't work with our schedules," Jack said, broaching the subject again.

The Bollinger arrived. They toasted to the future.

"I'll have the Shrimp Scampi," Claudia ordered.

"I'll have Gazpacho and the Sea Bass."

"Very good, sir," the waiter said, taking their menus.

"What day will you be leaving for Paris?"

"I haven't booked the flight yet. It'll probably be on the eleventh. I have to get there a day or two before the show to set up. My assistant will already be there, but you know how I am," Claudia said.

"Why don't you travel together?" Jack suggested, trying to get Claudia to fly sooner without mentioning the reason.

"I don't see how I can; but like I said, the flights haven't been booked yet."

When the lunches were served, Jack changed the topic. They talked about the heat outside. In the summer the city was unbearable, though they only suffered a few moments from the curb to the building.

After lunch, Jack's limo went one way and Claudia's the other. Back at the fashion house, she had hardly put down her clutch bag when the seamstress walked in.

"Ms. Lei, here are two more sketches for you to consider for the show," the head seamstress said, hoping that her boss would be more receptive today than she had been last night.

Claudia took the poster board over to the window to shed natural light on the drawing. She glanced at one, then the other, not noticing the WTC in the distance. It had long lost its novelty. The twin towers only impressed her clients.

"Okay. This one will do," she said, handing the sketch back. "Start cutting and I'll adjust it as we go."

"I have one of the other dresses ready for your approval. When would you like to see it?"

Claudia looked at the clock and answered, "Three."

The seamstress nodded her head and scurried away.

Claudia picked up the inter-office phone and buzzed her executive assistant. "Bring in your calendar; we need to set some dates."

"Yes ma'am?"

When the assistant arrived with the calendar, Claudia instructed, "Book the airfare for our trip to Paris. The show's on the thirteenth. Maria needs to be there by…" She paused and looked at the desk calendar. The thirteenth was a Thursday. "Oh dear, I was going to say ninth, but that won't work. You better get her over there the Thursday before. Make my flight for Tuesday, the eleventh."

"So, Marie goes the night of the sixth and you want to fly the night of the eleventh, giving you jet lag on the day before the show?" The assistant asked, glad that it wasn't her.

"Oh, you're right. Book me Monday night, the tenth. Good thinking," Claudia complimented, "At least someone is clearheaded."

Punctually at three, the head seamstress came back with the model. She was dressed in the gown that the seamstress was working on. They went directly into Claudia's workroom, which sat adjacent to her office. Claudia was seated at the table, waiting for them.

Immediately the model went into motion. Claudia watched the model walk first toward her and then away, as she'd do on the runway at the show. After three passes, Claudia motioned for her to come close.

"Look," Claudia said to the seamstress. "I want you to add a sash here; trim it with sequins. Then bring it back for me to see."

"I think the sequins will be too much," the seamstress said, relatively sure Claudia wouldn't like them in the end.

"No, I think it's needed in order to see the movement as she walks. The chiffon flows. I want the audience to see it."

"Okay, Ms. Lei. I should have another dress for your approval tomorrow," the woman promised as they left.

September 10, 2001

Claudia was relaxed and hopeful as they rode to JFK. Maria had called on Saturday to tell her that all the dresses had arrived in Paris, putting her at ease. Jack was seeing her off, which was a bit unusual. He seemed relieved that she was taking this earlier flight.

"Send me a postcard," Jack joked, as he waved good bye at the gate. "Break a leg."

"Bye," she said and waved as she boarded.

Claudia took her first-class seat and buckled up. They taxied down the runway and were in the air within minutes. The flight attendant, who was assigned to first-class, began serving French champagne.

Claudia pushed her seat into a slight recline. She took a sip, musing at the setting sun in the West. In a few more days, her stress would be over until the next fashion show.

"Beef Wellington, Rice Pilaf, and Broccoli," the attendant said, setting the plate on the table. She replaced the empty flute with a large wine glass. She held up two open bottles of French red wine made from different varietals.

"The Cabernet Sauvignon," Claudia answered the unspoken question.

Since they were flying north, night would appear to be short when judged by the sun. For Claudia, this was a short overseas flight compared to the ones she remembered when she was younger. Her parents had wanted her to see the China they knew, since Claudia had been born and raised in America, Mei Guo: the Beautiful Country. On the trip, she saw a way of life that was very foreign to her, even though she looked like everyone there. At least, she knew the language. Her parents had made her speak three languages as a child: English, Cantonese, and Mandarin. To Americans, Cantonese and Mandarin seemed the same, but it was far from it. Claudia had been so good with languages that she took two more in high school, adding French and German to her repertoire. She had perfected them in college, which only made it easier on her as she traveled around the world.

The flight attendant asked as she removed the half-eaten dinner, "Would you like anything else?"

"Yes, Bailey's on the rocks, s'il vois plait," Claudia answered, noticing that the attendant was from France by her accent.

"I'll be right back," she answered, not noticing that Claudia had spoken in French. The attendant spoke both languages fluently. From time to time, she used both languages in one sentence as well.

The cordial was placed on Claudia's table, but she had already drifted off to sleep. She hadn't had any rest the night before, due to the anxiety that the show caused her. On the outside she seemed calm, but inside she wasn't. Her Asian heritage helped her to mask anxiety and fear.

In several short hours a different flight attendant came around the cabin, bringing sausage and eggs, and fresh hot coffee.

"Do you have any croissants?" Claudia asked, removing the sleep mask that she had put on during the night.

"Of course, Madame; un moment."

Technically, Claudia was a Mademoiselle; but at her age, the use of Madame was to be expected.

"Here are your croissants and some preserves. Bon Appetite."

"Merci."

Claudia quickly ate the breakfast. Afterward, she went to the restroom to freshen up. It wouldn't be long before they landed.

"*I'm glad I got here a day earlier. I'd hate to feel like this and have the show tomorrow*," she thought as she combed through her long black hair, noticing the bags under her eyes.

She returned to her seat and buckled up just as the bell dinged, announcing their approach.

CHAPTER 6

September 11, 2001
New York, New York - 6 a.m.

Jack didn't know exactly what would happen, but he was smart enough to stay home and not go into work. His apartment across town was obviously safe; if it weren't, the note would've mentioned it as well.

Jack placed his first call and spoke hoarsely. "Chef Jean, I won't need you today. I have a cold and I'm staying home. It must be the change in the weather."

"I can make gourmet chicken soup for you. You know that's always a good remedy," the chef suggested.

"No, that's okay. I just want to stay in bed. I'm not hungry. You know what they say 'starve a cold, feed a fever', or is it the other way around?"

"I'm not sure. If you really don't want anything, then I'll leave you alone. If you get hungry later, give me a call."

"I doubt that I will, judging by the way I feel right now. I'm heading back to bed as soon as I call the office," Jack lied.

"Well okay; I'll see you tomorrow."

Jack hung up. He went to the kitchen for water. Imitating the hoarse voice made his throat sore. He downed a half bottle of water as usual, and then took out food for breakfast. It'd be awhile before he could call the office. His assistant, Jeff, wouldn't be in until 8:45 a.m. Jeff faithfully arrived fifteen minutes earlier than Jack each and every day.

He turned on the little television that the chef used in the kitchen. Jack usually didn't have the time or want to watch television. He thought the shows were mundane and stupid. Yet, it served as a good advertising tool to reach the masses, expensive, but well worth it.

Jack's cell rang. He opened it.

"Are you at home?" The boss, Mr. Egypt, asked.

"Yes. I'm doing what you advised and calling out sick. Never have before, but there's always a first."

"Where's Saudi Arabia?"

"In Paris, at a fashion show; she flew yesterday."

"Great! Have a nice day."

The call ended.

Jack placed the cell phone on the counter. He cracked several eggs into a bowl and beat them with a whisk. He poured them into a warm skillet, after placing a whole-grain bagel into the toaster. Stirring the eggs with one hand and sipping his coffee with the other, he looked quite competent in the role of cook.

After breakfast he showered. While toweling his hair, he decided what to wear. He tossed the towel on the stool and selected his comfortable nightly garb of loose slacks, pullover shirt, and slip-ons.

It felt strange to him to be home during the day and all alone. "*What can I do today? Can't go out to lunch and what about tomorrow?*" Jack questioned, as he aimlessly walked around the apartment, waiting for the minutes to tick by so he could place his call.

Turning off the TV, he poured another cup of coffee to take across the hall. Entering the relatively empty space, he set down his mug and placed the call early. He couldn't wait to get it over. The phone rang several times as Jack sipped the coffee and gazed out the window. The day had turned out to be clear and beautiful. He stared at his office building in the distance as he heard the phone ring again.

Jeff ran down the hall, sloshing water from the coffeepot as he came, not wanting to miss the call. He got it on the fourth ring. "Hello, Mr. Jones' office," the assistant panted, "Jeff speaking, how may I help you?"

"Jeff, I won't be in today. I have a sore throat and need to rest. You know I never get sick, but it seems that I must've finally come across a really bad bug," Jack lied, using his rough sounding voice again.

"Rest up, sir," Jeff suggested, hearing how bad his boss sounded.

"Maybe I'll be back, in a day or two. Please don't call me with problems. I plan on going back to bed. I'll call you."

"Take care," Jeff said.

Before the handset reached the phone base, Jack heard, "Oh, no!" It was the last sound that came across the line.

Jeff's acknowledgement of what was about to happen never registered in Jack's brain, because the sight of a plane hitting the north building of the WTC shouted louder.

"Oh, my God!" Jack called out, dropping his coffee mug in shock.

But it was too late for Jack; he sold his soul to the devil years ago and his chance at redemption had crumbled like the buildings soon would.

September 11, 2001
Magdalena, New Mexico - 7 a.m.

Ted was stepping out of the shower when he heard his wife Freda scream. Throwing the towel around his waist, he ran to the kitchen, thinking she was cut, or possibly burned by hot coffee.

He surprisingly found neither. She was staring at the television screen. Immediately, he turned his attention to the CNN report. Feeling lightheaded by what he saw, Ted staggered towards Freda. He pulled her into his lap as he sat on the nearest kitchen chair. They watched in shock as smoke poured from the building.

Their son, Teddy, slowly stumbled into the kitchen, his hair in disarray. Not a first-responder type, Teddy had surmised his mother's scream was her overreaction to something non-life threatening, like she often did. When he saw a replay on the set, his eyes almost popped out of his head. The camera returned to the live shot, as he questioned, "What in the world?"

His parents silently watched the screen, ignoring his rhetorical question. Now adequately startled awake, Teddy ran into the living room to turn on the big set. The little black-and-white portable wasn't big enough for that kind of news.

"Come in here, guys!" Teddy urged.

His parents broke away from the small set and joined Teddy. They arrived just in time to see another plane crash into the second tower.

"Whoa! What's going on?" Freda asked, plopping down on the sofa beside Teddy.

"We've got to be under attack. Two planes can't accidentally hit both buildings. It's got to be deliberate," Ted answered.

"But who, Dad?"

"Who knows, Son? Someone will claim it; you can count on that," Ted said as he sat on the arm of the couch.

Thick smoke reached the living room at the moment the detector screamed its alarm, pulling their attention from the television screen. They ran to see what it was.

Freda ran toward the kitchen, realizing what it was. She yelled, "The bacon!"

Ted reached the stove first. He turned off the burner and opened the backdoor to clear the air. Teddy flipped on the ceiling fan and opened the front door. Freda briskly fanned the smoke alarm with a tea towel. Thankfully, the blaring screech stopped.

The attacks had drawn them away from their normal morning activities, placing the family into motionless shock. The burning bacon snapped them out of it, and now they were extremely sensitive and alert.

September 11, 2001
Paris, France - 4 p.m.

It was late in the afternoon when Claudia finished looking over the clothes for the fashion show. Just as Maria had told her, everything was fine. She wanted a pick-me-up so she started down the Champs Elysees to find some cappuccino.

"The walk'll perk me up; besides, it's gorgeous out."

Claudia turned the corner in search of a street café and spotted one up ahead. When she reached it, she sat down and waited. She had been working on New York time and resolved to go to bed on Paris time that evening. The jet lag was beginning to take its toll.

As she waited to place an order for a double-shot espresso, she rubbed her temples. Glancing around, she noticed that no one was sitting at the sidewalk tables. She wondered why; it was a perfectly lovely day. Turning her attention to inside, she saw people gathered near the bar.

"*How odd*," she thought and dismissed it as she opened her show brochure for Thursday. Once she read it over, she set the pamphlet on the table. She drummed her fingers on the tabletop, perturbed with the non-existent wait staff.

"What am I going to have to do, go get it myself?"

Fed up, she stomped into the café. Once inside, she saw the special news report.

"The World Trade Center was hit by two airplanes," the reporter said. Two still photos of planes hitting the buildings came on the screen. "It is thought to have been done by terrorists."

"Quoi?!" she asked in shock.

No one answered.

She recognized the two different buildings. One had the communication tower and the other didn't. She listened along with the other Parisians until the regular programming resumed.

The waiter finally turned, noticing her. The young man sincerely apologized, "Pardon moi, Madame. May I help you?"

Claudia was quite shaken. Espresso no longer fit the mood. She ordered, "Un dry vodka martini, s'il vous plait," and walked back to the outside table.

She dialed Jack, knowing that he had to be trapped in the building. It rang once. He picked up.

"Are you okay?" Claudia asked with concern.

"Yes, I'm home. I was sick so I called in; must've picked it up at the airport yesterday, when I dropped you off," Jack explained with healthy exuberance, watching the smoke pour from the two buildings.

She wrinkled her brow and didn't answer. *"He never takes off. This can't be a coincidence.*" Quickly putting two and two together, she thought, "*Did my contacts a few years ago have something to do with this, something so destructive? Did the boss of GUILE orchestrate this? Jack must've known.*" She furrowed her brow even more deeply.

Jack's voice interrupted her train of thoughts. Nervously, he continued, and acted as if he was concerned about her, "Are you okay? Obviously, you arrived okay. Mr. Egypt was glad to hear you flew yesterday."

"*The boss said that? Now that says a lot.*" She needed time to think this through. "I've got to go Jack, busy you know; glad you're okay; check with you later," she said, ending the call.

Claudia sat at the café, pondering all the scenarios. Her martini was delivered. She lifted it to her lips with a shaking hand, spilling some on the table. She thought about gulping it and ordering another, but her better judgment took over; she had to keep her wits about her. She nursed it slowly, thinking, and rethinking, every possibility of GUILE's and Jack's involvement before walking back to the hotel.

"*I won't have to worry about not getting much sleep tonight. I'll be lucky if I sleep at all,*" she thought, entering the lobby.

September 11, 2001
Magdalena, New Mexico - 8 a.m.

Ted dialed his secretary. She picked up on the first ring. Ted hardly waited for the customary hello and started right in, "Hi, sorry to bother you; I'm sure you saw what's happened."

"Yes. Isn't it awful?"

"Awful doesn't even begin to describe it. Look, call each of the division chiefs and tell them the offices are closed today. Tell them to pass the word to their staff. I'll ride over and place a note on the door, just in case someone doesn't get the message."

"Will do," she replied, fumbling in the drawer by the phone for the list of home numbers.

"Thanks. Talk to you later."

Ted hurriedly dressed, eager to get the message posted.

"Breakfast's ready," Freda called.

Ted came to the kitchen to grab a piece of toast as Teddy yelled. They ran into the living room in time to see the first tower collapse.

"My word!" Ted exclaimed, shaking his head.

"Dad, that's impossible. That steel can't drop like that, even if they did get hit," Teddy declared in disbelief.

"Well, it did. Look, I'll be back. I've got to go post a message that our office is closed until further notice. I'm sure both of your schools will be closed. I don't want you two leaving, understand? Stay here until I get back," Ted ordered, wanting to protect his family.

He ran out the door just as the phone rang. Freda answered, "Hello?"

"School's closed today," the principal's secretary told her. "Please call your staff. I have to finish calling the department chairmen."

"Sure thing," Freda agreed.

Teddy took his plate to the living room to eat the cold eggs and toast. His mom had forgotten to make the coffee in all of the excitement.

"Mom, come sit down," Teddy told her. He couldn't remember ever seeing her look so pale.

The local television station was running cancellation captions at the bottom of the screen. It looked like everything was closing. All county and state offices were closed, along with the county school system and his college.

Freda was brewing the coffee when the second building collapsed.

"Mom, come on, you're missing all this," Teddy said, regarding the live shot.

"I see it, Teddy," she yelled back. "The little set is on. As soon as the coffee's ready, I'll be back," Freda informed him, as she steadied herself against the counter.

September 11, 2001
Naval Academy
Annapolis, Maryland - 11 a.m.

The Academy students had been informed of the incident and were told to all report to the auditorium. They filed silently into the field house and took their seats. A pin could've dropped.

The admiral was about to address them collectively.

Mary Matthews sat with her fellow first-year midshipmen, waiting to hear what he'd say.

"*Will we be going to war*?" She wondered in fear. She didn't have enough military experience for early graduation, like the Academy had done during World War II. Theorizing the possibility of her involvement, she thought, "*Maybe the senior midshipmen, possibly third-year, but not us, not now.*"

The admiral took the podium and tapped the microphone.

"This facility is in complete lockdown. You'll not be permitted to leave and no one except persons with naval identification will be allowed on the Academy grounds. There will be no use of cell phones at this time.

"In case you haven't already told your parents that you are fine, your parent's home phones are receiving an automated voice message as I speak, saying that you're here and safe at the moment.

"You're ordered to give your cell phones to your floor leaders for safe keeping until later notice. This goes for all midshipmen, including seniors. This is an order. It is to be carried out once you are in the dorms.

"It is felt, as you already well know, that we are under attack. Therefore, we are about to take arms, as if at war, and need to be standing ready. John Paul Jones, who is laying at-rest under our chapel, once said, 'I have not yet begun to fight,' and neither have we.

"Dismissed!"

September 11, 2001
Christiansburg, Virginia - 2 p.m.

John Germaine was a sophomore at Christiansburg High School. News had spread around the school that something had happened in New York City.

"Hey man, did you hear what happened?" A fellow student asked, as they entered the English classroom.

"What do you mean?" John answered, puzzled at the question poised him.

John and his mother had moved over Labor Day weekend from Virginia Beach. Their boxes were only half unpacked. He didn't know many people in school; he safely assumed the student in the next row wasn't asking him about the latest school gossip.

John's grandfather was in the hospital with COPD, and in need of full-time care. The responsibility fell to John's mother, since she was the oldest and divorced.

"I heard the Capitol got bombed," the boy said anxiously.

"You're kidding!"

"Class, let's take your seats," the teacher said, clapping her hands to get their attention, "quickly!"

Half of the students were nervously chattering; the others were quietly waiting to find out the truth.

The bell rang. The teacher ushered in the last student. She shut the door, her face void of all expression.

"I've heard that the country has been attacked and there'll be an announcement on the PA in just a minute. Please be quiet and respectfully listen. I want to know exactly what has happened as well as you."

The speaker above the chalkboard squealed. The principal created the feedback as he adjusted the volume. He moved the microphone away from the control panel and the piercing noise ceased.

"Students, we're in an emergency situation. The county Board of Education has called and given instructions for complete lockdown. These are the facts that I have been given permission to disclose to you at this time:

"This morning, shortly after your second-period class started, a hijacked plane hit one of the World Trade Towers. Then a few minutes later, another plane hit the second tower, killing many people. Both towers have collapsed. It's reported that another plane has hit the Pentagon. No one is permitted to leave the school without your parent coming to sign you out. Your safety is our prime objective.

"Now, I know that most of you seniors drive your cars to school, but you will not, I repeat, you will not, be allowed to leave early. Your parent must come in to check you out. We'll be dismissed whenever the county deems it safe to close school for the day.

"I will come on the PA periodically, to call names of those students whose parent reports to the office. I don't know how long it'll be before the entire school is dismissed. The county bus drivers are being notified of a possible early dismissal.

"Teachers with TVs in your classroom may group classes together to watch the news reports, or you may use radios."

There was a pause in the principal's address as if he was evaluating whether he had covered everything. The sound of the open microphone was evident. He then announced, "That is all for now." As soon as the PA was turned off, the teacher took her group across the hall to the Social Studies class to view the historical events.

They filed over, carrying their chairs, and placed them around the perimeter of the room. The television was already on. The usually active teenagers sat quietly, watching the replay and listening to the reporters repeat what was known.

Every ten minutes the principal came on the intercom, announcing the names of the students whose parents were able to come get their children. The teacher muted the television by remote each time; and the students held their breath in hopes that their names would be called.

John's name wasn't called; he knew his mother wouldn't come. She was at the hospital. He patiently waited for hours before being dismissed with the handful of students that remained. He wasn't anxious to leave as usual. There was nowhere to go, except home, where he'd sit alone and watch the news. At least here, he wasn't alone.

The school was finally dismissed at noon, as if for snow. The principal called the students with cars first, before releasing the rest by bus numbers. John's bus was the last to arrive.

The school looked eerie to John as he boarded the bus. It was totally void of cars and students, which hardly ever happened at a high school. There was always something going on: sports, kids with cars, groups of teens gathered talking. He was the only student on his bus.

As the bus left the school grounds, John gazed out the window in silence at the blank parking lot. When the bus stopped, John exited and walked down the deserted street to his grandfather's house. He immediately turned on the television once inside, and stayed glued to the set for another hour.

After that, he couldn't take any more. His life was already depressing enough. His dad had left right before Christmas last year, and as if that wasn't bad enough, his grandfather turned ill within a few more months, and now Gramps was too ill to live alone. John was force to leave behind all his friends. High school would be spent in a strange school, no friends, no favorite teachers, just strangers.

John turned off the TV. He turned on his radio to listen to rock music and drown out the unpleasantness. But the only thing he could find was the news coverage. He shut it off as well.

He began digging in the boxes for his cassette tapes and a Walkman. He found an old family picture album instead. Turning the pages, he looked at pictures of a happier time in his life. He laughed at some of the fond memories of him and his dad. They had made a car for the soapbox derby races in Cub Scouts. He was holding the winning car, and his dad held the trophy.

There was a photo of his catch after going fishing with his dad and grandfather. They had camped at Smoke Hole, West Virginia, near Staunton, Virginia for the Easter break in late April that year. The trees were just sprouting leaves. Everything looked so bright green.

They had hiked to the top of the hillside and found a cave. John had wanted to go inside, but his dad told him a bear might live inside. So they hiked back down the steep slope, never knowing for sure. By the time they reached the river's edge, John looked up and swore he saw a black bear. It might've been because his dad planted the suggestion, or it might've been reality; he'd never know for certain.

John spent the rest of the afternoon buried in the past, when life was happy and full of hope for tomorrow. He blocked out the present, forgetting about his and the country's woes.

CHAPTER 7

September 12, 2001
Lima, Peru

Juan Perez awoke to a beautiful September day in Lima, Peru. He walked down the circular staircase and into the kitchen area to pour a cup of steaming fresh coffee. He was about to take a sip, when the maid walked in.

"Oh, Señor Perez, you're a little early this morning. I have the table set. Go; I'll serve you," Señora Gomez said, shooing him out of the kitchen, embarrassed that her employer was waiting on himself.

Juan took his cup to the dining room and sat at the well-appointed table. The morning paper was lying beside his place setting of fine china and silver. He finished his coffee as he read the headlines: NY World Trade Buildings Collapse After Attack. He had no idea that GUILE had caused it.

He read the article without much emotion. Opening the paper, he checked the current price of gold on the market and smiled. Stocks were down; metals were up. The maid brought in the breakfast while he compared precious metal prices. Satisfied, he turned to other international news.

Juan tapped his spoon against his soft-boiled egg and removed its cap, as the maid exited the room. Tasting the bland egg white, he decided to add a sprinkle of salt. His blood pressure was high and his doctor told him to avoid it, but he used it anyway. He buttered his toasted points, without another thought to health, and dipped them into his egg.

He folded the paper to a story on page three, propped it against the silver service set, and read while he ate. Pouring a last cup of coffee from the shiny pot, he finished breakfast and tossed his linen napkin on the table,

He had a mine tour planned for the day. There'd be no fine office clothes for him today. Pushing his white shirts aside, he selected a sturdy blue denim work shirt, a pair of twill pants, and his thick leather hiking boots.

He showered quickly in the brightly colored ceramic bath. The fixtures were made of copper from one of his many mines; the plush towels were monogrammed with the letter P in gold.

Juan pulled on his khakis, glancing outside at the countryside. A soft breeze blew the branches of the trees; the cloudless spring sky was a vivid blue. "*Too bad I'll be spending most of my day underground. But, such is the life of an owner of gold mines,*" he thought, and grinned with a wink. "*It's hard work, but someone has to do it.*"

Juan buttoned his shirt to the top and tied his boots snug. He descended the stairs with a spring in his step, even though the boots were constrictive. He grabbed his hard hat from the closet by the front door. Outside he waited for the chauffeur to pull up in the Rolls-Royce Silver Shadow four-wheel drive.

It was one of his better purchases in life. The car could tackle the roughest of rock-strewn roads like a tractor or heavy-duty vehicle. Yet, it still spoke of his wealth and importance. In order to get to some really remote areas though, he resorted to a less expensive vehicle.

"Good day, Señor," the driver greeted.

"Take me to the Guadalupito District," Mr. Perez directed, climbing into the back seat.

They drove through several seaside towns on the way up the coast of Peru: Huacho, Huarmey, and Chimbote. Juan reviewed the geological reports. His research team felt that the new area held promise for the future. By evening, he'd know for himself.

Chimbote was the largest of the villages on the coast. He was born near there. In 1970, there had been the Great Peruvian Earthquake where many had lost their lives. He was only ten at the time. Seventy thousand people had died; his parents were two of them. Fifty thousand were injured and eight-hundred thousand were left homeless. He had been one of the lucky Peruvians. He'd never forget the feeling of the 7.8 quake, and how the old adobe houses fell apart. Chimbote was devastated, and so was he.

Yet, the Perez estate had provided for the orphaned boy. The parish priest, who had known Juan's wealthy family, was the appointed guardian and cared for him. In time, Juan was sent away to boarding school in Europe; he had shown too much promise to stay in Peru.

Knowing he'd want to return home to Peru some day, Juan had selected an undergraduate in Mining Engineering at the University of Witwatersrand, in Johannesburg, hoping for hands-on experience in the South African gold mines; he wasn't disappointed.

Upon returning to Peru, Juan found a new Chimbote. Buildings constructed after the quake met the specifications to endure another such incident. Even so, he decided not to live there, but settled in the Lima area instead. Three of his gold mines were south of Lima. Only one was in this not-so convenient area.

"I'll have lunch in Chimbote, before continuing on to the prospective mining site," Juan instructed his driver.

He opened his phone and dialed.

"Hi, Father, this is Juan Perez." He smiled as he looked out of the window at the waves lapping the seashore.

"Hi, Juan! It's been a while. You know I'm getting old and would love to see you sometime." The priest lovingly urged, "Why don't you plan soon to come and see me?"

"How's lunch today? Is that soon enough?" Juan laughed.

"Whoa, that is soon. No problem; I can make it." The Father smiled and asked, "What time can I expect you?"

"How's a little after noon? Don't worry about preparing me anything. We'll go out; my treat."

The priest laughed, "I'd hope so, Juan."

"See you then, Father." Juan snapped his phone shut, ending the call.

For the next hour Juan recalled university days with his old friend, Paul Beorg, who now owned mines in South Africa. They hadn't stopped at an undergraduate degree, but had gone on to earn a Master of Science in Engineering, and then a Doctorate in Mineral Economics. It had paid off. Of course, family money hadn't hurt either of them.

"Thank God," Juan said, crossing himself. The priest had made it all possible by seeing his potential and sending him away to study.

Juan dialed and placed the phone to his ear. "Hello, Paul; how are you?"

"Mr. Morocco, is something wrong?!" Paul asked, surprised to hear from him.

"Oh!" Juan said, realizing what he had done. He quickly replied, "No Paul, no alarm. I was thinking about our college days in South Africa and thought I'd give you a call."

"Good. Glad to hear you're just feeling a little nostalgia, my friend. Is all else fine?"

"Sure. I'll get my contact names tomorrow, when I get back home from my road trip. I'll move forward as planned then."

"Well, it's a slow plan, but I think it may work if mine doesn't work first," Mr. Afghanistan taunted and laughed.

"We'll see. I'm on my way to lunch with Father Paola. You remember meeting him at our graduation?"

"Sure, he's your dad. Well, have a good lunch. I've got work to do; it's late here. Remember?"

"Sorry, bye," Juan said, closing the phone and placing it in his pocket.

The driver pulled up to Cathedral De Nuevo Chimbote. Juan jumped out and gave Father Paolo a warm hug and pat on his back.

"Hi, Juan," the priest greeted, and returned the pats.

They climbed back into the car.

"Take us to Don Filippi Restaurant Grill for lunch, please. It's just around this next corner. Is that okay with you Father?"

"Sure, sure, it's fine," the old priest agreed.

They spent lunch talking about the old days at the orphanage, when Juan was just a young boy, before he had gone away to Europe. After lunch, the priest asked Juan to let him off at the Plaza Mayor de Nuevo Chimbote; he wanted to walk for awhile. He waved as the Silver Shadow headed on to the mining area.

After touring the mines, Juan spent the night in Chimbote so he could visit with Father Paolo a little longer. Who knew when he'd get a chance again?

Juan had reservations for a room on the top floor at the Remanso Hotel, across from the Plaza. The executive suite had a small balcony facing the ocean. His chauffeur had a lesser room.

At six the next morning, Juan checked out to catch the flight at seven. The driver dropped him off and began the long trip home alone; he wouldn't arrive in Lima until around noon.

Juan's flight took off on schedule. He arrived at eight and took an airport limo home.

"Good morning, Señor. A large package came for you yesterday. I placed it on your desk," the cook informed him.

"Excellent," Juan said with a smile.

"Did you have breakfast yet?"

"No. I'll want some after I get dressed for the office," he answered, heading to his study.

Opening the box, Mr. Morocco found the binder and disk. He leafed through the pages, knowing one day that he'd be called on to execute a backup plan.

He placed a call from his cell. "I want you to begin working on some contacts. If we get called on to go forward, we'll be ready. I may never have to call on you if all goes well, but you never know."

"Yes, understood, Mr. Morocco," answered the operative, who was actually in Morocco.

"I'll email some names for you to start on. The list includes their expertise, which should be helpful when enlisting their assistance," Juan informed him.

"Excellent. Have a good day."

The phone went silent.

Juan Perez dressed for his office in downtown Lima. By the time he was finished, his cook had his breakfast ready. She poured him a cup of strong coffee as soon as he sat down at the dining table. While he was drinking it, she brought his eggs.

He ate leisurely while reading the morning paper, paying close attention to metals on the stock market and only glancing at the headlines. When it was time to go into work, the gardener acted as a substitute driver. Juan rode into town, calculating the number of men to contact at this time.

"Oh, I'll think of that this evening," Juan absentmindedly said aloud.

"Señor?" the gardener asked, unfamiliar with driving his employer around.

"Oh, I wasn't talking to you," Juan apologized. He hadn't realized he had spoken out loud.

As soon as the car reached the curb Juan got out, not waiting to be let out as usual. Waving the gardener on, he headed into the tallest office building in Peru. Because it too had been built after the big earthquake, Juan felt safe.

He took the elevator to the top floor.

"Good morning, Mr. Perez," the head receptionist greeted.

Juan nodded and walked on to his large office, which looked out over the city.

His executive assistant greeted, "Good morning, Mr. Perez. I placed the list of yesterday's calls you'd be interested in on your desk. All others have been forwarded to your individual directors of mining for them to handle. You had one urgent call this morning from the Cathedral of Chimbote. Here's the number," she said, as she handed him a slip of paper.

"Very good," Juan said, walking into his office and closing the door behind him.

"What could Father Paolo want?" Juan mused aloud, a bad habit of his.

Juan dialed the number. "Hello, this is Juan Perez. I believe Father Paolo called me this morning."

The secretary answered, "Please hold for a minute, sir."

Juan could hear her place the phone on the desk; her heels clicked on the tile floor as she walked away.

The Monsignor came on the line, "I'm so sorry to bother you, Juan. I must've just missed you this morning."

"Yes; what is it?" Juan asked, beginning to worry.

"Father Paolo slipped away during the night. When he didn't come down for Mass this morning, we checked on him. We found he had died sometime during the night. I knew you would want to know."

"I was just with him yesterday," Juan said, shaking his head.

"I know it's a shock, my son, but Father Paolo was an elderly man. It's so good that you were here to see him. You can rest assured, he died a happy man. You meant the world to him. He's in the Savior's hands now.

"I'll call when we have made funeral plans."

"Thank you," Juan said. He plopped down in his chair, unable to stand any longer. Shaking his head in disbelief, his tears began to flow.

CHAPTER 8

September 12, 2001
Virginia

John and his mother sat watching the television throughout the next morning. They wanted to learn who had caused this terrorist act, and what the United States was going to do about it.

At noon, Emily went to the hospital. John turned off the television and searched for the tape recorder again. This time he was successful. He took his tapes to his room and lovingly placed them one by one on the bookshelf, the way they had been at home.

He popped in a cassette, put on the earphones, and pushed play. Metallica instantly blared into his ears, blotting out the other noise in his head. Before long, he was head-banging to the beat of the heavy metal tune. He jumped onto the bed in a prone position, like a WWF wrestler executing a dropping head lock. John flipped through an old magazine as he listened to the music. It was comforting to escape reality.

The phone didn't ring all afternoon. John couldn't hear it if it had; the walkman's volume was as loud as it would go. No friends were calling anyway, and his grandfather's condition had stabilized.

His mom arrived home around six. She prepared a quick version of tuna fish casserole. While the macaroni noodles boiled in the water, she mixed a can of tuna and cream of mushroom soup together in a large bowl. When the timer buzzed, she poured off the boiling water. As she tossed all three together, she yelled for John to come to the table. When he didn't come after three minutes, she went to get him.

"Didn't you hear me calling you?" Emily scolded, snatching the headphones off of his head.

Nirvana's song, "Smells Like Teen Spirit," came blaring out.

"Turn that thing off and come for dinner. I've been calling you; I'm too tired to have to come get you all the time," Emily complained and headed to the kitchen to eat the now cooled tuna mixture. "Since your dad left, that's all you do is listen to that stuff. I don't know how you can stand it."

John sat at the table and ate the casserole without saying much. He knew his mother really didn't want answers to her questions. He knew she was in as much pain as he was. Only his dad coming back could solve the pain they felt. John and Emily didn't feel safe. There was not an active father-figure or protector for either of them. They were alone.

September 12, 2001
Maryland

The Academy had collected the cell phones and issued all the midshipmen real guns, not drill rifles. Each company was instructed on the use and care of weapons. Some already knew how, but the Navy wanted everyone trained and ready. They didn't want a midshipman with a gun who didn't know how to use it properly.

Mary's company marched in formation back to Bancroft Hall; and for the first time, she realized what military life really meant. It was more than being on a ship or aircraft carrier on the open sea, or being a pilot flying in the great blue yonder. Being part of the military was being a part of the *armed forces.* It was about defending the country. War was not impersonal. Guns meant shooting to kill and that was very personal.

"Boy that was intense. It was so real," she confided to her bunkmate when they were back in the room.

"Yes, it was. But we knew we entered the armed forces, and now we're finally armed," the other female midshipman said, happy with the turn of events. She was ready to kick butt.

"Well, I did do well. My trigger squeeze was excellent the instructor said," Mary replied. She didn't want to give the impression she was a wimpy girl.

"Did you hit anything on your target? I missed a lot. I've got to get my aim perfected."

"I hit the body circle every time, even if I didn't get the bull's eye," Mary said proudly.

They stopped their conversation when the Battalion Commander glanced in, looking for one of the other two midshipmen who bunked in the room.

"It's almost time for dinner," Mary said, looking at her watch. "I need to use the head first."

When Mary returned, they filed out into the corridor to go to King

Hall to eat. They marched over with their company. Sitting together, they ate family-style passing the bowls and platters of food. Even though Mary, and the rest of the midshipmen, consumed nearly four thousand calories a day, no one gained weight due to the amount of rigorous activity that was required of them. The meal conversation centered on the topics of target practice and when they would be given their phones back to talk to the outside world.

September 12, 2001
New Mexico

Since no other events had occurred the next day, Ted decided to go into work. It seemed safe to leave Teddy and Freda at home.

"Ted, I wish you would stay home. I want things to feel normal. I can't stay away from the television; I want to know everything. But I'm getting stressed out seeing the planes crash into those towers over and over and then seeing them collapse. It's like a bad nightmare that I can't wake up from," Freda admitted at breakfast.

"I know. That's why I'm going to the office. I think everyone in America has to have seen the replay at least twice. Why they continue showing it is beyond me. I want some normalcy. And the only way I can do that is to do something normal."

"I hope school opens again soon, so I can experience that," Freda said, stirring her Cheerios around in the skim milk, never taking a bite.

Teddy ate his cereal and didn't contribute one way or the other. He seemed interested in staying with the News. As soon as he finished, he placed his bowl in the sink and headed back to the living room to watch the latest.

By afternoon, he was tired of it and needed a break. He called a friend. "Hey, do you think they might have the golf course open even though classes are canceled?"

"Nah; I already drove by there to check. A sign 'Closed until campus is reopened for all activities,' was posted. I'm thinking they'll open for classes tomorrow."

"Maybe," Teddy responded, not as hopeful.

September 12, 2001
New York

Jack hadn't heard from any of his main staff from the office. He called Jeff's home phone, but there was no answer.

He refused to watch the television, but continually listened to radio talk shows where persons in the buildings called in to report their miraculous escapes.

One woman was saying, "I felt the building shake above us and knew something was wrong and headed to the stairs. I wasn't waiting for anyone to tell me to get out of there. My office was on the eighty-fifth floor.

"When I got in the stairwell there was smoke and people were hurriedly running down the stairs. The pace was unbelievable. I really don't know how I did it.

"I just kept moving and some people were saying, 'go, go, go,' and that's the rate I matched. It seemed like eternity. Eventually, I got to the bottom. Once outside, I saw the debris and started running away. I just couldn't stop. When I got two blocks, I turned and saw the one building start to collapse and went back to running with all the others.

"Before I knew it I was all the way to the Brooklyn Bridge. When I got home I was covered in white dust. I quickly showered it off and got into bed. My body started shaking uncontrollably. It's the next day, but I can't get out of bed. I just can't believe it. I can't believe I made it," she said and started crying.

"Thank you for calling in. Swift thinking really saved your life." the host said. "The next caller was in the North Tower…"

Jack started lying to himself. He began thinking that maybe Jeff could've made it. He walked down to the area and posted a picture of him with others, even though he was sure he hadn't made it.

Jack saw many mourning persons in the street, posting pictures of their loved ones who would never come home.

September 12, 2001
Paris

Claudia had slept better than she thought she would, considering the news and her concerns about GUILE. She pulled on her red silk kimono and twisted her hair into a knot, using a chopstick-like hairpin.

Dialing room service she ordered, "Good Morning. Please send up a croissant and egg sandwich, a large glass of orange juice, and a pot of strong coffee."

"Do you want cheese on your sandwich, Madame? And cream for your coffee?"

"Yes, I'd like Brie on the sandwich and no cream," she answered.

If she were in New York the show would've been canceled, but here in France, everything was normal, except for the flights out to the United States, and the occasional special reports on the television.

Before long there was a knock at the door. "Room Service."

Claudia opened the door and the bellboy rolled in the cart.

"Out or in, Madame?"

The French doors were open; it was another lovely day in Paris. "Out," she answered.

He rolled the cart onto the small balcony. After she handed him the tip, he discretely disappeared.

The morning view of the Eiffel Tower went unnoticed as Claudia read the international newspaper. She learned of the plane that crashed into the Pentagon and another that crashed in a field in Pennsylvania. As she ate her breakfast sandwich and drank the coffee, she pieced together GUILE's involvement. Over the years, they had ever-so-slowly orchestrated it. She had definitely played a part. She hadn't known that it would've ever led to something so drastic.

"*I wonder if they had a hand in the first bombing attempt a few years ago*," she thought, then nodded her head affirmatively. "*Money is important, but not that important.*"

She compartmentalized her new awareness in her mind, at least until the show was out of the way. She came here to do business, and business was what she was going to do. As they say, 'the show must go on' and hers did now.

After showering and dressing, she walked down the street to get to work. There was much to attend to before the show started.

"The set is fantastic. I love it. It's a perfect backdrop for my dresses in this show," Claudia told Maria, approving the execution of her idea.

Maria smiled and was glad no changes were needed. "Good. Sign this please, Ms. Lei," she said, handing the clipboard to Claudia to sign-off on the set design. Maria could cut them a check and get that off her plate.

"Now let me see what the stylists are doing with the models."

They walked back stage to the numerous hair and makeup booths. Ten models were standing waiting their turn. Five were sitting in the chairs as the hairstylists and makeup artists worked their magic, giving each a touch of radiant beauty.

"I don't like that look. She's going to be wearing something that is flowing; I don't want her hair to be more noticed than the dress. Do you understand?"

Of course, the stylist did. He had been working in the fashion field for many years; hardly anyone ever complained. He rolled his eyes in his head as he turned toward the model and took a few clips out of her hair and reset it again.

He wasn't as pleased with it, but he had to please Claudia, even if he didn't like it himself. "Will this do?"

Claudia had already turned her attention on another girl's face. She glanced and made a sound of, "Aha," then turned back to the one she was dealing with at the moment. She had hardly noticed the change.

The stylist placed his hands on his hips, rolled his eyes, and exhaled loudly. Then he said under his breath, "I could have left it, for all she would have noticed."

The fashion industry was made up of many temperamental artists, who liked it their way. He was no different. It all came down to who was the head artist in charge.

Claudia worked with the dressers last. When initially satisfied, she took a seat in the front row to evaluate the total run through. She gave constructive comments to the models with certain dresses, and not-so constructive criticism of others, making the model do the catwalk a second time. Claudia was a perfectionist. It was a trait that had gotten her where she was. Sometimes, it was a fault.

CHAPTER 9

September 13, 2001
Paris

Claudia awoke the morning of the show to the sound of the American National Anthem being played. She looked out to see that it was coming from the Arc d' Triumph. She felt proud to be an American and a New Yorker. This attack was personal. It was her America, her New York.

On the other end of her emotional teeter-totter was fear. She was now afraid to be a member of GUILE. As she showered and dressed she couldn't keep her mind off of it. How could she go home and pretend that she wasn't responsible? GUILE would continue to use her to meet their agenda; of that she was sure. She no longer wanted to be a part of it, but what could she do?

A limousine picked her up from the hotel to take her to the show. "*I guess this is my swan song*," she thought and smiled. She was filled with so many mixed emotions. When she arrived, she saw the place was packed with celebrities. Many she knew. Several gave her a hug or kissed her cheeks. Others shook her hand, showing their support. She had designed many items for all of them over the years.

The house lights lowered and the bright lights hit the catwalk. The audience hushed and took their seats. Claudia went back stage and managed the show from there. Most everyone was ready and lined up. With a wave of a hand, the music started. The thin models slinked onto the stage and down the catwalk one by one. They twirled at the end, pausing for a moment, just long enough for the photographers to catch a shot. Then up the other side they went for the audience on the left to get a better look.

On return, some were stripped out of the first dress and helped into another. Rapidly, they joined the line again. Judging by the applause, the audience loved it. The show was a success.

At the end, Claudia Lei took the walk and they all filed down and up, lining the complete catwalk. Photographers continued to snap shots of the group and the individual designs. The pictures would be published in magazines by week's end. The best would make it to the web.

After the show, Claudia attended a reception and sipped champagne, while the others rubbed elbows with fame. Claudia looked elegant in her long red silk brocade dress. The rush and long hours had been worth it. She loved this attention and the notoriety. But most of all, she loved designing. It was a shame that most of the show was blurred by the turn of events, and that she would have to give it up.

September 13, 2001
New York City

Jack selected several office-space properties for the real estate agent to show him. The realtor told him the number of square feet of each space that they had seen today.

"You can see that this space can hold twenty cubicles over here. It has two lavatories for the employees, and as you have already noticed, a private lavatory in your office," she added.

Jack had reviewed the sizing and feasibility of each potential office before he contacted her and knew which one he truly was interested in. But he had to do the customary 'sightseeing' as he called it.

"I like the view," he confided at the place that he was truly interested in. "How soon can I be in?" He didn't want to waste any more time. He needed to begin interviewing; and he needed this space to get started. Time was money and both were wasting away.

"According to the listing, it's ASAP. If you want to sign a contract, I'll take it to the landlord for approval. I'm sure there won't be a problem." She was eager to get the deal signed.

"We can do that at your office, or we can do the contract right now," Jack offered, trying to speed up the process.

"I don't have a contract with me. We'll need to go to the office to take care of that business."

"Okay. Let's go."

On the way down the elevator, Jack called his chauffeur to pick him up at the realtors in the next half hour.

After signing the papers, Jack said, "Here's my home number, call when you have approval."

Before the recent events in the city, she would've thought that comment was a come-on on his part, but she was aware that his previous offices had been in the World Trade building. She knew office space was going to be scarce and in high demand. The realtor was only surprised by the fact that he was shopping for it so soon.

Jack's chauffeur picked him up as requested and drove him across town to the usual restaurant.

"Good day, sir," the Maitre d' said as he walked Jack to his usual table. "Will Ms. Lei be with you today?"

"No, just me," Jack replied, making a mental note to call her.

He selected a soup, main course, and no dessert. After lunch Jack returned home; there was nowhere else to go at the present. It wasn't long before the realtor called.

"The contract has been accepted Mr. Jones. You can pick up the keys, or I can bring them to you."

Jack thought that she was coming-on to him. He wasn't interested, so he replied, "I'll pick them up at your office in the morning. Say around nine."

This was earlier than she usually arrived at work, but she agreed.

As soon as he ended that call, Jack placed another using his cell phone.

Claudia answered, "Bon Jour. What's up?" She was feeling a little paranoid.

"How was the show?"

"Great! How are you doing?"

"Fine; I picked out new office space today; soon there won't be any available. I needed to work fast before the shock wore off and the others got out there, grabbing everything up. I'll arrange a decorator tomorrow."

"Did any of your employees make it?"

"No, I don't think so. Many are missing."

"That's a shame," Claudia said, grossly understating her feelings for everyone, as a tear rolled down her cheek.

"I don't think any flights have resumed here," Jack reported.

"I thought not," Claudia said as she wiped the tear from her face. "Since I'm stuck over here, I've decided I might as well use the time as a vacation, like you suggested."

"Good idea," Jack commented. "See you when you get back." He closed his phone, ending their conversation.

Jack reviewed the paper and planned the number of essential employees he would need to start again. He still had current contracts in the works and that data was stored on his home office computer. All had not been lost. Those contracts in progress would directly deposit funds into the business account. Salaries were withdrawn automatically, including his. He immediately contacted the bank to stop all withdrawals until further notice, except his salary of course. They sympathetically assisted.

Next he placed a call to an office decorator.

The receptionist answered, "Corporate Decors, how may I help you?"

"I need to speak with one of your decorators. I have an office space that needs work. Is someone in or can you have one call me at the earliest convenience? I'm interested in beginning yesterday."

"If you can hold, we might have someone available to speak with you at this time. If not, I'll take down your number when I return. Could you give me your name please?"

"Yes, this is Mr. Jones, Mr. Jack Jones."

"Just a minute, Mr. Jones."

She placed him on hold and Jack began hearing Verdi's Rigoletto. That impressed him.

"Yes, Mr. Jones. I'm sorry to keep you waiting. I'm Gregory Michaels. How can I be of assistance?"

"I have just procured new office space. I recently lost mine in the attack. I need to have it done as soon as possible, so I can get my company up and running again in New York. Can you meet me there in the morning around ten?"

"Let me see," the decorator said, looking at his schedule for the next day. It was completely blank. "Yes, I can squeeze you in. What's the office address?"

Jack gave him the information and ended the call. He walked to the kitchen to let his chef know what time he'd be having dinner. Since he was spending most of his time at home, he was anxious to get the chef out of his way. He faked a cough as he entered the room, still feigning recovering from an illness that had saved his life.

September 13, 2001
Virginia

"John, the county Board of Education is reopening schools on Monday. I figured you didn't know because you've had on your headphones all day," his mother said.

"Great. Can't wait," John responded, sounding as if he were being sarcastic, but he was actually truly glad. He was bored. Nothing was worse to a teenager than boredom.

"How's Gramps?"

"He's being released sometime tomorrow. I'd like you to go with me and bring him home."

"Fine, what time are you going?" John asked, hoping for another day to sleep in.

"I can't imagine them letting him go home before eleven, so I'll go about nine or nine-thirty."

"That works for me."

"I'll heat up the tuna casserole. Would you take out this trash? It smells like the tuna cans. Please start helping out here. I can't do everything. I need your help," she said sincerely.

In the kitchen Emily plopped down at the table and began crying. She was emotionally drained and exhausted.

When John came out, he felt sorry for her and gave her a pat on the back. "It'll all work out, Mom," he said, hoping that someday soon it would. He gathered up the trash and placed it in the large container outside. He stuck his head through the open back door and asked, "Do they pick up tomorrow?"

The question momentarily pulled Emily out of her woes. She thought for a second and responded, "Yeah?" She didn't think John knew those things.

"I'll put it by the street and be right back," John yelled, as he dragged the large plastic container along the drive.

September 13, 2001
Paris

Claudia looked over the maps of Europe and Asia. She was planning her long journey. She placed a call. "I'd like a flight to Zurich. Do you have one in the morning in first class?"

"Yes, we do Madame. We have one at nine and one at noon."

"Please book me on the nine o'clock. My name is…," she gave the necessary information required.

Next she called Maria's room. "Maria, I'm taking a vacation. I'm not exactly sure when I'll return. Please take care of the dresses and clean up all the details here. Then get back to New York as soon as flights resume."

"Okay; anything else?"

"Yes; if by any chance I'm not back in time for the fall show in Los Angeles, set up everything exactly how we did it here. We'll repeat the show in all of our usual cities, an international show so-to-speak. Why reinvent the wheel, hey?"

"Yes, Ms. Lei," Maria said, relieved to hear such good news. She was tired and had been run ragged.

"Au Revoir," she answered, modulating her voice higher on the ending, sounding upbeat and carefree, all the while feeling quite the opposite. It was one of the blessings of an Asian heritage.

Claudia packed her bags for Switzerland. She was visiting her bank to take care of important personal business.

September 13, 2001
New Mexico

Ted took the U.S. flag used for holidays out of the storage closet and started out the front door. His son followed him to see where he was going. Ted unfurled it and placed it in the holder by the carport. While out earlier, he noticed many yards decorated with flags, showing their support and honoring those Americans who had died. He wanted to do the same.

"Hey Dad, that's a great idea." Oddly, it felt like they had done something to help.

"I wish it was my idea, Son, but I'm just joining all of the flags that are already out in yards and on posts. I saw them on my way into the agency today. I told the office to leave ours at half-mast on the pole 24/7 until we get this resolved."

"I know. I've been listening to families who have lost their loved ones and feeling like I want to help them. I'd like to contribute to some of the funds that are starting up."

"Sounds like a good idea, Teddy. Don't do anything about it until we find out which ones are legit. You don't want to give to funds over the web and end up funding the terrorists," Ted told him, advising his son on the ways of the unscrupulous.

"Okay," Teddy agreed as they walked into the house arm in arm.

Ted kissed Freda on the cheek and asked, "What's good for dinner?"

"Your favorite."

"Great. What did you two learn on television today?"

Teddy updated his dad on the latest news as he set the table. Ted poured iced tea in the glasses. Freda pulled the warm tortillas from the oven. She placed them and the skillet of hot chicken, onions, and peppers on the table for fajitas.

CHAPTER 10

September 14, 2001
Peru

Juan Perez had breakfast and prepared for the trip to Chimbote. He had arranged a private plane to fly him up and back. He didn't want to hang around for long, nor talk to others about Father Paolo.

His driver took him to the airport and waited until Juan's plane took off. He didn't have anything better to do.

"*I never had a family; Father Paolo was all I had. You took my parents when I needed them. Now you take him. Why?*" Juan thought, poising the angry question to God, while the plane seemed to float on air.

Juan didn't realize that one of the reasons he had a position with GUILE was due to the fact he was a loner. True, he had inherited his dad's position after he died; yet, sometimes GUILE ignored the inheritance rule when it wasn't convenient or didn't serve them well.

Juan's dad had died when he was young, giving him a fictionalized image of his father. Father Paolo had never wanted to change that image, or to tell him the stark truth. His father had been ruthless, and really didn't care much for his wife, or young son for that matter. Father Paolo had looked on his death as a blessing for Juan. It was such a shame that the earthquake had taken his loving mother, as well.

When the plane landed, Juan took a limo from the airport to the cathedral. A few days ago it was sunny and the trip was welcomed; now everything was gloomy. Even the clouds were hanging around the shoreline. The park looked dark and foreboding. The airport limo pulled to the curb. He waited for the driver to open his door.

"I'll need a return ride to the airport at four. Please come back for me then," he said, handing him a handsome tip to ensure his return.

"Yes, Señor!" The driver smiled when he saw the amount. He didn't realize that it was his total tip for that day's service.

Juan mounted the steps of the cathedral slowly and walked inside. Others from the parish had already gathered. They were seated and waiting, along with the Monsignor, who greeted Juan before he made his way to the Sacristy to prepare for the service. Walking to the fount, Juan dipped his fingers into the holy water and made the sign of the cross. He tried to inconspicuously make his way to the front row, but his soles clicked on the marble floor. Juan genuflected before entering the pew.

Once the priest had on his vestments, he and the altar boys circled around the building. They came in the vestibule entrance and carried the processional cross up the aisle to the altar.

Juan kept his eyes on the wooden casket, refusing to look at the crucifix. He no longer believed in God, and definitely not one that cared about him. He made all the right moves at the right times during the service; he had been well trained by Father Paolo.

As he knelt, he thought back to a time when he was assisting Father with Mass. Sometimes, he had nodded off almost missing his cue to ring the bell as the priest held up the host to be consecrated. "*Father Paolo had always been patient with me. He'd clear his throat or tap his foot on the wooden floor, causing a vibration to stir me awake*," Juan remembered and smiled.

"The Mass has ended; go in peace," the Monsignor said, drawing Juan out of his thoughts.

The funeral director walked forward and announced there was to be a wake in the adjacent parish hall. The Monsignor stepped down with the processional cross, leading the recessional down the aisle. The parish priests, who were pallbearers, lifted the casket and slowly followed. The director motioned for Juan to step out next. He followed with his head bent in mourning. He watched the casket as it was placed into the hearse. He walked on to the white limousine that waited behind.

The cars lined up. They drove a few miles out of town to the old cathedral's cemetery, where they circled the gravesite. His parents were supposedly buried there somewhere; where exactly he didn't know, neither had he or did he care.

The Monsignor said, "We commit the soul of our brother Paolo to God, in the name of the Father, the Son, and the Holy Spirit."

"Amen."

The casket was lowered into the grave. Juan tossed a rose on top of it and walked back to the car. He rubbed his arms. He felt as cold as his heart.

Once in the limousine, his cell phone rang.

"Yes?"

"Mr. Morocco, please contact your people and tell them to begin."

The phone went dead. Juan snapped it shut. He did nothing about the call.

"*It can wait. It's not safe to talk here,*" he thought.

Back at the Cathedral De Nuevo Chimbote, Juan got a drink of punch, wishing for something much stronger. He greeted most of the priests and gave them his condolences, only to have them returned. Everyone who knew Father Paola felt the loss.

Other well wishers who knew Juan's parents and Father Paolo said things like, "Juan, I'm so sorry for you. I know Father meant the world to you."

He smiled and said, "Thank you."

He thought, "*I wish this was over. I didn't even want to come. Death means nothing, just that you're dead. Then there's nothing.*"

He remembered when he was ten and stood with Father Paolo at the funeral of his parents. People then had said similar things. Some, who had gathered, handed him Mass cards. It hadn't helped ease the pain. Nothing ever could or would.

Before leaving, Juan gave the church a contribution to pay for all the funeral expenses, including the food. He departed sharply at four, when the driver pulled up. Once on the jet, he poured a glass of Jack Daniels, downing it in one gulp. Then he poured another, glad that the plane was whisking him away from the memories.

September 14, 2001
Paris

Claudia checked out of the hotel. Boarding a plane to Switzerland, she took her first class seat and buckled up. She downed a glass of champagne as soon as they took off. A plate of strawberries dipped in dark Swiss chocolate was on the side, which she only sampled. When the menu came for breakfast, Claudia selected an omelet and croissant. She had hardly finished, when they began their descent. The snowy Alps and the Italian/Switzerland border were in sight. She shivered at the sight.

Exiting through customs, she showed her U.S. passport.

"How long will you be staying with us, Ms. Lei?" The official asked.

"Just a few days; I'll be leaving for India the day after tomorrow."

"Reason for your visit?"

"Banking," Claudia answered truthfully.

"Have a good day," he said, as he handed back her passport; he then yelled, "Next," before she had moved on.

Claudia walked to the baggage carrousel. She placed her two large pieces of luggage on a rent-a-cart and wheeled it to the curb, where the limousines were lined up. She approached one. The chauffeur opened the door for her and placed her bags in the trunk.

Once in the driver's seat, he asked "Where to?"

"The Park Hyatt," Claudia answered.

The car headed for the city's center. Aside from wanting a five-star hotel, Claudia also wanted to walk anywhere in the downtown district easily. She selected a hotel that met both criteria. After checking in, she went directly to her suite. When the bellboy left, she quickly changed into a blue business suit.

Claudia walked to the Finter Bank Zurich. There she signed in and waited to be escorted to her safe deposit box on the second floor. The customary two keys were used to unlock the box, and she carried it to one of the private rooms. Once alone, she pulled several items from the box, checked to make sure she had chosen the right ones, and placed them in her purse. Claudia met the bank guard again and they returned the deposit box to the vault for safe keeping.

Downstairs she transferred funds from her personal account into the business account, matching the amount that was earned for the Paris show. She wanted her employees to be able to receive salaries for several months. By then, they would realize she wasn't coming back.

"*Knowing Jack, he'll buy the company out, let Maria run it, and continue using my name, sans the original owner, Ms. Lei,*" she thought. She had seen him handle other business buy-outs that way in the past.

Once the transfer of funds was processed, she withdrew currency to use in India. The teller efficiently made the exchange and Claudia left the bank, having completed what she had set out to do. On her way back to the hotel, she stopped at a favorite restaurant. She enjoyed an early dinner. Afterward, she walked back to the hotel feeling confident.

She ran a large tub of hot water and added bubble bath. She undressed and slipped beneath the white foam and soaked away any useless stress and anxiety that remained. As she looked out the large window at the colors of sunset, she calculated her next move, like an expert chess player.

September 14, 2001
Virginia

Gramps came home. He seemed to not be in too bad of shape. He had a nebulizer machine that he was supposed to use three times a day for treatments to help him breathe easier. When he wasn't using it, he used up what little breath he had relating his memory of the United States being under attack at Pearl Harbor.

"It was much different, John."

"How's that, Gramps? All those ships were sunk and so many

servicemen lost their lives."

"Well, John, we heard about it by radio. We didn't have any movies like we do of the trade buildings. We couldn't see it happening. It wasn't until Hollywood made a movie of that day a few years ago that we could really see it how it was.

"But even so, it was a different time. We were already worried about Hitler; now we had to get the Japanese. We had good American spirit. We ended up saving us, as well as all of Europe, because of it."

John was fascinated by Gramps' tale. "All I know is: it makes me sick to watch the video of Tuesday's attack. I hope that America can do something about it. A bully got us, not a country. They'll be really hard to find and get rid of. Bullies always are."

"That they are, John; that they are," Gramps said, shaking his head about the incident and the loss of so many innocent lives.

A news flash came across the bottom of the screen. Gramps turned up the volume with the remote. Several different congressmen announced that a bill had been introduced and passed. It was the Emergency Supplemental Appropriations Act for Recovery from and Response to Terrorist Attacks on the United States in the amount of forty million dollars. It was beginning to feel like America was doing something, especially when the two parties put down their usual differences long enough to unite in one cause.

September 15, 2001
Zurich

In the morning, Claudia ordered room service and read her paper. America was rallying, it seemed. There were photos of flags everywhere. Other countries were supporting the United States, England assisting them the most.

Claudia wore her long hair loose and dressed in a simple dress. She walked to the Lienhardt and Partner, not far from her regular bank. They spoke only German, but they understood her well enough when she asked the teller in English to exchange her Swiss bank check for Swiss Francs. She wanted one thousand dollars in small denominations of spendable money. For an additional small fee, they provided the cash in an easy-to-carry case that came complete with wheels, making it even easier to pull along back to the hotel. On the way, she shopped at several stores.

After lunch, she went to yet another bank. This time she exchanged cash for twenty-four-karat gold pieces in one-tenth of an ounce size. Only in Zurich could she exchange cash for gold. The small denominations would be easier to use for payment, to anyone, in any country. Outside of America, the rest of the world preferred gold.

The employees didn't lift an eyebrow at the exchange. Bankers in Switzerland had become accustomed to the rich doing odd things with their money. They had stopped asking questions long ago. They cared only about business and fair exchange; more than that, they didn't care to know.

There was no record of her name, and even a surveillance camera wouldn't have picked up Claudia Lei. She didn't look like her usual self. She wore dark sunglasses, a short red-haired teased wig, a false bra in size D cup, and a mini-skirt with stilettos. The appearance of a cheap hooker, not a wealthy socialite, was achieved, as evidenced by the men doing double-takes. They surmised that her cash probably came from her dealings on the street, possibly even her pimp's drug money, no doubt.

Claudia was escorted to a side room and given the gold. There she transferred the heavy bag of coins to the suitcase that she had brought the bills in.

"Will there be anything else, Madame?"

She only shook her head and started rolling the case out of the bank, smacking her large wad of gum. She blew a bubble near the door, making it explode right before she exited. The large pop echoed in the bare sterile environment of the bank walls.

The manager rolled his eyes and shook his head in contempt. Yet, he continued to watch her swing her hips as she walked down the street. He couldn't resist the attraction of the female body, classless or not.

CHAPTER 11

September 16, 2001

Claudia's bags were packed and ready to go. She was dressed and finishing her breakfast, as she waited for the computer to come online. Once on the Internet, she went to the bank's website and registered a user name and password.

"Great! I'm in. I knew I could count on the efficiency of that German Swiss bank," she said aloud.

"*Now, let's see if I can set up a wire transfer to my bank account in China. Of course, it'll turn the funds that I deposited into Yuans, and there'll be another exchange fee charged. But, hey, it'll be worth it. This way, no one can follow Claudia Lei into China*," she thought, clicking around her new online account page.

It took an hour for the complete transfer of funds. She glanced at the clock. There was still time to make her flight.

She dialed the front desk. "I'd like to check out now. Would you arrange a ride for me to the airport?"

"Certainly, Madame; I'll send the bellboy right up."

In minutes there was a knock at the door. The young uniformed man put her four bags on the luggage rack. She snapped her purse closed, as she handed him a banknote.

They took the elevator to the lobby in silence. She was greeted by the concierge, who escorted her to the limousine for the short ride to the airport. He had previously been adequately tipped.

At the airport, the hotel chauffeur loaded her bags onto a luggage rack. She tipped him and wheeled the cart to the check-in counter.

"I have a flight booked for Delhi, India," Claudia informed the airline agent, handing an American passport to the woman for processing.

"Yes. Here it is," she said, finding the reservation.

A punch-card ticket was produced and handed to Claudia. Tags were placed on her three pieces of luggage.

"Your flight leaves from Gate 8."

Claudia rolled the wheeled case of gold with her to the boarding area. She sat patiently, waiting for the arrival of the plane. Within minutes it arrived. She watched as it pulled up to the gate.

The stewardess announced, "First class passengers please line up for boarding to Delhi."

Claudia did so and watched the previous passengers disembark. When the line ended, she handed her ticket to the attendant and wheeled her small case down the jet way. She took her seat by the window.

The flight was a long one. It wouldn't arrive until almost midnight, so she slept. She would stay one night in another hotel before making her way to a spa.

That night she didn't sleep; she had lots of work to do. She began the long task of sewing the pieces of gold into the linings of some clothing that she would be keeping. At least one piece of luggage wouldn't be kept when she was finished. She had already packed the articles of clothing that she wouldn't need again, like the blue power suit. It wouldn't be needed where she was going. The wig and stiletto heels had been tossed in a dumpster earlier, erasing a link to the banking transactions.

In the morning, she shopped for Indian cotton and gauze fabrics by the bolt with thread to match. Her week at the spa wouldn't be all luxury as it was designed to appear. She would spend her nights sewing new clothes.

"*I hope one week will be enough time*," she worried, as she next waited in line to buy a ticket.

Finally it was her turn. "I'd like a round-trip ticket to Narendranagar please," Claudia requested with a smile. She knew she wasn't coming back here. Only her luggage would return, but GUILE and Jack wouldn't know that. She had other plans and was hoping the extra time would afford her the space to begin making that move.

"What day will you be returning?" The agent at the counter asked.

"Next week. That's umm," she paused.

"September 24th?"

"Yes, that's good."

She paid him for the ticket and waited another hour for the train. The ride by rail was four hours long. Upon arrival, she would have to charter a helicopter to Ananda Spa. They were exclusively an out-of-the-way spa and expecting her. She had been there ten years ago for a GUILE meeting. She knew what they offered and how she could use it to her advantage. Otherwise, she wouldn't have selected a spa in her plan of escape.

September 20, 2001
Washington, D.C.

The President's address to Congress was aired to the nation at nine. He declared America's future moves as 'War on Terror.' To Congress, it wasn't really a war; it was just appropriations.

"Tonight we face new and sudden national challenges. My fellow citizens, for the last nine days, the entire world has seen for itself the state of our Union, and it is strong.

"…We will come together to improve air safety, to dramatically expand the number of air marshals on domestic flights, and take new measures to prevent hijacking. We will come together to promote stability and keep our airlines flying, with direct assistance during this emergency…"

This was what John Germaine wanted to hear. This was what every American wanted to hear. More flags appeared on buildings and overpasses. Little flags were lining lawns; flag stickers were placed on car windows. The American Spirit was gaining strength. And those selling flags were making money hand-over-fist.

September 20, 2001
New York, New York

"Hey, Claudia, good morning," Jack greeted, as the airing of the President's speech ended.

"Hi, Jack," Claudia calmly answered. She was glad that he hadn't called during her breakfast or worse yet, during the wonderful yoga meditation period.

The meditations were helping her gain clarity on everything. She was seeing things for what they truly were. The massages helped each day to move the toxins of stress out of her body. The impurities that had built up due to her rich-food diet over the last few years were taking a hike.

Jack talked about the key points of the President's speech, as she took deep breaths and exhaled.

Trying to sound normal, she asked Jack, "Were you able to get an office up and running yet?" She was sure he had, knowing him. The truth was she didn't care.

"Yes; all the furniture is in. I have a skeleton crew of workers to keep my New York concerns running. The plane crashes were just a hiccup. I even got some of my factories to make little American flags that people can attach to their car windows. They flap in the air as they drive. It looks like the Presidential Limousine," he said, laughing at the absurdity and irony of it.

"*Wow. The loss of those many lives and all he calls it is plane crashes and hiccup. I can't believe this guy,*" she thought, shaking her head. "*And of course, Jack's making money.*"

"That's good. Well, I gotta run. It's time for my colonic appointment. Sorry."

Jack couldn't see her place her hand over the phone and say to no one, "I'll be right there."

"Bye, Jack."

He closed his phone and grabbed a bottle of water. After drinking half, he placed another call.

"I don't know when she's coming home yet. I'll let you know." He closed the phone and stared at the strange skyline. It was odd not seeing the twin towers. He finished his water and tossed the plastic bottle toward the recycle bin and made it.

"He scores!" Jack said, lifting his arms in victory.

After shutting down his computer for the night, he locked up the office. As he walked through his foyer, he took a sniff of the new flower arrangement that had been delivered that afternoon. He unlocked the elevator and headed for bed.

September 20, 2001
Annapolis, Maryland

Mary filed out of the field house. They had congregated to view the President's speech as a collective body on the large viewing screens. The Commander-in-Chief was bigger than life and the past nine-day's events seemed to be also.

Her group of midshipmen marched back to Bancroft Hall. She was still carrying a gun at her side, and would be for some time yet. Now that she had perfected its care and aim, she didn't feel as uncomfortable with it. It gave her a sense of security.

Before being dismissed to go inside to their rooms, the commander announced that their phones were being returned. "You'll be allowed to make one call home before retiring for the night. I'll bring the phone to your room. After that the old rule will be enforced. No cell use during the weekdays."

One by one each group heard, "Dismissed!" Breaking formation, Mary headed into the dorm, taking the nearest set of steps. Others took different hallways and stairs anxious to get to their rooms.

Before long she heard, "Matthews!"

"Yes sir," Mary said, accepting the cell phone, which was in a labeled zip-locked bag.

"Smith!" and on it went until all had their phones.

Mary placed the call to her parents in Massachusetts.

"Hello," her mother said as she answered the phone, wondering who was calling at that hour.

"Hi, Mom; I only have a few minutes to talk. We were just issued our phones and allowed to call."

"Thanks for calling, dear. We got the automated call last week and I wondered when I would hear from you."

"We're fine, Mom. Our classes have resumed. Things will begin to feel like normal again. Tell Dad I love him."

"I will, dear."

"I'll call again some weekend."

"Okay, Mary. Talk to you then. I love you," her mother said.

"Love you, too. Bye." Mary pushed the end-call button.

She turned her phone off and placed it back in the bag. She stored it in its normal place, her footlocker.

September 20, 2001
Ananda Spa, India

Claudia had to keep the pretense going with Jack until check-out day, September 24th. His call had destroyed the peaceful feeling that the spa had given her. She picked up the needle and began sewing the quilted jacket that she had been making. It held a piece of gold in each diamond section. It was rather heavy all in all, but when worn, it wasn't too cumbersome. She finished the body of the jacket and tried it on.

Looking in the bathroom mirror, she liked what she saw. She removed it and started quilting the sleeve. It was going to be more difficult. She had to avoid placing coins around the elbows. She needed freedom of movement. When she stitched the last sleeve in place, she packed the coat in one of the smaller pieces of luggage.

When it was time for her Tai Chi, she walked slowly down the hall to the pavilion. The views of the mountains gave a peaceful appearance, as the group moved as one.

"*This will bring back my old skills of Karate and Kung Fu,*" she thought, as she imagined blocking an assassin's moves with her arms in self-defense in a slow-motion sequence of a Jackie Chan movie.

Claudia had taken Karate as a child and had earned her Black Belt. She had been good at it, quick and agile. The Tai Chi was helping her stay focused as she gracefully changed positions and sifted her weight. The movements refreshed her muscle memory. It was truly being in the moment.

"*They'll come at me when I least expect it. They may even send Jack to do the job. They know I trust him the most, but that's all over,*" she thought, as she achieved inner peace and focus with each and every movement.

A gong sounded as they finished the session. They filed quietly to the dining room. She had signed an oath of silence during her stay. She didn't want to accidentally say anything that might incriminate herself, or accidentally lead anyone her direction when she left. She left her phone in her room so there would be no chance of her answering it in the open for all ears to hear, or know that she wasn't really remaining silent, just distant.

She was staying alert and on guard at all times. Even at night, she set booby traps to warn her if a window or door opened while she slept. With GUILE there was no such thing as being too careful or prepared. When they came, and they would come, it would be a surprise.

But GUILE didn't know that she had gone rogue yet. She was still Claudia Lei, doing Claudia-type things. She only hoped Jack didn't come to escort her back to the States.

CHAPTER 12

September 23, 2001
Ananda Spa, India

Claudia had packed everything into the two small suitcases that she would need for her long trip into anonymity. All of her New York clothes were packed in the large suitcases. Most of her travel-sized cosmetics had been used and tossed in the trash. Just a few of those remained to be sent back home.

She bought a new toothbrush in Zurich because she needed to have everything in the cases to give the appearance that she was really planning on going back. She reasoned that if she had taken it, when they checked the luggage, they would know right away to start a full-scale search. Instead, she hoped that they would give her the benefit of the doubt and think she had possibly missed the train or flight. That was a big 'if', but she was hoping for the best and planning for the worst.

She packed the cell phone in the large luggage labeled with the prepaid transfer tags. She had purchased a transfer for the baggage back to the airport for her scheduled flight to Paris. If all went well, the luggage would go from the Delhi station to the airport and be loaded onto a plane that she would never catch.

"*The phone's on so they can track the chip. This might buy me a little time at least,*" she thought hopefully, as she chopped off her long hair and fashioned a clip-on bun with the length. When she left tomorrow, no one at the spa would know the difference once she had her hairpiece in place.

In the morning, she made her way to the station. She bought several tickets. In case her trail was followed, she wanted it to point in several directions.

"I would like a ticket to Dedradun. And I would like to buy another for my friend who is going to Bareilly, please?"

The clerk took her money. All was within the Indian border, so he didn't bother to ask for identification. He passed her the two tickets.

She placed her small bags in a locker and turned the key. Next she boarded the Delhi train and placed her large suitcases overhead for the long night ride. She hurried to the lavatory before the train left. Once there she removed her makeup with her last moist towelette. She unclipped her faux bun. Her hair was just long enough to pull back in a band. She planned on cutting it much shorter. The train whistle blew a short toot and the conductor yelled the equivalent of 'all aboard.' She rushed to the door just as the train jerked forward, almost causing her to fall as she stepped from the car.

"Bye." Claudia waved as the train pulled out of the station, pretending she was seeing someone off. In a way she was; her previous existence and all she symbolized was departing. Walking past a trashcan, she tossed in the bun. She retrieved her small cases from the lockers and took a jeep forty miles to Jolly Grant Airport.

Once there, Claudia chartered a flight, using one of her many Chinese forms of identification. Over the years, she had procured several in different names by paying bribes to officials, in the event that she may need them someday. Her dad had taught her when she was very young to weave layers around her privacy. Her U.S. passport, the only proof of Claudia Lei's identity, was now sewn inside the lining of a skirt. Who knew? She might need it. But she didn't think that would happen.

She flew to Mahendranagar, Nepal. After two hours, and many questions, she received her tourist visa. Claudia made her way to the local bazaar to buy a few items of clothing for the winter in the mountains. It would be snowing soon where she was going.

Claudia downscaled again by bartering a trade of her luggage for one backpack. She went in the merchant's stall and unpacked the items that she would be keeping. She stepped into two long skirts and wore them over her jeans. She put both of her silk blouses on over her chemise top and then layered again with a new oversized tee shirt. She slipped on two new pairs of socks and jogging shoes.

The toothpaste, toothbrush, scissors, comb, and bar of soap were quickly transferred into the backpack, along with her handmade quilted jacket of gold and orange gauze fabric, which was wrapped around a gun. She placed her newly exchanged currency, visa, and matching identification into the front zippered pocket for easy access.

Releasing her hair, Claudia slipped the band on her wrist. She placed a cap on her head, pulling the bill down to shield her eyes. Tossing the backpack over one shoulder, she walked on through the bazaar. For the next hour, she bartered the few other garments she had over her arm for food, each time packing the provisions away for later.

Satisfied she was as ready as she could get, she found a place to sleep on the floor for the night. She was not the only one. Many had settled down to wait out the night. Claudia was no longer at an exclusive spa or fancy hotel. She was no longer a privileged American for that matter.

September 25, 2001
New Delhi

Jack was waiting in the morning at the train station just like Claudia thought he would be; she would have been shocked if he wasn't, even though she had planned for that as well. He had gotten round-trip first-class tickets from JFK to Paris to Delhi, in order to intercept Claudia and escort her back home.

He watched the last passenger leave the train. Claudia hadn't been among them.

"*I was afraid of that,*" Jack thought. "*Oh, Claudia, why did you have to go and do something so foolish?*"

He boarded the train. It wouldn't be leaving for thirty minutes. He walked through the cars, looking for signs that she had taken the train and skipped out somewhere along the way.

When he spotted the conductor, he asked, "Have you seen this passenger? I was supposed to meet her here and I didn't see her get off the train."

The man took the photo and looked closely. "Chinese, hmm?" She looked familiar. "I don't think I saw this woman when I was punching tickets; maybe I saw her at the station."

"Do you mind if I look through the train?"

"Go ahead," he urged Jack on ahead of him so he could finish checking the cars to make sure all had exited.

Jack looked in each of the private compartments. Then he decided to give her a call to see if she'd answer. Maybe he had misjudged her. Maybe she had only missed making this train. Her phone rang, but she wasn't picking up. Claudia's typically black luggage rolled by outside on a cart. Jack couldn't hear the muffled ring as it traveled through the busy station. His mind was pondering her strategy, as the phone went to voice mail. He pushed end-call. If all was well and her phone was within reach, she would call back.

He stepped off the train and dialed the boss.

"She wasn't on it. Where would you like me to look now?"

"Try the other end of the line and call me when you get there. We'll track the phone."

"Okay," Jack said with a grimace and closed his phone.

"*So, where did you go?*" Jack questioned, as he walked to the ticket counter.

"Give me a ticket to Haridwar. Is it the end of this line?"

"No, it goes one more stop after that to Dedradun."

"Okay, give me one to Dedradun," Jack said and slid him the money.

"The train leaves this evening. It's a night train and will get there around midnight," the ticket agent informed him. He slid Jack his ticket and change.

"Thanks."

Jack pulled out the brochure to Ananda Spa and called them next.

"Hello, this is Jack Jones. I won't be making it today. I'm coming your way tomorrow and staying in Dedradun tonight. Do you know of an acceptable hotel there?"

"There is nothing like our place, but I'll tell you the number of the best they have. You'll have to get a helicopter tomorrow or take the bus in order to get to us."

"Okay," Jack said and wrote down the number of the hotel.

He wiped his brow with his handkerchief. He didn't care for India. It was too dirty and poor for him. *"Claudia certainly won't stay around here long. You'd think she'd have detoured in a nicer place,"* he thought.

Jack went to a food shop and bought curried rice. He sat eating and thinking while he waited. He was losing time and she was slipping away.

"*If I can't follow her trail when I get to Dedradun or Ananda Spa, then we'll turn it over to our other blood hounds. I'm not going to hang around this disgusting place.*"

He tossed the paper plate in the trash and wiped his mouth on a rough paper napkin before tossing it in as well. He searched for a restroom to wash up. After seeing the color of the water that came out of the faucet, he decided not to wash his hands after all. They were cleaner as they were than what they would be if he did that.

Jack walked around for the next hour. The environment and wait was killing him. The longer he waited, the antsier he became. Finally, Jack retrieved his luggage case from the station locker and took a seat to wait for the train. He nodded off and was awakened by the loud announcement of his train.

Rolling his luggage along, he located the sleeper car. He stowed the suitcase in the rack and took his seat. The conductor punched his ticket. Before long, the rocking of the train put him to sleep.

September 25, 2001
Hong Kong, China

"Hello, Mr. Tunisia. I have a task for you."

"Yes?"

"I need you to track Ms. Saudi's cell phone SIM card. It seems she has gone rogue on us."

"I can arrange that."

"One more thing; I doubt she still has the phone on her, but it doesn't hurt to try, just in case. Please be ready with your Chinese contacts in case I need you to do a more personal land search. She'll be coming from the south."

"I'll put them on alert at the borders," Mr. Tunisia said, as he heard the boss hang up.

Just like all the rest, Mr. Tunisia had never been there personally, and couldn't speak the language. He was only in charge of setting up operative contacts in the country.

Chen Hui Long's factories made computer chips for everything, from SIM cards for phones to the computerized systems for car repair diagnostics. His offices were located in one of the tallest buildings in Hong Kong, the International Finance Centre.

He looked out over Victoria Harbour and placed several calls.

"I want you to be on the lookout for a Chinese-American woman around fifty years old. She's quite attractive. I'll send you a picture by fax. Detain her and call me immediately for future instructions."

"Yes, Mr. Chen."

Hui Long closed his phone after he had covered the most frequented crossing locations from India and Nepal into China.

"*Why in the world would she be on the run? I'd have never guessed she was skittish and I know Chinese women*," Hui Long mused before returning to his work.

When his day ended, he took the long elevator to the lobby.

"Good night, Mr. Chen," greeted the doorman.

Hui Long only nodded. Walking on to the curb, he entered his limousine for the not-too-long ride to The Peak. It was on the Hong Kong side of the river and towered over Central from high on the hillside.

He had a large mansion with lots of space, unlike others in the area. Most Chinese lived with as many as seven to ten relatives in a one-bedroom apartment. Even though a unit was located in an old high-rise, they called it a house. That was how Hui Long's grandmother had lived many years ago. He remembered visiting her house when he was a young boy and listening to her stories of poverty as a child.

Hui Long glanced out the window and thought of his father, who had been a brain surgeon. When Hui Long was thirteen, his dad had become the head of a hospital. That was when their way of life had improved even more. His parents had thought they might go to America, but they passed up the chance in order to buy Hui Long a future in advanced electronics. This elevated him to a higher stratum of life on Hong Kong Island.

Hui Long had developed computer microchip technology during his research project for his Doctorate degree at the University of Hong Kong. Upon graduation, he was ready to build an empire, and his father was ready to invest in it. Hui Long started his company on the ground floor, or so it seemed. But it rapidly skyrocketed, thanks to his father's connections. Unfortunately, Mr. Chen senior died suddenly of a heart attack. And a year later, his mother died of a broken heart.

He never felt close to them, like he had his grandmother. They hadn't shown any interest in him as he was growing up. Thinking about them never saddened him. On the contrary, he was happy that he inherited all their wealth and prestige, and that included his father's ruthlessness and position with GUILE.

The chauffeur pulled up to the mansion and opened the door. "Will there be anything else this evening, Mr. Chen?"

"No. I'll be staying home," Hui Long answered and walked inside the spacious house on two acres of well-manicured lawns and gardens.

CHAPTER 13

September 28, 2001
Ananda Spa

Jack had gotten nowhere. There was no sign of Claudia ever being in Dedradun. He checked into the hotel. It would be lucky to receive a one-star rating as far as he was concerned, even using European standards.

In the morning, he chose a helicopter instead of the bus; he had wasted enough time. When he finally arrived at the spa, he felt like a wet noodle that had been hung out to dry.

After contacting the boss, he arranged a one-night stay before moving on. He scheduled as many activities as possible with instructors, and questioned them regarding Claudia's possible whereabouts.

"I know Claudia had to have enjoyed your strong hands. Your deep massage is working wonders on my tired body. No wonder she recommended it," he lied.

"Claudia, sir?"

"Yes, my friend who was just here. She mentioned how great the massage was. You probably don't recognize the name. She's Chinese, about fifty, and thin."

"Yes, now I remember."

"She planned to go somewhere afterwards, making a longer vacation of it. Did she mention by any chance where? I was hoping to catch up with her so that we could travel together. I really hate for her to travel alone," Jack said, which wasn't lying.

"No, sir; we never spoke. She just came in and relaxed on the table. I worked on her tight muscles."

"Oh," Jack replied, disappointed.

Next he went for his colonic. He knew she went there. She had said so on the phone. A colonic wasn't appealing to him, but yesterday's curried rice hadn't set well with his stomach; the enema would help flush it out of his body.

The nurse didn't remember her at all, disappointing Jack.

"*How odd*," Jack thought, sitting on the toilet and expelling the fluid. When he could get up without having an embarrassing accident, he went directly to his room to rest for a while.

Once there, he visited his private bath for yet another long spell. He complained, wishing his intestines would stop grumbling, "How much did that nurse give me?" The enema literally wiped him out; he got into bed. After a twenty-minute powernap, his bowels calmed down. Jack thought it now safe to try yoga.

At the end of class, he asked the instructor about Claudia.

"Yes, I remember her. She was very agile. But as you know, we don't talk during yoga in order to stay focused. I don't remember her talking at all."

"Thank you, anyway." "*Well, at least she was here. She wasn't faking that*," Jack thought, as he walked to the front desk.

He questioned the new receptionist, who had just replaced the one that was working when he arrived.

"Oh yes, Ms. Lei, very nice lady. She signed a vow of silence while here. She ate by herself, scheduled massages, and joined the large groups in Tai Chi and Yoga."

"Thank you," Jack said and thought, "*That explains it.*"

He ate the special diet food which they served for dinner. It had an appealing presentation, but it wasn't very filling. He preferred Chef Jean's cooking and couldn't wait to get out of India; at least it was better than the train station. That's when Jack noticed the no-flys zone. He hadn't seen a single fly since arriving on the Ananda property.

"*It seems all the flies have gone to the rest of India. They must not like the food and the cleanliness here. Certainly in this Zen/Buddhist-like place, they haven't used pesticides to keep them out?*" Jack chuckled at contradiction of the thought.

Jack went to his room and called the boss. "No one knows anything here. Were you able to track her phone?"

"Yes, it was packed in her luggage that showed up in the Paris airport. She knew we would be following her. I just don't understand what set her off and made her do this." The boss was beginning to think Jack must have.

"Well, her show went fine, according to her assistant, Maria. So, who knows?" Jack played innocent.

"Did you tell her anything at all about the plans we executed in New York?"

"No. You said not to, so I didn't," Jack answered.

"Okay, go home. I'll have Mr. Tunisia work on it in China. I'm sure we've lost her for now," the boss paused and then added, "and that could prove very dangerous for us, all."

The inference shook Jack a little. "Since you don't want me to follow her, I'll leave for New York tomorrow," Jack informed the boss, and closed his phone.

"*He's always trusted me.*" Jack fretted. "*Now he has doubts.*" He turned on the television, hoping to lose himself in an old TV show like "I Love Lucy" or "Star Trek." All he found was tranquil music and pictures of pastoral scenes. Eventually it worked; he drifted off to sleep.

September 28, 2001
Nepal

Claudia stretched her back, trying to straighten her spine. She had spent the night on the floor at a youth hostel. It wasn't too uncomfortable for her. She had slept on the floor at the spa, getting used to it again. At the spa she used a real pillow; last night her backpack served as her pillow, and would from now on. It brought back memories of traveling around Europe during the summers before she ever met Jack, or been approached by GUILE. She hadn't winged it like this for years. It was starting to come back to her. A smile appeared on her tired face.

"*Hitch a ride, take a crowded bus, or even walk. It didn't matter if it rained, I just kept moving forward toward my next destination. Beauty wasn't important, no makeup and expensive creams, no fancy clothes, just the bare basics. That was how it was in the past,*" she thought and smiled. "*And it was for pleasure. This is for self-preservation.*" She shivered at that thought and the smile faded.

She hitched a ride out of Mahendranagar bright and early; she'd be long gone should anyone follow her that far. The truck she was riding in hit a pothole, jarring her thoughts back to the present. She unfolded an old map of Nepal that she had bought at the bazaar, and studied how far she thought she might make it today.

When the old man saw the map he asked her, "Where exactly are you going?" He was probably younger than Claudia; eking out an existence in a less affluent land had aged his skin more than hers, making him look her senior.

"Not sure, maybe to Jumla for a while."

He shook his head and returned his attention to the switchback road. They were beginning to climb higher into the mountainous area that Claudia had seen in the distance from Mahendranagar. Everything was becoming greener. She hadn't seen any houses for hours. After about five more kilometers, she saw some buildings ahead. They were tucked in between two mountains with tiered-crop areas on either side of the road.

"This is my village. It's on your map. It's called Budar."

Claudia traced the road they had been on and found it.

"I'll be stopping up ahead. There aren't any hotels here, but you are welcome to stay for one night. I'm sure my wife won't mind."

"Thanks, that's very kind of you."

"Probably no one will be going anywhere until the morning at this hour."

Like he told her, Budar consisted of only a few houses here and there. It wasn't really a town, and hardly a village. It was just on the road to somewhere else, and a little farther down the mountain than other places in Nepal.

Tomorrow she would move on. Traveling this way kept her off the grid, no credit cards, no cell phone, and no hotels that required her to sign in. There would be no record of her. The trail would consist of just a few kind drivers, helping an old woman walking with a backpack. The drivers would be too difficult to find, let alone question where Claudia might be going.

September 28, 2001
New York, New York

"*It's been two weeks. I thought Ms. Lei would've been back,*" Marie thought. She flipped the calendar. The Fall Fashion Fling in Los Angeles was in one month. "*Of course, Ms. Lei did tell me to do everything all the same way. She must have thought she wasn't going to be back by then, or she wouldn't have warned me,*" Maria reasoned.

As she took phone messages from their sponsors, it finally registered with Maria that she in charge. No one was going to tell her when to do something. She was the boss for now. She had coordinated all of it for Paris, so she'd do the same for L.A. The only difference was no one would ask if she had done it yet.

Maria phoned the staging company. "I'll send you drawings of how we want the catwalk for the show. If you have difficulties let me know immediately. If you can't do it tell me, so I can hire someone else."

"Fax us the sketch and we'll get back to you with an estimate of time and expense."

"I'll be sending it shortly," Maria said, gathering up the sketches.

She went to the facsimile room and dialed the company's fax number. When she heard the shrill sound, she pushed send. The drawings began feeding through the machine.

Within an hour they called back. "No problems on this end. We can have it ready for you to inspect when you get to town."

"Okay, that sounds great. I'll contact you later with my arrival date,"

Maria said and hung up the phone, feeling more confident than she had earlier that morning.

The rest of the day she coordinated the brochures with the printers, hired the models for the dresses, and contacted the hair stylists and makeup artists for the models. She booked the hotel and bought the plane ticket for herself.

As a second thought, she called the hotel and airlines again and made reservations for Claudia too, in case she came back by then. "*Maybe she'll just fly straight to the show*," she thought.

"Tomorrow, I'll make the guest list and begin the invitations," Maria told herself, as she closed up the office for the night. When she got into the elevator, she realized she was the last to leave. The door closed, ordinarily signifying the end of the workday for her. Now, her mind was still planning, setting tasks to complete for the next two weeks.

September 28, 2001
Christiansburg, Virginia

"John, it's time to get up," his mom yelled.

John staggered out to the kitchen and poured himself a bowl full of Wheaties. Topping it with whole milk, he returned the carton to the refrigerator before sitting at the table with his mom. He took a heaping spoonful of the crispy flakes and said, "I've got practice today."

"Have they decided about the games? I thought they didn't want large gatherings of people, anywhere, anymore."

"I don't think they're worried about a little place like this, Mom. They're worried about NFL games in big stadiums," John said, thinking his mom silly.

"Do you think they'll let you play this game?"

"Who knows, Mom? I'm the new kid on the block and I don't mean the group either." He chuckled at his own joke, as he crunched on the cereal.

"If I knew you'd play, I'd bring Gramps to the game."

"If the coach gives me a hint, I'll let you know."

John went to the sink, washed his bowl, and put it in the drain, leaving his mom drinking her coffee. He dressed for school in his old jeans, tee shirt, flannel shirt, and Nike's. It was his standard uniform. The only thing that changed was the color of the shirts.

He threw his backpack on his shoulder and adjusted his headphones as he left the house for the bus stop. Walking to the end of the street, he waited with two others. The bus arrived later than usual and John picked a seat near the rear of the bus. The bus was never full; most students drove their cars or rode with friends. John never had to share a seat with anyone.

He stared out the window, continuing to listen to his tape as the bus pulled away.

CHAPTER 14

Thanksgiving 2001
New York, New York

They still hadn't heard from Claudia. The West and East Coasts' shows went off without a hitch. There had been enough money in the business account to keep them open and salaries paid, but Maria didn't know how long that could go on. Claudia had said that she was taking a vacation, but something bad must've happened. She would've returned by now.

Jack seemed interested in taking over 'in memory' of Claudia, or so he had mentioned to Maria. She was meeting him to watch the Macys Parade in an hour. It wasn't really a date, more like a schmoozing employee/employer activity. Maria felt compelled to attend. She dressed and placed a small hen in the oven. It could bake while she was gone.

Since it was a beautiful brisk day, Maria decided to walk to the parade. The grandstands, lining the parade-route, were for paying customers. Jack had arranged seats in front of Macys on Broadway and 34th. She had never attended like this before. Usually, she watched on TV like most Americans did, who weren't stuck in the kitchen preparing the traditional meal.

Maria was a little late. She saw the first float in the lineup move, so she began to run. Arriving out of breath, she asked, "Did I miss any of the Broadway acts? I heard someone from Mama Mia was going to perform here."

"Hi, Maria; take a seat," Jack replied, instead of answering her question and jumping right into the conversation without a proper hello.

"Thanks, by the way. I've never been right here before," she said, taking off her glove and patting her damp brow with her bare hand.

"Well, that's what's great about New York. We've got it all."

"So, did they perform yet?"

"Who?"

"The cast from Mama Mia."

"No, haven't seen them. You missed Tony Bennett, though. Did you know they have been doing this parade for seventy-five years?"

"Yeah, when you asked me to come, I read in the paper that it was the 75th Macys Parade. I couldn't've turned you down even if I wanted to," Maria joked truthfully. "Whoa, Jon Secada; I've got his album."

Jack hadn't heard of him. He only knew classical music and opera performers. He decided to get down to business. "I was thinking, Maria; I hold shares in Lei Fashions, and I don't want to see it go under."

"Yeah, I know what you mean. What would I do?"

"I have checked with the lawyers. They said if I buy the controlling share of the stocks, I can begin running it."

"But you don't know anything about fashion designing."

"I may not, but I know how to run a business."

"There's Billy Ray Cyrus," Maria announced, interrupting the conversation again.

"And who is he?"

"You don't know him? He's famous for Achy Breaky Heart," Maria said, shaking her head. "And you thought I didn't get out much."

Jack simply said, "Oh." He still didn't know who he was. He decided to try again. "If I have controlling stock, I can run the business until Claudia shows up. I'll leave the name as Lei Fashions, and you can become head designer for the winter show. If that is too early for you, you can start with the spring collection."

Boys II Men were next, but she didn't mention it; this time she responded to his proposal. "Wow! I hadn't thought of something like that, hmm?" She was stunned, but quite interested.

"Well, think about it."

She wanted the position, but she didn't want to admit Claudia wasn't going to be found, or coming back. It was all too unreal. When she saw the next float, she changed the subject, avoiding the emotional tug-of-war she was feeling. "Oh, look, it's Kenny G. You know him, don't you?"

"Does he do children's music?"

"No, silly! Why did you say that?"

"Well, he's with the Three Little Pigs," Jack said, raising his eyebrows.

Maria laughed, "Just listen."

Jack decided to let the business proposal rest and watch the parade. The plan had been laid out. He would take care of the buy-out the following week.

Maria enjoyed the rest of the parade, knowing the inevitable would happen.

Thanksgiving 2001
Christiansburg, Virginia

Emily was in the kitchen stuffing the turkey. John and Gramps were watching the parade on television. Gramps' oxygen cord ran all around the floor. John had to be careful not to trip on it.

"Mom! You're missing it. Billy Ray Cyrus just went by with the New York Firemen. We'll help you later. Come watch with me and Gramps," John yelled.

"I'll be there as soon as I get the bird in the oven."

Emily sat on the sofa just in time to see another one of her favorites, Kenny G, on the Three Little Pigs float.

"That's kind of odd. What statement are they trying to make?" John had a puzzled look on his face.

"Well, it could be that he's a pig, or either that he's pig-friendly, since he's Jewish and probably doesn't eat pork," Gramps laughingly said. He stopped quickly, when he wasn't getting enough oxygen.

"Serves you right, Gramps," John joked, thinking the retribution of a lack of oxygen a funnier joke. "Yeah, but the mean old wolf huffs and puffs and blows the house in so he can eat them. Is Kenny G the wolf? He blows his sax, meaning he's long-winded like the wolf. See what I mean?"

"There's your float, John," Gramps said.

"What do you mean? I only watched World Wide Federation of Wrestlers when I was a kid."

"Yeah, but that's what got you to take up the sport of wrestling, didn't it? His mother reminded him, "Did you forget all those trophies you've got on your bookshelf?"

"I'll be glad when football ends soon. I can't wait to get back on the mat. Guys around here haven't seen me wrestling. They don't know my moves and strategy. I'll be able to win hands down."

When the parade ended at noon, John and Gramps went to the kitchen to help Emily prepare the food, before watching the first game.

"Here, Dad. Fill the celery for me." Emily said, giving him the celery, Philadelphia cream cheese, and a silverware knife.

Gramps said, "I guess I can do that."

"John, you can peel the potatoes and put them in this pot of water," Emily said, setting the pot on the table and handing him a paring knife.

Emily opened the Campbell's Cream of Mushroom soup and used the rubber scraper to empty it into the Corning dish. She tore open the package of Lipton Onion Soup mix, poured it on top, and stirred the mixture together. She added the Del Monte Blue Lake green beans and topped it with a can of fried onion rings. Covering it with the lid, she set it aside until it was time to bake it in the oven.

John placed the pot of potatoes on the burner and headed out to the living room.

"He's a pretty good boy. You know, Em?"

"Yeah, I guess. At least he hasn't caused me any trouble, like some of my friend's kids have caused them. Gosh, they don't even know where their kids are today. They started using drugs and ran off somewhere."

"He's doing good with the football, too. I'm glad the coach played him last week. The boy's got potential. I can see it. He must've gotten his dad's arm. Have you heard from him lately?"

"No, Dad. I think he's married by now. It just goes to show that he didn't even love John, or he would've contacted him by now. We won't even talk about helping with child support, knowing I'm not working since I'm taking care of you," Emily said. She was feeling sorry for herself, and thinking of all the happy families having turkey dinners together.

"That's okay, Em. I love you and John. And I'm thankful this year I've got the two of you," Gramps said, realizing he shouldn't have asked.

Emily wiped the tear from her check with her hand. She quickly stood and said, "The celery's done. Go on and watch the game with John. I've got to get busy on the pies." She waved her hands, shooing him out of the kitchen.

Gramps moseyed into the living room, pulling his oxygen tubing with him. "Game on yet, John?"

"Not really. It's just pre-game stuff right now. Does Mom need any more help?"

"Nah! I kind of think she wants to be alone right now. Maybe you can help, once she gets the crust in the pie pans."

Gramps plopped into the recliner and pulled the lever to lift his feet. It wasn't long before he was asleep. John went to the kitchen during the next commercial break.

"Perfect timing, John; could you open the Libby's pumpkin for me, while I gather the rest of the ingredients?"

"Sure, Mom." John turned the key on the can opener, and once around, the lid popped up on a slant. He dumped the contents into a large bowl sitting on the enameled tabletop.

"Let's see. I've got cinnamon, nutmeg, and what's that other spice? Read the can for me, John," Emily asked with her head still in the spice cabinet.

"What?"

"The recipe's on the side of the label; at least it always has been."

"Oh, here it is. It takes, hmm, cloves, and evaporated milk."

"Here, open the evaporated milk for me," Emily said, setting it on the table and turning back to the cabinet to dig for the cloves.

"Hey, Mom? It says here you need ginger, not nutmeg."

"Oh, goodness; see what I told you? You've got to read the recipe every year to remember. Some people nowadays use pumpkin spice, but I don't like it as well. Guess it's made up of all three, but why buy it for only once or twice a year at the most?

"Go ahead, dump in the cream, and I'll measure the spices," she said, getting the set of measuring spoons out.

John read the amounts to her and Emily put in the cinnamon, ginger, and cloves.

"Okay, we need eggs next," John reported.

"How many? Three?" Emily asked with her head inside the refrigerator this time.

"Nah, two."

Emily broke each into a bowl and whisked them with a fork, before pouring the scrambled eggs into John's bowl. He stirred until they were blended.

"Now pour it into these two pie crusts."

"But they're not cooked yet," John noted.

"Read the recipe. That I know. They're unbaked pie shells, John. They cook with the filling."

"Yeah, you're right," John said, after checking the recipe.

"Okay, let's see if this bird's ready." Emily lifted the covered roasting pan out of the oven. The gauge had popped; the turkey was done. She reset the temperature for the green beans to bake and tented the turkey with foil to keep it from drying out. She sent John out to watch the game while the potatoes boiled.

It wasn't long before all was ready and the pies were in the oven. They sat down to dinner. They prayed, thanking God for their family unit and that there had been no more attacks on America.

November 2001
Nepal

Claudia wasn't sure if it was Thanksgiving or not. She knew it was a Thursday. She didn't know why she bothered at all to know day or date. Somehow it made her feel that she was on top of things and in control of her life, when it was so far from the truth.

"*Is it this week or next? I don't remember. Can't tell around here. No one celebrates Thanksgiving but us, thanks to the pilgrims. I'll be like them. Thankful if I make it through this winter alive,*" she thought, as she rode along with yet another stranger, who had picked her up, and moved her further along on her continuing journey.

Each morning she woke, she was glad to be alive. It was amazing she had eluded GUILE this long. Every day was one she could be thankful for. And sometimes when she felt tired and miserable, she remembered how lucky she was to have had the life she experienced all her life. She hadn't had to eke out a living, like the people in that part of the world.

She had been privileged; and that privilege had linked her with the greedy, those who wanted it all and wanted it their way, the spoiled. On Thanksgivings in the past decade or two, she hadn't even considered the thought of thankfulness.

Today she was thankful that she was starting to look less and less like herself. If people came asking about her, she wouldn't fit the description. Her roots had grown out without having her stylist to color them. Almost three inches of her hair was gray and white; a few more inches and she could cut off all of the dark ends. Then she'd look totally different. Claudia pulled her cap down to cover the gray, not for vanity's sake but anonymity's.

The truck slowed. They were approaching the driver's village. He let her out on the main road. She thanked him and began walking, hoping to get another ride before nightfall.

Thanksgiving 2001
Cambridge, Massachusetts

"It's so good to have you home, Mary. I'm glad they didn't change their minds with all that has happened," her mom said, giving her a hug.

"We didn't know for sure until the last minute that it was going to be after last obligation. My obligations meant I had to stay and fly today. I'm glad you were able to get me a flight," Mary said appreciatively.

Her dad asked, "How did you get to the airport, honey?"

"Jeff's sponsor family in Annapolis took both of us. They said they'd be at the airport at two on Sunday when we get back. You don't have to worry," Mary said, easing her dad's mind.

Mary went upstairs to her room, unpacked her toiletries, and got out of her dark winter uniform. She replaced it with her jeans and an old tee shirt, before heading back downstairs.

"Do you know if Janie came home for Thanksgiving, Mom?"

"I don't think so. Her parents are probably getting her airfare for Christmas. We're a long way from Berkley, you know."

"Yeah! Some of the plebes can't go home; they're from California. Even if they did, they'd have to turn around and come home Saturday in order to get back to the Academy by six Sunday night. It's hardly worth it, especially when you figure they'll spend more time flying than being home," Mary stated very practically.

"So what are they doing?" Her mom asked, as she prepared the dressing for the dinner.

"What can I do to help?"

"Set the table with the china from the cupboard, and use the silver from in there, too. Your grandparents will be over soon, so set the table with five place-settings."

"Okay. To answer your question, some of the guys who have that coast-to-coast dilemma are having Thanksgiving dinner with their host families. I'm glad I could come home."

"It's nice there are people in Annapolis who are willing to help middies like that."

Mary was already in the dining room getting out the dishes. Her mother used them rather often. "Hey, Mom, do you want bread plates and butter knives?"

"They could get in the way with all the food on the table; we can place the serving dishes on the sideboard to make room. What do you think?"

"It's up to you. Both are fine with me."

"Well, we have to have the turkey on the table for your dad to carve, so let's just put all of it on the table and pass it, instead of making a cafeteria line out of it."

"So bread plates?"

"No, don't use them."

Mary finished placing the silver and folded the cloth napkins that matched the tablecloth. After she placed them in the center of each plate, she returned to the kitchen.

"Anything else you want me to do?"

"No, you can visit with Dad. He'll make time for you," Mary's mom urged.

Mary's dad was in his study, grading the papers that he had assigned before the holiday, when Mary came in. "How many more do you have, Dad?"

"Two more classes' worth," he moaned.

"You'd think you'd know better by now, Dad. You assign them during the holiday, not before. That way you get to take the holiday and forget the students," Mary suggested laughingly.

"Well, some professors do that but I can't; I want the kids to have a good time with their families. Heaven knows families hardly get together for a meal anymore. I don't need to add to the downfall of the American family. Now do I?"

"What time are Grandma and Grandpa coming over?"

"I think at five for a happy-hour drink. I've got to get more of these done before they get here. You know if I don't, Mom'll say I did it on purpose in order to avoid her parents." He smiled, dismissing Mary gently.

"Okay. I'll tell you when they get here."

"Deal."

Mary turned on the television and caught the first game kick-off. Before long she was wrapped up in the game. She rooted for her team to make the touchdown as the quarterback ran down the field and crossed the goal line. Mary cheered loudly, and the doorbell rang.

CHAPTER 15

Christmas 2001
Magdalena, New Mexico

"Merry Christmas, Dad!" Teddy said, handing his father a large box.

Freda watched with a smile. She knew what the gift was.

Ted loosened the bow and removed the paper. Opening the lid, he read the contents. He questioningly looked at Teddy, and then to Freda, who was now laughing.

"How do you have a diploma? What's this?" Ted asked, pleasantly puzzled.

"I graduated early, Dad, with honors. There's only one graduation ceremony a year in May. This is your surprise present. I can go when you go to Houston. I want to check out the program at the University of Houston. They have a Master's and Doctorate program in Mechanical Engineering. Who knows, I might take the interdisciplinary program of Astronautical Engineering? I have to take a look first," Teddy said, admitting his true incentive.

"Well, we can't ***both*** leave your mother behind," Ted said and looked to Freda for validation.

"It'll all work out, honey. Here, open my present next," Freda said excitedly, and handed him a small box. She sat next to him on the arm of the upholstered chair.

"Okay, but we'll discuss this more later," he promised.

They nodded their heads, and smiled in agreement.

Ted gave Freda a kiss before opening the lid. "Thank you, honey."

Inside he saw a library card. He wrinkled his brow. Squinting his eyes he read, "Book Title: Freda French. Did you publish an autobiography that

I don't know about?" He was confused, but marveled at the idea.

"No," she said, laughing at the thought. "Maybe one day, since life's getting so interesting, I'll write about you. Read on," she urged.

"'Checked Out' is stamped Dec. 31, 2001 and 'Due Back' is blank." He turned the card over; nothing was on the back. "What does that mean?"

"It means that, as of the last day of the year, I'm unemployed."

"What?! What happened? They wouldn't fire you."

Freda explained, "When you told us the good news this summer, I asked if there was any way that I could quit as of the end of the year. The principal checked with the county board of education. And they began looking for a mid-year replacement. Last week, they found one they liked. She was hired and begins as of January. So you see, I can go with you, too," Freda said laughingly, and gave him a big hug.

A tear rolled down Ted's check. It had been a hard month. The last few employees had left. Luckily, one division chief got a job with The Weather Channel, another with a TV station in Albuquerque, and a third went to the Miami Hurricane Center.

Most of the secretarial staff found jobs with local government agencies, which agreed to credit the same government years of service after reading Ted's glowing recommendations.

All of the staff at the AWA was top drawer; no one had a poor rating in all his years. If they had, they would've been replaced long ago. The office may have been lax in dress-code, but not in output.

"So, when should we go? Or do you guys have that all planned, too."

They laughed.

By their laughter, he thought they might've actually planned it. "Is anything up to me to decide?" Ted asked, laughing now with them.

Freda expressed her desires. "I thought that after Christmas, when we take down the decorations, we'd keep boxing the house since we'd be on a roll.

"Starting January, you can help with some of the larger items like all your books and telescope, that kind of stuff."

"Yeah, Dad, I'm not touching some of your equipment. I know how precious it all is to you," Teddy said. He had enough to pack in his room.

"Okay. We'll plan it as we go. We'll probably have it all done by the end of January. We can wait until then to put the place on the market," Ted said, roughly sketching a plan in his head.

Now that that was settled, Ted clapped his hands and stood. "Now for your presents."

He walked to the carport and retrieved a large box from the trunk of his car. He carried it in and set it on the floor in front of Freda.

"Before I let you open this, I've got to have some eggnog."

"That's a great idea. Big or little glass?" Freda asked.

"Medium-sized tumbler for me, Mom."

"Tall for me, please," Ted requested.

When Freda left for the kitchen, Teddy asked, "What is it, Dad?"

"You'll see soon enough," Ted said and chuckled.

The hot chili pepper lights on the live pine tree blinked on and off, making the room magical. Christmas was always special to Ted when he could smell the scent of a live tree. Freda returned with a tray of eggnog and served it to each of the men folk.

"To a new life," Ted said.

They toasted and all took a sip of the eggnog. Freda set her glass on the end table, after she'd taken another slow sip. She liked drawing out the suspense.

"Okay, open it."

She slit the paper folds free, lifted the flaps on the box, and looked inside. She couldn't tell what it was, until she reached in and lifted it out of the box.

Teddy and Freda looked at the model, then at Ted. It was a box with glued on photographs of a house. Each photo corresponded with each side of the house. The front view had a realtor's sign in the yard with a red 'sold' sticker over it.

"Does this mean what I think?" Freda asked.

"Yeah, Dad. Does it?"

"Yep! I have a signed contract on it. The gift to you, Freda, is that you won't go homeless for months in Houston," Ted said and chuckled. He had promised when they married that she'd never have to worry about a roof over her head. And he wasn't kidding then, or now.

"My gift to you, Son, is the mother-in-law cottage in the back. It even has alley parking. If you attend the University of Houston, you can live there. Otherwise, we'll rent it out." Ted was looking ahead to a time of retirement. The cottage would give them an income after Teddy was gone.

"So, when is closing?" Freda asked.

"The day after Valentine's Day. I figured I'd have to be here then with you," he said, giving Freda a kiss on her head, "and I thought I'd fly back on the fifteenth. Because of your gifts, I won't need to. We can all be there. Oh!" Ted had almost forgotten. "And Teddy, this house is less than five miles from the College of Engineering, too!

New Year's Eve
New York, New York

Jack was looking out at Times Square filled with people. The police had everyone cordoned off. The barricades made him laugh, thinking they looked like cattle going to slaughter. Once loaded into the makeshift stall, they couldn't leave. All alcoholic beverages had been confiscated, and everyone was frisked down to make sure there were no guns, knives, or suicide bombers in the crowd.

The foolish people were waving American flags that some vendor had sold on their way to the square. The flags were actually the end of the production of Jack's short-term opportunist venture.

Jack smiled with pleasure and drew his attention back to the clock in his daytime office. This space still seemed not as appealing to Jack, but at least he had a great view on New Year's Eve.

Chef Jean's dinner had arrived at ten-thirty and was being kept warm on stereo burners on Jack's office credenza. He had Jean work late since the chef would have off the following day. Jack's champagne was on ice, waiting to be opened. He had his chauffeur on standby to pick him up as soon as the street below was cleared.

The cell phone rang.

"Hello, Mr. Tunisia."

"Happy New Year, Mr. Iran."

"Any news for me?"

"Still no trace; if she's in the heights of the Himalayas, we'll have to wait for spring before she budges again," Hui Long reported, giving his prediction.

"I'll check with you before that. You know we work on the New York minute over here," Jack said jokingly with disappointment, and closed his phone. He was hoping to celebrate in 2002, knowing Claudia was no longer out there, like a loaded loose cannon.

"*Oh, well, I do have her company and it seems like it's doing well. I've got Maria running the show very nicely*," he thought, unfolding his napkin and sitting down to the tablecloth-covered card table that was appointed with Holiday Lenox and Waterford crystal.

He poured the Pinot Noir that the chef had sent over from the wine cellar to compliment his Filet Mignon. Jack took a sip and swished the wine around in his mouth, savoring the taste.

January 24, 2002
Nepal

It was Chinese New Year. 2001 had been the year of the dragon and GUILE had certainly breathed fire upon America. Claudia hoped that 2002 would be better. It was the year of the snake. Maybe she could slither away and hide. Today's celebration was slowing her progress, making her rest. She hadn't taken a break since she began this journey into oblivion months ago; and who knew when she would again.

February 2002
Magdalena, New Mexico

The house was packed. The movers had just finished loading the contents and Teddy's old car. The French's belongings were the first on the truck, and would be the last off, as the moving van made its way to Houston.

Since the house had no mortgage, they listed it: Rent with an option to buy, with the French's holding the financing. They weren't burning any bridges. If no renters desired to buy, Ted and Freda could come back to Magdalena in their retirement years. The word had gotten around; and the town's people knew they were going. Two days after the house was listed, the French's had an annual lease signed.

They started on their journey from Sorocco, New Mexico to Houston, Texas. They pulled out of the drive shortly after the moving van had left. They planned to only drive six hours a day, and rotate drivers and passengers every two hours, breaking up the boredom of interstate driving. Tonight, they made it only as far as Truth or Consequences. The center of town had seen better days. There were a few locals and it still had the usual interstate travelers, stopping due to the unique name of the town.

"If we knew that this place would pick up again someday, it certainly would be the time to invest and fix something up," Ted said, thinking of additional retirement income.

"Maybe it will, but what would ever happen here?" Freda asked, as she climbed into the full-sized bed across from the one Teddy was sitting on, watching a movie.

"Who knows?" Ted rolled over ending the thought, wanting a good night's sleep before the drive the next day.

February 15, 2002
Houston, Texas

It was the end of the week and they had arrived in Houston. Ted and Freda were sitting at the table, waiting to sign the closing papers. They had left Teddy at the house after the walk-through.

"Hi, I'm Jane. I'm your closing agent. I have all the papers ready. Are there any questions before we begin?"

"No. Everything looked fine to us," Ted said, looking toward Freda.

She nodded in agreement.

"Fine then; the sellers already signed. Since, as you know, they moved out a few months ago. So, all we need to do is have you sign here, here, and here," she said, sliding him the papers and showing him the little yellow arrows, pointing to the signature lines.

Ted signed and passed the papers to Freda to add her signature. In a few minutes everything was completed. The agent handed him the keys with a handshake and, "Congratulations. Welcome to Houston."

Freda and Ted left the office as excited as first-time buyers.

"Let's pick up a pizza and celebrate," Freda suggested, as Ted opened her car door.

"Okay. Do you have any idea where we might find one?"

"I saw a Papa John's on the way here from the house. You ought to be able to find it on the way back, if we're lucky."

They found it and purchased a two litter bottle of cold Pepsi, some cups, and a large 'everything' pizza, without much of a wait. Teddy was sitting on the front porch as Ted and Freda pulled up. He looked like he had grown up there. Once inside, they sat around on the hardwood floor in the large living room and ate their first dinner in the new house.

"The moving van will be here in the morning. Let's walk around and discuss where the furniture should go. I don't want to make you two rearrange it after they leave," Freda suggested.

"Sounds good to me, Mom."

"Where do you want to start?" Ted asked, washing down his last bite of pizza.

"Let's start at the top and work our way down," Freda said, beginning to climb the stairs.

Teddy followed, even though it didn't matter to him where she wanted things. This was their house. His was out back. The furniture placement went rather quickly; within an hour all was decided. That night they slept in sleeping bags in their new homes, Teddy in his, and Ted and Freda in theirs. Teddy was amazed at all the space he'd have. For the first time, it wasn't just one bedroom that was his; it was a two-bedroom house!

March 2002
Houston

Teddy took a tour of the university. He was impressed as much as he had been by reading their online presence. He enrolled in the program at UH, and was accepted for the next term.

Ted checked into his new offices at NASA. There was a message from Director Haynes to call as soon as he arrived. "You said I should contact you upon arrival. Is there a problem?" Ted feared he'd be told that he was laid off as well, after making the move across country.

"No. All's fine. Matter of fact, it's so fine, that you have the task of hiring."

"Really?"

"Yes. You need a complete or should I say small unit of AWA there to work with NASA. This is a joint effort. You're allotted two secretaries, one meteorologist, one environmental scientist, and two mechanical engineers."

"Okay. Are there any applicants?"

"No, that's up to you to flush out. Have fun. Let me know when you have the skeleton crew up and running."

"Is there a deadline for this?"

Ted knew Haynes. There was always a deadline. This wasn't a surprise to Haynes either. Ted was sure that he had known all along. Ted didn't like how the 'Haynes' people of the world did business; and that's exactly why he hadn't wanted to go to Washington and play politics. It was bad enough to do so over the phone.

"The sooner the better. Well, must run, I have appointments, you know."

"Sure. I'll let you know when I have everyone hired. Bye."

Hiring suited Ted's personality better than laying-off. It was a shame he had let some good people go. There were several he could use now. Besides, some of his old people might've wanted to transfer, if he had had a chance to have asked them.

April 2002
Houston, Texas

Freda applied for a librarian position with the county public library system and had been placed in a position at the main branch. She worked a full schedule Monday through Friday and half day on Saturday, in other words, every day that the library opened.

Unlike school systems, she worked summers as well and only got two week's worth of vacation time, which she'd qualify for after a year of service. She was on the go so much that she hardly had time to fix dinner, except on Sunday.

Ted had been busy meeting the staff at NASA, interviewing, and hiring his small roster for AWA. Ted hired back two of his associates that hadn't found placements. He interviewed and selected a secretary for himself. He decided to let the other two men hire the other secretary, once they had settled into the Houston area.

He visited UH and met Teddy at the College of Engineering.

"Dad, I'll introduce you to the head of the department. He'll be able to help you, if anyone here can," Teddy said, as they walked down the hall to Dr. Johnson's office.

"Well, that's why I got you involved, Son," Ted said, and lifted his arm to rough Teddy's hair before he realized what he was doing.

Teddy saw it coming out of his peripheral vision and ducked saying, "Dad!"

"Yeah, sorry Son. I'll have to work on getting out of that habit."

"I'm not a kid anymore," Teddy pleaded his case.

"I know, I know. I won't do that again. Promise." Ted had actually embarrassed himself, when he realized what he was doing. Teddy looked more like his mother than Ted; and he didn't want someone in this new area to think that he was sweet on good-looking men at the university. Rumors started easily, spread like wildfire, and were near impossible to squelch.

"Dr. Johnson, excuse me," Teddy said, interrupting the professor talking with an undergraduate.

"No problem, Ted. We were just finishing. Arai, I'll see you later."

"Sure thing, Dr. Johnson," the student from Turkey said, and hurried down the hall.

"This is my dad, Dr. Ted French, Dr. Johnson," Teddy said to the professor.

Then he addressed his father saying, "Dad, this is Dr. Johnson."

The men shook hands. Dr. Johnson said, "Call me Lyn."

"I've got a class. See you later," Teddy said, excusing himself.

"Come into my office, Ted," Lyn Johnson offered.

Ted followed behind and got comfortable in the chair across from the desk. It was loaded with stacks of papers, a blotter, and the latest large screen monitor computer.

"Yes, Lyn does stand for Lyndon; and no, I'm not related in the least. Persons often joke about it, especially the undergraduates when they first find out. I try to nip it in the bud, keeping the chuckles and questions down a bit."

"I can imagine. I guess your mom was a loyal Democrat and Kennedy/Johnson fan."

"Yes, she was. Now what can I do for you today, Ted?" Lyn said, getting down to business.

"I'm on a special project here with NASA and need to hire two mechanical engineers. I don't have the budget to be able to hire anyone with a Master's degree, but I was hoping to find two recent graduates you have had from the undergraduate program. I'm interested in hiring from the top five pupils," Ted said, getting to the point and sensing that Dr. Johnson was pressed for time.

"Some of them may have already been placed into programs or moved away, but I can supply you with those names and contact information. I'll get my secretary to fax you the information by close of business today; you won't need to wait around wasting your precious time."

"Thank you; that would be great." Ted stood and handed him his business card. "Thank you for your time. I'm glad you could make this appointment for me." Ted let himself out.

"You're welcome," the professor said, picking up the phone to return one more of his many messages.

Ted contacted and interviewed the top five graduates and hired one. He was having trouble deciding on whom to hire for the other position.

Director Haynes phoned. He asked bluntly, "Ted, do you have all your people hired yet?"

"I have one more to go. I'm trying to decide which to offer the position. I'm not as impressed with them in person, as I was with their transcripts."

"Is someone already in the field that would do better?"

"I'd have to post the position through the government channels and that would just take too much longer. I was trying to speed this up," Ted said, expressing how Haynes felt.

"Yes, time is of the importance. I'm being pressured here in Washington to get the show on the road. Congress wanted to have reports of the project by now." Director Haynes needed bottom line results to report to his constitutes on Capitol Hill.

"I'll make a decision by the end of the week, sir," Ted said and hung up the phone.

Capitol Hill and GUILE were anxiously waiting.

That evening, Ted offered the other position to his son.

"I'd love to Dad, but how can I do my Master's and work, too?"

"Plenty of people have gotten a Master's while they worked. Did you forget that's what your mom did?"

"Yeah, that's right. Well, it looked simple to me then, but I can't understand how you could have, Mom, thinking about it now," Teddy said, puzzled by the whole idea.

"It wasn't easy Teddy. You were young then. I'd do all my reading and assignments late at night, once you had gone to bed. If I had waited until you were older it would never have worked out, having to chauffeur you to games and practices," Freda admitted.

"Oh wow! I'm glad I don't have a family. That sounds even worse," Teddy said, taking a bite of a taco that he had picked up from the local Mexican restaurant for the family's dinner.

"This is how I think you can work it, Teddy," Ted said, starting to give suggestions to ease his son's mind. He needed him to accept the position. Ted wanted the brightest and the best for the project. The Weather Space Lab was going to be his claim-to-fame.

"Look, schedule all your classes either first thing in the morning and come to work at noon. Then do your eight hours and eat dinner at nine. You'll get your assignments done between nine and midnight and so forth.

"Or come into work at six and get off at two. Eat dinner early and take night classes doing your assignments once you get home. That's how most people do it," Ted explained.

"Well, won't people think it nepotism?"

"Your credentials were more impressive than the other four I interviewed and I know I can work with you. That's something I can't be assured of with the other four. Besides, I'll keep all the files on the applicants in case someone complains. Now, what do you say?"

"Okay. When do I begin?"

June 2002
Nepal

Claudia spent the first winter held up in Jumla. She learned of company-led tours each summer for die-hard adventurous types. They hiked from Jumla to Nepalgunj, visiting monasteries and meeting locals. The group met in Kathmandu and flew to Jumla to start. The company furnished the camping equipment, three meals a day, cooking utensils, and supplies. An English-speaking guide accompanied them. Porters, Sherpas, and pack animals were also provided.

Over the winter, Claudia's appearance had changed. She looked more like a local, even though it was obvious she wasn't Tibetan but Chinese in ancestry. She paid the guide company the fee, which was equivalent to three-thousand American dollars, and signed on for a second team leaving in June.

When the group flew in, they brought with them a pair of hiking boots in her size in trade for the price of the initial flight. Since she was meeting them in Jumla, she had bartered for the flight/boot exchange when the first group came in May. Now that it was summer, she needed to move on. It wouldn't be long before the snows stopped her for another winter. It was good that the tours kept far off the beaten path, away from the roads.

At the first Buddhist monastery, and all that followed, she made inquiries about her half-brother. When she had visited China many years before with her parents, her father had revealed the story of his life there. When he was young, he had been married. He had left his home to make it in America, and had promised to bring his Chinese wife some day, if ever there was a chance. At the time, only one family member was allowed to leave China. He didn't know when he left that she was expecting at the time. The communication tended to be one-way. Many years passed. Eventually, her father met Claudia's mother in New York's Chinatown and married, having Claudia. Her mother was aware of his previous marriage. Many in Chinatown had similar stories.

When they visited China, they searched for Mr. Lei's first wife. What they found instead was Mr. Lei's thirty-five year old son. His mother had died the previous year. They urged him to return with them to America, but he had made his decision to become a Buddhist monk. He was making his way to a monastery in Nepal when they had found him.

No one had kept contact with him after that, and Claudia was hoping to come across him now. Since she was fifty-two, he would be sixty-six. She was hoping that he was still alive.

When the twenty-two day journey ended, Claudia hadn't found her brother at any of the monasteries. But she had learned how to camp. She purchased a light-weight tent to carry atop her backpack in Nepalgunj, and flew with the group to Kathmandu.

GUILE had someone waiting in Kathmandu. They were watching the hotels and hostels, figuring she wouldn't be dumb enough to charter a private plane. They didn't expect her to travel with a group. Unknowingly, Claudia had slipped through their fingers.

After landing, she caught a ride with another hiker, who was anxious to get to Bhaktapur. From there, she walked and hitched a ride, making her way toward the Kopan monastery. Claudia knew she needed to keep moving while the weather was relatively warm, permitting travel. She hoped that if she could find her brother, maybe he would allow her to stay at the monastery, as long as she helped in some way. Even if it were to wash floors, she wouldn't mind; at least she'd be safe. That night, she slipped off the road and pitched her new tent. In the morning, she'd continue her solitary journey toward Kopan.

September 2002
Houston, Texas

The newly-formed smaller branch of AWA had its first meeting with the NASA group on the project. They were drawing up plans to include everything the scientists would need on the lab and everything that NASA would need to make it function.

"Of course, we need on-board computers. Let's start there."

"The question is what do we need them to do?" Ted answered. "Can one computer do it all?" Ted was unsure of NASA's capabilities.

"How large of a capacity will be needed for data storage?" The NASA computer tech asked.

Teddy put in his two cents worth. "We will need downloading and uploading abilities, along with storage."

"What resolution will you need?"

It was going to take hours to work up the complete list of computer requirements. Each group had to work separately to finalize that piece of the government wish-list. When each was finished they'd brainstorm together again, eliminating duplication and adding overlooked items. They started with the computer system; without it there would be no project.

This drawing board stage would take the next year. Each and every step in construction had to be submitted for approval before they could move to the next. With each approval came the funding necessary to build the WSL piece by piece.

GUILE's contacts in Washington were aware of every appropriation.

CHAPTER 16

March 2003
Houston, Texas

Arai was taking his second semester courses in Mechanical Engineering at the University of Houston. One of the directives for him and the others from Turkey, after learning English, was to learn pre-assigned topics. After he earned a degree in Mechanical Engineering, he was assigned to go on to Astronautical Engineering. He wasn't sure where this was taking him, but he didn't mind. He found it challenging and quite interesting.

What he did think strangely odd was that he was told to infiltrate a Christian church. He joined a campus ministry group for evangelical Christians, and acted like he had accepted the faith. He learned their ways and studied, of all things, the Bible. Under no circumstance was he to go to a mosque. Instead, the Imam came to him for monthly reports on Christianity.

May 2003
Blacksburg, Virginia

Arai's friend from home, Mustafa, took longer to grasp English. He had just started his engineering studies at Virginia Polytechnic Institute in Blacksburg during the summer session. He, too, was ordered to join a Baptist campus ministry and attend church. His reports were emailed to someone he had never met; there were no mosques in Southern Virginia.

He called Arai, frustrated with it all. "Arai, this is starting to get to me," Mustafa admitted.

"What do you mean?"

"There's no mosque here. I was given orders not to be seen saying prayers. I'm living in a dorm and it's impossible to pray. I'm afraid Allah is not being praised at all."

"I can understand, especially since we're attending the infidels' churches. I think of it this way. In the Bible it says to pray in the closet and not to let others see you. I think this is a good idea. Sometimes when my roommate is out, I go into the walk-in closet, shut the door, and pray to Allah. I know it's not at the correct times, but I think it's better than not at all. If I get caught in the closet, I'll quote the Bible."

"I don't have a walk-in. This closet has sliding doors; it's too small. I feel like a traitor," Mustafa continued to complain. Just the thoughts of the small closet triggered his claustrophobia; he involuntarily shook.

Arai explained, "At noon when we're to pray, I sit still at a cafeteria table and think my prayers in my mind. I see myself praying. I think that's what Allah may really want us to do. It's our mind that Allah wants. We constantly remember him in our minds. Do your best Mustafa. We're serving..." Arai paused. He was no longer alone or able to talk. "Yes, praise the Lord; you've found a church. Keep attending my brother; God will honor your fortitude. Look, I must go."

Mustafa understood by the change in the conversation that someone was within earshot. "Okay. Bye. Go with Allah, my brother."

June 2003
Los Angeles, California

Gani, Ediz, and Derin were still having difficulty mastering English. They had been given an ultimatum, practice for six more months, or go home. Gani decided to stay and the other two went home to Turkey. Without his pals to talk to, Gani had to use English all day long. The total immersion was helping. He actually dreamt the night before in English, a true sign of progress. He reported the good news, in English, to the Imam at the mosque.

"Keep speaking only English, Gani. I'll notify my contact; he'll tell me where to send you next."

Gani kept practicing. In a month, he received instructions to take pilot training at a flight school in Florida. He had seen the New York buildings come down, and thought they were assigning him to do the same. It would be his punishment for taking so long to learn English. He tried to convince himself that he was willing to die for Allah.

The Imam saw him off at the California airport. "Your new contact will meet you at the Florida airport when you land. He'll set you up. Follow everything he tells you, no matter how odd. It is for Allah."

Gani boarded the plane. During the flight, he psyched himself to do the task, whatever that may be; he was serving Allah. As warned, the contact told him the oddest thing; he was to attend a church and not a mosque for any reason.

Fall 2003
Paris, France

Maria passed through customs at the airport, followed by Jack. He placed his recently-renewed American passport back in his pocket, picked up his leather attaché bag, and walked with Maria to the baggage claim area. Swiping his credit card in the machine, Jack released two carts. He placed his attaché on one, and the other was for the boxed fall fashion collection.

"There're my bags," Maria said, pointing to the cheetah-spotted pieces of luggage coming into view.

Jack snagged each quickly off the turnstile, setting them on the floor, as Maria rolled the cart closer. She placed the smaller pieces on board and Jack lifted the large bag.

"*What does she have in here, a ton of bricks?*" "There's mine," he said, retrieving his one bag and adding it to the full cart.

Maria kept her eyes on the lookout for the boxes of dresses. She had packaged them carefully in the shop for the transport. She used hot pink packing tape to make them easy to differentiate from others at the airport.

Lei Fashions didn't show in Paris the year before and only showed on the east and west coasts, staying away from the European market altogether. Maria felt insecure without Claudia's touch. Now that more than a year had gone by, she was finally beginning to believe in herself. Jack did his best to boost her confidence through it all; his stock would've gone down if he hadn't.

The boxes were loaded into the van going directly to the location. Marie rode with the driver, not willing to let the creations out of her sight. They were too precious and needed her immediate attention.

Jack took a limousine with the luggage to the hotel. He had reserved the large suite with two bedrooms and an adjoining living room for himself and Maria to share. Once in the room Jack undressed, showered, and got into a fresh change of clothes. Bundled in a thick hotel robe, he drank a Perrier while he unpacked. Once settled in, he dressed casually chic in black tee shirt and sports jacket. Filling his glass with the complimentary French wine, he stepped out on the veranda. He admired the view of the Eiffel Tower, and thought about Claudia. "*Where did you ever get to, my dear?*"

Hui Long hadn't found her yet; and the hired hands in Nepal hadn't been able to pick up her whereabouts either. Jack came to Paris on the hunch that Claudia might contact Maria.

He placed a call to Ananda Spa perchance she backtracked. "Hello, this is Jack Jones. I was there a few years ago and was wondering if my friend, Claudia Lei, had made it back again. I was hoping to meet up with her. It seems we can never schedule a vacation at the same time. We just take time together if it happens," he lied.

The receptionist replied, "I don't think Ms. Lei has, but I'll check the record of her last stay. Hold the line please." In a minute she came back on and said, "No sir. She hasn't been here since September 2001. I don't see any pending reservation. Should I put a note here to contact you if she should show up?"

"Yes, that would be so kind of you. I hope I can be there soon."

"I can make a reservation now if you want?"

"I'm sorry; I don't have my itinerary with me at the moment. I was taking a chance that Ms. Lei was there, and changing it anyway. I'll be back in touch."

"Thank you, sir. Goodbye."

As Maria unboxed the dresses, she gently removed the packing tissue. When finished she left them under lock-and-key at the show sight, satisfied that the security staff were competent. She hopped a cab to the hotel. Once there, she was escorted to the suite.

"I'm here," she announced as she walked in. "Do we have a great view?"

Her room had been nice two years ago, but it was far from a suite, and it didn't have the fantastic view that this one had. She smiled with pleasure. She liked the benefits of being the head designer, with a boss who really didn't know much about creating anything, but money.

"I thought the view of the Eiffel Tower would be to your liking. I have reservations for dinner. How long before you can go? I'm afraid I didn't account for the time you'd spend with the fashions."

"How much time do I have?"

"The reservation is in an hour. If that isn't enough time I can call and ask if they can move it," Jack said, hoping she wouldn't make him do that.

"I can be ready by then," she said, heading for her room to quickly touch up her makeup. She unpacked her clothes and set out the toiletries, noting the large soaking tub. She quickly changed; she could relax later.

November 2003
Christiansburg, Virginia

John arrived for his senior appointment with his guidance counselor.

"Have a seat, John. How's everything with you?"

"Fine," John answered, quickly scanning the small office as he sat across from Mr. Albright's desk. This was the first time he had been there.

"Have you applied to colleges, John? I haven't gotten a request for a guidance recommendation or for your transcript from any school."

"I haven't applied anywhere," John said and added, "yet."

"You've taken the academic track for college; your grades are good," the counselor said, studying his school record. "You only needed English to graduate, yet you still chose a rigorous class schedule this year. That looks impressive to admission counselors at good colleges and universities." The counselor looked up with a puzzled look on his face. "Why haven't you applied?"

"I thought I'd like to go to Virginia Tech."

"Have you been to the campus for a game or walk-through?" Mr. Albright looked directly at John, trying to access his sincerity. He heard it all the time. Many students in the area thought they wanted to go there after attending one game. Very few had the credentials to get in the door, let alone be accepted. John did.

"No, I haven't. Most of the time their games are when ours are; you know I'm on the football team," John said, having a feeling that he didn't.

"Aha," Mr. Albright said, unaware of John's athletic abilities. He didn't follow the sports of the high school. He left that to the coaches and the scouts. He concerned himself with the students' grades and credits to meet graduation requirements. Extra-curricular activities, as far as he was concerned, were only for students who had good grades and the time to pursue more. Thankfully, that had been true for John.

"VT has Campus Tours for juniors and seniors, and their parents. I can call them and set an appointment, if you're serious about applying, John," he said with a strange subtlety, wanting to encourage this worthy candidate, and not scare him away. "The deadline to get your application in is Thanksgiving." He turned toward the large calendar on the wall, causing John to look as well. "And it's rapidly approaching. You'll need an essay, recommendations from a teacher, coach, and me, and one from someone outside of school, like an employer, pastor, or scout leader."

John felt overwhelmed, "I didn't realize all of that was required."

"Are you the first in your family to attend college?"

"Yes."

"Well, there are first-generation scholarships that you can apply for. They'll help with VT's tuition; they're a private college. The tuition is higher than a public institution." Mr. Albright sensed other reasons for John's stalling.

"I can't go away. I'm needed to help at home here in Christiansburg."

"Well, living off-campus does save on room-and-board," the counselor said, helping John to share other financial needs.

"My mom takes care of Gramps, who's very ill. We don't have much family income. Are there any other scholarships?"

"Sure, I'll give you applications to ones that meet your circumstances; there's also the Army after graduation."

"What? I don't want to go to the Army; I want to go to college."

"What I mean is, John, the Army has an incentive program for those who graduate from college with student loans. Up to forty thousand is taken care of, after enlisting and serving one rotation of duty in the Army."

"I see," John said unenthusiastically.

"You'd have officer status after basic training. They'd mark you as a leader of men, not just infantry."

"Oh, hmm?"

"But first things first; I can call over to VT and put you on Friday or Monday's tour; you can take a personal fieldtrip. They'll give you an application at the end of the tour, and answer any other questions you may have at that time."

John agreed to take a tour. He accepted scholarship applications and a questionnaire to fill in for those he'd request a recommendation from. On Monday, John and Emily took the campus tour. John decided to major in Mechanical Engineering, which was a five-year work-study program. The income earned during the employment semesters, he'd save and apply to the next tuition bill. John completed his application, including the essay that took him several days to produce.

"Mom, read over my essay and see what you think."

Emily sat down and read it over. She was proud of his work. She was amazed at his ability. She didn't know where he got it. Obviously, he had paid attention in school. "Sounds great to me; have you gotten all the recommendations the guidance counselor told you to get?"

"Yeah; they're in sealed envelopes for me to put in this packet. Can you run me over to the campus to drop it in the admissions office mail slot?" His friends had cars, but John didn't.

"I'm going across town tomorrow morning. I'll give it to them in person while you're at school."

As promised, Emily dropped the package off on Thursday, beating the Thanksgiving deadline by a week.

It had been a busy week for John. There was a Friday night football game. He was on the active bench now, no longer sitting on the sidelines at the games. After the game, he'd get off for a week's well-deserved vacation from school and practice.

Emily and his grandfather were in the habit of attending his games. Gramps had to bring his travel tank of oxygen. The school allowed him to sit in a wheelchair beside the fence that circled the field, instead of climbing the bleachers. Gramps liked the location; he felt a part of the game.

Friday night, the high school team ran together from the locker room to the stadium. John glanced around, once the team reached the field. He didn't see his family. It was obvious that they were running late.

The coin was tossed and the game began. It was a game of tug-of-war; one team gained yardage, and then lost ground again the next down. Each side struggled to get the upper-hand by scoring a goal. It was a long first and second quarter with few time-outs. The score was nothing to nothing.

At halftime, his mother and grandfather still weren't there. Where could they be? John was worried.

When halftime ended, his team took the field again. The ball was snapped. John glanced around; the intended receiver couldn't take the pass. John was open. The ball was thrown to him. He caught it and ran down the field, hoping to pass off the ball to the star player. Linebackers were charging toward him. He managed to avoid one, then the other. There still was no one to hand off to. He had no choice but to run, avoid being tackled, and get down the field as far as he could, while his other teammates blocked. Nothing was as planned. John ran as fast as he could.

His path was clear. He resisted looking back; he knew it would be a mistake. He envisioned players diving toward his feet, trying to bring him down and missing, others being blocked by his teammates, the perfect scenario, everything happening to make it as he saw it now, absolutely clear. His uncanny sense was dead-on accurate. He gave it all he had; adrenalin made him run even faster. His heart was pounding like a runaway train.

Touchdown!

As he turned, his eyes darted to the fence, searching for his family. No matter how hard he looked, they weren't there. The fans in the stands were jumping up and down, yelling, and cheering for the new hero. John held the ball up to please the crowd as he jogged back to the bench. Somehow the cheers didn't matter. He was worried about Gramps.

The rest of the game was a blur. All the plays were by the book, exactly as they had practiced them. John performed his rehearsed moves, even though his mind was far away. His team won the game.

John bummed a ride home. When he saw the dark house, his heart sank. His fears were confirmed. They weren't at the game and now they weren't at home. There was only one place they could be. John let himself in and read the one word note left on the kitchen table: Hospital.

He ran next door and hitched a ride from the neighbor. He found his mom in the ICU waiting room.

"John! I'm glad you're here. We were coming to your game, but Gramps couldn't breathe. I had to call for the ambulance. I followed them to the hospital. He's intubated and on a ventilator. The doctor told me there's no point of leaving him on the vent indefinitely. His COPD has progressed and Gramps can no longer breathe on his own."

"If you take him off the vent, he won't be able to breathe!"

"Right; he won't. He'll have a mask for oxygen to help, but they'll have to start the morphine drip to help him not feel the pain of basically suffocating. Gramps and I knew this day would come, John, and he's ready to go. We have to let him go with as little pain as possible. The sooner we do, the better it is for him."

John sat down with his head in his hands and cried. He had been on an emotional rollercoaster this evening, the pinnacle to the pit. Emily rubbed his back in sympathy, not realizing all the turmoil that her son felt.

"How was your game?"

"We won. I made a seventy-yard touchdown."

"Oh, John; I'm so sorry we weren't there to see it," Emily said, giving John a tired and sympathetic look.

By Wednesday, Gramps was taken off of the ventilator. No other family was coming. He hadn't spoken since the intubation and didn't seem to know they were there. Emily and John stayed all night, sensing his time was near. In the morning, they watched the Thanksgiving parade on the hospital TV. At noon, monitoring alarms sounded; Gramps was slipping away. The staff rushed them out of the room.

When the nurse let John and Emily see him again, he was peacefully lying in bed, no tubes, no mask, and no ventilator noise. A quiet calm existed in the room. They stood on either side of him, holding his hands for awhile. When he started feeling cold, they were ready to leave. They went home in silence, each processing their individual thoughts and memories. They ate peanut butter and jelly sandwiches for dinner. Neither felt like a traditional Thanksgiving meal.

The arrangements had been pre-arranged. They never saw Gramps again. He had been taken from the hospital and cremated. They picked up his ashes during the holiday season.

Emily's brother and sister-in-law didn't bother to come. She wasn't surprised; her brother hadn't seen their dad in years. His share of inheritance was in the form of bank CD's. He had no reason to come as far as he was concerned, or so he had said when Emily had called apprising him of Gramps' condition in the hospital. "The 'old man' isn't long for the world and there's a branch here in town." Gramps left Emily the old house.

John and his mom were numb. They didn't put up a tree. There were no lights or decorations. John thought it was sad when they first moved there, but now it was worse. Gramps' social security income ended with his life; they had no means of support. During the Christmas break, John boxed Gramps' clothes and medical equipment. And he cleaned and rearranged the house, while Emily searched for work.

CHAPTER 17

Early January 2004
San Diego, California

The Pakistanis in California were given assignments that split up the group. Abdul applied and was accepted into the Meteorology program at University of Oklahoma. He was told to find and attend a Church of the Nazarene. Mohammad needed to master English before he could be used. He agreed to try harder. Sabur was sent to pilot school in Salt Lake City, Utah. He was instructed to join the Mormons. Naji couldn't speak English well enough to do any assignment that GUILE had at the time. He went home, never to return. He only wanted to use guns and felt it useless to speak English. And Ahmad went to Penn State to major in Mining Engineering. He was assigned the job of infiltrating a group of Pentecostal Roman Catholics.

Each kept their contact updated on developments and progress, just like their Turkish Islamic brothers, whom they had never met.

Late January 2004
Los Angeles, California

The Imam answered his cell phone "Hello."

"This is Mr. Morocco," Juan Perez said, identifying himself, as he sat in the back of his Rolls Royce Shadow. "How are my young Moroccans working out?"

"Jamal, Omar, and Nassim have all mastered English. They have passed their GED and are ready for assignment. Tarek and Karim need more time."

Juan looked at his mining map and said, "Send Jamal to Virginia Tech for Mining Engineering and Omar to Penn State for Meteorology. Nassim will learn to fly. I'll get back with the name of the flight school soon.

"What for Tarek and Karim?"

"Pick one to send home. Let the other learn English alone. We've found it works better that way."

"Thank you. Good Day, Mr. Morocco."

Juan closed his phone and looked out at the Peruvian sky. A storm was brewing.

April 2004
Christiansburg, Virginia

John came home after baseball practice. He was the star pitcher. *"I should have my arm insured,"* he thought, as he chuckled and rubbed his biceps.

He had the best arm for long passes in football, and threw a really mean curve ball. His baseball coach wanted him to take the scholarship to the University of Virginia in Charlottesville. John had been accepted at Virginia Tech and wasn't interested.

May 2004
Houston, Texas

Ted's AWA staff and the NASA crew had worked well together. They were almost finished with construction. The red tape, waiting for Congress' appropriations, had made the project slow and arduous. Teddy had one more final exam to take; and his master's program in Astronautical Engineering would be finished.

"Gotta leave now, Dad," Teddy said. "I have my final this afternoon."

"Okay, hope you ace it like you did all the rest."

Ted was proud of his son. He had been so busy between the courses and work, that he hadn't the time for a girlfriend in his life.

Ted wondered, *"Did I do my son a disservice by hiring him on this job?"* He shook his head, realizing no one would ever know the answer to that question.

"Ted, you couldn't have asked for a better son," Stan, the NASA chief engineer, said as he patted Ted's shoulder and watched 'Junior', his nickname for Teddy, go out the door.

"His mom and I will be at his graduation next week. You don't need to tell me."

"I wish they made more like him," Stan said, and turned his attention to the blueprints.

When Teddy finished his final, he checked on his academic advisor, hoping he was free. He found him at his desk, behind a stack of thesis papers.

"Do you have a moment, Dr. Johnson?"

Lyn Johnson looked over his reading glasses and said, "For you, Ted, I certainly do. I'm sure your parents say it all the time, but you've been a great addition to our university. How can I help you?"

"I wanted to begin my doctorate studies and use the project I'm working on with NASA over at Johnson Space Flight Center. Since you're my advisor, I thought I'd clear the idea with you, before spinning my wheels in the wrong direction."

"I think that could be a fantastic project. Go ahead and write up the proposal."

"Thanks, Dr. Johnson. I'll let you get back to your papers. See you next week at graduation."

"You're attending? Most students don't anymore."

"I wasn't able to go to my undergraduate graduation. I finished early and then we moved here in February. I couldn't see the point of the expense to go back. My parents deserve to see one ceremony, don't you think?"

"Yes, all parents like to be proud of their kids. Give your parents my best, and don't forget to pick up your gown," he said, and turned his attention to the next paper to be graded.

Teddy dropped by the graduate studies office and picked up his cap, gown, and hood along with the schedules of practice and actual ceremony.

June 2004
Christiansburg, Virginia

John's mother was seated in the bleachers on the warm Sunday afternoon of his high school's graduation. Emily was fanning herself with the program, waiting for the seniors to process into the stadium. "*Too bad Daddy didn't make this. Of course, the heat would've been unbearable for him,*" Emily thought, as a welcomed breeze whisked past her cheek. "*Did you just give me a kiss, Daddy?*" Emily smiled warmly at the thought.

'Pomp and Circumstance' came blaring out of the stadium speaker system. The Class of 2004 processed onto the field and took their seats, the white-gowned girls to one side, and the navy blue-gowned boys to the other.

Tears gently flowed down Emily's face, as they did for most of the proud mothers in the stands. The Valedictorian of the class stood to give a speech. When she was finished, John walked up and gave his Salutatorian speech. The ceremony ended with the class president saying, "Graduates, turn your tassels."

All the new graduates of Christiansburg High School moved their golden tassels to the opposite side on masse. There was only a split second before they tossed the caps away into the air, cheering and hugging each other. The music signaled an end to the jubilation. They quickly joined the recessional line, and filed out of the stadium, eager to attend graduation parties.

Emily met John at the car. They rode home talking and laughing, something they hadn't done for some while. Once home, Emily handed John his card and gift. He opened the envelope as he sat down in front of the graduation cake his mother had baked for him.

He read aloud, "Congratulations!" He opened the card and laughed. Inside it read: 'We Did It!' He unfolded a piece of paper that had fallen out when he opened the card. There was a clipped picture of the nation's Capitol glued to it. Below was printed the reservations for a hotel in Washington, D.C. John looked to his mother for an explanation.

"I'm taking you on a vacation," Emily said excitedly. "We'll be gone only one week. I'm hoping we can see all the monuments and the Smithsonian while we're there."

"You got off?" John asked, surprised that after only a few months Virginia Tech was letting her have vacation time.

"Yeah, the cafeteria supervisor said I could take one week this summer and then two next; otherwise, I would've made longer reservations."

"Great, Mom," John said without sarcasm; he truly meant it.

"We'll go during the July 4th holiday. I'm off on the weekend and Monday. I thought I could stretch our vacation time if we went then. We can leave on Friday evening. We'll even get to see all the fireworks on the Mall and the Beach Boys too, I hope."

"Oh, great," John said a little sarcastically that time, making then both laugh.

July 2004
Washington, D.C.

Emily and John checked into the hotel across from Arlington Cemetery. They visited the Tomb of the Unknown Soldier and the Lee Mansion first thing Saturday morning, since they were close by. In the afternoon, they rode the Metro and visited the Holocaust Museum.

They noticed the stage being erected on the Mall for the festivities. The Fourth was the next day on Sunday. Thousands were going to be at the celebration, since they'd all be off on Monday.

"We'll have to get over here early in the morning, John, if we want a good seat."

"No problem, Mom," John said, happy to get the chance to see the

Mall and the monuments in person, and not in an encyclopedia or textbook picture, or on the Nightly News.

They had a great time the next day. Emily brought a quilt and they picnicked. They purchased ice cream and sodas from the vendors that lined the Mall. When the Beach Boys played John didn't mind, but he wished that Brian Wilson was among them. Emily didn't even seem to notice, as she danced and sang along.

"Fun, Fun, Fun, 'til her Daddy takes the T Bird away…" As Emily sang, she thought of her own dad taking away her privilege of using his Mustang when she was a teen. Every time she heard the song, she remembered getting busted for not going where she said she was; yet she still liked singing along. It had changed into a fond memory, now that she was older.

John was glad that she was enjoying herself. It had been a hard four years on her, on both of them for that matter. The Mall was like a large yard party. Even he was enjoying himself.

The day slipped into darkness. As they watched the fireworks explode over the Washington Monument, they both welled up with pride for America.

"Did you see that?" Emily asked.

"Yeah, I like those that spiral down."

"Oh my goodness, this must be the finale."

The fireworks went off three at a time, and one rapidly after the other. The smoke drifted off with the breeze that came up, making the heat of the day less oppressive. The last series of red, white, and blue bursts cascaded down from high above the white obelisk, signaling it was time to go.

On Monday, Emily and John took the Metro early again, spending the day in the Museums of American History, Natural History, and the American Indian. On Tuesday, they dedicated their touring to Art. They saw paintings and objects of art at the National Gallery of Art, the Hirshhorn, the Sackler, and the Freer.

"Mom, I'm like art and museumed out."

"I have to say I am too," Emily agreed as they rode the Metro back to the hotel.

Wednesday, they did the monument route. They started at the Lincoln Memorial and walked to the Washington Monument. They took the elevator to the top of the tallest building in D.C. They looked out of the little windows at the bird's eye view of the Mall. They hadn't realized how far they had walked.

"The tourists on the ground look like ants," John commented. "If they look like ants, then the Reflective Pool is longer than I thought."

"Let me see," Emily said, and John stepped aside, allowing her a view. "They really do."

Back on the ground, they walked past the Bureau of Engraving and Printing to the Jefferson Monument.

"I wish we could stop and fill our pockets," John joked.

"Do you think they give out free samples?" Emily ask the deliberately silly question, making them both laugh, as she noticed that there were tours.

"It would be nice, but since they won't, I don't care to see the place," John said seriously, even though he was laughing.

Their laughter lightened their spirits in the humid summer air of Washington. They were so tired that they rested on the steps overlooking the Tidal Basin. They ended the day by taking a paddleboat and having fun.

That night, Emily's legs were achingly sore. "I'm getting too old for this much fun, John."

"I know we covered a lot of ground today, but it's been easier than ball practice," John commented, as he fell asleep. He was dead to the world, and the city noises in the distance, in less than five minutes.

"I've saved the Air and Space Museum for last." When John didn't answer, Emily turned out the light.

Thursday, John loved the Air and Space Museum and joked, "One day, Mom, I'll be in space."

Emily laughed, but knew her son could do anything he set his heart and mind on.

July 2004
Nepal

Claudia didn't find her brother at the Kopan Monastery, like she had hoped, but she stayed at the retreat and meditation center, anyway. She felt at one with herself and the world there. What really sunk in was a posted message by Shantideva. The first section she memorized and meditated on often.

'Whatever joy there is in this world
All comes from desiring others to be happy.
And whatever suffering there is in this world
All comes from desiring myself to be happy.'

Claudia spent the winter, volunteering in the Nunnery. The number of orphaned children moved her; fifty percent were orphans and twenty-five percent more only had one parent. The monastery educated them in English, Math, and Science. She helped teach English and Math.

Warm weather returned, and she stayed. She shaved her hair and wore the clothes of the nuns. She awoke at four thirty in the morning and retired at eleven. Claudia felt at peace and sensed no urgency to leave.

CHAPTER 18

August 17, 2004
Somewhere in the Atlantic Ocean

Mary Matthews was aboard ship for the required summer cruise. They had been gone a week. She had her sea legs, and walked like she was born on the water. During her free time, she strolled around the ship, breathing in the fresh salt air.

"*One more year at the Academy, and I'll go to flight school in Pensacola,*" she thought, as she stared out at the rough seas. She couldn't wait to learn how to fly and land on an aircraft carrier. Mary thought it'd be the best of both worlds: one at sea *and* one in the air.

"Did you see the weather report?"

"What? Hurricane Danielle?"

"Yeah; she's a CAT 2 and might be coming our way. I'm from Miami," her fellow midshipman, Sara said; her eyes were steady and focused, but it was obvious that she was concerned.

"I don't think we'll have to worry. I think our waters are cooler here; and she'll get downgraded in a day or two. Besides, I think they're predicting for her to go to the Azores. That's where we were two days ago, so we're headed in the opposite direction," Mary said confidently.

"Well, I sure hope so," Sara said, heading through the door in the bulkhead, leaving Mary on the deck alone.

The next morning, Hurricane Danielle had changed course, as Sara had thought it might. The midshipmen were given orders to head home to Annapolis. By the following day, Danielle had weakened and was downgraded to tropical storm status.

The Academy had the ship continue their course home, anyway.

October 2004
Lima, Peru

Juan finished his breakfast. He went to his room and placed a call to the boss.

"Yes, Mr. Morocco. Do you have some news for me?"

"Yes, I do. I've been studying your idea regarding fault lines. I've worked up some models. I think it just might work."

"Do you have a suggestion of location for testing?"

Juan scratched his head, smoothed his hair again, and answered, "Well, I think we can trigger one from a mine. That's why I suggested this before, but only as a test, hmm?"

"Would you feel better if it was a small test?" The boss said, sensing Juan's hesitancy.

"That might work if we use explosives near some island areas which are relatively sparse in population. That way we don't cause anyone to wonder, or report loss of life on the News. If I do that, we won't be using a mine for the test. I don't have contacts for sea craft."

"I'll handle that and get back to you. You work on the plan for a water test."

When the call ended, Juan searched his world map for just the right islands to use. After an hour, he decided on the Solomon Islands.

"*Now for the execution; what can I use?*" He contemplated the answer, as he created the initial test.

November 2004
Solomon Islands, Pacific

A special crew of demolition experts had been gathered. They were not the normal Navy Seal types. They were mercenaries, who asked no questions. Just show them the money, and the job would be done. They planted the charges and were standing clear, waiting for the go-ahead.

The phone rang.

"We're ready," the captain said, answering the call.

"Do it!"

The explosives were detonated many fathoms below on the sea floor. A wave caused by the quake rocked the boat thirty miles away.

Juan waited for the outcome nervously. He didn't want the boss to be disappointed. He stood by the wire service to see if any earthquakes were being reported.

Finally, it came.

Nov 09 23:58 hours Solomon Islands 1.0 magnitude 11.150 S and 163.706 E. No one injured.

"*Good, no one hurt. But it wasn't strong enough,*" Juan thought.

Juan placed a call to the mercenaries.

"Good job. I need one a little stronger. Can you give me another in a few days? Can you get together the materials necessary?"

"Sure, I'll get it together, maybe by the eleventh. I'll call you when we're ready."

"Good work."

On November the eleventh, the second test results came in. The quake registered 1.1 in magnitude.

"That's good enough for now," the boss said.

Juan replied, "I know it was only a small test the first time, but we proved that an additional charge under water can increase the magnitude. I think the water softened the blow."

"I'm confident you can make it stronger when the time comes."

"We can perform a larger test from a mining location when we get closer to the deadline," Juan added, knowing that he had assured GUILE that one of the components of a very large plan would work.

December 2004
Houston, Texas

"We're putting the final touches on the WSL, Director. I need your go-ahead. Can I begin to hire and train the two meteorologists and two engineers for space travel?" Ted asked his boss in Washington.

"Well, Ted, Congress isn't seeing the necessity of this project lately. They're also cutting some of the space funding," Director Haynes said, as he looked disappointedly out the window at the Capitol building. "I've been talking it up, but it looks like we're not going to have enough to pay that many salaries. What bare-bones personnel will we need?"

"That is the bare-bones!" Ted was frustrated, and didn't mind letting Haynes know it by the tone of his voice.

The director looked at the figures on his desk asking, "Can one meteorologist and one engineer handle it?" Haynes only had enough in the most recently approved budget to add two more to the staff.

"Possibly; I guess one meteorologist in the lab can discuss things with a team on the ground; and an engineer can work with NASA's team, if problems arise," Ted said doubtfully.

"Maybe after it's up and running, Congress can read the reports and see the merits. Then we'll be able to fully man it," the director stated, promising the unlikely. "In the meantime, find two who can train for the positions," he ordered, ending the call.

Ted hung up, red in the face, and left his office. He needed to take a walk and blow off steam. He didn't want to unintentionally attack his staff.

Christmas 2004
Monte Carlo, Monaco

Jack walked into the casino and right away spotted Andre Grimaldi. He nodded his head and went to the table to play. In a short while Andre walked over.

"How have you been?"

"Quite well; and you?"

"Fine. What will you have; champagne, perhaps?"

"Yes, that would suit me."

Andre made a gesture and a man was there in a moment.

"Please, bring my friend all the French Champagne he wants."

"Yes sir," the well-dressed waiter said.

"If there is anything else that you want while here, be sure to let me know. Are you staying close by?"

"I have rented a yacht in the harbor for the holiday season. Please join me sometime while I'm here."

"What time do you get up for the day? Maybe I can drop by before going home one morning."

"Tonight, I'll be out late, but the other evenings I'll go to bed at a reasonable hour. You understand; we're getting old, my friend."

"Americans age; we French only mellow like fine wine," Andre joked and left Jack to play on his own.

Before Jack left the casino, he gave Andre the location of the yacht and contact information.

Several days later, Andre made a stop at the piers and rode a small craft out to the large yacht moored several hundred yards offshore.

The yacht was owned by one of their other GUILE associates, Paul Beorg, aka Mr. Afghanistan. Paul was currently experiencing summer in South Africa and would come to the Cote d'Azur for the Cannes Festival, as he did each year.

"Why didn't you say you were staying on Paul's yacht? I would've known right away how to get out here. Paul has me over each year when he's in town for the film festival."

"That's right. I forgot he did that. Since I live on the other side of the Atlantic, I don't get over here that often."

Even though the meeting seemed social, it wasn't. Mr. Iran and Mr. Pakistan compared updates on all of the operatives' progress in the States.

"So the majority of our recruits have mastered English well enough to enter all the programs we need to train them in?" Andre asked, seeking clarification and assurance.

"About three out of each group of five did, yes. We have sent them on to different universities in the States to get the degrees necessary to apply for the jobs we'll need to manipulate. It'll take years for this training; we must all be patient," Jack confirmed, sipping his cold champagne.

"Please stay for brunch before you rush off. You must eat, before you go to bed for the day like a vampire," Jack invited and laughed at his own joke.

Andre didn't take offense and accepted the invitation.

Jack had his staff bring fresh chilled glasses and a full bottle of Krug.

The server removed the empty bottle and opened the new bottle with a slight pop. After pouring the bubbling wine into the glasses, he set the bottle into the ice bucket. He returned with fresh strawberries that had been flown in from a warmer climate. Then, he left the men to talk.

Jack sat comfortably in his terry robe and Andre in his tuxedo in the salon, looking out at the many other large boats in the harbor.

"Do you feel these men can accomplish these hard subjects?" Andre asked, while he ate the omelet.

"The initial program I used to find these last operatives had a criteria regarding intelligence quotient. We were only looking for muscle the first time," Jack explained, and took another sip of his champagne.

"We had them take the TOEFL to enter the school as well as an aptitude test. From there we selected the subject for them to learn. We feel they'll do well. Some still had problems with English; we have let them return to the Middle Eastern country they came from."

Andre commented, "Besides, we can manipulate the results when they apply for the positions in the end."

"Just the same, they'll know the subjects and will be well versed in interviewing when we get to that point," Jack replied, confident that the operatives would succeed on their own.

Andre apologized, "I'm sorry. I asked too many questions. This project seems to be much more complicated than before."

"It will work out. We have every confidence," Jack assured him.

In time, the subject changed to the projects and efforts of the past.

"Have we heard anymore on Claudia?" Andre asked. He didn't like that she had slipped through their fingers so easily.

"I'm sure she'll turn up soon."

"Where can she go?"

"She has to be making her way to China and Chen Hui Long has that covered. I have every confidence in him," Jack said, and bottomed his glass.

"China is a big place with a lot of people. It's like looking for a needle in a haystack. Is that not how you say it?" Andre expressed it as it was.

"Hui Long has many operatives. I'm betting on him for the time being," Jack said, bringing the reference back to Andre's world. It was a reminder that he should take his leave before the night called again.

"I don't think we would run a 'Claudia' table at the casino, the odds aren't good enough for me," Andre added with a smile, "But who am I to say? Thanks for having me out. It was nice visiting. Enjoy your stay."

With that, Andre left the yacht. He had to rest before returning to his tables. He stepped into the dinghy and donned a pair of dark glasses. He wasn't used to the bright sun on the Riviera. He saluted Jack as the boat pulled away to shore.

CHAPTER 19

January 2005
Houston, Texas

"Teddy, I have some serious decisions to make about the project and I need your input. Do you have a moment?" Ted asked his son.

Teddy was going over the lab with a fine-tooth comb before placing his initials of approval on the completed work. Everyone on the project had to sign-off before the lab was transported to Cape Kennedy. Once there, it would be checked over again to make sure nothing had shaken loose from Texas to Florida.

"Sure, Dad; I'll be free around five. Will that do?"

"Actually, I want to talk with you in private. Do you mind if I come to your house directly after work? I don't even want your mom to know about this until we've spoken."

Teddy stopped what he was doing. His eyes got big as his eyebrows raised. "You've got my attention now, Dad. Is everything okay with you and Mom?"

"Nothing like that, Teddy; this is shop talk, but I don't want it interrupted by anyone here; and I don't want your mom in on it yet, either. Okay?" Ted asked again.

"Sure, no problem; how about we meet at my alley parking at six?"

"Good. Six, it is," Ted slapped his son's shoulder and walked back to his office desk.

When six rolled around, they met at Teddy's place as planned. Ted went directly to the kitchen table. Teddy handed him a cold Corona with a slice of lime. He felt Ted was going to need it; he seemed so serious and uptight about something. After pouring some tortilla chips in a bowl, Teddy joined his dad at the table. He pushed in his lime and took a sip.

"Okay, shoot. What's up?"

Ted munched on a chip and washed it down with a swig of beer before he began. "Teddy, our funds have been cut. I didn't want to ruin Christmas for everyone on the staff, or here at home either. I've just been sitting on this, waiting for some miraculous solution, but I've got to get moving on it. Time's wasting."

"How much did we get cut?" Teddy asked.

Ted raised his brow and answered, "A couple of positions that we need." He took another drink and added, "I can only send two to train for the space lab: one meteorologist and one engineer. We'll have one backup on the ground."

"Goodness gracious. All this time and money, and they're not going to man it properly. What in the world is Washington thinking?" Teddy asked, shaking his head. He took a large swig of the beer to push the bile down that was threatening to rise.

"Exactly; they're not thinking. They only look at dollars and how much it's going to cost." Ted nibbled on a few more chips before he continued. "I was wondering; since you have no wife and kid, would you like the position in space for the first year?"

"What?! Me?!" Teddy rubbed his head and expelled a deep breath. "Whoa, no wonder you didn't want Mom, or anyone else for that matter, to hear this."

"I know you're qualified. You built it. I'd like you to be able to take it for the test drive. Besides, it'll make a heck of a doctoral dissertation, I'd say."

"It sure would. Wow! I don't know what to say."

"Well, think about it. If you can pass the training, it's yours."

"Who's going to be the weather guy?" Teddy had worked with the other two on the project. He wasn't so sure that he'd want to spend a year with either of them in space; yet again, he didn't want to pass up such an opportunity either.

"I know I'm not a spring chicken, but I'm in shape and…"

Teddy cut him off, "What?! Did you ask Mom?!"

"No!" Ted lifted the bottle to his lips and placed it down again adding, "I don't want to spend a year with anyone else but you, or your mom, but she's not in the running here. Could you see her in space?"

They laughed at the thought.

"If you agree to be the engineer, I'll see if I pass the muster."

"Mom may not like both of us in space, leaving her alone, you know?" Teddy said, stating the obvious.

"If you agree to go, you and I can go see if she agrees tonight. If she does, we'll see what Director Haynes in Washington thinks. I'm hoping we can cut a deal, one where both of us win."

"And what's that?" Teddy's interest was piqued, again.

"Haynes told me I could hire two. My plan is to hire one other meteorologist for the group team, then use the other funds for our insurance policies. If we don't return to your mom, she'll have enough to retire and not have to financially suffer."

"That totals the same as the project."

"Not really. They don't have to cover unemployment insurance, any other medical, or retirement; they'll save in the long run."

"Good plan; I'm in." Teddy said, shaking his dad's hand.

May 22, 2005
Naval Academy, Annapolis, Maryland

Sunday afternoon, Mary could hear the Navy's precision jet team, the Blue Angels, as they practiced up and down the Severn River. For a minute her mind wandered, as she daydreamed she was flying one of the F/A-18 Hornets herself. She snapped mentally back to attention outside Bancroft Hall; any moment she and her fellow classmates would be dismissed. It was hard to stay focused; graduation was nearly here.

Her mom and dad arrived the next day. Her parents rented a house for 'June Week' in Cape St. Claire from a neighbor of a host family. Every year, the couple rented it out and got enough for that one week to pay the month's mortgage, plus take a modest vacation. Many in Annapolis took advantage of the opportunity to get far away from the Academy crowds and the Route 50 gridlock.

"Hi, honey. We just arrived and are unpacked. We'd like to meet you for a little while. Is that possible?"

Mary answered, "Sure, Mom. I'm free for the next two hours. You can pick me up in front of the Chapel."

"Okay, we'll be there shortly," her mom said, ending the call. "She's got two hours free; she'll be at the Chapel entrance."

"Then we better get moving," Mary's dad replied, grabbing the keys to Mary's new car.

They locked the front door to the house, pulled out of the driveway, and headed out to Route 50. At the on-ramp, they turned right and merged with the very limited traffic. It appeared that most were going east to the Bay Bridge. They got off at the Pendennis Mount exit and traveled over the Old Severn River Bridge. Her dad entered at the Hospital Point gate and proceeded to the Chapel, avoiding Rowe Boulevard traffic.

"Mary!" Since they weren't in the family car, her mom had to wave her arm out the window of the silver sports car to get her attention.

"Wow! Did you rent this for the week?" Mary asked, not expecting her parents to give her a BMW M3.

Margaret Matthews opened the door without answering; Mary slipped into the seat behind her mom.

Her dad explained as he drove away from the Chapel area and headed toward the seawall. "We got this for you. It's your graduation present. We figured out how much you saved us. We haven't had to pay tuition or for you to have a car all these years. That's when we realized this car was actually cheaper than a normal college education. Hope you like it!"

"Are you going to use it during the week?" Mary asked, admiring the leather upholstery and the open-top convertible view.

"No; we need to rent a car. We're going over to the car rental place now. Your mom can drive you back here and park the car for the night," Michael explained.

"It has to be parked here along the seawall," Mary said, aware of the rules and regulations and proud that her car would soon be there among the others.

"I know; I've been reading the Midshipmen Parents' blog. That site answers all your questions," her mom said.

"I don't know if I've got time for you to get all the paperwork filled out for a rental," Mary said, nervously looking at the car's clock.

"As soon as we get there, I'll turn the car over to your mom to drive you back. She can wait for me."

"Sounds good, Dad," Mary said relieved, the beaming smile returning to her face.

They changed drivers at the car rental place and Margaret drove Mary back onto the Academy grounds. When Mary left, she gave her mom a big smile and wave as she made double-time across the field.

The following day they enjoyed the Blue Angels air show; the jets flew up and down the Severn River, performing aerial acrobatics. There was a full week of activities that culminated with the graduation ceremonies. By the end of the week, the Matthews were seated in the stands of the Navy-Marine Corps Stadium on Rowe Boulevard. The graduation got under way with a twenty-one cannon blast, followed by a fast and low fly-over by the Blue Angels in formation.

"Oh my goodness," Mary's mom exclaimed.

"I can't wait to hear the President make the address," Michael admitted. There was always a good speaker at the graduations, but it wasn't every day they were this close to the Commander-in-Chief. Before the President spoke, the ebullient midshipmen got several rousing rounds of 'the wave' going around the stadium. Mary's parents joined in the merriment.

President Bush came to the podium and made his speech. He reminded them, "The U.S. military is on the offensive in the War on Terror to prevent terrorists from reaching America's shores." He added later,

"Twenty years from now, historians will look back on the Iraq war as 'America's golden moment.'"

Michael Matthews leaned toward his wife and whispered, "I doubt that."

Margaret Matthews quietly said, "Ssh!"

When the speech ended, almost a thousand graduates were given their commissions. They hurled their white hats into the blue sky and left the Academy for their new status as military officers. They were no longer plebes, midshipmen, and underclassman. They were officers, special officers, with a very prestigious ring, the Navy's elite. Mary was proud to be among them; she was ready for her four years of flight school in Pensacola.

June 2005
Cape Kennedy, Florida

They were ready and waiting for the last clear-to-launch and go-ahead signal. All systems had been checked and double-checked. The launch was advertised in the papers and news media as just another satellite. The public didn't know it was manned. The American Weather Agency didn't exist, neither did the Weather Space Lab; at least, not until they had success.

"We are ready to resume countdown, all systems go. Repeat, all systems are go. Do you confirm?"

Ted French answered, "A OK here. The Frenchs are ready."

Teddy had an anxious look in his eyes and butterflies in his stomach, as the countdown resumed. In less than twenty minutes, they'd be lifting off into space for a one-year tour.

"This is the last time they'll let me speak to you two. Remember, don't pick up any space gals while you're up there."

"I'll watch him, Mom."

"What? You don't want an alien daughter-in-law?" Ted chuckled and then turned serious, "I love you, Freda. Thanks for agreeing to let us go."

"Ten minutes and counting. Systems go," a voice said.

The private communications were over. There was a job to be done. The control room was buzzing with activity. All were at their posts and monitoring the constant flow of data on their computer screens.

Ted and Teddy were seated inside the Weather Space Lab. After this launch, the crew would be replaced by shuttle transport. Freda was nervously watching from the VIP section, acting brave. Mentally, she was praying that her husband and son wouldn't meet any calamity on the launch pad or in the air as they headed into space.

Johnson Space Flight Center followed along, waiting for the lift-off, and the moment they took over. GUILE watched with great expectations.

June 2005
Nepal/China Border

No one had been following Claudia for years; she thought it safe now to enter China. She used her Chinese passport to cross the border. She showed the false visitor's visa from Nepal. Even though she had spent time in the monasteries and practiced tranquility, she hadn't lost her survival instinct of self-preservation. Her heart beat rapidly as she unknowingly made her first mistake. She used papers with her real Chinese name.

Few Chinese had a passport and a 'Residence ID Book' like hers. The small brown plastic-covered notebook, which had a record of where she lived and had traveled inside the country, was procured for her years ago by her father. For a few more Yuan, she had regularly sent it to be updated, as if she were still in residence until 1990. China had become much more open, but she wanted to appear authentically Chinese.

"Claudia, when someone living in China leaves home and checks into a hotel somewhere, they need to bring this book with them. They have to go to the local Security Bureau to get a visa on official letterhead that carries a stamp of approval. Without it, they could get arrested," Mr. Lei instructed her many years ago.

She knew it wasn't as necessary these days, but everyone still needed to have one. Her father's words were engrained into her as a child and had instilled much fear of travel in his strange country-of-birth, with all of its restrictions. She was desperate, but China wasn't the threat, GUILE was. Her documents were returned, and her heartbeat returned to normal as she passed over the border. She walked away and breathed a slow sigh of relief.

"Mr. Chen, an old woman passed the border today at Zhangmuzhen that had the name Li Mei Lian. You said to inform you if a person with that name should pass through. She didn't meet your description, so we didn't detain her. She may have been a decoy. I'll continue to watch for one meeting your description. The woman today said she was making her way to Yushu, to the monastery. She appeared to be a nun."

"Thank you. Good work. Keep looking and tell me when a woman appears meeting the description."

"Yes, sir."

Chen Hui Long looked out over the Victoria Harbour and placed the call. "I may have good news. An old nun passed the south border today from Nepal. Her passport had the Chinese birth-name of our Claudia Lei. She must be a decoy; Claudia may arrive soon."

"Follow this one to make sure. Don't harm her; just have her watched."

"It shouldn't be hard. She's going to the Yushu Monastery. It'll take her some time on foot. We'll keep an eye on her."

"Good work." The boss closed his phone. *"As long as she keeps quiet, living a miserable life, I'll leave her alone, at least for now,"* he thought and then let out a sinister laugh of satisfaction.

August 2005
WSL in Orbit

Ted and Teddy had gotten used to the routine on board the orbiting weather lab. Since there were only two of them, they alternated shifts of sleep and wake time. In a twenty-four hour period, each slept six hours. The clock was divided into quarters. They shared the wake times of the first and the third quarter.

Ted slept during the second quarter. During his alone time, he concentrated on developing modules to aid the existing program in tracking and predicting weather systems.

Teddy slept during the fourth quarter. He used his private time to work on his dissertation and grant project. The university knew that these graduates would derive their livelihood from government money. The grant writing course was added to the required program several years back. Teddy would be competing with the other students in the program. Just like real-life government grants, the lowest bidder won. But in the case, the winner only received a plaque.

He had written his rationale and included all the necessary budget needs for the project. He had checked over the assignment several times. Teddy could've low-balled his proposal, but that wouldn't mean he would score well if in reality the project couldn't fly. In Astronautical Engineering, what good was a project that couldn't get off the ground?

The sun came into view just as Ted awoke. He didn't need to stretch; in the weightless environment, the joints never compressed. He did want his caffeine though. He took his first sip through the straw as he floated over to Teddy's desk to gaze out of the porthole.

"Dad, look over this proposal and see what you think. If I've missed something let me know. Don't tell me what to do, just point me in the right direction." Teddy didn't want to have his dad's work. What he wanted was to know what he'd need to use in his near future.

"Sure, let me see. I'm not about to do your work for you," Ted said, as he drew his attention away from the view and sipped on the coffee.

"While you were sleeping, I've been running the different scenarios on Katrina. I think almost all of the Gulf should move back, especially areas like New Orleans. Look over my work while I read over the grant," Ted suggested, strapping himself into a chair to concentrate.

Teddy moved to his dad's computer and started studying the many different screens. He was no meteorologist, but he had to agree it looked bad.

Ted was pleased at his son's work. "If someone else gets this grant, they'd be cutting way too many corners is all I can say."

"Thanks, Dad. This doesn't look good," Teddy said, tapping the monitor picture, "especially since they sit on top of all that water."

"That's what I think. I sent an email to your mom to book a hotel further in for next week, just to be safe. It might've only been a CAT 1 when it crossed over Florida, but now it's in that hot bath water of the Gulf. It's being fed the food champion hurricanes eat."

"Too bad we can't push it out of there," Teddy said wishfully.

"Yeah, too bad. The best we can do at this point is to tell everyone to get out of the way, and pray they listen."

September 2005
Dondrubling Monastery, China

It took Claudia all summer to reach Yushu. Out of habit, she checked at the monastery for her brother, no longer expecting to find him. She was pleased when she did.

"You may not recognize me, Ci An; I'm your half-sister Claudia Lei, Mei Lian. When we met I was twenty-one and you were thirty-five."

"That was a long time ago," her brother said, staring strangely at her clothing. "Did you become a bhikkhuni?"

"No, not exactly. I've been performing a nun's activities at the Kopan Monastery for the past two years, but then I pressed forward into China to find you. Now I have. May I be of service here in some way?"

"You may stay for one night and visit me only occasionally. Try at the Temple of Princess Wencheng. Maybe they can use you there as a jushi, a devotee lay follower," he interpreted for her benefit.

She had hoped for more. "Okay. Thank you, Ci An"

In the morning, Claudia arose early. She made herself useful until it was time to leave. She walked to the temple and met with the head nun. They accepted her offer of service. She was given a different robe to wear only in the temple. In China, the temple robes weren't worn outside.

As she changed, she wished she didn't have to stay somewhere else. She'd only see her brother once a week this way; she had hoped to see him more. At least she had finally found him; she was thankful for that. He reminded her of her father, who passed away of cancer shortly after their visit to China. Her father must've known then that he was ill. Maybe that was the reason for the trip; her mother never said. Unfortunately, she passed away while Claudia was in Cambridge, earning her degrees.

It was moments like this when she felt so alone.

CHAPTER 20

September 2005
Los Angeles, California

Maria had the new collection ready for the next day's show. She had run through everything with the models, makeup artists, and stylists. She was ready.

Once she was settled in at the hotel, she called Jack. "Everything's set. It really looks good."

"Glad to hear it, Maria. Your decision not to go to Paris this year was a good one. I think it's best to only show there every other year. We'll make a bigger profit in the long run. At least that's how a projection model looked, using the data since 2001."

"Well, you won't get any objection from me. If we can turn the same profit with one less show, it means less work for me. I'm all for it."

"Glad you agree. Call me tomorrow when it's over and tell me how it went," Jack said, only concerned about the bottom-line, and hung up.

October 2005
Blacksburg, Virginia

John began his classes with trepidation. He wouldn't admit it to anyone, not even his mother, that he was afraid of failure. "*I think I've bitten off more than I can chew? Some of these guys have had harder classes in their high school than I did; at least that's what they're telling me.*"

The following day the head of the department came into his classroom and tapped him on the shoulder. He whispered, "Come with me."

"*Oh, no. They're going to kick me out of the program. They made a mistake when they accepted me,*" John told himself, as he followed the professor to another room.

"John, we've reviewed your first exams and realized we've misplaced you."

"*See. I knew it.*"

"We want you to sit here and work with these students. Would you like some coffee or anything?"

"No, sir." John was extremely puzzled; there had to certainly be a mistake now.

He took his seat and the professor brought him several assignments to work on independently. After he left, John glanced around. One fellow caught his eye.

"Don't worry. We've all felt that way. This is a special independent study class. We work on the assignments individually and next semester they'll adjust our classes to the appropriate level. My name's Ryan; that's Jason; he's Mustafa; and that guy over there is Aaron."

"Hi, I'm John."

"Nice meeting you," Ryan said, turning his attention back to the formula that he was trying to get his head around.

October 2005
WSL

"I was awarded the grant," Teddy proudly said to his dad.

"See, I told you. You've watched me most of your life; I guess it's rubbed off on you," Ted joked, and tousled his son's hair.

Teddy flipped and rolled away into the end of the cabin. They liked playing around on occasion. Most of the time, they were all business.

Katrina had proven to be as ugly as they had feared. Many persons had suffered and died in its aftermath. It would be years before the people of the Gulf could return to their property and way of life, if ever. FEMA and other organizations had stepped in to relocate displaced citizens in hopes to keep them away permanently. If they didn't live there, it couldn't happen again - that was the philosophy. But heritage and culture has a way of surviving. Some were still hoping to return one day.

Ted had been thinking for months about what Teddy had said and had worked on a program. "Teddy, you know I've been running these modules of the satellite images. I think I might be able to write a better program. I want you to help me with this."

"No problem. Let me finish this workout, and I'll take a look," Teddy said, as he used artificial intensification to simulate weight lifting.

Ted typed more lines of code as he waited.

"Okay, let me see what you have," Teddy said, wiping his brow before a bead of sweat could float off into the module.

"Well, that ought to make AWA and FEMA happy," Teddy replied, as he moved the cursor around the program, checking some of the lines of code to ensure accuracy of input.

"If we use this laser-driven program to follow the hurricanes from up here, we might be able to nudge those eye walls around, or at least diminish their strength. Maybe next season, we can keep them out at sea, saving lives and property damage." Ted stated the obvious outcome, unconvinced that it was possible.

"I think your work is fine. The predictions will be dead on the mark. We'll be home before we can try them out, though. The equator and the oceans are cooling down," Teddy prognosticated.

"Actually, we've got a storm heading for the Yucatan. I don't want it to even get into the Gulf."

"Send it down to AWA. Maybe they'll approve its use in time to try it on this late storm. After Katrina, they might figure they've got nothing to lose."

"Too bad we can't test it before asking, like in lab work," Ted said, attaching his data to the daily reports with a red alert flag for immediate attention.

GUILE reviewed the intercepted copy of the report. "We may be taking small steps, but one good thing that's come out of 9/11 is easier spying access in the name of homeland security," Jack said to the boss.

"So you have looked at the program and think we should let AWA approve it?"

"Yes. We'll be able to manipulate it in the future to our advantage. In the meantime, it may save some of the insurance companies that we have holdings in."

"Good."

The boss placed the next call, giving this item a thumbs-up.

Three days later the approval reached Ted on the WSL.

"Teddy, I can't believe this. We've actually gotten government approval to try this out," Ted replied to the communication on the computer screen, shaking his head.

"After what Katrina did to New Orleans, did you have any doubt?"

"Washington never moves that fast. That's something you'll learn over time when you get in the field. Only private business can do that. Washington only has red-tape and moves like molasses in January."

"Might be, but you got approval. Now what are you going to do? Complain? Get busy, old man," Teddy joked, "or you'll be as slow as they are."

Ted ran his first program and reviewed the satellite images again. Hurricane Wilma was growing and looked like it would be heading for the peninsula. He had to wait for an eye wall to form before he could try weakening the wall, or nudging it. When the wall formed, he locked on its exact coordinates, and radioed clearance of all aircraft for one hundred miles.

"Okay, you are all clear," Houston said.

"Okay, here goes nothing," Ted said, and pushed the enter key.

A laser beamed into the center of the storm. From space it appeared as a huge lightning bolt sent by Zeus, or so Teddy thought as he watched through his tinted face shield. From earth, it appeared as electrical activity in the storm.

An hour passed. The wall didn't weaken. It had actually strengthened. Ted worked through all the formulas again. He sent his findings to the ground. They confirmed.

"All we can do is to wait. Maybe by tomorrow it will downscale in status," Teddy said to his dad, as he turned in for his six-hour sleep period.

Time passed quickly. Ted was at the monitor again. Wilma was now a CAT 3 storm and maintaining its position over Cozumel.

"Ted, try it again," Houston ordered.

Ted called for clearance. He repeated the procedure from the day before with the same results. Hurricane Wilma remained a CAT 3 storm on the coast of Cozumel. Ted didn't see that the process had changed anything except to lower the pressure. It didn't weaken it or move it.

On the fourth day, the normal prevailing westerlies of fall came into play. Nature pushed Wilma back towards Florida. Ted's plug was pulled and testing ended for the season. The meteorologists on the AWA team on the ground were assigned the task to figure out why it hadn't worked.

Christmas 2005
Mission Control

"Merry Christmas, Freda," Ted said over the direct intercom system that WSL used to communicate with Houston Command Center regularly. NASA had arranged for Freda to be able to come in and talk with her husband and son, since it was Christmas. Most of the time, she received email-like printouts originating from Ted, which were delivered through the U. S. Postal Service from NASA.

"Merry Christmas, boys. It's good to see you. How are you feeling?"

"We're fine, Mom. It gets a little boring, but it is really cool to see the earth from way up here."

"I guess you'll have to wait to give your dissertation when you get back down to earth," Freda said, making an unintended pun.

"I have sent in data once a month to the doctoral committee, keeping them posted on my progress, but you're right, the dissertation in person will be the thing that gives me the degree. Have you been keeping busy?"

"Well, the house is totally clean, even the fridge. I have gone over to your house once a month to dust and clean the bathrooms."

"It isn't getting dirty. No one's there," Teddy protested, not wanting his mother to clean for him.

"It still gets dusty with the air handler blowing. The toilet gets a ring and kind of slimy without use. I don't want foreign organisms growing in the cottage. Otherwise, I wouldn't go over actually, Teddy. I can appreciate your privacy."

Ted broke into the conversation. "Other than cleaning, what have you been doing?"

"I joined Curves and was going by there every day to get some of my old accumulated weight and flab off. Now I go three times a week. It's really nice. Whenever I arrive, I just get on whatever equipment is free. When the music changes, I move through the circuit until I get back to where I started again. I think I'm ready for a gym for weight training now. Maybe after the holidays I'll join one of those.

"My doctor said I needed some weight-bearing exercise. I have some osteopena showing up and he doesn't want it turning into osteoporosis, since I've taken off the fat."

"How much have you lost?" Ted asked concerned.

"Only fifteen pounds; you probably wouldn't even notice it much. I'm eating better now too. I don't have you two around buying all that fast-food stuff."

"Believe it or not we have to exercise regularly up here as well. In weightlessness we can suffer bone loss, too. I guess we can say the family is all on controlled diets and exercise programs," Ted said and laughed.

"Well, they're giving me the signal to wind it up. I love you and can't wait until you get home," Freda said with a tear in her eye.

"We love you, too," came across her headset in harmonious stereo.

Everyone displayed big smiles and waved goodbye.

The video-feed went blank.

Freda wiped her tear from her cheek, thanked the technician, and walked to the car, feeling more alone than before the call. She had adjusted easier than she thought she would've to single life in an oversized house.

She drove home listening to "We Wish You a Merry Christmas" by the Chipmunks on the radio. She sang along in a falsetto voice. Even though she tried to have the spirit, it just wasn't there.

She drove past the other houses on their street. They were decorated and the lights and displays in the yards were starting to come to life. She pulled into the driveway. Her house was still dark. When the garage door opened, she pulled inside and turned off the engine. As she walked into the house, the timers snapped the interior and exterior Christmas lights on.

Freda placed her keys beside the little artificial tree that she had bought at the local Wal-Mart for ten dollars. She didn't feel like going to the effort of the full-sized normal tree, when none of her family was there to enjoy it.

CHAPTER 21

February 2006
Pensacola, Florida

Mary completed the first set of classes. She'd have a full set of classes for each of the four types of fliers, one each year of the program. She had been using simulators to fly ever since she arrived. Last week, she was finally given the privilege to fly in co-pilot student status with the instructor.

Today, she was in the pilot seat with the instructor as co-pilot. She was buckled into the sleek red and white plane. Her helmet was in place, and she was anxiously waiting for the go-ahead.

"Mary, have you checked all of the gauges on the instrument panel?" The instructor asked, knowing she had.

"Everything is ready for take-off, sir."

"Have you filed your flight plan with the tower?"

"Yes, sir."

"Okay, taxi out to the runway and take-off. I'm right here if you need me," the Captain said, tightening his seat belt.

Mary lined the plane up on the tarmac and revved the engine. The plane rolled down the runway increasing speed as it went. Near the end of the pavement, she pulled up on the throttle. The landing gear gently left the ground. She raised the plane into a steep ascent, leveling off when they reached the desired altitude.

"Great, Mary. Good take-off. Let's take this baby down to Key West and back."

Mary smiled as she looked through her face shield at the beautiful small clouds and answered, "Yes, sir." She banked the T-45 Goshawk south. If it weren't for the loud roar of the jet engines that Mary could hear through her helmet, she'd almost believe they were gliding through the air.

The sun glistened on the blue waters of the Gulf, like diamonds on dark blue velvet in a jeweler's shop. The white powder of the sandy shore was clearly visible below, as Mary raced high above it to the Keys. She turned her attention back to the instrument panel, and checked the gauges.

"Do you see the aircraft carrier down there?"

Mary answered, "Yes, sir."

"Eventually, you'll be landing on one of those."

To Mary the anticipation was going to be worth the wait.

March 2006
Salt Lake City, Utah

Gani had joined the Mormons as originally assigned and the flight school training was on hold. He first was serving God on mission, since he was still young and had a sponsor. The next two years of his life would be spent walking 'two-by-two' from door to door in a white shirt and tie, trying to win converts to Mormonism.

Gani would go over drills in the morning before heading to the street. The two of them drilled each other on scriptures that they used when coming to a house where someone answered the door.

He was walking with a twenty-two-year-old initiate from the Jewish faith. Gani was overwhelmed with the assignment, but he was determined to serve Allah.

"*Surely the Imam wouldn't have told me to do this if it wasn't praising Allah*," he thought, as he walked silently beside Ivan, a Russian, who hadn't lived in America long.

"What was it like in your home country?" Ivan hoped to get to talk about his. He was homesick and hoped that one day he'd take his faith home to Russia.

"It was different than this. We didn't have red rock, like here. How about you?" Gani asked, not really wanting to say much.

"We had mountains, but not like these. I think we had more snow. I don't mind snow; I miss my home," Ivan admitted.

Gani replied, "I understand. Yet, I could do with less snow myself. I think liking our home country is normal, even if we're supposed to be happy in this new faith of ours."

"There are so many rules. I thought Jews had a lot of laws from God, but the Mormons have more. I'm trying to follow them, but how can you do everything?"

"I don't think it can happen all at once. I think it's going to take time. We're being tested. God wants to see if we're sincere," Gani said, summing up what he had gathered so far, as he shifted his backpack to the opposite shoulder.

"Well, at least it didn't snow today, my friend. Spring is on the way."

"I think you're right," Gani said, stepping on the porch of another house, and boldly knocking on the door.

They waited.

Ivan knocked a second time, and silently waited again.

No one answered.

They wiped their feet on the doormat, and walked away.

April 2006
Houston, Texas

"Hey, Freda, since we usually lunch at the same time, why don't we go to dinner sometime on our way home; maybe Debbie can join us? I get so tired of going home and eating alone," Jim, Freda's fellow librarian, suggested.

"What day? I go to the gym on Mondays, Wednesdays, and Fridays," Freda said, scanning in the returned books.

Freda didn't think of it as a date; she was rather sure that Jim was gay. Most of the men librarians she had ever met were. Granted, they were very intelligent and avid readers, but she didn't know why they didn't put their good talents to better use and write like Truman Capote or Gore Vidal.

Besides being intelligent and kind, Jim was good looking, a good dresser, and had never been married. "*Add that all up; it can only mean one thing*," Freda thought, stacking the books on the cart and waiting for Jim to select the day.

"How's Thursday next week sound?"

"Okay, Thursday's good. Jim, I don't want to sound picky, but I don't want to go somewhere that serves fast-food fare. I've lost some weight over the last year. I don't want to put it on in one night out."

Freda started to wheel the cart to the shelves. She paused again when Jim responded differently than she had expected.

"I didn't want to mention it, but you have been looking great. I noticed the weight loss, but when you started changing the soft appearance you had before, I *really* noticed. Your gym workouts are worth every ounce of energy you've put into them. I wouldn't think of spoiling your progress."

"Um? Thanks." She resumed pushing the cart to the fiction aisle to shelf the books.

"*Did he just say he thought I was buff? If I didn't know better, I'd think he was a normal hot-blooded male after a good time. Must be my imagination*," she thought, shaking her head and placing the latest books from Patricia Cornwell and Dean Koontz in the New Releases section.

Good Friday 2006
State College, Pennsylvania

Ahmad was at the service, kneeling and repeating the words from the small paperback missal for the Lent Season. He had been baptized and confirmed last month. Sunday, he'd receive Holy Communion.

"We adore you, O Christ, and we bless you. Because by your holy cross you have redeemed the world," the congregation said in unison.

Ahmad had attended every Friday during Lent, and almost had the Stations of the Cross memorized. He stood, as the priest came up his aisle and stood in front of the first station.

Ahmad followed along, as the priest described the story, and marveled at the gruesome death. "*This is their God's son? No wander they're so fanatical about their faith, like we are about ours,*" he thought.

They knelt again and prayed.

Ahmad had given up pork for Lent. Since he didn't eat it anyway, he really didn't have to give up anything. He hadn't suffered or denied himself in the name of Jehovah; he was suffering this religion for Allah.

At the end of the last station, instead of filing out of the sanctuary the people remained. So, he did too. "*What are they doing now?*" He questioned and watched.

He was amazed and almost became sorrowful in sincerity when the priest and altar boys stripped the altar. No ornamentation remained. "*It's like the light of the world has been snuffed out,*" he thought.

Ahmad didn't realize that his sentiments were exactly what the early followers of Christ had felt. He filed out of the church very solemnly. No one chatted outside. The parishioners went to their cars in solemn silence.

Walking back to the campus at Penn State, he thought about a paper which was due the next week.

Friday Evening
Houston, Texas

Freda and Jim made a habit of going out to dinner every two weeks, even though that had only added up to three times by Easter. They ate their lunch together every day in the library's binding room. Everything had been harmless and above board.

"Freda, instead of being alone for Easter, why don't you come over to my place? I'll grill us a nice dinner and we can sit on my porch and enjoy it. It beats being alone, while the rest of the Christian world is celebrating, especially here in Texas," Jim said, as they walked out the door for the day.

"You do have a point there. No greasy hamburgers, right?" Freda asked, as she turned the key, locking the library for the night. She didn't want to blimp out with only two more months before the guys were back.

"No, I was thinking Crab Salad with Asparagus Tips, Grilled Salmon, and Sautéed Squash. For dessert, we could have a light Sorbet."

"That makes my mouth water, thinking about it. I'll bring a bottle of Chardonnay and my appetite," Freda teased.

"I hope so. How's two o'clock sound?"

"Great," Freda said, unlocking her car and starting the engine.

Jim opened his car door and waved as she pulled away.

Easter Sunrise Service
Norman, Oklahoma

Abdul was up before sunrise and had privately said his morning prayers to Allah without a roommate to notice. Josh had gone home Thursday evening, while Abdul was at church for the special Lord's Supper service.

Finding Christianity less demanding, Abdul was taking an easy ride. He felt he understood why this Christian nation was a bunch of infidels. They made no real demands on themselves, no sacrifices.

He didn't like ending his prayers early this morning to attend a sunrise service at the Church of the Nazarene, but at least he'd be able to have that off of his plate for the day. Then he could return to his own religion, which he hadn't been able to do with so many people around. He'd file his weekly report with the Imam hundreds of miles away by email when he returned.

Abdul walked to the service and put on a fake smile as he reached the early risers of the church. He took his seat on the folding chair, and listened to the choir sing, 'Up from the Grave He Arose.'

Early Easter Service
Houston, Texas

Arai had taken the public bus to Lakewood Church at the old Compaq center in Houston. He got off at the corner and took the tram through the huge parking lot to the large building. Inside, he made his way to a seat in the upper rows, looking down over the stage.

The trip took over an hour. He had to arrive an extra hour early, since it was Easter. At the Palm Sunday service, everyone had been asked to attend the early service today, and leave room for first-time attendees at the normal service.

Arai spend the time reading his new Bible. He treated church like one of his classes at the university. He was studying Revelation and finding it very confusing. The book was coded with images and some were beginning to stand out to him. The hour passed quickly once he became absorbed in

John's dream.

The choir was in the stands. The praise team came out and everyone was rejoicing and happy, even more than usual. The citizens of Houston, who attended this mega-church smiled all the time, but today Arai noticed a definite difference. They were acting as if they had just won a million bucks.

Arai had tried to imitate the big smile. The first month he thought his cheeks were going to ache forever. His face muscles were now getting used to it.

The music started. He forgot everything else and began singing the words on the overhead screen, clapping to a new song about the risen Jesus.

Arai filed his report later that afternoon.

The operatives' reports filtered through the appropriate channels and GUILE was pleased with their obedience and discoveries.

Easter 2006
Houston, Texas

Freda had bought a pink chiffon dress with an invisible zipper on Saturday. When she got dressed, she had trouble pulling the zipper up. She had caught it on the fabric. She couldn't get it up or down. The side placement had made it impossible to work with. "*If only Ted were here, he'd fix it for me*," she thought. Suddenly, it broke free.

She grabbed the bottle of wine and made it to Jim's by two-fifteen. Freda was fashionably late, but he didn't answer the doorbell. She walked around the nicely manicured lawn and found him on the deck, setting an arrangement of flowers on the table.

"I rang but you must not have heard me, so I came around," Freda said, explaining her traipsing through the yard. She now had cut particles of grass on her heels.

Jim looked up and noticed her grassy shoes.

"Sorry about that. I didn't realize. Here take this napkin and wipe the grass off your shoes. I'll go get another for the table, and bring out the glasses. I'll be right back," he said and disappeared inside.

The house was shielding the afternoon sun, making it perfect for grilling on the patio. Freda wiped the clumps of debris from her shoes, as she sat in the patio chair waiting for Jim's return.

He soon reappeared with the glasses and a corkscrew. Opening the bottle, he poured them each a taste and toasted to friendship.

"I hope you're hungry, Freda. I'm starved. Do you mind if I bring out our appetizer?"

"No, I don't mind. I didn't have breakfast. I'm kind of hungry as well. Is there anything I can do to help?" She asked loudly as he went into the house again.

"No, just sit. You're my guest," Jim yelled back.

Jim returned with the crab salads.

"Boy, this is a work of art. You're good with cooking," she said, amazed at his gourmet ability. She reminded herself, "*But of course, he's gay.*"

"Well, I got this recipe from Bon Appetite magazine. The only hard part is removing the membrane from the orange sections. It's kind of messy, but well worth it," Jim said, taking his seat and laying a napkin across the lap of his linen slacks.

"This asparagus is cooked to perfection, crisp, yet tender, even though it's cold. And it's so artistically placed," Freda complimented, taking another bite of the crab mixture.

"I was hoping you'd be impressed. I like to cook, but when you live alone it's hardly worth it. I'm glad you came over to share this with me," Jim gently placed his hand on hers to show his sincerity. He removed it as quickly as he had placed it there.

It was so innocently done, that Freda didn't register another small line being crossed.

When the salad was done Freda followed him into the house. Jim gave her a short tour of his home. Freda admired the artwork. She noticed that the watercolors were originals and painted by Jim.

"Do you paint much?"

"I took classes for several years at the college. I used to practice quite a bit. It really takes a technique that you have to develop. The right paints, paper, and brushes make a world of difference, too. Anyway, that's when I really began to get good at it," Jim said, admiring a piece of his work.

After a moment of silence, Jim snapped back to the present. "Let's go back out and fix our meal." He raised his up-turned palm, indicating for Freda to walk back down the hall and that he'd follow.

Jim placed the fish on the grill, and prepared the zucchini and yellow squash. He poured them both a second glass of wine. They talked as they waited for the salmon and the squash to cook.

They enjoyed the day and laughed easily.

Jim quickly cleared the dinner plates and returned with two small cups of the promised sorbet.

"Did you make this, too?" Freda asked, amazed at his cooking talent.

"Actually, I bought this. I have a recipe that I tried that isn't too hard. But I thought I'd make it a little easier on myself, and just purchased this one."

When they finished the sorbet, Freda thanked Jim for the invite and fabulous meal. He walked Freda to her car and waved goodbye as she backed out of the drive and headed home.

CHAPTER 22

May 2006
Virginia Tech

The first year was over. John found placement for the co-op portion of his five-year program. When he graduated he'd have a degree and work experience. John was looking forward to his first assignment. He'd work at a government-contract facility near the Patuxent Naval Air Station.

John, and his mom Emily, had befriended a first-year student named Jason, whose family lived in Hollywood, Maryland, not far from PAX, as Jason said the locals called it. They worked out a barter-like system between them. Jason lived in Gramps' room while taking classes at VT and John lived with Jason's parents while out on co-op.

"John, I've talked with my advisor. I'll continue classes during this summer and fall term while you're away; that way you can just use my room at home, and I'll continue the work position when you're back here for two terms," Jason said.

"I don't know what Mom and I would've done without you?" John said, smiling at the good fortune. He didn't want to compete against Jason for the same job. This way they'd share the position, as if the company had a full-time employee.

"This is your last box. I'll let you unpack while I go load up my last stuff for the trip tomorrow."

Emily brought Jason clean towels and explained how the faucets in the bathtub were plumbed backwards, so that he wouldn't freeze himself to death, or worse, scald himself when taking a shower.

They ate dinner together around the old enameled-topped table and laughed. It was as if John had a brother.

"Ms. Emily, I'll be back next week. I've got to take some of this stuff back home and visit my parents before the summer term starts. Don't worry about John. I'll show him around Hollywood."

"Ha," Emily chuckled, "Hollywood. I knew John would go far, but I never thought Hollywood," she said thinking how she couldn't believe how much Jason resembled John. He was like a twin brother lost at birth.

"That's what my Dad says all the time when he tells people he lives in Hollywood. There's even a town called California up the road from us. Whoever named those places had the West Coast in mind, that's for sure."

Memorial Day Weekend
Houston, Texas

Freda invited Jim over to celebrate the holiday at her house this time. She liked having someone to pass the time with. She couldn't wait for the boys to come back and have everything normal again.

"Thanks for bringing the red wine, Jim. It'll go great with the steaks," Freda said as she accepted his bottle and walked him through the house.

In the kitchen, she asked him to open it while she finished wrapping the potatoes. She hadn't had one in so long, that she decided she could afford the transgression.

Jim handed her a glass of Pinot Noir and asked, "Is there anything else I can do?"

"No, the layered salad is in the fridge." Freda lifted her glass and toasted, "To those who have given so much for our country and those who have gone before."

They both sipped the wine and it was obvious that Jim had selected well. Freda hadn't expected less.

"I'll be right back," she said and carried the potatoes out to the patio. She placed them inside the preheated gas grill. Closing the lid, she set the timer and returned to her guest.

"Now, let me give you a little tour of my place."

"I noticed you have a cottage out back. What a wonderful idea," Jim commented.

"Yes, it's currently occupied by our son, Teddy."

"When did they get back?!" Jim asked with an amazed expression on his face. He was hoping to be alone with Freda.

"Oh, they're not back yet. They'll be back in June," she said answering his question and continued, "To help Teddy out while he finished his Master's and Doctorate, we let him live there rent free."

Relaxing a little, Jim calmed down. "I thought he was employed by NASA."

"He is; he attends school at the same time. He's really a good boy. I mean young man. You know moms; we never think our children are grown. Let me show you the rest of the house while the potatoes are cooking.

"Obviously, this is the great room connected to the kitchen area here with the breakfast nook over there near the slider."

Freda led Jim through the dining room and formal living room, circling back to the foyer. "Over there's the master bedroom and bath and upstairs are the other four bedrooms. Living here alone this past year, I realize that it's actually a rather large house."

"Yes, I'm sure it has felt that way," Jim agreed and took another sip of his wine.

Freda followed the hall back to the kitchen to check the timer. "Here's the powder room, if you'd like to wash up before dinner."

"Thanks, I think I will," Jim said and stepped inside, closing the door.

Freda seasoned the steaks and placed them on the grill, timing the meat and the potatoes to be done at the same time.

She had set the table in the kitchen nook instead of the dining room. It was too formal for Memorial Day, and it was too warm in Houston to eat on the patio.

"Please pour us another glass of wine and place them on the table, while I get out the salad and check the steaks. How do you like your meat?"

Jim chuckled, but she didn't notice. He answered, "Warm and red, but not bloody."

"Okay then I'll go pull yours. I'm sure it must be ready. Please take this sour cream and butter to the table for me."

Jim completed the tasks and sat patiently at the table, waiting for Freda's return with the rest of the meal. In minutes she was back with the steak and potatoes. They ate and comfortably talked about work. After dinner, Freda cleared the table and opened a second bottle of wine. She served a few pieces of chocolate, another luxury she hadn't had for months.

"Let's take this to the living room," Freda said, liking the smaller room without the cathedral ceiling. It felt less like two small people in a large space.

Jim sat on the opposite end of the sofa, since Freda placed the plate of candy on the coffee table.

"Oh, I could offer you coffee, if you prefer."

"No, this red wine is nice with chocolate."

They talked comfortably and sipped the wine. Before long, the wine clouded their judgment. Jim moved closer as Freda showed him a book that she kept on the table for guest's viewing. He thought it an invite and moved closer. When they had finished looking at the book, Jim moved into her personal space; she didn't move away, so he kissed her.

Freda was shocked, but didn't go ballistic over his approach. She was mostly confused about his sexuality or her misreading of it. She backed away. "Jim, I like you, but I'm not interested in ruining my marriage. We can remain friends; that's all."

"I understand. I thought you might be lonely and miss the physical touch," he explained lamely.

"Well, I do, but not enough to throw away everything. I love my husband."

"Under the circumstances, I think I should thank you for a delicious meal and say good night. I'm afraid I've gone too far. I don't want to end our friendship, or cause any tension at work."

Freda rolled her eyes; she hadn't thought about work. "Yes, I think it'd be best to call it a night." She stood and walked him to the door.

As soon as Jim walked through the door, Freda closed it. She didn't wait to wave goodbye. She secured the locks, and walked around the house turning off the lights. She checked the slider, and turned down the charley bar. She took her glass of wine to the bedroom.

She crawled into bed and thought through all that had transpired. "*Did I cause this? Was it something I did or said?*" She didn't know what to do. This had never happened to her before.

Freda evaluated Jim's advance and was satisfied she had handled it maturely. She thought everything would be fine at work. She'd continue to eat lunch with him; nothing needed to change, except no more dinners out. She'd tell Ted about it when he got back. Or should she? She had a month to think about that. She turned out the light and went to sleep.

June 2006
Washington, D.C.

A year had past and funding hadn't come through. The Frenchs had to wait for the next shuttle. The government had robbed Peter to pay Paul when they funded the experimental use of the laser on Wilma last October. NASA promised they'd be home before Christmas.

Teddy disappointedly filed an extension with the University of Houston on his dissertation. "This has been a once in a lifetime, or several lifetimes, chance, but after a year, this is getting old," Teddy said, as he hit enter on his email to the school.

Ted agreed, as he sent the bad news email to Freda.

NASA printed them both and placed them in the mail.

"Guess we've got hurricane watch again, Teddy," Ted said, trying to sound thrilled. He just wanted to retire and be home with Freda.

Looking on the brighter side Teddy replied, "Maybe we'll get to try the laser out again."

September 2006
Naval Air Station Patuxent River
St. Mary's County, Maryland

John was comfortable in his first job assignment, gaining practical knowledge about Mechanical Engineering in the field. Even though he worked for a government contractor, he reported to a building directly adjacent to PAX. John had a security badge with a low security-clearance for this first year.

Besides a good size room at Jason's, he had his own bath, even if it was in the hallway. There were no other children left at home. Mrs. Leonard wasn't quite ready for an empty nest and was thrilled John was taking Jason's place.

John pulled out the lunch he had prepared the night before and a frozen egg sandwich from a spare refrigerator in the garage. Stepping back into the kitchen, he placed the breakfast into the microwave to nuke, as he filled his travel mug with the already prepared coffee. Mrs. Leonard always had the coffee ready for him in the morning, and home cooked dinners in the evening. They ate sharply at six each weekday.

The bell dinged and John carried his sandwich, mug, and lunch out to Gramps' old Buick parked in the Leonard's side drive. He opened his sandwich while the car idled and warmed up. The last two days of rain had turned things cold and damp. "*At least we had good weather the Labor Day weekend and I got to see the air show with the Blue Angels,*" he thought as he placed the car in gear.

He pulled out of the drive and onto Route 5, heading in the direction of the base. At the light, he took a sip of coffee and another bite of rubbery sandwich. Mrs. Leonard said she'd cook him breakfast if he wanted, but he didn't want to bother her.

His cell phone rang.

"Hi, Mom, what's up? Are you okay?"

"I'm okay. I just wanted you to know we are in a lockdown. There has been a bomb threat on campus and they're doing a sweep of all the buildings. I just think it's a sick joke, but I thought I'd let you know just the same."

"You can't go home?"

"No, they feel we'll be able to go back to normal in a few hours. So we're going ahead with preparing the food for lunch. We've checked all the stoves and things. Everything looks normal."

"Call me tonight and let me know that you're okay. Have you heard from Jason?" John asked worriedly as he turned onto the secured facility.

"I don't know about him, but I'll call tonight. I love you," Emily said to her son.

"I love you too, Mom. Bye," John said, ending the call and passing his badge to the guard.

The Marine waved John to enter and said, "Moms are always worried about us."

It didn't apply in this case, but John responded with a short, "Yeah," and a nod of his head as he rolled his window up.

At the end of the day, all was well.

CHAPTER 23

October 2006
Cape Kennedy, Florida

The radio silence was a little unnerving, but it didn't last as long as Ted and Teddy thought it would. The first voice to break it came by radio from Alamogordo, which was comforting and made them feel right at home. Within minutes, their transport touched down.

After the main shuttle crew left the runway, the camera crews and media followed behind. It was now safe for Ted and Teddy to disembark. They were assisted into a van since their ability to walk was limited. They were taken to temporary quarters until they could reacquaint themselves with the earth's atmosphere and gravity.

After a debriefing, they were free to contact Freda.

"Hi, honey. Did you see us land today?" Ted asked, excited to be back on the ground, even if he wasn't home yet.

"Yes. It was great. I'm glad they had clear skies. I was afraid they'd send you around one more time to get the right conditions for landing."

Since the call was on speakerphone, Teddy piped in. "They tell us we should be home in time for Halloween; so let's plan a party, Mom. Dad and I can be astronauts," Teddy said in a good mood. He couldn't wait to socialize. The almost solitary confinement had gotten to him. It hadn't been as much fun as he had hoped. Even if it had been a unique once-in-a-lifetime experience, it would never show up on his résumé.

"Think of whom you'd invite; I'll send out the invitations," Freda said, thinking it'd only be the AWA team.

"Everyone we worked with at NASA, of course, the AWA team and their spouses, and the head of my department at school. That's all I know. You and Dad can add any others."

"Whoa, that'll be a house full. I've gotten used to being alone too, you know. Haven't you?" Freda asked, feeling apprehensive and overwhelmed with the thoughts of that many people in her house.

"You've gotten to go out and see people, Mom; we didn't. Remember?" Teddy pointedly reminded his mother.

Ted took over. "Okay. Freda, you do what makes you happy, honey. I'll be a mummy. I'm tired of being an astronaut and a meteorologist."

Once Freda heard Ted's suggestion, she warmed up to the idea. "How about, I'll be Cleopatra, and you can be Mark Anthony?"

"That would be scary," Ted said, and laughed at the thought of him looking young and sexy.

Their time was up so they ended the call for the day. They had strengthening exercises to do.

The following week, Freda placed the invitations in the mail. She planned grueling foods, like Bone Dry Red Cabernet and Ghostly White Chardonnay, Green Slime Punch, Graveyard Dip with Witches Fingers, Spider Web Dip, Beefy Eyeballs, Spaghetti Worms, and Freaky Fudge with Gummy Worms. There'd be the customary washtub of beer on ice on the patio. She bought cardboard tombstones and white batting to decorate the cottage, turning it into a haunted house. She placed the grave markers in the backyard between the houses and spread batting all around the railings and trees, too.

Decorating had kept her busy until the guys got home and now homecoming day had arrived. Freda headed to the gym after work and got in a quick workout. On the way home, she picked up a loaf of fresh Italian bread for the French's reunion dinner. She had made lasagna and salad that morning. After placing the baking dish in the oven, she showered away her perspiration and anxiety. She couldn't wait for them to get there.

While drying her hair, she thought she heard something. She paused, and then dismissed it since the guys weren't due for another half an hour. She applied her makeup and slipped into a new sleek black dress. As she crossed the tile floor to check on the lasagna, she saw suitcases by the door, but no other sign of them. She rushed to the slider and saw the open cottage door. Running over in her bare feet, she charged inside.

As soon as she stepped across the threshold, they yelled, "Boo!"

Freda screamed with joy. Ted snatched her up and spun her around.

Teddy laughed. "I like the decorations, Mom. This is great." Then he said seriously, "Is something wrong with my electricity though? I tried the lights upstairs. Did you shut off the electricity while I was gone?"

"No, I just threw the main circuit breaker to the cottage for the 'haunted house' effect so I wouldn't forget. You'll have to use the guestroom upstairs in our house for tonight," she explained. "Come on, I've got dinner ready. I'll tell you about the foods I've got planned while we eat."

Freda ran across the grass, looking barefoot and beautiful to Ted.

"Hey, honey?" Ted called, stopping her in her tracks. "Give me a kiss."

"Oh, my goodness, I got so excited I forgot."

Freda ran back and they embraced, as Teddy wished he had a special someone to welcome him home.

They ate, laughed, and chatted until they were thoroughly exhausted.

At the party the next night, Lyn Johnson, the head of the Astronautical Engineering program, who was dressed as Dracula, greeted Teddy in his astronaut suit. "Welcome home. By the way, when can you schedule your dissertation? You have probably been the only student in the history of the college to say they needed an extension due to not being on the planet."

They both laughed, as Teddy replied, "The sooner the better."

The party was a huge success. Everyone attended, except Jim. Freda hadn't noticed, and she was too busy to care.

April 16, 2007
Virginia Tech
Blacksburg, Virginia

When the spring semester started, John and Jason traded places.

"Boy is it ever cold this morning, Mom. I'll be glad when summer gets here," John commented, as he drank his coffee and ate his homemade egg sandwich.

"Summer? I'll be happy for spring. They said it might even snow today," Emily replied, shivering as she ate a bowl of oatmeal. The doctor told her that her cholesterol was getting high, and she read in a magazine that oatmeal would lower it; only time would tell.

"I'll see you tonight," John said, heading out to start the Buick.

"I'm right behind you," Emily replied, filling her bowl with water to soak.

She grabbed her purse. John pulled out of the drive, as she locked the front door. Snow flurries danced on the cold wind. Emily shivered again.

"Guess a saint will die today," she said under her breath, as she started her Toyota and placed it in reverse. As a child, she had heard that whenever someone died when there was an unseasonable snow that they were a saint. She couldn't remember whom her mother had been talking about, but she'd never forget the feel in the air.

She walked through the cafeteria's back door, as the first saint died that day. Emily and the majority of the school were unaware. She put a large pot of water on for the grits that they'd serve with the fried eggs. Very few came to breakfast, or the first class of the day for that matter, but some did. Emily stirred the pot, thinking of Jason. She always saw him at breakfast his first year. "*That's how I knew he was a rare kid.*"

Across town the police received a 911 call. "We got a report of a shooting at one of the dorms on Virginia Tech," the operator told the police officer. They grabbed the keys and ran for the car. By the time they arrived on campus, the assailant was gone.

The officer radioed the station. "We've got two dead students over here at VT. Please send an ambulance and back up." He secured the one dorm, but decided against locking down the whole campus. They had been over cautious before.

The general staff weren't informed. Emily continued preparing and serving meals for breakfast, as the snow outside continued to fall.

John watched the flakes outside the classroom window and noted that it wasn't sticking. When class ended, he made his way over to Norris Hall for his next class of the morning. John climbed the stairs to the second floor and followed the others, making their way to the other classrooms.

"*I'm not sure whether I like working, or sitting in class. Both aren't easy, just different,*" he thought, as he took his seat.

The last student closed the wooden door behind her. The lecture started and John scribbled notes on his paper. There was construction and constant hammering noise somewhere on campus.

"*Gosh that's distracting. It's getting annoying. Why can't they do that in the summer?*" John thought.

The noise got louder.

"*Hold it; that's not construction! That's gunshots! A lot of gunshots.*" John glanced quickly around at his fellow students in disbelief. John's heart raced and his eyes got wild. He doubted he was right, yet feared that he was.

"*What should I do?*"

Everyone in the room was thinking the same thing.

John looked to the professor for direction. The instructor had frozen in place and was quietly listening. They all were listening. Then as if on cue, John and the rest of the students jumped up and quickly got under their desks. A fellow student named Frank called 911.

Suddenly the door flew opened. A crazed student dressed in black shot the professor in the head. John closed his eyes, as if that would make the shooter disappear. John felt a strange tingle go through his body as his heart got caught in his throat.

"*Oh, God!*" John opened his eyes slowly. He watched as the assailant walked around the room, emptying his 9M handgun and reloading it with another cartridge to fire more.

"*Stop it; get out of here. Why doesn't he say something?*"

Then suddenly the guy in black left the room.

John quickly got out from under his desk. That's when he noticed that he had been hit; blood was staining his shirtsleeve.

"*What can we do*?" he frantically questioned himself again.

He looked wildly around and said to two other girls, "Help me move the teacher's desk to the door to keep the gunman from coming back."

They pushed the desk against the door, exposing the dead professor's body. John and the girls sat behind it, listening to shots in the next room. Glancing around the room, John saw that fifteen fellow classmates had been shot and probably weren't going to make it. John shook his head in disbelief. He was in shock. The two girls, who were in shock as well, were crying silently, waiting for it all to end.

Outside, the officials ordered lockdown of the school, after receiving the second 911 call. The head of the cafeteria followed the instructions from the administration to lock the cafeteria doors and not let anyone enter or leave. When she told John's mother that students were being shot in Norris Hall, Emily fainted. She caught her as Emily slid down to the floor.

When Emily came to, they were beginning to get reports.

"One of the professors advised his kids to jump out of the second-floor windows. He's the one that survived the Holocaust," the student repeated what he was being told by cell phone. "Some kids have gotten away."

Emily knew that John didn't have the teacher they were talking about. "Have the police gotten the shooter yet?"

One girl shook her head and shrugged. No one had that answer.

"My friend says they've sent rescue vehicles. It looks like they're putting some of the injured kids that jumped into them. Does anyone know Mustafa? He's okay," the girl relayed the message via her phone.

That spurred students to ask who of their friends that took classes in Norris Hall, were safe or uninjured.

Jamal, who was another GUILE operative majoring in Mining Engineering, was in one of the classrooms on the second floor. When his professor heard and recognized the shots, he reacted quickly. He directed, "Jamal, Mike, Sam, help me push my desk against the door."

As they held the barricade, the gunman fired shots through the wooden door, trying to gain entry. Splinters flew everywhere. Jamal felt him push against the door. Since the gunman couldn't gain entry, he moved back to John's classroom.

John heard him reloading another cartridge clip outside the door. When the shooter couldn't get in the second time, he began firing through the door in anger. Then, he moved on.

To John this whole morning was moving in slow motion. It seemed like it would never end.

Finally it did; the madman turned the weapon on himself, ending his spree of violence. But most of the students in the building didn't know. Even the officials were unsure.

It was quiet for some time before the police entered the building. John hadn't heard anything for awhile and thought the shooter had left. Yet, he didn't want to leave the classroom until someone confirmed it was safe to do so. John watched some of the severely injured students in his room die from their wounds, while they all waited for help. All John could do was to hold the barricade until that help arrived.

Many 911 calls came in, but the authorities didn't storm the building, feeling they'd cause more deaths not knowing where the gunman was.

"There haven't been any shots for an hour," a student in the cafeteria reported. "The police are starting to go in now."

Students were taken to several area hospitals. The unconscious students couldn't tell the hospital staff their names and had no identification on them. Even the school officials, who knew the student enrollment of the affected classrooms, didn't contact the parents. Most parents learned of the attack via television news reports.

When the school ended the lockdown, Emily drove to all the area hospitals to find John. She found him at the one furthest from the school.

"Why did they bring you this far?" Emily asked angrily. She had been franticly searching for him. "They should have at least called the other hospitals and told them who they had; then I wouldn't have had to drive all over worried about you. I'm in no shape to be on the road after all this." Emily stated the truth.

"Mom, don't be angry. At least I'm alive," John said with a sober look on his face and a tear in his eye. "I could have been Frank, or Susan, or Jane. They didn't make it. It was so surreal Mom. The guy never even spoke. He just fired over and over again, and then he'd reload. No one even screamed." John placed his face in his one hand to hide his emotions, since his other arm was bandaged and in a sling.

Emily realized how upset John had to be. She tried to comfort him with a modified hug. She couldn't really get to him lying in the hospital bed and didn't want to touch his injured arm.

A nurse entered the room. "You won't be comfortable, but you can sleep in that chair if you like. We'll be keeping him for observation through the night." Then she administered a shot to help John slip into slumber, even though he thought it impossible.

Emily held his hand and didn't say anything. She wanted her son to be the one to talk if he felt the need. She had almost lost him and it was more than she could bear.

When John fell asleep, Emily cried silent tears. Finally at three in the morning, she gave up and took the chair, falling into a fitful sleep.

CHAPTER 24

April 2007
GUILE

"Did you hear what happened at Virginia Tech?"

"Was it one of our operatives?" Juan Perez asked.

"Of course not," Jack answered. "We almost lost two of our boys. The darn South Korean kid almost ruined some of our hard work. We had one of your kids from Morocco. Jamal's his name; he's studying Mining Engineering, and there's one from Turkey, named Mustafa, studying Mechanical Engineering."

"Were they injured?" Juan asked, now interested.

"Not really. Fortunately, Jamal's fine. Mustafa has a twisted ankle from jumping out a two-story window to get away. Good thing his professor had his class jump, or he might be dead like so many of those other kids."

"When are they due to graduate?" Juan was thinking if it was earlier than GUILE needed, he could use Jamal at one of his mines.

"If everything goes well, and those small town cops keep the place safe, they'll be graduating in two more years," Jack said in criticism of how the event was handled.

"Keep me posted." Juan closed his phone and went back to reading his morning paper.

May 2007
Houston, Texas

By the end of first semester, Teddy had given his dissertation to the committee and was granted his long-awaited Doctorate. The graduation ceremony had been held at ten and he was still wearing his new style of black gown. It had velvet stripes on the sleeves and now he would forever wear a soft velvet hat when in his formal robes of academia, which would not be often. With his added Master's hood he really looked impressive, or so Freda thought, because she kept snapping pictures of Teddy. She wouldn't let him get undressed.

"Okay, Mom. The guests will be here soon. I'd like to get out of these hot robes. This sun is more intense in black, you know," Teddy pleaded.

"Just one more with your dad."

Ted ran over and smiled as Freda said 'cheese' for the twentieth time. It was obvious he was as proud as she was.

"Okay, Son. Go get out of your robes," Ted directed, as he gently removed the camera from his wife's hands and coaxed her inside.

The AWA team was invited for a cookout to celebrate. The first car pulled into the driveway just as they crossed the threshold, followed by two more.

Teddy greeted them at the door, thanking them for their cards of congratulations. "Dad's in the great room. Go on in."

When all had arrived, he joined the party. As Teddy stepped onto the patio, one of the secretary's husbands handed him a cold beer.

"Did you hear the report? It seems they've made some progress on the guidance system."

"I hope so. Hurricane season's fast approaching; last year was a humdinger. With global warming, we can expect more."

"Do you really believe in that global warming stuff? Whatever is happening to our world is exactly what God intended. If anything, we're close to the Tribulation."

His evangelical views were falling on deaf ears in this scientific community, but he liked to espouse them, if only to the youngest on the team.

Teddy responded with, "Uh ha," and moved over to talk with one of the meteorologist on the subject.

"Hey, I was told you've been working on the weather guidance system. What was wrong?"

"Well, I'm not sure why it didn't move. But something was right about it, if after three pushes it didn't move at all. That gave us a lot in the way of data, too!"

"But it got stronger?"

"Anytime something sets in that hot Gulf water, it has to get stronger. That wasn't our fault. We changed a line to make the push stronger. We were all thinking timidly, but it's almost better to err by doing too little than too much."

Before the party ended, Ted announced his retirement to everyone. "It'll coincide with the fiscal calendar for those curious. It's been great working with all of you, here on the ground and up in space."

They raised their glasses and toasted, "To happy retirement!"

Christmas 2007
Yusha, China

Mei Lian realized it was Christmas, even though there were no decorations and ornamented evergreens. Buddhists didn't celebrate Christmas, obviously, and they weren't like American Jews, who did in a secular Santa Claus kind of way either. This area of China had no holiday displays, no Macys Day parade, and no Christian traditions.

Claudia was missing it, yet as Mei Lian, she had gained such good wisdom during her stay at the Temple. Oddly enough, she was feeling the need to move on. A spirit or ancestor perhaps, was nudging her to go. But she didn't want to leave her brother. He was getting old and he wouldn't outlive her; so she decided to stay until he passed.

"Hi, Ci An, how was your week?"

"The same as every week; will you never learn?" He asked gently, not meaning to insult her.

"I'm learning, Ci An. It takes time."

They sat together for the next hour. Even though they said nothing more, just being together brought her pleasure.

When her time was up, she bowed and walked back to the Temple of Princess Wencheng. The cold air blew over her, making the feeling of dread return. She willed it to leave her and returned to her normal duties.

February 14, 2008
Houston, Texas

Ted did freelance work for AWA for the past year; Teddy stayed on in the engineering capacity; and Freda remained the head of the public county library system.

Teddy walked into his dark house at the end of the day. It was Valentine's Day and he still didn't have a girl. Sure there were some at work, but none whom he was interested in, even though they had hinted plenty of times that they were interested in him.

He went to parties and out with groups of young people, but he didn't date anyone, or double-date either. He didn't like getting involved when he didn't feel anything. He was a rather unusual man of twenty-eight.

Glancing over at his parent's house he saw his dad placing a bouquet of roses in a vase. The candles were lit. Teddy looked in his freezer. He pulled out a pizza with 'The Works' toppings. Placing it on a pan, he popped it in the oven and set the temperature and timer.

He pulled a Coors Light out of the fridge. Removing the cap, he pushed in a slice of lime, assembling his brew, and walked into the living room. Teddy grabbed the remote and channel surfed. Everything on the large screen reminded him that he was alone.

The timer buzzed, calling him to the kitchen. Cutting the pizza into large slices, he lifted one and sampled. He placed another slice on a dinner plate. He returned to his recliner, eating one slice while he carried the plate with the other.

He rummaged through the DVDs stored in the side table. He placed the "Apollo 13" disk in the player. Watching it, he forgot about his situation and remembered his days in space.

When the movie ended, Teddy had made up his mind. He was moving back to New Mexico. He had grown up there and he liked the people there better. He felt more at home in the dry high-desert. He was tired of Houston. As he climbed into bed, he decided to tell his parents the next day.

Across the lawn

Freda got home late but was pleasantly pleased with Ted's attention to romantic details.

"Thank you, Ted. This is nice," she said as she gave him a kiss. "Let me slip into something more comfortable."

Ted yelled at Freda as she headed for the master bedroom. "Don't take too long, the dinner's ready to come out any minute."

Freda returned in a new long red satin Harlow gown. It displayed all her curves, as well as the hard work that she had continued to maintain since their arrival home.

"I swear you get better looking every year. What a lucky guy I am."

"No, I'm the lucky one. What's for dinner?"

"We're serving tonight for your lady's pleasure: Shrimp Cocktail, followed by Coconut Crusted Tilapia on a bed of Wilted Spinach. But first, let's toast."

Ted poured the chilled split of Pierre-Jouët into two cold flutes and said, "To us, my love."

"To us." Freda took a sip and sat in the chair that Ted had now pulled out for her. She placed the cloth napkin in her lap, as Ted served the appetizers.

"I was thinking, Ted."

"Oh no, that's a problem," he said, and they laughed.

"I'm due to retire soon. Why don't we move back to New Mexico?

We don't need this huge house. We'll never be filling it with guests, or Teddy, his wife, and kids visiting on holidays, it seems. What do you think?" She dipped her shrimp into the dollop of cocktail sauce in the center of the plate.

"I'm tired of doing the little bit of freelance myself. Even though Houston has been good to all of us, I'm ready to go home; maybe not the old house, but certainly back to New Mexico. How about the Cloudcroft area?"

"That'd be too cold with all that snow in the winter. How's Alamogordo? You could do docent work at the Museum of Space History. They'd like a man with your experience." Freda laughed, licked her fingertips, and dried them on her napkin.

Ted cleared the plates, and served the fish on a bed of spinach. Sitting down he said, "You know, that's not too bad of an idea. I couldn't say I've been in space, you know, but I could give my experience here at NASA. That would get me in the door at least."

"Do you think Teddy will mind? Where will he live?"

"He's twenty-eight now. He has a doctorate and a good paying job, thanks to his father," Ted said with a chuckle. "He can find a small house. I'm sure he has saved money for a down payment by now. He certainly didn't use his salary shopping when we were in space."

Freda laughed at the image of Teddy shopping online and getting free delivery.

"This is good fish. Did you do this?"

"No. I saw it in the fresh seafood section, and thought it wouldn't blow your healthy diet too much. All I had to do is bake it, and throw the spinach in the skillet with a splash of water. Viola, a gourmet dinner is born!"

"Are you ready for dessert?"

"That's breaking my diet."

"Not really. Chocolate protein bar anyone?"

February 15, 2008
Washington, D.C.

"AWA will be downscaling again for a short time. We'd like the Frenchs to really retire and leave town."

Director Haynes answered, "I see. That can be arranged."

April 2008
Pensacola, Florida

Mary was in her third year of the naval aviator program. Today she was on her solo flight in the F/A-18 Hornet. The Hornet was a supersonic carrier-capable fighter jet and was designed to dogfight and attack ground targets. It was the aerial demonstration aircraft for the Blue Angels since 1986.

Mary paid close attention to her flying, but she couldn't help thinking about the day she graduated from the Academy and the squadron of navy blue Hornets flying overhead. Now *she* was flying at the supersonic speed of Mach 1.8. The two engines delivered almost eighteen-thousand pounds of force and each had afterburners giving the aircraft a high thrust-to-weight ratio. Of course its main purpose wasn't to impress the crowds at air shows but to carry a wide variety of air-to-air and air-to-ground bombs and missiles. It was also equipped with a M16 Vulcan cannon in case the pilot needed it for close range objects.

The Hornet had excellent aerodynamic characteristics and would someday aid her in missions such as fighter escort, fleet air defense, and aerial reconnaissance. Its versatility and reliability proved it to be a valuable carrier asset.

"*I better turn around; I've heard these Hornets criticized for lack of range.*"

Mary rolled the aircraft and turned for home.

CHAPTER 25

January 2008
New Mexico

In New Mexico the Commissioner of Public Lands had signed off on an agreement, granting the Spaceport Authority access to nearly fifteen thousand acres of state trust lands near Truth or Consequences in January 2006. Two years later, they were ready to begin the ground breaking of the proposed site for the Southwest Regional Spaceport. As usual, projects moved slowly when involving governmental offices, especially when they worked with the private sector.

The project was a daring futuristic move on the part of New Mexico, and all concerned. Director Haynes heard of it through the grapevine and let Jack know.

Jack was ready to buy a ticket and go into space. He was always looking for unique and different things to interest him. He relentlessly inquired until he found out who was selling tickets, and he put his money down on a one.

May 2008
The Operatives

At Virginia Tech, Mustafa was graduating from the five-year program for Mechanical Engineering; Jamal graduated the same day with a degree in Mining Engineering. They hardly knew each other. They had no idea they were both GUILE operatives. They only knew that they were among the few lucky ones in their fields of study to survive the massacre.

Juan Perez attended the VT graduation ceremony. He had interviewed Jamal the day before for a position with his mining company in Peru. Jamal had previously been informed by email to interview and to take the offer. Juan interviewed three other new graduates to make the interviewing process seem legit. Jamal accepted the position as instructed.

At the University of Houston, Arai graduated with his Master of Science in Astronautical Engineering. He graduated previously in 2006 with his bachelor's in Mechanical Engineering. He had been informed that he'd be interviewing for a position with AWA shortly, as a vacancy would be opening up soon.

At Pennsylvania State University, Omar graduated with a degree in Meteorology, but was continuing on for a Masters. He wouldn't finish until 2011. Ahmad received his Mining Engineering degree and interviewed for a pre-arranged position. Ahmad and Omar had never met either. Paul Beorg from South Africa, aka Mr. Afghanistan, attended the commencement, and would finish his bogus interviewing later that week.

At the University of Oklahoma, Abdul graduated with a degree in Meteorology. GUILE decided he'd continue his education and graduate with a Master of Science in 2010. His church family from the Church of the Nazarene attended his graduation ceremony. This cover pleased GUILE.

Gani finished his flight school in Florida years ago and trained to fly commercial jets as well. He was employed by Allegiant Air, a smaller craft airline not associated with GUILE.

Because his old Turkish buddy, Mohammad, had needed longer to master the English language, GUILE decided to save him for a job that required muscle. Currently, Mohammad was employed at Bally Total Fitness in Culver City, California. Because Karim, of Morocco, had the same difficulty with English, his muscles were receiving a workout daily at Gold's Gym not far from Mohammad in Culver City. They hadn't heard of each other.

Sabur, who was from Pakistan, completed his two-year mission for the Church of Jesus Christ of the Latter-Day Saints as well as flight school in Salt Lake City. Currently, he was a private pilot for extended acquaintances of GUILE in Utah.

The last operative for GUILE, Nassim of Morocco, had also learned to fly private planes. He was under the employ of Paul Beorg in South Africa.

July 1, 2008
Houston, Texas

The Frenchs had everything packed and ready to move out. The house was sold without a hitch. They practically had doubled their money. It had proven to be a good retirement investment after all.

Ted French received sixty percent of his three highest-paying years of employment with the federal government. Freda had a small pension that would be saved for a rainy day; and in New Mexico they didn't have many of those.

Teddy was slightly unsure of his future at the moment. He knew he'd find something, even if he was over-qualified.

They decided to use this last time together as a family to take a well-deserved vacation. Soon they'd be parting, and life would take on long awaited changes. Ted and Freda, who thought they knew an empty nest, would soon find out what it was really like.

They spent July Fourth in Roswell. When they visited the Art Museum, the men enjoyed the Dr. Goddard exhibit while Freda liked the Native American exhibit best.

They couldn't resist visiting the Alien Museum, even though they didn't really believe there had been a cover-up.

"Look Mom. I'm an Alien," Teddy said, with his head behind a large-eyed green mask.

Freda laughed as she pushed through the tee shirt rack, trying to find just the right shirt as a souvenir. Ted bought them each a bottle of UFO H_2O. Seven years in humid Texas had made him extremely thirsty in the dry climate of New Mexico.

"Here everybody, I'm sure you have to feel as parched as I do," Ted said, handing them each a bottle.

"Thanks Dad." Teddy gulped down several swigs of the refreshing water.

"Honey, what do you think of this shirt?"

"Who for?"

"Me!" Freda frowned. "Who else?"

"It isn't bright enough. The gray and black is too drab. Is there a bright colored one? Those usually set off your dark hair and complexion."

Freda placed the one back on the rack, and thumbed through one last time. "Nope, I don't see any in my size."

"Okay, let's head on out Frenchies," Ted said, wanting to get out of the souvenir shop.

The next day, they moved on to New Mexico Skies for a three-night visit. It was an astronomy resort outside of Cloudcroft, high above Alamogordo. They had rented a twenty-four inch Dobsonian telescope for two of the nights.

The couple running the place were a little older than Ted and Freda and their son was around Teddy's age. During the daylight hours Teddy had struck up a friendship with Michael.

"So your parents run this place?"

"Yeah, one day it might be mine, so they have me employed to take care of the scopes. Maintenance around here is a fulltime 24/7 type of job. We hire a man for the night hours.

"My dad stays in the office and monitors by computer. He picks up communications from our foreign clients if there is a problem. Sometimes I call him a vampire; he's up most of the night and asleep a lot of the day.

"We rent a large portion of the facility to persons and entities that aren't physically here like you. One guy lives in Saudi Arabia and another is in Tokyo," Michael explained. "All these pods view remotely."

About twenty white domes came alive along the red lit drive each night. Even a member of GUILE rented a view of the dark sky.

"I see NASA has a pod there. I used to work at NASA in Houston on a project. That's how we learned about this place," Teddy admitted.

"Gee that must've been great. Did you actually use our scope?"

"No. This seems like a nifty job you have."

"To tell the truth, I'd kind of like to have a job somewhere else. I was hoping to go to Truth or Consequences and start a space motel there. They're projecting a large influx of people coming to New Mexico when that spaceport is finished. If I got in on the ground floor, the property would still be cheap. The place kind of went by the wayside years ago. But it'll be booming again before long."

"What spaceport?"

"You haven't heard of it? Well, they're building a commercial transport to outer space. It'll cost people two hundred thousand dollars for a ticket to outer space."

"That's an expensive ticket," Teddy replied and thought, "*Glad mine was free.*"

"I better let you get back to work. Nice talking with you, Michael."

"How long will you be here?"

"Three nights."

"You'll have a clear night each of them. What did you rent?"

"The twenty-four inch."

"Good. My mom'll check you out on it around five. I'll get it out of the shed around four. You're welcome to come back and watch."

"Okay. See you then."

That night the sky was crystal clear. The Frenchs remembered what they had been missing. Houston had so much humidity and light pollution that they had almost forgotten that the Milky Way could be seen from Earth with the naked eye.

A few days later they shopped for real estate in Alamogordo. They found a nice four-bedroom home with a garage for half the price of Houston. Ted visited the Museum of Space History and signed on as a guide. Teddy applied for an engineering position on the spaceport building project. They welcomed his experience in the field of space and hired him.

September 2008
Truth or Consequences

Teddy moved into an adobe-like building in the downtown section of the T or C. Most of the area needed renovating. Speculators would soon be buying the properties up and making improvements. Ted now understood what Michael had described to him. There were several locations needing rehab that could easily be turned into rental motel space.

Teddy contacted Michael by email:

Michael,

I understand living near your parents and working hand-and-hand with your dad. I've done it for years. It's nice to know I'm not the only guy in the world that has, who's not gay, or retarded.

I've attached the listings and look forward to being a neighbor of yours, should you make the move away from home like I finally did.

Your Friend,

Ted French

Teddy clicked on send and went to dinner at the new local restaurant in town. They had his favorite food on the menu, pizza, along with other Italian dishes. He filled out his voter registration form as he ate his food.

"I see you're planning on voting," the waiter said, then asked, "Do you mind if I ask you whom you're voting for?"

"No problem. I'm a registered Democrat. I'll be voting for Obama."

"Great. Someone said you were from Texas; I figured you were a Bush fan."

"No. I'm not; I'm ready for change. Actually, I'm from Magdalena, New Mexico, born and raised. I've only been away for six years, working for NASA. My name's Ted by the way," Teddy said, shaking the guy's hand.

"I'm Josh. Are you working for the spaceport?"

"More or less, I've got the job building it."

Another couple entered the restaurant and the waiter was also covering seating the customer, since the hostess had called out for the night.

"Sorry to bother you. Hope to see you again." The waiter left to take care of the new arrivals and then another table.

The next morning, Teddy drove thirty miles southwest to begin work at the spaceport outside T or C. The two-lane country road was in good shape and didn't have any traffic to speak of, nothing like Houston.

November 2008
United States of America

The Barack Obama and Joe Bidden ticket won the election. Blacks and whites, old and young, and rich and poor were ready for a change.

George W. Bush was now the lame-duck President. Yet, he still made some decisions that benefited GUILE in his last days in office, totally unaware he was doing so.

CHAPTER 26

The GUILE operatives infiltrated the Orthodox Synagogues, the Conservative Catholic Churches, Mega Evangelical Churches, and Christian sects alike. Since America was known to be Judeo-Christian, the organization had to understand how religious America thought.

Several presidential elections ago, GUILE successfully got the politicians to woo the Christians into voting for them. In studying history, GUILE noticed how Billy Graham had repeatedly tried to sway the presidents in their spiritual lives. That gave the members of GUILE the idea of manipulating the religious leadership in America.

They steeple-jacked the Southern Baptist Convention and manipulated the leadership of the organization. The organization urged pastors; and pastors encouraged their congregations to become politically active.

The Christian Americans supported the Republican Party in the 2000 election, achieving GUILE's goal. The citizens had truly believed that Bush had been God's man for America. GUILE manipulated their puppet; and the Christian audience accepted his actions with applause.

GUILE had backed the political powers in the past election in order to put two things on the ticket which these Christians and other Americans wanted: a woman and a fundamentalist. She was even attractive, which was a big plus among the redneck Americans. But the Republicans didn't win the election as GUILE thought they would.

GUILE wanted to control this segment of the American population; they tended to be the ones with guns and processed a survivalist mentality. The operatives reported that this mindset prevailed in the outlying metropolitan areas: the 'Bread Basket' of America, and the South. After four or more years of personal first-hand study, the Turks, Moroccans, and Pakistanis had reported that the book of Revelation in the Christian Bible, also called the Apocalypse in the Catholic Bible, would make the perfect guide for GUILE to use to support the plan for global takeover.

GUILE read it closely and decided to use NATURE to do their dirty work. Scientific-minded people would blame mankind for global warming. The Christian Fundamentalist would credit and praise God for punishing the evil-minded politicians; and they'd pray for the Rapture to come soon. Either way, the world would be GUILE's.

In the meantime, they'd have to keep this new President from accomplishing much.

January, 2009
Washington, D.C.

All Federal Government offices in Washington, D.C. were closed for the inauguration. Most non-government offices in the area had closed as well.

Jack Jones was seated next to a stylishly-dressed woman on the main stage.

"Isn't this an experience of a lifetime? I can't believe that Mrs. Obama selected my design for the Swearing-In."

"So you're a designer? What a coincidence, I have a close friend who's a designer in New York City. You may have heard of her label, Lei Fashions of New York?"

"Yes. I used to love Claudia Lei's work. I own one. But I must say that the work they've been producing for the shows the last five years aren't what they used to be."

"Hmm," Jack replied, and turned his attention to Director Haynes, retaking his seat on the other side of him.

"Director Haynes, what great seating. Thank you for inviting me," Jack said graciously.

Haynes only nodded, since the ceremonies were beginning. The Bush's and the Obama's were taking their seats.

Jack leaned over to the designer and whispered, "We'll have to talk after this about the possibility of you coming to work with Lei Fashion in New York."

She quickly nodded, not wanting to talk at such a time.

The first black President was sworn in. During the luncheon that followed, it seemed Obama had already begun work on his medical reform plan by the looks of the invitees. Jack was observing and enjoying it all. The public had no idea how capitalistic GUILE had made a killing in the banks. Soon things would change. Jack knew downsizing would be coming to stay off a great recession. In two more years, they'd put the brakes on this runaway train. The casualties would struggle to stay alive. The ranks of the middle class where going to thin out.

February 2009
Houston, Texas

The second-in-command meteorologist had moved up to Ted French's position as head of the division. Arai had been hired, as promised, as the astronautical engineer for AWA, even though he had little experience. His excellent grades from the University of Houston, and GUILE recommendations, won him the position. Washington also directed that more engineers be hired as the WSL aged. So Mustafa with his mechanical engineering work-experience from VT was hired, as well. Director Haynes reported there was a good chance that funding would follow in a few years to fully man the WSL with two meteorologists and two engineers, as originally planned.

May 2009
Virginia Tech

John Germaine and Jason Leonard graduated with honors and their parents were delighted.

Emily said, "It's so nice to meet you, after all these years of us trading sons."

Mr. and Mrs. Leonard responded with a laugh, followed by Calvin Leonard's compliment. "John was rather self-sufficient really. We hardly knew he was there. He actually did more work than Jason did around the house when he was home. So I'm afraid we got the better of the deal."

"Jason was a dear for me to have around. After getting a divorce and losing my father a few years ago, I wasn't ready to lose John. It would've been so lonely. I'm glad Jason was such a disciplined kid that he came to breakfast, or I never would've met him." Emily felt that she might've over-shared her true feelings, but she felt like she knew the Leonards.

"I know, after that massacre happened, we realized how blessed we were as well."

John and Jason found their parents chatting in the parking lot. "You ready to go?" Jason asked.

"Now that you two are here, we are," Julie Leonard responded.

They piled into the cars and drove back to the Germaine's for a small celebration of coffee and cake.

"I understand John's going into the Army. Whatever for?" Calvin asked, as they sat around the living room.

John answered, "It's always been part of my plan. We weren't quite as equipped for me to go to VT as you were for Jason; I have student loans to pay off."

"Well, certainly your first few years of income as a mechanical engineer ought to pay that off," Julie said.

Jason had used his work experience money to pay toward tuition, just like John. But he had additional help with tuition from his two grandparents and aunt, who wanted him to go to a good school. Jason's remaining loans would be paid off in his first year of employment at the PAX facility. He had been fortunate enough to be permanently hired for the position that he and John had shared the last four years.

"The Army has the GI Education Bill. It gives forty-thousand as an incentive to those with degrees, so we can pay on our loans. That'll almost cancel my debt. Besides, I'll only have to give a two-year commitment."

"But with all this fighting, you might not be lucky enough to dodge a bullet again, John," Mr. Leonard responded, telling a truth that most didn't want to speak out loud.

"After 9/11 I felt helpless. I think a lot of Americans did, too. Then when that guy came into our classroom with a gun, I personally felt threatened," John said, as he rubbed his arm in remembrance of the day he'd never forget. "I don't want to ever feel that way again. I want to be trained to take charge, to be able to do something, something to save lives."

Jason felt the conversation had gotten too serious and tried to change the subject. "Hey, John, did you see the team's car that's going to the show in Chicago next week? I think they might win it for VT this year. Heaven knows, we tried last year."

"Yeah, but we lost. That darn engine crapped out on us." John said, remembering how they worked on the problem several times without success.

Fortunately, the conversation lightened up after that. They enjoyed the time together before the Leonards left for the hotel.

The next day, they loaded Jason's belongings into his car for the five-hour trip back to Hollywood, Maryland.

Emily gave John an orange Mustang for his gift. One of the students on campus had purchased it to show his VT spirit. He was unable to keep up with his car payments, and the dealership had repossessed the car. She used the old Buick as a trade-in and supplied the down payment as his graduation present. The rest would be his responsibility.

When June arrived, John left for boot camp in South Carolina. The army trained new recruits at Fort Jackson in Columbia.

July 2009
Flying high over the Gulf of Mexico

Mary was flying the EA-6B Prowler, which was known as the "Electric Intruder." The forward fuselage allowed a rear area for a larger four-seat cockpit; and an antenna fairing had been added to this model of plane. The two turbojet engines gave Mary the ability to fly at high subsonic speeds over open seas. She had taken off from an aircraft carrier and would be returning for her landing soon.

Although this aircraft was designed as an electronic warfare and command-and-control aircraft for air-strike missions, the EA-6B was also capable of attacking some surface targets on its own. Mary had already practiced that feature at sea. She knew the real targets would someday be radar sites and surface-to-air missile launchers, but she was hoping to mostly be used to gather electronic-signals intelligence, or to support ground-attack strikes by disrupting enemy electronic-magnetic intelligence from within a combat zone.

Today, she was flying with a simulation crew made up of three electronic countermeasures officers. When she was over the Atlantic, she was able to bring her speed back to five-hundred miles per hour, even though she knew this plane could do ninety more.

At the end of summer, she'd be officially winged a Naval Aviator. Mary could hardly wait. It had been a long four years, but at least she was enjoying flying high above the ground. After graduation, she'd get a long-awaited furlough. Afterwards, she'd report to her new assignment.

She saw the carrier. She made the necessary changes in speed and altitude for the approach and landing. She made her pass over, and circled down, like a bee returning to the hive. The tires touched down. The guy wire caught. The ride came to an end.

Mary stepped down from the plane onto the flight deck. She removed her helmet, and placed it under her arm as she headed to the stairs.

Once inside, she received the message. "The Admiral wants to see you ASAP, ma'am," the young swab said with a salute.

"Thank you; as you were."

The young man went back to his normal duties.

Mary reported to the Quarter Deck. There, she found the Admiral meeting with his other officers.

"Admiral," Mary said, saluting, still holding her helmet under arm as some women did a baby.

"Yes. I've just gotten your orders. I've reviewed them, and think you'll find them most rewarding."

He handed the papers to her. "That is all."

Mary saluted again, and took her leave.

Once in her bunk, she opened the papers. In the fall, she was to report to Cape Kennedy for further training. To say she was surprised was an understatement.

"*Wait until Mom and Dad hear this*," she thought as she folded the orders with a smile.

October, 2009
On the road in the South

John traveled the undulating interstate through the foothills of South Carolina, coming ever closer to the repetitive waves, where muscular youth rode on brightly-colored surfboards to the shore. As he listened on his orange Mustang's radio, he imagined the rocket's fiery tail that would signal another launch tomorrow to the space station that orbited forty miles above the earth.

He couldn't wait for his astronaut training to begin. He graduated just a few months ago with honors from Virginia Tech with a Mechanical Engineering degree, and a hefty student loan, that his enlistment in the Army would pay off. He had completed his basic training in Columbia, South Carolina and scored well on his aptitude test. The results didn't peg him to be on a shuttle, but he was to serve his country as one of the first commercial-pilots at the spaceport in New Mexico. It wasn't a military operation, as such, but the brightest and the best were being trained. The Army was sending him.

CHAPTER 27

October, 2009

Now that flight school in Pensacola was finished, the Navy assigned Mary a new duty. She was currently driving across the panhandle on Route 10 to get there. She wanted to make Cape Kennedy before nightfall.

She couldn't believe it. She had been tapped for the astronaut training program for future commercial flights from the spaceport. Her excellent grades at the Naval Academy must've made the difference, along with the fact that she was a woman, no doubt.

Mary pulled into the rest stop. She had been driving for five hours and needed a break. She used the restroom and then walked back to the snack machines, hoping to find some caffeine to keep her going.

"Excuse me miss, do you have change for a twenty? I've been driving since South Carolina; and I need some caffeine bad," John said.

Mary hated talking to strangers, but she wasn't afraid of defending herself, if need be. After all, it could just be another come-on line. Yet, she believed it was best to give people the benefit of the doubt.

"I think I might. Wait here; I'll be right back," Mary said, jogging off to her car.

John watched, thinking that Mary was actually going to get in her car and drive off, but she didn't. She jogged back with five ones, a ten, and a five dollar bill, flapping in her hand. John watched her as she approached him.

"Here; I gotta get going," Mary said, conscious of the time.

John quickly handed her the twenty saying, "Thanks," and giving her a salute.

Off she ran again. She hopped in her car and revved the engine before leaving the rest stop.

John bought a Red Bull. He popped the top and took a sip as he walked back to his car, thinking about Mary as her silver BMW M3 entered Interstate 95.

Mary set her cruise control for five miles over the speed limit. She didn't want to get a ticket. Cops loved to ticket sports cars. She set the radio to a classic rock station, after scanning for local stations.

She was taking a sip of Pepsi and thinking it odd that the good looking guy had saluted her as she left. She glanced into her rearview mirror to straighten a stray hair that had come loose from her ponytail. Her eyes picked up an orange Mustang that was approaching rapidly in the left lane.

John caught up to her. He noticed a Naval Academy sticker as he came along side of her car. He stayed parallel for long enough to jiggle his Red Bull can, showing her his purchase. He gave another salute of thanks and resumed his faster speed.

Mary nodded, acknowledging his actions, but didn't give any more feedback or encouragement. She noticed the large VT sticker on his bumper as he picked up speed again. She thought she had detected a southern accent. That explained it.

"He must've been in the Corp of Cadets," she said aloud to herself, as his car slipped out of sight.

John's cruise control was set for nine miles over the limit. He had released it to maintain speed when he was beside the girl. He thought about slowing down to keep her car in his rearview mirror. Then he decided against it. He had to keep his mind on reaching his goal.

Mary sped up until she could just see the back end of the orange car. She set the cruise control speed to maintain tracking. This was a pleasant distraction; and she'd get to the Cape a little sooner too.

At the Naval Academy, she hadn't dated anyone who attended the college and neither had she at the flight school. She didn't like complicating work with relationships that could end.

She noticed that the orange Mustang had taken an exit. She read the next green interstate sign, "Cape Kennedy. Not my exit," she said, as she glanced at her directions on the passenger seat. "Yeah, mine's Exit 205, guess there're two ways," she said, disappointed that it wasn't this one.

Mary drove on. And in fifteen more miles ramped to the east onto Interstate 528. "Ten more miles," Mary said with a smile.

She took the ramp at Exit 49 and headed north to Cape Kennedy. She pulled up to the guard shack.

"Good day, Ma'am. May I help you?"

"I'm here for training," she said, and handed him her military ID.

The guard looked at the ID, comparing her face to the picture. "Excuse me, Ma'am," he said before stepping into the booth. He scanned the list of names on his clipboard and found hers.

He handed back her credentials. "Go one mile up the road and turn right. The barracks will be ahead on the left." Then he saluted.

She returned his salute before raising the window again. She followed his directions to the building and parked the car. Pulling out her duffel bag from the truck, she walked to the entrance, just as the orange Mustang pulled into the lot.

She paused.

John parked the car, and walked straight towards her.

"Please, allow me," John said, opening the door.

"Why are you here?" Mary asked.

"I could ask you the same question," John answered, just as they reached the front desk.

Then in unison they both said, "I'm reporting for training, Sir," as they stood rigid, waiting for further instructions. Glancing over at each other, they controlled their urge to laugh.

The instructor said, "At ease. This isn't really being run as military, so we can dispense with military formality. I see you have your gear, Ms. Matthews. You can take it up to your room. Here's your folder and the key."

Mary stepped forward, and took the folder and key with her free hand.

"Take those stairs over there; you'll find it on your left, facing the Vehicle Assembly Building. I sure am glad the two of you made it here early to see the launch tomorrow morning. A little later today, you'd have found yourselves in traffic."

"Okay," he said, turning to John, "Now for you, Mr. Germaine. Where's your stuff?"

"In the car, Sir."

"Let's go get it. I'll show you to your quarters," the instructor said, walking toward the entrance.

Mary unlocked her door and set her gear on the double bed. It looked like a regular hotel, which surprised her a bit, since she was expecting a single bed made up like she had learned at the Academy.

The assembly building was impressive, standing five-hundred and twenty-six feet in front of her. She couldn't even see around it; it was so wide.

"So much for a room with a view," she said, and unpacked her stuff, hanging it in the closet.

It didn't take long before she was ready to shower. She got out of her driving clothes and started the water. It was taking awhile to warm up, so she wiped her hands on the towel and opened her folder.

"Dinner at 1900 hours; good; plenty of time," Mary said, pulling the band out of her hair.

She climbed into the shower and ran the warmth over her head and down her back. She opened the complimentary bottle of shampoo and lathered up her fine blonde hair. Readjusting the water to one or two degrees cooler, she rinsed. She opened the bar of soap and washed away her weariness.

The knob squeaked as she turned the water off. She threw open the shower curtain and grabbed the bath towel on the rack. Mary roughly dried her wet hair and wrapped it into a turban on her head.

She pulled the other bath towel off the rack and dried her long legs and polished toes. She tossed the towel over her head and dried her back with a sawing motion. Stepping out of the tub onto the floor mat, she hung the folded towel back on the rack again.

She directed the hot air from the hair dryer onto the mirror and removed the steam. As her image appeared, she saw that her sky blue eyes looked a little bloodshot.

"Not enough sleep, Mary," she told herself.

Her friends had taken her out the night before as a farewell gesture. She didn't get to bed until 0100 hours and had to hit the road at 0700 hours.

She combed through her hair as she heard the plumbing squeak next door, indicating someone was in the adjacent bath. Mary turned the dryer on and styled her hair.

John was stepping out of the shower onto the mat, when he heard a TV in the next room. He wrapped the towel around his waist and unpacked his bag. He laid his shirts and tee shirts in the top drawer in very neat stacks. He placed his shorts and socks in the middle drawer, and his pants in the bottom.

He sat on the bed and read through his folder. The instructor had already told him that dinner was at seven o'clock, so he had another half an hour before he needed to meet him downstairs.

John turned on the television just in time to see the launch announced on the news. It never ceased to amaze him. And now he was going to be trained to go into space too!

He walked over to the window and looked at the VAB, wondering if they'd get to see inside. He sure hoped so. He left those thoughts behind, and went to the bathroom to brush his teeth.

After spitting his toothpaste in the sink, he rubbed his jaw, deciding whether he should shave. Thinking he ought to, he picked up his shave cream and lathered up. He didn't want to make a bad impression at dinner, especially since they had been given time to freshen up.

At six-fifty he stepped out of his door and was turning the key, when Mary Matthews exited her room next door.

"Gee, I'm surprised he put us so close together," John said.

"I am too, but maybe he figures we're going to be working together so we might as well get used to being near each other. No need for mystery," Mary said matter-of-factly.

They walked down the stairs side by side and found Mr. Jacobs waiting for them.

"Well, I'm glad you're punctual."

"One thing the Navy teaches is punctuality," Mary said.

"Army," John said, correcting her.

They all laughed.

"Follow me. I'll be taking you to your last meal," Jake Jacobs said.

"What?" John asked.

"Well, tonight is a treat. You'll eat normal real food just like everyone does, but not after tonight. You're going to be on a strict astronaut's diet starting tomorrow morning."

Jake unlocked his car doors with his remote key, and they all climbed into his SUV. He started the engine. Placing his arm on top of the passenger seat back, he reversed the car.

"So, tonight I want you to pick anything and everything on the menu that you want. Money is not an issue here. It's all in the budget."

"Anything, Sir?" John asked.

"Yes, John, you can even order a Martini if you want or pizza until your stomach explodes; whatever you want. After tonight you aren't getting any."

They pulled up to the restaurant and got out.

The waiter brought the menu, which was rather extensive. It even had Hasenpfeffer! Mary began first noting the group divisions: Appetizers, Entrée, Beef, Chicken, Fish, Poultry, Game, and Pizza, as promised.

John glanced quickly for the names he recognized and liked. As soon as he saw them, he moved to the next. He closed his menu; he had made his choice.

Jake kept his head in the menu, noting John's quick decision-making. He had read it many times before and could've rattled it off verbatim. Jake waited until he saw out of his peripheral vision that Mary had lifted her head.

"Well, have you decided?" Jake waited, wondering what the selections would be.

Mary nodded her head.

John said, "Yep."

The waiter approached. "Would you like something to drink?"

Jake responded with, "Are there any specials this evening? I'd like to hear them first."

Mary nodded her head in agreement. She always wanted to know all the options before making a final decision.

John smirked a little and rolled his eyes. He was ready to place the order. He was hungry.

The waiter recited the specials and glanced once at his notepad to make sure he had said everything. "Do you need a moment before ordering your drinks?"

"No, I'm ready," Jake said, looking to Mary and John for confirmation.

They nodded.

"We'll first have a bottle of champagne to toast the occasion." Jake ordered.

"Anything else for you at this time?"

John and Mary shook their heads, 'No.'

"I'll bring your glasses and the ice bucket. I'll be right back." The waiter scurried off to the kitchen.

"It's important that you kids recognize how special this is in your life. Don't take a moment of it for granted. It's important to celebrate it responsibly, and mark this time in your memory for life."

"Yes, Sir," Mary answered.

John sat quietly with his arms folded over his chest.

The waiter brought out the chilled champagne and popped the cork. He poured the three glasses. Laying the bottle in the bucket of ice, he placed a napkin around it and left.

Jake held up his glass, and John and Mary did the same.

"To your accomplishments and the future. May the world come to depend on it."

The glasses rang as they gently touched. Each took a sip.

The waiter came back. "Are you ready to order?" His pin was perched, ready to write. He took the orders, and went off to place them.

"Mary, tell us about yourself," Jake said, wanting the two to get to know each other. He had already read the dossiers on both; and of course knew all about them. It was always interesting to listen to someone tell their own life story, especially in a capsulated version.

"I was born in Boston and grew up around Cambridge. My dad is a professor at MIT and my mom is a housewife. I graduated high school with honors and was the valedictorian."

When Mary divulged that much John had to have another gulp of the champagne, even though he didn't drink.

Mary continued, "I received an appointment to the Naval Academy in Annapolis, and continued onto flight school in Pensacola. I was then told that I could be the first commercial woman pilot into space; so I jumped on the opportunity." Mary smiled shyly, and took a sip.

"Now, John, fill us in on your life," Jake said, giving him all his attention.

John started to speak and the waiter interrupted with the tray of orders.

"Here's your Stuffed Portabella, ma'am. Watch it, the plate is hot," the waiter warned.

"And your Filet Mignon, sir, medium rare." The waiter placed the dish in front of Jake.

"And you, sir." The waiter turned and picked up the last dish. "Here're your Filet Burgers. I'll be right back with your drinks; other than that, will there be anything else?"

"Yes, some ketchup and steak sauce please," John quickly said before the waiter could run off.

"Certainly."

Jake lifted his glass and said, "Bon Appetit! Okay, now where were we? John, it's your turn," Jake said, cutting into his steak to make sure it wasn't raw and red inside. It wasn't.

"I was born in Richmond, but we moved to Virginia Beach when I was young. Then we moved again when I was a teenager to Christiansburg, when my grandfather took ill. My mom had to care for him," John said as the waiter returned.

"Here's your ketchup and sauce sir." The waiter set small ramekins beside John's plate. "And here is your large Coke Classic. Your Chardonnay, ma'am, and your draft beer, sir," the waiter said, as he placed the glasses. "Is everything to your liking?"

"Yes, all is fine," Jake said.

Mary and John nodded.

"Continue," Jake urged, slicing another piece of tender beef.

John swallowed his food and continued. "I graduated high school with honors in the top of my class. I studied Mechanical Engineering at Virginia Tech, graduating with honors again. I then enlisted in the Army."

"Why the Army?" Mary asked.

"They had the best tuition plan. I had a sizeable student loan that I wanted to cancel and the promise of forty-thousand dollars for my time was worth the trade," John explained before taking a large bite of his burger.

"Do you have any questions, Mary, about the program?"

"No, not really, at least not now, but I would like to know if we could have a tour of Kennedy. I've never been here before. Actually, Pensacola was the first time I've ever been south," she said.

She had joined the Navy to see the world. But she wanted to see her own country first.

"You're ahead of me. We're going on the tour first thing after breakfast."

"Will we get to see inside the VAB, Sir?" John asked with a gleam in his eye. He wanted to see some of the nuts-and-bolts of the space program.

"Yes, we can arrange that."

"Dessert?" The waiter asked, as he cleared the table.

"I'm fine," John said.

"What do you have that's really chocolatey?"

"We have Chocolate Muse and Chocolate Decadence."

"I'll have the Decadence," Mary said and added, "Please bring three forks, in case the two gentlemen change their minds."

Jake went back to business. "We'll meet for breakfast at 0600 hours, so I want you two to get a good night's sleep. Please be sure to read over the information in the folders I gave you, if you haven't yet."

The dark chocolate flourless cake came to the table. Mary took a bite and rolled her eyes, indicting it was sinful. She chased it down with the last of her now warm champagne.

"You have to at least taste this. It's to die for," Mary said, taking another bite.

"How is it?" the waiter asked. Do you want anything else before I bring the check, sir?"

Mary answered first, "Wonderful. I'd like a cordial of Frangelica, please." She thought the hazelnut liquor would go great with the rest of the chocolate. She wasn't about to let the remainder of it stay on the plate.

The men said they were fine.

The waiter brought back the small glass and the check.

After dinner, they drove back to the Cape and retired for the night.

Stepping out of her dress and getting under the covers in her slip, Mary read over her folder. The alcohol had done its trick. It had made her relaxed and sleepy. When she finished reading, she turned out the light and pulled the covers up tight, drifting off to sleep with the TV in the other room acting as white noise.

John wasn't sleepy. He was too excited and wired with the caffeine of the cola. He had already glanced over the folder, so he watched a movie. It was a grade B sci-fi, making him laugh at the actors and the script. Before long, he fell asleep with the television still on.

CHAPTER 28

Kennedy Space Flight Center

The alarm sounded and Mary jumped in the shower. After toweling off, she combed her wet hair into a tight ponytail and knot, the way she did at the Academy. She dressed in her khakis and headed out the door.

"Good morning, Sir," Mary said to Jake.

"Did you sleep well?"

"Yeah, like a log. Where's John?" Mary asked.

"Right there," Jake said, glancing toward the stairs.

"Good morning, Sir. Good morning, Mary."

Jake and Mary answered, "Good morning."

"Okay. Come with me," Jake said. He walked out the door and they followed him over to the VAB. "As you probably read in your folder last night, the Vehicle Assembly Building is five-hundred and twenty-six feet tall, seven-hundred and sixteen feet long, and five-hundred and eighteen feet wide. It's the largest one-story building in the world."

They walked through a normal-sized door that looked like it belonged in "Alice in Wonderland" when she was small. It was dwarfed by the immense size of the building.

Inside was huge. There were gray steel girders lining both sides of the building connected with catwalks at one end, and a large door at the other end that ran from floor to ceiling.

"The complete Saturn Five rocket, among others, was assembled here in one piece. As you can see, the next shuttle is being worked on at present."

John was impressed. Mary was amazed. They took an elevator to the floor that led onto the shuttle wing, and into the cockpit.

After allowing them to look around for ten more minutes, Jake said, "I think it's time for breakfast."

The Cape was busy with activity. The launch was scheduled for four. They would view it later as VIPs. For the time being, they went to a special mess hall that not many had ever seen. They took their stainless steel trays and proceeded to the counter.

The nutritionist greeted, "Good morning, Jake. Are these the new recruits?"

"Yeah, this is John and Mary. They'll be starting into full training tomorrow. I want you to give them the first-day pack that I ordered last week."

"No problems. Coming right up," she said, reaching in the refrigerator and removing four cold foil packets. She went over to the warmer and pulled out two breakfast packs already heated. She had been expecting them.

She placed the items on their trays. "See you at lunch," she said and left them to eat.

They walked over to the table and sat down.

"Aren't you eating, Sir?" John asked.

"I had my breakfast before meeting you. Now let me describe your packets to you. These are your liquids. This one is orange juice with calcium, and this is your Vitamin D-enriched milk. They are a little more fortified than you can get at the store. You need to support your bones in space."

"It looks like you open it here," Mary said before testing it.

"Yes, you pull this open and use this straw to suck out the liquid. It has a one-way value. It will only come out by you sucking on it. You can't have loose bubbles of liquid floating around in the cabin."

John nodded his head, taking everything seriously.

"Now these warm packs are your bacon and eggs so to speak. It's a nutrition-packed combination of egg and protein, simulating the taste of the traditional breakfast food."

"How do you get it out?" John asked this time.

"This one has a nozzle, too. It's wider; you have to squeeze the contents for it to come out. Be sure to chew it well with your mouth closed. No talking and eating, like you did at the meal last night.

Mary nodded.

Jake added, "I did notice that last night you both talk with food in your mouth. We need to break you of that habit, first."

John wrinkled his brow in disbelief. "Are you saying I talked with my mouth full?"

"No. I'm saying you talk and still had food in your mouth. You must swallow everything before talking in space.

"So lesson one: try eating your breakfast and not talking until you have thoroughly swallowed."

Mary and John opened the packet stems and began having breakfast. They didn't talk at all. They continued quietly until Jake broke the silence.

"Now, remember I didn't say no talking. I said no talking with food. Let's try some conversation."

Mary took a sip of milk and swallowed, clearing her mouth. "John, did you see the launch pad towers?"

John took one minute before his mouth was clear. He answered, "Yes, I did when we came out of the VAB." Throwing it back at Mary he asked, "How many hours did it take you to get here yesterday?"

Mary chewed, sipped her orange juice, and swallowed. "Nine. How about you?"

"Ten," John answered.

Jake told them to finish up their meal so they could get on with the tour. He left to talk to the nutritionist about lunch.

John and Mary's packets where flat, indicating they had finished. They carried the trays to the counter.

"Just leave 'em there; come with me," Jake ordered.

When they got outside, the sky had changed. It was no longer a clear day. Large clouds were forming. It looked like it would rain at any minute.

"Here; take these ponchos in case it starts pouring. Florida weather, you know. It rains buckets for an hour; then it clears; otherwise it's just liquid sunshine. You'll need to be prepared."

They climbed into the SUV and headed to Launch Complex 19. They read all the names of the two-manned flights, starting in 1965 with Grissom and Young and ending with Lovell and Aldrin in 1966. The history was intense.

"This all happened before we were born," John said.

"Speak for yourself, kid," Jake said jokingly, pulling his cap off and straightening his gray hair. "Next stop: Launch Complex 34."

They sat quietly in tribute to the tragedy of Apollo 1. Jake stopped the car. They walked around and reflected on the seriousness of space flight.

"I wanted you to see and realize; this is not all fun and games. You are putting your life on the line. There is the prestige and notoriety of it all, but there can also be death involved," Jake said. He placed his cap back on his head as he walked to the car.

"Now, let me take you near the Launch Complex that's operational."

John wanted to see the launch site. "Where is that?"

Jake pulled up between two launch gantries. "You can see that's the one for today's possible launch."

"This is way cool. So there are two launch pads this close together?" Mary asked.

"Yes. They make the decision which one to use. Then they roll the shuttle out on these tracks here," Jake said, pointing to the parallel roads running up to the launch pad.

There was a loud clap of thunder. Jake added, "We probably only have a few more minutes. Go ahead and get the ponchos on."

They pulled the blue plastic ponchos with the white NASA insignia out of the pouches. Unfolding them with a shake, they quickly slipped them over their heads just in time for the downpour. Another lightning bolt went straight for the ocean, not far away. The smell of ozone hung in the damp air.

"The water usually keeps the lightning from the towers, but sometimes they do act like lightning rods. Luckily, we haven't had too much damage that way."

When another bolt hit nearby, Jake said, "This tour's over."

They quickly piled into the car.

"Any questions?" Jake asked now that they were out of the cold rain.

"So Cape Canaveral and Cape Kennedy are separate?" John asked, wanting to set the record straight in his mind. "My grandparents called Kennedy, Cape Canaveral."

"Yes. A lot of older people used to call it that. Canaveral is mostly for shooting small satellites; Kennedy is for the large payloads, like the shuttle and manned vehicles."

Jake glanced at the car clock. "Is anyone hungry? It's time for lunch." He drove back to the mess hall.

The rain ended. The launch was still on schedule. As they ate the astronautical packs of food, the clouds moved offshore.

"Now, let's get you over to the VIP viewing center for the pre-launch hoopla. I'll meet you afterwards or sooner if it gets scrubbed."

Jake made introductions at the center and left Mary and John to appreciate a scene that he had seen way too many times. He'd never get tired of seeing liftoff, but he had grown tired of the press, and the dignitaries and politicians from Washington.

Mary and John noted that there was a reception table of food for the guests.

"Do you think we get any of this?" John asked, feeling hungry for real food.

"Jake said last night was our last meal. He didn't mention anything about this, one way or the other. I think we shouldn't."

"I'm glad we can agree on that. Let's walk over here then, and get away from it. It's too hard to not want any when you can see and smell it."

They walked over to the corner of the room, staying to themselves. They watched people more than they actually talked.

Two men entered the room. Both were well dressed. One was in a pinstriped suit, which looked odd when everyone else in the room was more casually dressed. The other man wore an obviously custom-tailored suit of linen and wore kid-glove leather shoes.

"They must be some really big wigs from Washington," John whispered to Mary.

"I think you're right," Mary answered. She opened the program that Jake had given them. She read it and chuckled.

"What's funny?" John said, thinking she laughed at what he had said.

"Look at the bottom of your program."

John glanced down at the brochure. He didn't see anything amusing on the cover. He opened it and chuckled too. Handwritten on the page next to the word Reception it read, "I was joking last night, help yourself. See you later."

They got plates from the table and placed on a few canopies. Picking up a glass of punch at the end of the line, they overheard the two well-dressed men talking.

"Thank you for getting me this VIP invitation to the launch Director Haynes. I've always wanted to see one of these live."

"I haven't seen one myself. Since we're sending a new crew up with this shuttle, I was invited by NASA to bring along one guest. I thought you might enjoy this, Jack." Director Haynes wanted to continue to make friends and influence people, especially those who seemed to have the power to control the purse strings. "I just hope it gets off today. I'd hate for you to miss it."

The last hold was lifted. The countdown resumed. They had twenty minutes before the show. The VIPs were escorted to the seats in the next observation room.

Mary and John filed in and took a seat along with the rest of the people in the room. The shuttle lifted off amid the fiery exhaust. The stream of white smoke trailed through the sky. It could be seen for a long time after the shuttle could no longer be seen with the naked eye.

Mary and John watched as the first stage dropped away. They were in awe. They might not get into space this way, but in the near future, they would be taking a commercial flight there.

Jack, who was seated in the front row with Director Haynes, said, "Now, that was impressive. I can't wait until I get to go into space."

"You?"

"Yes, I already bought my ticket. It won't be too long before they have the spaceport complete and the aircrafts ready."

Director Haynes was now the one impressed. He played it off as if he knew all about it. This was something Haynes had perfected in Washington. If you wanted to know anything in D.C. you listened, absorbing information like a thirsty sponge, and adding two and two together. Before divulging anything though, you verified it first.

Mary and John were unaware of their conversation, or they may have entered into it. They were thrilled to have seen the launch and to have been included with the VIPs.

The next day, a special NASA transport carried their cars to Houston. They were transported by a military flight from Patrick Air Force Base to Texas to begin the real training. This had just been a teaser of an introduction; one they'd never forget.

CHAPTER 29

February, 2010
30 miles outside T or C, New Mexico

Ted French, the younger, had been busy with the spaceport building project. Virgin Galactic had quite a unique and futuristic design in mind. The runway was two miles long.

Gerald Martin Construction Management had been chosen in December 2008 to oversee the construction of the spaceport. The groundbreaking ceremony marked the beginning of construction for Spaceport America's permanent facilities on June 19, 2009. The goal at that time was to have construction completed by December 2010. Ted was beginning to wonder if they'd accomplish it on schedule.

Last October, the spaceport announced that paid tours of the facilities would begin in December. The concrete dust was swept around on the dry air when the tour buses drove by. Since concrete dust was a carcinogenic, this caused a problem. Now, while tours were in progress, they had to stop work. This really slowed the construction down.

The need for concrete was such an essential part of the project that the construction company had its own plant. Now in February 2010, they were only in mid-construction. The budgetary estimate for completion was one-hundred and ninety-eight million dollars.

"Ted, we'll be ready for some decorating proposals soon. I'd like you to post this announcement for any local decorators to submit plans and bids. It would be nice if we had somebody from this part of New Mexico to win the project," the head foreman confided.

"No problem. I'll post this to the website and around the neighboring towns," Ted answered. He headed to the construction trailer office to get right on it.

He placed a call to Michael. "Hey, they're ready for local proposals for the job of decorating. Would you still be interested? I know you're rather caught up in your motel, but I think some photos of your different rooms might impress those deciding who gets the contract. I can even help you write it up. I have grant writing experience," Ted added, hoping that his friend wouldn't shy away from the political aspects of getting a bid.

"Actually it's a perfect time. The motel's almost running itself. Between the old mineral-spring baths, and those spaceport tours, my business is steady. I'm glad I acted on your email when I did. To tell the truth, Mom and Dad don't even miss me. They hired some other tech to do my job. It was as if they never needed me.

"Besides, even if I get the bid, it'll be a few years before I'm actually needed. By that time, I could hire employees to handle guest check-ins and housekeeping."

"Check with me later tonight over at Joe's. I'll give you some pointers over beer and pizza." Ted smiled, happy to help someone out.

"Who's buying?" Michael asked.

"I am, of course."

"Well then, I'll have bells on."

"Later," Ted said, ending the call. The announcement was on the web, so he left to post in the surrounding towns.

March, 2010
Lima, Peru

"Yes. We're sure she's in Yushu, China. She has been spotted several times visiting her brother at the monastery. I don't want her contacted. Just go to the mines in the area and try out your test," the boss said. "It's on a major fault line, right?"

"Yes, it is. I'll take Jamal with me and fly to South Africa. We'll pick up Ahmad to help us with the job. I'm sure Mr. Afghanistan will let Nassim fly us into China," Juan Perez stated, explaining his plan of action.

"Mr. Tunisia will take care of any paperwork for entry into China from his Hong Kong office. We'll take care of two birds with one stone: actual ground test results, and terminating our loose cannon by natural causes."

"Yes. This test will be better than before," Juan assured.

"Hopefully, it will be, Mr. Morocco," the boss said, ending the call.

April 2010
Yushu, Qinghai, China

Mei Lian was helping the girls in the dorm when the earth shook violently that morning. It threw them all off balance. She reached for anything to stabilize her until it stopped. The never ending quake broke a slab of ceiling loose. It came crashing down, hitting her in the head and knocking her unconscious. When she came to, most of the temple was destroyed, as well as the village. Children and nuns were trapped under the rubble. She worked feverishly to free the injured. Others were dead and could not be helped.

When she uncovered all that she could, she ran to her brother's monastery. It had also collapsed. Many priests were dead. Searching, she found her brother. He was trapped under debris. Pieces of wall lay across his chest and legs. She freed him as best she could.

"Ci An! Ci An, can you hear me?" Mei Lian asked frantically.

He opened his eyes when he heard her voice. A moment later they locked open in a blank stare. She closed his eyes, but they wouldn't stay shut. There was nothing more she could do for him, so she turned her attention to others. After checking many, she found very few had made it. Her work there was done.

Claudia ran back to the temple and gathered her belongings. Even though she was in shock, her survivor instincts were still keen.

"*A major earthquake like this will draw the attention of the government within China and agencies far away. When rescue teams get here, I'll lose my security of anonymity. I've got to get far from this place as quickly as possible.*"

One of the nuns, who had perished in the quake, was around her age and size. This terrible tragedy was a perfect opportunity for Claudia to exchange identities, swapping Mei Lian for Xiang Ping.

Claudia dug out her old backpack from under the debris that used to be her room. She changed her clothes and instantly no longer looked like a nun. She switched her Chinese passport and papers with the other nun's ID book in the process. Hopefully, when the agencies started clearing, they'd identify the Xiang Ping's body as Mei Lian; and Claudia could stop looking over her shoulder.

She grabbed her backpack and walked down the road. Many families passed her by, leaving the area. She was fortunate to catch a ride. She climbed into the back of the pickup truck and sat down. Her scarf and quilted jacket warded off the wind.

"This had to be the fault of the mining company," one of the other occupants said, needing to place blame for the loss of so many lives.

"Yes, the capitalistic mine owner only thinks of money, not about the people, our homes, or the land," another said.

Claudia, now Xiang Ping, (Fragrant Peace), nodded in agreement. That set her mind to wondering if indeed GUILE had caused this. "*It fits their MO*," she thought, shaking her head. It seemed death was following her. "*If they did do this, why have they let me live this long?*"

Many days later, when Xiang Ping was miles away, Chen Hui Long reported to GUILE, "A body of an old nun Claudia's size was found. The surviving nuns believe it to be her. Rescuers found the ID book for Li Mei Lian in a nearby room. The woman has been cremated in a mass grave, along with the other thousands of recovered dead bodies."

"Thank you for the report. Good work," Mr. Egypt said, ending the call from his office phone in Brussels. The boss was busy making financial deals in Belgium's Finance District, and was glad to have one less thing on his plate to worry about.

"Would you call my car around? I have a business lunch to attend," he told his executive secretary.

May, 2010
University of Oklahoma

Abdul received his Master of Science in Meteorology from the University of Oklahoma that morning. The day was clear with no threats of tornadoes. Spring in Oklahoma was a rather exciting place. The Meteorology Department and Research Center was funded by grant monies from the government for that very reason.

Abdul packed. He had been hired by the AWA. Director Haynes conducted a phone interview with him two days ago and gave him a position in Houston. Abdul accepted as he was instructed to do.

"*I wonder what Texas is going to be like. Mr. Pakistan assured me I was going to be working with other meteorologists on a very intriguing project. I guess time will tell,*" he thought, as he folded his last shirt and placed it in the suitcase.

The older members of AWA in Houston had retired and the newly hired meteorologists of the last few years had perfected the guidance system. There had been no major storms to cause damage. This had saved the American Insurance Agencies millions of dollars.

Soon GUILE would have their crew serving on the ground, and in space on the WSL.

July 2010
Wuzhong, China

Claudia was making her way slowly, but methodically, across China. She was hoping to settle down, get a job, and blend in with the crowd. Feeling the need to be creative again, Claudia thought about the fine rugs she once had in her New York City apartment. She had imported each from the four major rug cities in China: Guangzhou, Shanghai, Tianjin, and Beijing. Maybe she could find work in one of the factories.

"Guangzhou is the closest, but it's too close to Hong Kong. Hui Long lives there and I don't want to take any chance being seen by him or his men," she thought, reasoning out her plan of action.

Her dyed black hair was, after four months, long enough to tuck behind her ears; though it wouldn't stay there long. Using bobby pins, she clipped it in place and studied Xiang Ping's ID book again.

"She lived there, right between Tianjin and Beijing," Claudia noted, tapping her ragged map. "Not bad. I wanted to assume as much of her identity as possible. Perfect! I always liked the carpet designs that came out of the northern factories the best. Now I know where I'm going."

She folded the map and placed it back in her bag. Her new goal was to make Tianjin, or perhaps Beijing, by winter. After slipping her arms into her jacket, she placed the backpack over her shoulder and started walking.

October 10-17, 2010
Houston, Texas to Mojave, California

Mary and John finished the astronaut training and were given orders to move to Mojave, California. They had one week between locations. Packing their limited belongings didn't take long. They sat down together to look over traveling by car. The temporary housing would be furnished, but it wouldn't be available until late next week.

Mary preferred to tour the country, taking the trip west slowly. John agreed, not wanting Mary to travel the road alone. They sat down and planned the travel route, including the stops of interest.

"I'd love to see the spaceport, but that'll come in time," Mary said pulling up the computer map of their route.

John said, "I want to see Goddard's Lab in Roswell," making his wishes known. "How far is it off the path?"

"Ok. Let's see," Mary entered the info on the search engine and looked at the map. "We'll need to stop at Fort Stockton, Texas. That's already an eight-hour day. We can get to Roswell the next day. I'd like to have fun and see the UFO Museum, myself," Mary said.

"It looks like we can go over the mountain to Las Cruces the next day. We can stretch our legs at the Space History Museum in Alamogordo," John said, pointing at the map on the screen.

"And I'd like to see White Sands."

"Ok. We'll stay over in Las Cruces then. How far is Phoenix?"

"Says it's six hours," Mary answered.

"Ok. Let's stop there and then how long 'til Mojave?"

"Um, let's see," Mary said, as she tapped in another destination and waited for the results. "Seven hours."

"Then let's do two nights in Phoenix. That way we can look around Arizona."

"I would've liked to see the Grand Canyon," Mary said.

"Tell you what; let's go that route when we make the move to the spaceport area?" John suggested, waiting for her approval.

"Deal," Mary said, and printed out the map and directions for the trip.

Visiting the Museum of Space History the third day, they passed Ted French leaving his volunteer docent position. He held the door as they walked in.

"Thanks," John said as he passed by.

"No problem," Ted responded absentmindedly, heading to his car. Freda wanted him to pick up some items at the Wal-Mart before he got home; and he was preoccupied with finding the list.

They paid the admittance fee; and another interesting docent took them on the tour. After hearing Mary was in the Navy, the frogman from the Mercury Manned Space Flight Missions told them how he had known most of the seven astronauts in the program. When they got off the elevator, he showed them a photo of himself placing the inflation collar on one of the capsules, keeping it from sinking upon splashdown.

"Boy, that was before we were born," John said.

"You sure do make it come alive," Mary responded, not wanting to insult the man who was in his eighties.

"I want you to understand real people went into space. They were pioneers and heroes. Now, come with me," Frank responded.

They followed up the spiraling aisle in the museum. They looked out over the rockets on display below.

"Now, that is a V2 rocket brought here for Van Braun to work on after the war."

"Wow. Just think, if we hadn't gotten him, some other country may have been to the moon before us," Mary stated, realizing how it would've impacted on her life.

They spent a wonderful three hours of real history with Frank before leaving to view the rockets up close.

"I'm glad we aren't using any of these to take us into space," John joked.

"Without them, we wouldn't be going at all," Mary said, understanding that she stood on the shoulders of giants, especially after this tour, and seeing Goddard's Lab the day before.

At the end of the week, they were settled into their separate residences that were supplied for them by the military. Before long, they would move to Spaceport America.

Even though they worked for the commercial company, the paychecks were issued by the armed services. It was a joint endeavor.

October 22, 2010
Spaceport, New Mexico

A ceremonial flyby of the spaceport was made by Mary Matthews to celebrate the completion of major construction at the facility. A statement was released about the event, saying that the world's first commercial spaceport runway reached a significant milestone in Spaceport America's construction.

"Do you see the runway?" Mary asked through her headset.

"Yeah, I see it. One day we'll take off from there. I can't wait until they let us actually take a test flight," John said excitedly, smiling down at the landscape.

"That's affirmative, co-pilot."

They could see the terminal building. It was now under active construction. The budgetary estimate for completion was two-hundred and twelve million. Approximately two-thirds of that was coming from the state of New Mexico. The remainder was coming from construction bonds backed by a tax approved by voters in Dona Ana and Sierra counties. Local residences were eager for America to get off the ground and into space, knowing they'd bring their dollars to New Mexico.

Mary and John headed back to Mojave.

Below, Michael received word that he was awarded the bid for the spaceport's motel. Customers taking flights into outer space would spend the nights prior to and following at the planned location. Teddy had liked Michael's planetary design for the rooms, and apparently so had Virgin Galactic.

It was Friday. The local single-professionals had made Joe's place the hotspot in town. Ted met his friends, as usual, for dinner at the bar. They left the tables for the couples and tourists.

"Congratulations, Michael. I knew they'd like it," Ted said, as he joined the group.

"It's hard to say which room I like best. I like the full-wall murals in the earth room. The underwater scenes with marine life swimming around, enhanced with bluish lighting, are so tranquil and refreshing here in New Mexico," Jane, the realtor, commented.

Joe was preparing his friends one of his specialties. He responded from the Vulcan range, "I liked the moon room."

Jessie, another friend who ran a new-age shop in town, piped in. "I like the Venus room."

"You would; you're a girl," Michael said, teasing her.

"I resent that. She's not the only gal here," Jane joked.

"It's not a girl-thing, it's the crystal. I held it over all of your sketches. Venus gave off the most response. That's all it took for me. It gives the best vibes," Jessie explained, fingering the crystal hanging around her neck.

Ted refused to comment on Jessie's crystal. "Hey, Joe, it won't be long before they need proposals for the food concession restaurant. Would you be interested?"

Michael urged, "Go for it, man. Ted's good at writing bids. You'll help him, won't you Ted?"

"Sure."

"I'll think about it," Joe answered, setting the hot plates on the granite bar.

Jessie took a whiff. "Great as usual, Joe. You could call the meatballs Joe's Moon Rocks."

Everyone laughed.

Wrinkling his brow and shaking his head, Joe began preparing the order that the waiter had just handed him.

"Add dough rings around 'em and make Saturns," Michael suggested.

Ted defended his friend, "Hey guys, I wanted him to try for the job because of his gourmet cooking skills, not haunted-house ideas."

"My rooms don't look like a haunted-house," Michael protested.

With that comment, they all laughed and dug in.

They had become great pals and joked around a lot. Only Jane and Joe dated. Michael had taken Jessica out a few times, but it didn't seem they'd really be a steady thing. Ted was still waiting for the right one.

When Ted got home there was a message on the recorder. He pushed play and listened.

"We hadn't heard from you for awhile, Teddy. . I saw an article about hitting some milestone today. I knew you wouldn't be home yet. Don't really want to bother you. Dad loves the docent's job. He meets some rather interesting people. Speaking of meeting anyone, have you yet?" We're planning to do a little maintenance on the old place next week. Thought maybe we could stop and see you on the way home on Sunday afternoon. I'll give you a call when we're leaving Magdalena, and give you an approximate time for our arrival. Call me back if that doesn't work for you. Otherwise, we'll see you then."

CHAPTER 30

April, 2011
Mojave, California

Virgin Galactic planned to provide sub-orbital space flights to the paying public. The original mission passengers, who weren't professional astronauts, would be flown to an altitude slightly over sixty miles, allowing them to experience weightlessness. These initial seats had already been sold to persons ranging from sixteen to ninety years of age. Jack Jones was one of them. As the general public became aware of this unique opportunity, more pilots would be trained. The first flights had been originally planned for 2010. That projected date had come and gone.

Test flights had been performed on the specially designed aircraft called the White Knight. A safe and controllable rocket engine, benign fuels, an air-launch system, a feathered re-entry system, strong lightweight composite construction, and lastly, a simple design to maximize safety was being used. Despite all the safety precautions, they hadn't gotten total approval yet.

Others at the plant were test flying it, but Mary and John hadn't had their chance.

"I really can't understand all the delays," John complained.

"I guess you weren't in the service long enough to learn the philosophy of 'hurry up and wait,' huh?" Mary asked jokingly. "Before long, we'll get our chance at a test flight; don't worry."

John smirked and nodded his head, showing his disappointment.

"Even after basic test flights are completed, they'll need to move a team to New Mexico to conduct operational tests. Maybe we'll get to be that team," Mary told John, trying to get his spirits up.

"I hope so," he replied.

John was smitten with Mary. He knew he didn't have a chance. He had several strikes against him: he was younger and she didn't date workmates. He liked being near her, but why be punished daily?

Looking at the situation realistically, he reasoned, "*She's to fly the White Knight and me the Space Ship. Different cockpits oughta help.*"

Late April, 2011
Southern United States

A historic tornado outbreak took place across much of the South at the end of April. There were more than three hundred confirmed tornadoes and just as many fatalities. The outbreak ranked as one of the worst in United States history.

Omar was graduating with a M.S. in Meteorology in another week. He had already been hired at AWA - Houston. As he watched the information coming into the Tornado Center, he thought, "*There must be some way to deflect them; seems like all we can do is blast a warning horn to seek cover.*"

Education in America had temporarily softened his heart.

May Day, 2011
Houston, Texas

The new slate of GUILE employees finally met their quota at AWA. They had two Meteorologists and two Mechanical and Astronautical Engineers. The original secretaries in the division had been transferred to other government positions for NASA. Only one replacement secretary was hired. She was a Muslim, but she didn't wear a burka.

"You have a call, Doctor, from Director Haynes," she said to Arai, the new director-in-charge of the Houston unit.

"Thank you," he said as he took the transferred call.

"Good afternoon, Sir."

"Arrangements have been made for the switch of staff on the WSL. We have been cut some funding again. I want you to take one of the positions. You select the other from your small staff. Have you met Omar?" Director Haynes asked, unsure if he was on board yet.

"Yes, he began last week. When will I be going?"

"If all goes well with NASA, you'll be on the next shuttle. After that, the transfer of duties will be done by a commercial source," the director said, staring out of the Washington office window. The azaleas were just starting to bloom.

"Commercial? Not NASA?"

"Apparently, the powers-to-be think it'll be cheaper. They've signed contracts with the commercial subsidiary to take payloads into space to the orbital stations."

"Do they still take off from Kennedy?" Arai asked, concerned about the changes.

"When it goes commercial, it'll leave and return in New Mexico. But as I said, the next one's going up from Florida. Make your selection and let me know. By the way, once you're up, the men coming down are being cut. Don't say anything. I'll take care of it."

"Who will man the operation down here?" Arai asked, confused by all the change.

"The two you have now. They'll be doing only nightshifts after this. You'll only be able to communicate live during those hours in Houston. You should get used to this. Congress pays some years and not others. No real rhyme or reason to it, even though I'd like to think that my bartering helps," Director Haynes said, smoothing his hair with his hand. "At least, we haven't had furloughs like the rest of the government here in D.C., or worse, been shut down totally. Get back to me with your partner in space by the end of the week."

"Yes, Director," Arai said, hanging up. He was already contemplating whom he'd rather spend a year with, confined in space.

May 15, 2011
WSL

Arai and Omar were now aboard the WSL. Arai had decided to leave Adbul with Mustafa on the ground. He had worked with Abdul for the past year and felt better with the two of them monitoring and supporting the WSL from Houston.

They had only been in space for a week when AWA spotted a tornadic supercell causing a swath of damage. A tornado emergency was issued. Omar was aware that WSL had been used to divert hurricanes.

"Let's try to move or disrupt the tornado," Omar suggested over the station's link to Houston.

"We have never tried that. Do you think we'd need Washington's approval, Arai?" Mustafa asked as Abdul glanced his way for the answer.

Arai discretely whispered to Mustafa, his fellow countryman, "I think Allah would be pleased."

Mustafa smiled. Finally they were able to do something against the infidel. If it went poorly at least Mustafa and Arai would have satisfaction.

Late that afternoon they used the laser to disrupt the cyclone's movement. This caused it to become very large. An intense multiple-vortex tornado formed, resulting in catastrophic damage in Joplin, Missouri. Many houses and businesses were flattened and some were totally blown away. The main hospital was heavily damaged and many people were trapped in destroyed houses.

Now GUILE had evidence that WSL could be used to cause destruction. They were pleased with their team's initiative.

Omar said worriedly, "Do you think they'll fire me?"

"Even if they wanted to, it'll be another year before they'll come up and take you off the job. I think you're fine."

The operatives from the different countries had never been introduced. Omar thought about Arai's response. *"Obviously he's from the Middle East; we all are. Maybe he's really Islamic,"* he reasoned.

Omar wanted to ask, but he didn't want to blow his own cover.

Because of all the cutbacks in government spending, no one ever knew that the WSL had tried the laser on a tornado.

Some of the news reports, that they received the next day from the South's Bible Belt, indicated that the tornadoes were perceived as just another sign that the End Times were near, exactly what GUILE wanted them to think.

Ten Year Summit
GUILE

An out-of-the-way resort was found for the summit, thanks to Claudia. When GUILE had been scouring the countryside of Tibet for her whereabouts, the boss had found an exclusive spa resort. They used their private jets to get to the region, not wanting to be inconvenienced.

Jack Jones noted the table was full. Only one person wasn't there and he didn't know where she was. The membership was varied. It represented major business interests all over the world: London - Insurance; Paris - Art; Hong Kong - Computers; Tokyo and New York- Stock Exchange; Monaco - Casino; Peru and South Africa - Gold; Cayman Islands and Zurich - Banking; and Utah - Weapons. The group was steered by Belgium Finance.

"I'm glad you could all put your businesses on hold for this special meeting, gentlemen," the boss, Phillipe Peeters, said opening the meeting.

"I'd like an update from each of you on our current state of affairs. Then we'll set our focus on the next decade. But first, let's begin with evaluating the past ten years. Mr. Chen, would you begin?"

"Thank you for the opportunity to address everyone first; I can answer the question that you may all have. As you may or may not be aware, I was assigned the task to track and find Claudia Lei. She was found in the rubble after the Yushu earthquake. Her remains were cremated with many others who succumbed to fatal injuries. This, literally, puts the issue to rest."

Jack listened. *"I don't believe that for a second. She's much too cleaver."* Jack had been working on a composite picture of her father, mother, and Claudia to give to his own private spies. He was continuing the search for her. *"Hui Long didn't have his high-tech group take a picture. He just jumped to the exact assumption Claudia had hoped he would."*

When Jack and Claudia graduated from the university in England, he had seen a picture of her deceased parents. He scoured her apartment until he found it. She mostly favored her father. *"I won't rest until I have concrete evidence that she's alive, or dead."* He brought his attention back to the meeting.

Juan Perez was standing and explaining the technique he had used to cause the earthquake in China. "As you can see, we've proven it'll work. I've researched all the fault lines in the world, especially the U.S., and think we should try it on the East Coast next."

Everyone was listening intently, wondering how it would benefit them.

"So much of America is run in the mid-Atlantic region and seaboard. There's the government in Washington, D.C. and Naval installations in the Hampton/Newport News/Virginia Beach area; and of course, there's Wall Street in New York. Wipe out money and politicians and the only thing left in America would be the film industry. No one takes them seriously," Juan said laughingly and added, "at least not to make major decisions regarding the economy and the world."

Phillipe Peeters said, "Thank you, Mr. Perez."

Juan smiled and took his seat.

"Our operatives have been performing insider-research while we educated them to serve us. Their reports have led me to conclude that weather and earthquakes are a better solution than our plan was ten years ago with the World Trade Buildings. By manipulating weather, and other normally natural causes, we can fool the Christians into thinking it's the Tribulation, or at least the End Times, and scientists into thinking it's just the result of global aging and warming," the boss admitted.

"Jack, would you explain your part next?"

Jack stood and reported the success of his last initiative. "The operatives, who were selected for our upcoming coup d'état, graduated with honors. They've been placed into corresponding jobs. The demographic program predicted an eighty-percent success rate and our results confirm our expectations. The twenty-percent have been sent home."

Next, Phillipe called on the London Insurance CEO.

He reported, "No one buys insurance like Americans. We have managed to instill the fear that drives people to buy insurance: the fear of losing it all. For instance, flood insurance in mountainous regions that happened to have experienced a once-in-a-lifetime flash flood; rental car insurance when normal car insurance will cover the driver; travel insurance; title insurance; children's life insurance; college tuition insurance; and so forth. The list could go on forever.

"As we previously recommended, all of you are invested in the selling of each of these products, and even the great idea of insurance on the derivatives.

"Soon we will recommend you terminate policies in regions that have been targeted. Therefore, you will get out before it's going to cost you. It will fall to the new insuring company. This will save you from having to shell-out when the damage occurs."

They all applauded. Nothing excited them like making easy money.

When the applause died down he continued, "In some cases, natural disaster is not covered. For example, when earthquakes are rare in a region, meaning not on the hundred-year record, we don't sell a policy to cover it. Once it occurs, we can provide policies for the eventual next time. Insurance works a lot like Andre runs his casino. The odds are we never pay out."

As he took his seat, one of the bankers commented, "That's what's so great about the U.S. mortgage crisis. We directed them to give the mortgages to those not truly qualified. Then we bundled them and sold them off, taking our cut before they defaulted. The closing fee was cash up-front for us, and we sold them title insurance, making money a third time. Insurance and Banking have always worked well together."

The meeting continued around the table. Each piece of the plan divulged. It was left up to each member to connect the dots.

Lastly, the boss disclosed, "Just like before, we'll monitor our weak companies and give each other the chance to invest appropriately, whether it be in stocks, derivatives, or insurance. I'm keeping a watch from this side of the Atlantic. Mr. Chen and Mr. Kazuhiro are watching from the Pacific. Mr. Jones is monitoring from Wall Street. We'll notify you before major financial events happen. That way, you can move or sell your assets, maximizing your profits."

The meeting ended. They divided into groups for golf, drinks, and massages before dinner. Jack followed the group to the bar. He downed a cocktail quickly, feeling frustrated by the continual responsibility. He lived in New York and invested in the stock market, but he wasn't really part of Wall Street. He left the others at the bar. He needed a massage to relax his uptight muscles.

CHAPTER 31

August 21, 2011
Mineral, Virginia

Juan Perez's men were in place. They had set the charges in the caverns and grottos not far from the Richmond/Washington corridor, along Interstate 95.

"According to this fault line, I think they'll feel it shake all the way along the mountain ridge into Pennsylvania, sir," Jamal reported.

"Great. Wait for my word. Pick a place close enough to detonate, and safe enough to survive for your next mission."

"Okay, will do." Jamal closed his phone and got into his rented SUV. He had selected just the right motel in Northern Virginia.

August 23, 2011
Virginia

John Germaine was on vacation at his mom's.

"It's so nice that you were finally able to take some time off," Emily said with a smile as they road along the highway. John hadn't been home since he had left for boot camp.

"The other weeks I was off, I was driving from Houston to Mojave. Then the next time I was moving from Mojave to Truth or Consequences. This is my first real two-week vacation.

"Maybe next time you get vacation time, you can come out to see me in New Mexico," John said, parking the car in the visitors' parking lot at the Madison Mansion.

"At least, I was able to take today off," Emily said, as she stepped out of the car. "This reminds me of our vacation in D.C."

John purchased the tickets. "Seems like we like being tourists at historical places," John commented and handed his mom a sticker badge for the tour.

In the middle of the tour they felt it. The ground began to shake. Everyone in the group looked to each other with quick glances, wanting an explanation. In unison they all yelled, "Earthquake!"

The guides began catching antiquities as they fell from the tables. Some couldn't be rescued from the fate of smashing on the floor.

One guide ordered, "Everyone come with me." The house was still shaking and she didn't want anyone injured.

They were gathered into the one room in the house which had the best structural support until all settled down again. The guides gathered up the artifacts, laying them gently on their sides until they could possibly be repaired. Those that couldn't were swept up, placed into boxes, and labeled. When the tours resumed, the tourists were now more interested in what had just occurred, than in the past.

August 23, 2011
AWA Headquarters
Washington, D.C.

Director Haynes and his secretary, Jaime, were at the computers in the Top-Secret room when the building began shaking.

At first, they didn't notice the movement. Haynes saw the coffee sloshing in the pot as he approached. He straightened his glasses, thinking it was his vision. Then he felt it.

Jaime thought it was possibly a bomb exploding, or maybe an airplane crash nearby. She turned from her computer monitor and looked to Director Haynes for an explanation. She saw his puzzled expression. He suddenly declared, "Earthquake! It's an earthquake. Start locking down. We need to get out of the building."

Jaime began the shutdown process. Director Haynes locked the file cabinets in the room. The monitor blinked off and they rushed into the main office space. Many were screaming. Cubicles were shaking. The shaking had intensified.

"Listen, everyone. This has to be an earthquake. Please, evacuate the building," the director said as the fire alarm now sounded loudly.

The employees grabbed their belongings and headed for the stairs. Outside, they waited with other government employees. An hour later, directors received word that all government offices were closing for the day. They passed on the news to the employees.

Jaime was happy to get an unexpected day off. She waved good bye and walked to her car which was parked several blocks away.

Haynes went back inside to study the track of Hurricane Irene.

August 23, 2011
New York

Jack felt a slight tremor of his building. He glanced at the clock. When it ended he thought, "*Good job, Juan. Thirty seconds, just enough to shake up the Washington bureaucrats.*"

August 23, 2011
Bay Ridge, Annapolis, MD

The television news station from Baltimore showed a cute pre-school child. "The ground was shaking at our school," the little girl told the reporter, who said, "Over to you, Ted."

Mary turned it off to answer the ringing phone. Surprised to see it was John calling, she answered, "Hi, what's up?"

"Did you feel the earthquake today?"

"No, we didn't feel it here near the Bay, but I understand that all of the Washington area did. Did you feel it in Blacksburg?"

"We were visiting Madison's place at the time. Artifacts were falling and everything. It was rather exciting actually."

"The TV reports said people from Pennsylvania to New York could feel it. Did you see the cracks in the Washington Monument?"

"No, were they bad?" John asked with a frown, remembering his high school graduation visit there.

"Bad enough; they can't use the elevator. From the shots I saw, they are quite visible. Really seems a shame."

"Yeah, it's an iconic symbol."

"Call me if anything else happens. I'm watching Irene. I think I might have to help my parents prep this place. Looks like it might hit Carolina, but you can never tell. Talk with you later," she said, ending her call.

Mary pulled up the NOAA satellite on her computer to check the track of Irene again. This was something she hadn't given up doing, even though there was nothing to track in the desert of California.

"*Yep, it's going to come close enough to cause us trouble*," Mary thought.

"Hey, Dad come look at this!"

August 23, 2011
WSL

Omar said, "Arai, I've been trying. All I can do is to make the outer bands wider."

"From the images that we're receiving from the hurricane center at NOAA, I see that you've created a large mass of clouds with a small center wall. Keep trying," Arai said, turning in for his six-hour sleep period.

To qualify as a Category 5 storm on the Saffir-Simpson hurricane intensity scale, maximum sustained winds had to exceed one-hundred and fifty-five miles per hour. Only thirty-two Atlantic storms in weather history had reached that intensity. GUILE had given the directive to achieve it again if they could.

The operatives kept firing the laser every three hours. The storm stayed off the coast of Florida. They thought it would probably track close to the Outer Banks.

August 26, 2011
Annapolis

After breakfast, Mary and her parents watched The Weather Channel. The TV gave warnings for the Outer Banks and coastal areas.

The reporter said, "There is a mandatory evacuation for the coastal areas in North Carolina. Remember, if you ignore the evacuation, the first seventy-two are on you. This means the first seventy-two hours local people will have to help themselves. No one from the power or emergency-rescue crews will be able to get to persons who do not evacuate.

"We are expecting serious flooding due to the rain that Irene will deliver over the next two days, as it approaches and passes by us. New York is already announcing that mass transit will be shutting down later this weekend."

Mary turned off the television and set down the remote. "Mom, take the patio furniture into the family room. Dad and I will get the dish removed from the roof," Mary directed.

Outside, the winds were already picking up and the sky was cloud covered.

"Are you sure this is necessary?" Mike Matthews asked his daughter. He had agreed the day before, but he hadn't thought it would come to fruition.

"Yes, Dad, this is a very large storm. The winds could gust up to one-hundred. That would rip the dish and the corner of the roof right off. You don't want rain flooding into the family room do you?" Mary asked. She placed the ladder beside the house and started climbing, ignoring his protests.

Mike watched her as she unscrewed the bolts with a wrench. Mary's hair was blowing lose from her ponytail, causing her to pause. She tucked the annoying pieces in place. She dismantled the dish by noon. Of course, without the dish there was no TV or Internet.

"Mike, Mary, lunch is ready," Margaret yelled out to them over the sound of the wind. The Bay was very choppy.

"Okay, Mom. We'll be right in; after we get the cars pulled in."

Mary and Mike moved all the objects off the floor in front the two cars. They placed the boxes in the trunks and back seats. Mary got behind her dad's wheel. He guided her close to the wall before moving out of the way.

"Okay, just a bit more. Ho!" Mike yelled, stopping Mary.

"Okay, now help me pull mine in," Mary said, slipping into her economy rental. She carefully pulled in beside the other car.

"Okay, you got it," her dad directed.

Mary rolled up the window and exited on the passenger's side.

"Now I'll move Mom's back in and we'll go eat lunch."

"It's amazing how you turned this two-car garage into a three-car garage."

"Well, it helps to have bought an older house with a garage made for those big cars of the fifty and sixties. Besides, a Smart Car is the size of a roller skate. It's not all that amazing really, Dad."

Mary disengaged the garage door and pulled it down by hand. "When the power goes out we'll still be able to get to our cars. I noticed you don't have a back door."

"I would never have thought of that. The cars would've been locked inside. In our Massachusetts home we could get to the cord, since it was attached." Mike followed Mary into the house.

The first rain band came while they ate their lunch. The Chesapeake Bay Bridge was hardly visible through the window.

"The waves are picking up," Margaret commented as they ate.

"We need to check the moon placement," Mary answered.

"You won't be able to see it tonight, not with all those clouds and rain," Margaret answered Mary.

Mary laughed. "Mom, I don't want to look at it. I wanted to know if we're going to have high tides with the storm surge. If we are, we might want to make sand bags to protect against flooding."

"We won't have problems out here like in town near the city dock. That's why we bought out here and not downtown, dear. We loved the old brown stones and the older framed houses from the eighteenth century, but we knew that there might be too many flooding issues. We didn't want to deal with that at our age," Mike said, finishing his sandwich.

Mary checked the paper anyway, just to be safe. She re-evaluated the slope of the lawn from each of the windows. When she was satisfied that the Bay wouldn't reach their doorstep, she went around to each bathroom and filled the bathtubs with water.

"What are you doing now?" Margaret asked.

"I'm storing water for when the power goes out. You've got a well now. You're not going to have any running water without power. You won't be able to flush the toilets without running water. We'll use the tub water to flush toilets."

"Oh, my goodness! We never had to think of that in Cambridge."

"No, you lived in the city then. Now get some containers so we can store extra drinking and cooking water."

The next morning, the power went out as soon as the breakfast was prepared. Mary and her family sat at the kitchen table, watching the rain beat against the windows as they ate by candlelight. The Bay Bridge was no longer visible.

August 26, 2011
AWA/WSL

"The boss was happy that you made Hurricane Irene one of the largest area hurricanes on record," Mustafa said smiling.

"We did our best," Arai replied with disappointment.

Omar listened. He shrugged his shoulders, nodding agreement.

"He knows. This isn't a criticism. He's glad you were able to keep it a CAT 1 in the cooler Mid-Atlantic waters. Washington will be without power for days. Apparently, he wanted to cause disruption, not disaster," Mustafa surmised, still unsure of those in control and their motives for Allah.

August 29, 2011
Virginia

"Hello, Mary. Do you have power yet?" John asked, aware of the conditions along the coast of North Carolina and above.

"No we don't, but it isn't too bad. We were all prepared. A gas grill helps, too. I triaged the food in the fridge. I hope we get it back soon. BG&E says it'll be back on tomorrow, or so the online instructor who lives next door, told us. She's been going to Mickey D's in order to get an online connection. She's our link to the outside world."

"Other than that, how's everything else?"

"I'll probably get the cars out of the garage, and put the satellite dish back up today. I'll be glad when we get home to New Mexico, so I can have a vacation," Mary joked.

John laughed. "Okay, I'll see you at Reagan National as planned."

"Yep, I'll be there with bells on," Mary said, ending her call.

John turned back on the TV and watched the reports of flooding. There were pictures of roads cracked and a large tractor-trailer truck floating down a highway. It was carried along by the muddy water rushing through the town's street.

Another man had sent in a video of the water in his elderly father's house. The retirement home was built in the Outer Banks region of North Carolina. His house was constructed over the garage for the simple possibility of flooding. The water was up to the fifth step of the two-story house.

They had been prepared, but they were trapped in the upper floor until the water subsided. "We'll clean up the garage and all the boxes in a day or two when the water goes down. I'm sure we didn't get everything picked up before the storm," he said as the video ended.

The reporter said, "That's why we told the people before the storm to remember the seventy-two rule. It's on them until crews can get trees cut and power restored. Others are staying at hotels or with friends and families until they can go home again. When they do, they'll find mud and settlement in their first floor. Carpets will be ruined if you aren't as fortunate as this man to have built with flooding in mind."

The anchorwoman added, "It's my understanding that reacting too soon and doing clean up isn't always the wisest thing; FEMA has to evaluate your damage. If you have cleaned up on your own, you'll receive no help or reimbursement."

"Yes, that's true Donna. With FEMA dollars locked down by government impasse, who knows how long it'll take for these people to get any assistance?"

John turned off the TV. He couldn't stand to watch any more bad news.

CHAPTER 32

October 2011
Spaceport America, New Mexico

There were speeches from congressmen and the governor of the state at the official opening of Spaceport America. An aerial show demonstrated the acrobatic qualities of weightlessness. The owner of Virgin Group ended the show by dropping down on his own rope and dedicating the building with a bottle of champagne.

Jack was standing in the audience looking up at the show with the rest of the dignitaries and 'future astronauts,' as they were being named. He and everyone else were impressed with the new facilities.

Being friendly, Ted leaned over and commented to Jack, "This is a rather spectacular sight. Isn't it?"

"Yes, it is. I bought my tickets years ago. I can't wait until I'm on one of the first flights."

"Nothing's like it," Ted said from experience.

Jack thought he was just making conversation.

Ted moved into earshot of a reporter covering the story. "Regulatory arrangements are just beginning. They'll have to get approval from the FAA before commercial operations can begin." The reporter made the cut-throat motion. The cameraman stopped shooting.

The reporter then complained, "This morning I tried to get a breakfast in Truth or Consequences and the only choices I had were McDonald's and Wal-Mart."

Ted spoke up, trying to be of assistance, "Well, if you're staying for dinner I know a great restaurant in town. You would consider it more to your liking, I'm sure."

"What's it called? I'll be ready for a dinner, even though this reception should be good by the looks of things."

"Take Route 51 into downtown. Bella Luca is on the left side of Jones Street. You can't miss it."

The reporter replied, "Thanks," and turned to talk with his cameraman. "I want an angle of…"

The White Knight approached for its flyby. Mary and John flew slowly over the facility as the audience applauded. Mary banked and landed to everyone's delight. They rode up to the front of the Spaceport amid cameras flashing shots of the memorable occasion.

John and Mary waved from their respective cockpits.

The reporters rushed over to ask them questions.

Later, when they were free to enjoy the reception, Ted said to John, "Great flight by the way."

"Well, I wasn't the one flying it. It was really Mary over there. I was just sitting in the Space Ship and wishing like most of you," John replied, thinking Ted was one of the many 'future astronauts,' since he wasn't taking notes and didn't have a cameraman in tow.

They moved up in line, coming a bit closer to the reception table. "Oh, I don't have that kind of money. I've been part of the construction aspects of this project. But I'm sure the passengers will have to get minimal emergency training and sign releases acknowledging the inherent risks," Ted answered, now close enough to pick up a drink.

"I wasn't lucky enough to get picked for the first test orbital launch; but one day Mary and I will get there. Here comes Mary now."

Ted watched as Mary walked his way. His heart sank. He knew in that instant that she was the girl of his dreams. No one had ever made his heart descend into his stomach and leave him breathless before.

"I see you found refreshments, and someone to talk to for a change other than me," she joked as usual. "Hi. I'm Mary, Mary Matthews," Mary said, placing out her hand to greet Ted. She wasn't about to let this guy get away without knowing his name.

Mary had seen him as soon as she stepped out of the aircraft. When she noticed John had struck up a conversation with him, she had to make her way over.

Ted shook her hand and said, "Sorry," to John, remembering he hadn't introduced himself, "I'm Ted French."

"I'm John Germaine," John said shaking Ted's hand next. He could see right away that Mary had taken a liking to this tall dark stranger.

"If I understood right, you two took off from Mojave. Will you be moving here for flight testing, now that it's officially open?" Ted asked, hoping it was the case.

Mary replied first, "I believe it's in the works as we speak." She took a sip of the champagne.

"We'll be here for a few days before being transported back to California to make the final move," John said.

A reporter who wanted an interview with Mary and John interrupted them. Ted made his leave for the time being.

When all the hoopla was over, Ted headed to the restaurant to meet with his regular friends for the evening. The place was packed. He was glad Jessica had saved him a seat at the bar. Ted saw the reporter from earlier. He waved from a distance, not wanting to bother his dinner.

"Hi, Jess. You should've been out there today. You would never believe it. It was really great. I bet you could've gotten some good vibrations today," he said jokingly, lightly punching her arm.

A couple came through the door. Jessica replied, "Hellooo courageous."

Ted turned to see John and Mary enter. "I guess you're talking about her."

"No silly, him."

"I met them today. Want me to introduce you?"

"Is the Pope Catholic?"

"Okay, once they're seated I'll take you over."

The host greeted them. "Welcome to Bella Luca. How many?"

"Two."

"I'm sorry, but we're very packed this evening. There'll be a wait for a table unless you want a seat at the bar. Two seats just opened up there."

John decided before he saw Ted, "We'll take the bar."

"Help yourself," the host said, greeting the next in line.

Mary and John made their way to the two seats.

"Wow, talk about good luck, Jessie, your dreamboat is coming this way," Jane said.

"It might not be her luck but yours," Ted said. "They'll be moving here before long. You have a sale walking this way." Ted turned straight to the bar, playing like he hadn't noticed them.

Mary sat on the stool next to Jane. John walked down to Ted. "Nice to see you again; is there anything good on the menu?" John asked.

"Hi, John. Everything's good here. This is Jessica, that's Jane down there, Joe's at the grill. He runs the place. This is John Germaine," Ted finished the introduction.

Jessica had a wide smile as she shook his hand. "Hi, nice to meet you." Before he released her hand, she felt a strange energy pass through his body. Something wasn't right. She wasn't exactly sure if it was his past, or the future.

John hadn't noticed. "Hi, that's Mary down there near the end," John said. He made his way back to the empty seat next to her.

Jane was talking with Mary. There were no strangers in New Mexico.

She gave Mary her business card and excused herself. She had other plans for the evening and needed to leave. "Nice meeting you. Give me a call when you're ready to see property. As you can imagine, it's starting to sell like hot cakes. You won't want to wait too long." Jane waved good bye to the crew at the bar.

Mary slid over one seat, pushing Jane's dessert plate forward. John followed suit.

Jessica shook Mary's hand just to see if she sensed the same thing. She sensed nothing strange, just warmth and friendliness.

"Ted tells me that you flew for the ceremony today. That must be exciting," Jessie said, hoping to hear more.

"Maybe one day soon I'll be able to carry John up in the SST and release him into space," Mary joked and hit John on the arm. Mary could tell Jessica was interested in him. She decided to help by playing matchmaker. Mary knew he liked her, even though he hadn't made his intentions known. "*This could be perfect. If someone else is interested in him, it might divert his thoughts away from me as the object of his affection,*" Mary reasoned to herself.

Jessie asked, "What happens then, John?"

John gladly took the bait. "The spaceship will drop down some. Then the rocket boosters will accelerate it vertically into orbit. It can nearly reach four times the speed-of-sound in seconds," John explained.

"Wow. Are you prepared for it?"

"Sure. We already did our astronaut training. I understand they've a G machine at the spaceport for the paying customers."

"You didn't get a chance to see that today? Oh that's right, you got there late," Ted said. "The crowds saw it all before you arrived. If you're here for a few days, I can give you the private tour."

"The original plans have changed. We're flying back tomorrow. So if we come early, you can show us," Mary said.

"Can I come too?" Jessie asked. She wanted to see John again.

"Sure. I can show you first thing in the morning," Ted said as the food was served.

"What time?" Jessica asked, not wanting to miss it.

"How about eight?"

"Works for us," John answered and took his first bite of linguini.

Spaceport America 8 A.M.

The next morning, they arrived as planned.

Ted gave the tour as if he were a professional tour guide. "Good morning; as you can see this massive low-lying structure blends in with our environment. At the same time, it gives a futuristic glimpse of the continued progress we'll see in our lifetimes. Follow me.

"As we walk down this way, you may not realize that it is actually made up of three floors. One is built into the ground for the hangar. The main floor is the terminal. The top floor contains the offices. When we get inside there's a spectacular view of the New Mexico sky and landscape."

"I like these tall walls. It really focuses my thoughts into what lies ahead and these exhibits," Mary added.

Ted led the way. Mary trailed close behind, followed by Jessie. John came last, taking in all the views, not just the building.

"This must take a tremendous amount of electricity to power the lighting and the HVAC," Jessica said, worried about the environment.

"Actually, it's eco sound. That was one of the things that attracted me to this job. The way it's built into the ground helps it utilize the thermal winds; and it buffers it from the extremes of our New Mexico climate changes at the same time."

John was intrigued. This information was right up his mechanical engineering alley. "So the air outside is naturally used for ventilating the building inside. Cool."

Jessica commented, "It can get very cold at night."

John smiled at her response, finding it endearing. He began paying a little more attention to the nice looking, Earth-Momma New-Ager standing near him. When he got a whiff of her perfume, it reminded him of his grandmother when he was little. "*What was it?*" He questioned himself. Without realizing it, he answered his question aloud, "Patchouli!"

Jessie smiled, "Yes, I put some on this morning. The scent lasts in the desert air for hours."

"Hmm," John said, nodding his head. He tried to turn his attention back to the tour.

"We were given the highest award for being the 'green'ist building at this time. We use passive energy for heating and cooling, and photovoltaic solar panels for electricity. We also have water recycling, making it a totally sustainable facility."

"I can feel the earth friendliness. I'm definitely drawn to the beyond," Jessie said, fingering her crystal amulet.

Ted continued without commenting on Jessie's strange comments. "Now, you'll see as we enter the terminal how all the skylights and large windows provide natural light for the seating and walkways inside."

"How many of our aircraft can we house inside the hangar?" Mary asked, encouraging Ted to move the tour along.

"Two White Knights and five Space Ships can be stored inside at one time," Ted answered. Gently placing his hand on her shoulder he urged her forward. The others followed behind. He knew they'd want to walk around, and sensed from Mary's question that their time was limited.

"So, this is where the suit-up area is," John said. He hadn't said much during the tour but had been quite interested. He occasionally opened doors that weren't locked.

"Yes, and over here is the centrifuge training room. We have to insure that your passengers are fit enough to survive your flights."

As they walked around, Mary noted that Jessica followed John around like a puppy dog. Ted was watching, as well. As if thinking the same thing, they looked at each other with smiles, hoping their friends had found someone.

"It's time for us to go, John," Mary said, taking the hallway to the hangar.

"Your plane is parked outside. It looks like you left it ready to go from what I saw upstairs. Just go through that door over there. Jessie and I will go up to the terminal deck and watch you take off."

Once in the White Knight, Mary placed on her helmet. She prepared for flight, flipping switches and checking gauges.

Jessica and Ted had ascended to the observation floor.

"You really like Mary. Don't you?" Jessie boldly asked.

"It was that obvious?" Ted asked. He thought he'd been rather cool.

"Don't worry, you weren't obvious. I have that sixth sense, you know, woman's intuition. Of course, I'm sure Mary has it too." Jessica laughed. "From the way it looked to me, she has the hots for you, too."

"It seems to me that you like John."

"Yeah, I was trying not to hide it. Some men have to be hit over the head and taken back to the cave," Jessie said joking around.

The aircraft began to move. The pilots waved. Ted and Jessica returned the farewell. The White Knight rolled down the runway. The engine revved and picked up speed. The craft lifted off at the end of the concrete. They circled back overhead. The surface of the craft glistened. The bright white stood out against the clear blue New Mexico sky.

Mary tipped the wings to wave goodbye.

"I better get going. I have to open my shop. Thanks so much for letting me come along for the tour. I would've come, even if John wasn't part of the show."

Aboard ship, Mary asked over her headset, "John, I'll be ready to make the move as soon as they let us; how 'bout you?"

"I think you already have. I was watching you. You don't usually make it so obvious."

"Well, when you meet the right one, you have to make it known. We don't want them to get away. I think that Jessie has her heart set on you too, in case you didn't already realize it."

John didn't answer; he just smiled and watched the controls.

CHAPTER 33

November, 2011
Europe

The grand plan to resolve Europe's escalating debt crisis was once again in doubt. Officials had decided that key parts of the package weren't ready in time for the leaders' summit. Earlier, the meeting of the European Unions' finance ministers had been called off. This aggravated the boss and GUILE. The summit was still held, but the grand plan remained vague without the technical work. This only made stocks on both sides of the Atlantic take a dive. GUILE members hadn't been warned about this possibility. Phillipe was livid.

Now, with the problems with Greece and Italy, GUILE could only hope an agreement could be reached. Greece had massive debts. Italy needed to take concrete action to control its debts as well. Changing to the Euro years ago was supposed to help all of Europe. GUILE wanted to do the same thing globally with one similar system. If the Euro wasn't successful enough, it might be hard to convince America's powers-to-be to go to a world monetary system.

"It's a real mess again," Philippe said.

"I understand some private investors will take the losses on their Greek bond holdings. The negotiations for the banks have indicated that they aren't willing to accept those losses voluntarily," Jack stated his understanding of the matter.

"Forcing losses onto banks could trigger big payouts of credit insurance and cause huge turbulence in the global markets. One is good and the other is bad. Pass the word."

"Okay, I will," Jack said and gladly ended the call.

November, 2011
New York

Jack watched the Occupy Wall Street demonstrators from one of his offices on Wall Street.

He listened to a demonstrator below. He said to the crowd, "The Banking Cartels today control the economy of all nations and the world. They fund the IMF and the World Bank. They dictate conditions for economic survival and structural adjustment to the majority of the world's nations.

"We, Americans, who make up the ninety-nine percent, are economically disenfranchised by the one-percent in this country, who controls the world's economic system. It's time the taxes on the top one-percent be raised, and close the tax loopholes for multi-national corporations that now pay little or no taxes."

Jack had heard enough. He went back to his desk and reviewed the figures on the stocks, ignoring the protestors for the time being. He had to decide whether they should pull the plug again on their insurance policies, or hold.

Before long another speaker took over. He was a middle-aged family man by the name of Charles Smith. He was fed up with both of the major parties and the past two administrations. He had served in Desert Storm and had been teaching Social Studies for the past twenty years. He taught and believed in the American System.

He held up the megaphone and said, "We should end foreign wars and bring those billions of dollars home to benefit the ninety-nine percent by creating jobs, a decent healthcare system, quality social services, and educational opportunities for Americans. We need to put Congress back in the democratic hands of the people, and curtail the influence of money and power over the political process within the United States.

"In other words, restore the promise of democracy. Establish a government truly of the people, for the people, and by the people. That is the very meaning of democracy."

The crowd cheered.

GUILE knew the irony of the Occupy Wall Street movement was that the majority of the protestors would no doubt substantially agree with each speaker, even though they weren't both true. GUILE and the one-percent did control the global system. There was no way that a protest movement within one nation could transform a global system that controlled and transcended that nation. There was no way to establish democracy and economics on behalf of the ninety-nine percent within the United States alone.

The one-percent that controlled the world also controlled the economic, military, and political system of the United States. Attempts at reform within the U. S. would only result in mere window-dressing.

Even if some economic gains were made internally to the U. S., the global system of exploitation and domination would remain. And GUILE knew it.

Jack placed a call. "The prices of gold should go up as a result of the Union's meeting. The boss isn't confident with the Greeks or the Italians. Derivatives should be high. Pass the word."

Juan answered, "I figured as much. I'm sure Paul did too, but I'll give him the other information as well. I'm sure Philippe has already informed Hui Long and Daichi when he called you. The rest are already close to the European Union, so they know."

"The bankers will all know. I'll contact our member in Utah."

November, 2011
Annapolis, Maryland

Michael Matthews was watching the news. "The White House announced we'll be downsizing our military efforts. The troops will be coming home by the end of the year."

"That's good," Margaret said, as she placed the dinner in the toaster oven to heat.

"Military men and women are beginning to show up at Occupy Wall Street. One Marine came in uniform today."

"Why did he do that?" Margaret asked, wiping her hands on a paper towel as she joined Michael to watch the evening news.

She saw the Marine look directly into the lens. He said with a stern face, "I took an oath when I put on this uniform. I take that oath seriously. It was to protect the United States from all enemies, foreign and domestic."

"That sums it up," the reporter added.

"This whole thing is going to grow into something big. Mark my words," Michael Matthews replied, shaking his arthritic index finger in the air.

Veterans had been returning home and finding no jobs. Unemployment for vets was high. They were getting angry. As the days went on, more veterans joined the protest, just not in uniform.

One day the police asked the crowd to disperse. One of the vets refused. He was arrested.

Michael and Margaret were watching the evening report as the man proclaimed to the camera, "I have an amendment right to peaceably protest." The Matthews agreed with him and so did most of America. But that didn't seem to matter to the mayors or police of the cities who were having 'Occupy' demonstrations.

Days Later
Occupy Wall Street

Protestors were tear-gassed and pepper-sprayed. Patience had run out.

Thanksgiving 2011
New Mexico

John and Mary had now officially moved to New Mexico, no longer renting, waiting to get settled. Mary bought a relatively new home from the original owner. She purchased brand new furniture in Las Cruces, and had it delivered the day after she closed.

Mary was on the ladder by the living room window. She had just turned the last screw in the drapery rod bracket when the phone rang. Stepping down off the ladder, she was glad it hadn't rung sooner. She glanced at the number display. "*I'll never get my place the way I want, if he keeps calling*," she thought.

"Yeah, John what do you want?"

"What time did Ted say he wanted us to come for dinner?"

"Five. Don't forget you're bringing the wine and bread."

"Yeah, I got two bottles of wine that the guy in the store said went with turkey."

"Was it a Gewürztraminer?" Mary said, hoping the locals knew their wine. She knew John didn't; he hardly ever took a sip. She studied the placement of the furniture as she listened and decided she'd rearrange it later.

John read the label. "Yeah that's it. I got some fresh bread this morning from the bakery. I figured he can heat up the rolls. Do you think I should bring butter, too?"

"Nah, he's bound to have that. Is there anything else? I've got some more things to get done."

"What are you doing? Do you need help?"

"John, I'll see you at Ted's at five o'clock. Bye."

"Okay. Bye."

Mary knew if she had told him what she was doing, he'd be right over, thinking she wanted help. She was completely capable. Besides, this was her first house. She wanted to do it herself.

John lived in an old fix-it-up house at the other end of town. He glanced at the clock and then at the living room. It had one wall with a picture window and a large opening leading to the eating area, basically two walls and a bit more that didn't add up to another.

"*I've got time to get the living room painted before getting cleaned up*," he thought.

Using his drill, he stirred the paint. He set the disposable plastic tray liner in the rolling pan. Pouring in an adequate amount, he wiped the drip with the practically new paintbrush. He climbed the old ladder that had been left with the house, and started cutting in the upper edge of the wall. He had painted the ceiling and the dining area last weekend.

In a short time, the room was a bright shade of red just like the eating space. John admired his handiwork from the kitchen as he cleaned the brush.

"I like these bright New Mexico colors. I wonder if the desert has something to do with it. The sunsets are really orange," he thought as he tapped the lid on the paint can with the hammer. He tossed the used paint tray and roller in the construction trash bag sitting near the yellow table and chair set that he had picked up at a yard sale.

"Off to shower and shave," he said as he glanced at the clock again.

Ted's Place
Five P.M.

"The turkey's ready," Freda announced after glancing at the pop-out thermometer that came on the bird.

Her son Ted got the potholders and lifted it out of the oven as the doorbell rang.

"I'll get it," his father said as he walked to the door.

"Hi, I'm Michael. I met you before, several years ago."

"Yes, your parents ran that wonderful astronomy village past Cloudcroft. How are they by the way?"

"Well, Mom is fine. Dad isn't doing well. His heart isn't what it used to be. These are the sweet potatoes. I better take it to the kitchen. Ted might want to put them in the oven soon to brown the marshmallows."

"Oh! Sorry. I should've thought about that. I see someone else is pulling into the driveway. Can you take them into the kitchen?"

"Sure. I know where it is," Michael said and walked on through.

Mary got out of her car, carrying a shopping bag.

"Hi, I'm Teddy's dad, Ted."

"Hi, I'm Mary. It's nice to meet you, sir. He often talks about you and his mother."

"Favorably I hope."

"Of course," Mary laughed, "or I wouldn't have mentioned it."

Ted laughed with her and added, "He talks about you and John a lot as well."

Mary heard a car pull up. "Speaking of which, here he comes now."

The orange Mustang pulled up to the curb. John got out with the wine and rolls as Mary headed for the kitchen.

"Hi, you must be Ted's dad. I'm John"

"So I gathered. Here, let me take this wine from you and open it. The others are in the kitchen."

Ted took the bottles to the dining room table. He used the corkscrew on one. The doorbell rang again. Jessie opened the door and passed on through without waiting.

"I'm here," she announced, taking the dish of green bean casserole to the kitchen.

Everyone else was crowded around the island in the kitchen. The spaceport was the topic of the conversation.

Jessica interrupted as she relayed the message. "Jane and Joe said they'll be here with dessert after the buffet group leaves. Joe thinks it'll all work out perfect, since you agreed to do it at the regular dinner hour, Ted."

When his dad walked in with a glass of wine in hand Ted asked, "Would anyone like some wine, coffee, sodas, anything?"

He had arranged the drink options on the island bar along with an ice bucket and cups. They helped themselves as Freda and her son arranged the food in order of heating, coordinating the actual sit down time.

"I have appetizers on the table in the living room everyone. Let's go out there. It'll be nice to actually use my entire house for a change."

"Next Thanksgiving's at my house," Mary announced as they walked through the hallway, meeting Ted's dad, who had gone through the dining area, followed by Jessie, who had filled her wineglass at the table.

"Only if we can all bring something," Jessie added. *"I'm glad Mary's volunteering. I don't have room for everyone at my little place above the shop. It'd be an awfully tight fit,"* she thought. She considered John's place next. Jane showed it to her before he had closing. *"That's too small for all of us for dinner. Joe needs the restaurant open for business; and Jane never entertains. Well, Mary or Ted's place is it."*

Someone spoke, pulling Jessie out of her thoughts and back to reality, a place she had difficulty staying in.

"Will you have your shop open tomorrow on Black Friday?" Ted Senior asked.

"Yes, I try to keep it open as much as possible. You never know when someone will be walking by; can't miss those little sales."

Ted joked with her, "Can't you feel buying vibrations? That way you could just open when you know they're coming?"

Jessie shook her head and chuckled, "You know my gift doesn't work that way." She didn't mind Ted's joking with her. She knew his spirit was pure; he only meant well. After meeting his parents, she felt the same vibration from them.

"Have you been out to the spaceport?" Mary asked Freda, who was sitting next to her.

"No, Teddy promises to take us tomorrow. I understand you and John fly the plane that will take the passengers to the edge of space. I've never been weightless before."

"I haven't myself either. I've been in the centrifuge; but that's it. I'm hoping to get in space one day. For right now, I have to fly everyone there. Do you have a ticket, yet?"

Freda laughed, "No. Ted and Teddy are enough." Then she realized she had said too much.

"You mean they have tickets and you don't?" Mary was appalled to hear of the sexism.

"No, I meant they talk about it all the time. It makes it seem like they'll be going, or even that they've already been," she said and laughed.

Mary laughed along not having a clue that they had been on the WSL, or that it even existed.

Ted came into the living room and announced that the food was on the table. Place cards were at each setting. Mary was impressed with his sense of detail.

They took their seats. Jessie was between Michael and John, across the table from Ted and Mary. Ted's parents were given the honored spots at the ends of the table. The empty place was used for serving dishes and the extra chair was in the living room.

"John, would you say the blessing?" Teddy asked.

He agreed.

Afterward, Ted Senior cut the turkey as they passed the serving dishes around the table, helping themselves. The platter of turkey was passed last.

"Tell us about Ted as a boy. I'm sure we all would love to hear the tale from your perspective," Mary said, curious about the guy she was falling in love with.

Freda answered, always proud to speak of Teddy as a child.

Finally, Ted interrupted her and said, "Dear, maybe we could learn more about Teddy's friends; where they're all from. John, I think I noticed an accent. Where are you from originally?"

"Virginia. I guess you can take a boy out of the country but not the country out of the boy, even after a college education," John said with a blush.

Jessie thought it looked cute. She volunteered that she had grown up in Sante Fe. Her mother was an artist and her dad a Native American.

"Is that Navajo or Hopi?" Freda asked.

"Navajo."

"That explains your gifts. You come by it naturally. I'm half Hopi, myself," Freda volunteered.

"*That explains the dark complexion and such dark hair. Ted and his mom both have nice bone structure*," Mary thought as she side glanced at Ted, not saying anything.

Jessica nodded her head. She had sensed it was the case.

The doorbell rang, announcing the guests with the dessert.

"We'll have to compare notes later. Joe makes a great crust. I can't wait to try his pumpkin pie," Jessie said, excusing herself to answer the door.

The women took care of clearing the dining table while Jane, Joe, and Ted arranged the dessert and dishes on the island.

Joe had prepared three pies: one pumpkin, one minced meat, and one lemon meringue. He served them up according to the individual orders. Ted delivered them to each person at the table as Jane told everyone about who all had been at the restaurant. It had been a very nice gathering.

"Joe, this lemon meringue is wonderful. Nice to have something different to finish this heavy meal," Ted said, taking another bite of the non-traditional bright-yellow pie.

"I like Joe's minced meat personally," Michael said. "He has a way with breads, pastas, and crusts."

Freda commented, "Well, they're all made with flour. Joe, do you sift your flour?"

"Always!"

CHAPTER 34

New Year's Eve, 2011
Alamogordo, New Mexico

"I have truly enjoyed spending Christmas with your family," Mary said to Freda. She hadn't spent Christmas at home with her parents for years. When Ted asked her to come with him, and that his parents had invited her as well, she jumped at the opportunity.

"It was so good to have Teddy home like in the old days. Maybe by next year you'll be engaged," Freda said hopefully.

In the living room, Teddy confided to his dad, "Mary's the one. I can't wait to meet her parents." He walked out to the kitchen to get the glasses and heard the end of the conversation. "Mom, don't rush us," he said, pulling Mary close to him.

Mary blushed. She liked the thought, but knew her first obligation was to the Navy, even if it seemed like she was a civilian. She had served almost eleven years; she needed to get twenty under her belt to make it worth it.

"Well, I'm in the Navy. If I was married and got transferred, Ted would have to ship out with me. How would you feel about that?" Mary asked, looking at Ted and then his mother.

"As long as you come visit so we could see the grandkids, it'll be okay," Freda answered, adding more 'what-ifs' to Mary's scenario and throwing the ball back into Mary's court.

"Okay, you two. Let's live one day at a time," Ted said. He hadn't even thought of having kids. He guessed he'd someday want one at least, but not anytime soon.

"Come on guys, you're going to miss the ball drop in Times Square, even though we still have hours before we'll bring in the New Year," Ted hollered from the living room.

Ted opened the champagne to toast New York's New Year. When they heard the pop, they all gathered around as he poured and handed them their flutes. In unison, they all counted down, "Ten, Nine, Eight, …"

The countdown made Teddy think of waiting for lift-off. He looked at his dad and said, "Remember when?"

Ted nodded and smiled knowingly. He said, "Happy New Year!"

They toasted and the men kissed the loves of their life.

March 3, 2012
Christiansburg, Virginia

Emily Germaine had filled in her absentee ballot for the primary that she'd miss while she was away. She really liked the independent candidate, Charles Smith. Emily had heard him speak at Occupy Wall Street. Too bad she'd have to wait for November to rally him into office.

She placed the envelope in the mailbox and the luggage in the trunk. She was off for spring break. It was early this year. She was a little nervous taking her first long trip on her own; but she couldn't miss the opportunity to visit John in his new home in New Mexico.

After filling up the car at the gas station, she turned onto the interstate and drove three hours to the closest airport. She parked her car in the small long-term parking lot. After double-checking where she had placed her ticket to retrieve the car when she returned the next week, she rolled her luggage up to the check-in counter.

"I have a flight to Las Vegas."

"It's a nice place. I think you'll enjoy it." The attendant labeled the bag and placed it on the conveyer belt, which carried it through the plastic flaps and out of sight.

"I'm catching another flight in Vegas to go to Las Cruces, New Mexico actually. My son lives near there."

"Oh, we don't have flights there."

"Yes, I know. I had to book it with another carrier."

"Here's your ticket. You can board your plane in another hour at Gate Three."

Emily took a seat and waited until the plane arrived. She watched the baggage handlers unload the previous flight's luggage. It didn't seem long before they announced her flight. When the passengers were allowed to board, she took her seat and tightened her seatbelt.

The woman next to her was with her husband. She leaned over to Emily and confided, "I've never flown before. I'm kind of nervous. My husband flew a plane in the Air Force many years ago. He said he was sure I'd be fine."

Emily felt better listening to her ramble on. When the woman came up for air, the plane had already pushed back and was rolling down the tarmac. Emily held her breath until she felt the wheels leave the ground.

"I haven't flown before either."

That comment acted like an open invitation for the woman to continue, since they shared the same anxiety about the flight. To Emily the five hours to Las Vegas seemed to end in no time, since the woman hadn't stopped talking. Her husband had taken the opportunity to sleep, relieved that he didn't have to listen to her.

"Have fun in Vegas," Emily wished, exiting the plane.

She followed the signs to get her luggage. She rechecked her bags for the next leg of the trip, got her ticket, and arrived at the gate just in time. The steward closed the door behind her; she was the last passenger to board.

This flight went back east. No one sat next to her. She rested her eyes until the coffee and snacks came around. The shorter flight lasted an hour and a half. By the time she had eaten the snack, they collected the trash. She used the restroom. When she returned to her seat, the pilot announced their approach. She tightened her seat belt, preparing to land.

John greeted her at the baggage claim with a big hug.

"You made it. I was worried you might get left in Las Vegas."

"If I did, I'd gamble away your inheritance," she joked.

"What inheritance?" John joked back.

"Exactly!" Emily chuckled. "Oh, there it is," she said, pointing to the bag with a green ribbon on the handle.

John pulled her luggage off the belt after double-checking the airline label. "That was pretty savvy for a first-time flier. How did you know to do that?"

"Jackie at work told me. She's flown plenty."

March 6, 2012
Tianjin, China

Claudia, aka Xiang Ping, had been working at the rug factory long enough for them to know that she had designing talents, even though they didn't know of her past. She had been moved back in the room several times. In America, the best get moved to the front. In China, the best were in the back of the room, where they wouldn't be disturbed. Now she sat at the rear of the room with two other designing masters at the factory.

She was honored that they had given her the position. It was better than when she had first arrived. Weaving has been arduous work. No one knew of her designing abilities. She had to prove her skills, and appear to be fully Chinese. After more than ten years in China, it was no longer difficult for her to continue her charade.

She could hardly imagine her old life in New York now. It seemed like it had been in another lifetime, or someone else's life. She occasionally awoke from a nightmare involving her prior life. But those had become less frequent.

Claudia looked up from her work. Several men in business suits had walked into the factory. It was obvious that they weren't from there.

"We're interested in buying rugs for an import business," they explained in Chinese to the head of the shop.

He directed them to follow him. He passed them off on Xiang Ping to handle.

"What exactly are you looking for?" she asked the Chinese-looking men whose Chinese wasn't as fluent as it should have been.

"Do you know English? Can we do business in English, please?"

"You are not from here," Xiang Ping boldly stated, switching languages, keeping her phrasing Chinese and her accent British.

"No. We're American of Chinese ancestry. We operate an import business of Chinese goods in New York City."

"I understand," Xiang Ping said guardedly. "What are you looking for?" She asked, maintaining the British accent as most Chinese would.

"We would like large carpets in very traditional-styled patterns that the U. S. customer would like."

"Come with me." Claudia walked them to an area that was used for American imports. "This is what we make."

They looked at the patterns, never checking the quality of the rug. That spoke volumes. She knew they didn't know much about rugs, or the import business.

"Have you visited any other factories? There are many in Tianjin and Beijing. If you do not see what you like here, you can try one of the others. Each factory weaves different designs."

She bowed, ending the conversation. They bowed in return, confirming her suspicions. It was a very Japanese move on her part, but she knew the men wouldn't notice. She returned to her seat and they left.

Claudia felt uneasy for the rest of the day, sure that they were GUILE's hired guns. They weren't body builders, and they didn't have enough muscle power; but she'd be ready nonetheless. She hadn't stopped practicing her Tai Chi or her Karate, for that matter.

As she walked home that evening, she kept looking over her shoulder. "*I wish they had left me at my table today. Now I'm spooked again. I don't trust those strangers.*"

The men had studied the six photos so long the images were etched in their mind's eye. One was of Claudia, one of Mr. Lei, one of Mrs. Lei and three composites. They were sure the woman had been Claudia. They called Jack.

"We have been to all of the factories, sir. We've seen many workers; but this is the only one that matches the pictures you sent."

"Keep surveillance at a distance until I can get there. I'm pleased with your hard work. I'll go to the factory myself and see. I'll place an order. If it's who we think it is, I'll know. Thank you. Your next installment will be in your account as soon as I finish this call."

"If we can get a picture without her noticing, we'll send it to your phone. We're positive it's who you're looking for."

Jack closed his phone and set it on the desk. He transferred the funds as promised, and booked a non-stop first-class flight to Hong Kong. He placed another call.

"Sorry to disturb you, Mr. Chen. I'll be in your area on business next Thursday. Would you please arrange an appropriate accommodation for me?"

"Yes, that would be no problem, Mr. Jones. Will you need limo service while you're here, or perhaps the use of my private plane?"

"I'll need a plane for a quick flight up to Tianjin to select a new carpet for my office. I'll tell you more about it when I get there. Thank you for your assistance."

"See you next week," Hui Long said, depressing the end call button.

March 8, 2012
Truth or Consequences, New Mexico

Emily made breakfast while John showered. She served it on the mix-matched plates. The royal blue placemats on the bright yellow table made the room look rather festive.

"Mom, this is your vacation. You don't need to cook breakfast for me every morning," John protested and sat down at the table.

"I know. I miss having you around to cook for."

"I don't remember you doing it much after we moved to Gramps'." John put a dollop of jam on his toast and spread it with his knife.

"I didn't. You tended to fend for yourself; and I let you. The divorce and Gramps' health really drained my energy. I wish I had though; so, I am now."

Taking a bite of toast, John chewed before answering. "Thanks, Mom. And thanks for helping me add the final touches to the place. I'm glad you came."

"I don't think these colors would go over in Virginia; but they look really great here. The bright colors of the Southwest look right here," Emily complimented. She took another sip of coffee.

"Now that we're done decorating, I thought you might like to come out to the spaceport and look around."

"I was wondering when you were going to take me. I've been dying to go see it."

They finished breakfast and John washed the dishes while Emily dried.

"You know, John, you really need some different dishes."

"What's wrong with those? They remind me of Gramps."

"That's what I thought when I saw them too." She chuckled at the thought. "They just don't work here. You've got it looking so nice. Maybe when we're out, we can find some that aren't too expensive."

"Okay. But if they aren't really going to look great, then I'll stick with these until I find the right ones. Jessie and I like these. They tell a story and have good vibes in them."

"And when am I going to meet this, Jessie? I've been here five days and go home the day after tomorrow. Have you been afraid to introduce us?"

"No. I wanted to spend most of my time with you. I can see Jessie everyday when you're gone. Last night when she called, she asked if you'd like to come to her store today. Maybe we can all go over to Joe's for dinner tonight. Most of my friends hang out at Joe's. You can meet them all there. Get ready and we'll go to the spaceport. It takes about forty minutes to get out there. I know you'll want to look around."

While Emily took her shower, John packed a lunch basket for their trip. He thought she'd enjoy having lunch in the big open desert. He pulled out a flat sheet and added it to the grocery bag with some plastic silverware and napkins. He heard Emily turn off the hairdryer as he placed the paper plates and cups in the bag.

"*It'll be about ten more minutes before she's ready. It never takes her long to put on makeup*," he thought, placing a call.

"Hi, Jessie; Mom said she'd like to meet you. We're going out to the spaceport and having lunch. We'll stop by your place about three or four. We can all go to dinner after that."

"Sounds good; you know I'll be here."

"Reserve us a table to hold the whole gang, okay? See you later."

March 10, 2012
Hong Kong

His hotel stay in Hong Kong was first-rate, and to Jack's liking. After his sixteen-hour flight, he needed to stretch his legs. He jogged on a treadmill located in an adjacent gym in his suite. "*Hui Long thought of everything*," Jack thought as he increased his speed by the push of a button. After a shower, he ordered room service before calling Hui Long.

"Mr. Chen, I've arrived and am very pleased with the accommodations. I'm waiting on my room service and wanted to call to thank you. I'd like to take the flight to Tianjin early tomorrow morning. Will that be a problem?" Jack asked, watching images on a muted flat-screen TV.

"No problem. Is nine too late?" Hui Long asked.

"No, that would be fine. If I'm able to obtain the rug that I'm hoping to get, I'll tell you all about it when I return. Perhaps we can plan dinner."

"I could have my limousine come for you around eight Saturday evening, if that's fine with you?"

"Eight would be great. I'll leave the location up to you."

There was a knock at the door. Jack said good bye. His dinner had arrived. He ate his meal on the penthouse patio, high above Hong Kong. He could see The Peak in the distance.

After a good night's sleep, Jack had adjusted to China's time and was now ready for his flight to Tianjin. The limo delivered him to Hui Long's jet. He was in the air by nine-thirty. Around eleven, they touched down at Tianjin Airport.

The prearranged limousine took him to his hotel. Even though the hotel had its own restaurant, he inquired of another.

The desk clerk was happy to tell him, "While you're here, you'll want to take a trip to Shipin Jie, which you'd call 'Food Street.' It's made up of a long, covered alleyway and has more than fifty different restaurants. The dishes are very diverse. The food ranges from soups, noodles, rice, and crispy duck. If you're adventuresome, you can find unusual dishes like dog meat, eels, and even snake."

Jack raised his eyebrows at the thought.

"I'm sure you'll find something you like." Noticing Jack's reaction to the previous food list, the clerk told him where to find American food like TGI Fridays.

"I wouldn't be interested in that either. I'll take the trip for lunch as you suggested. I'll have dinner here at the Xiang Wei Zhai."

She commented, "They have very good steamed dumplings. It's one of their specialties."

The clerk had been right; the afternoon was quite an experience. After eating fresh traditional Chinese food, Jack walked on toward the factory. He met his informants along the way.

Claudia had noticed that the two operatives had been watching her place and the factory for days. She had calculated that today Jack would arrive. She slipped out the back door of the factory to check the front corner of the shop each hour.

This time Jack walked up.

Claudia froze.

"We saw her go in this morning. We haven't seen her leave. She usually finishes at six."

Jack glanced at his watch. It was only four. "You wait out here. I'll go in and see if the one I'm looking for does indeed work here."

Neither of the men saw her as she waited for Jack to enter the building.

Jack spoke with the person in charge. He looked at carpets. There was a very modern design that hung waiting to be trimmed.

"This is nice. It looks very original," Jack knew it had to be Claudia's design. It screamed of her work to him.

"Yes, one of our new designers has begun a line of less traditional styles. This is not for American import."

"Can I buy it for myself? I want just one." He continued eyeing the shop. He hadn't seen Claudia or anyone fitting the composite images.

"Is the designer here today?"

"Yes. Every worker comes every day," he said, insulted by the accusation. The manager thought she was using the facilities. He didn't like this pushy American businessman.

As soon as Jack had entered the building, Claudia had quickly made her way down the alley and connecting streets unnoticed. Carefully crossing the street to her home, she saw that none of Jack's men were standing guard. She knew it was not long before they would be there. She grabbed her backpack and quilted jacket, and disappeared.

CHAPTER 35

March 9, 2012
Tianjin, China

Jack arranged for the informants to watch Claudia's residence through the night, but he knew she had already been there and gone. If indeed it was Claudia, she wouldn't return to the factory or her home again. But he had to be sure.

Claudia had boarded the first train for Beijing. She had to distance herself quickly. She was on the run again.

Jack had a poor night's sleep. He knew he had been close and it was eating him up inside. She had slipped through his fingers. After breakfast, he went to the factory and made the purchase. He knew she wouldn't be there.

"Can you tell me which photo best represents the designer? I want to keep it with the authenticity papers on the rug," Jack lied as he signed his name to the credit slip.

"Yes, this one is Xiang Ping. I don't know why she is not here today. She is never ill. She has worked here for two years. Never once has she not come to work." The shop manager didn't think to question why Jack had pictures of her.

"That's a shame. I hope she feels better. I look forward to unpacking my rug when I arrive back in New York."

Jack left. Checking out of the hotel, he caught the private jet back to Hong Kong. He met Hui Long as planned.

"Mr. Chen, I purchased a unique rug in Tianjin. Unfortunately, I was hoping to catch our elusive Claudia also."

Hui Long looked shocked, "What do you mean? She died in the earthquake three years ago."

"I know her a little better than you. I went to school with her. We've lived in the same city for twenty years. She's very smart, shrewd, and slippery. That's why she was one of us. She has proven that she is as wily as a fox and apparently, also has nine lives. Without a body, there was no way to prove her identity. Given the circumstances, we jumped to the conclusion that she hoped we would.

"I had composites made. My guys have been looking for her in all the factories that use designers. I knew she'd return to her love. That's where she almost messed up."

Hui Long worriedly asked, "What are you going to do now? She has never blown the whistle on us. I think she knows better. If she got spooked, she won't surface for a while."

"Don't worry, Hui Long, I'll not report this to the boss. I made the mistake of not letting my men do her in. I was keeping the pleasure for myself."

They finished the meal in silence.

Chen Hui Long thought, *"Once he gets Claudia, he'll come after me next."*

Jack thought, "*Fear. Good. I'll let him live. No reason to lose another GUILE member. He's too valuable.*"

May, 2012
New York

Charles Smith didn't win any primaries. He was an independent candidate and not on any ballot. But he certainly had the eye of the American people and the news media.

"You sound a lot like President Obama did in the last presidential election," the reporter on the morning show commented. "What makes you different?"

"Well, for one, I was never a politician. I'm a simple Social Studies teacher with two sons and a wife, who deserve a better way of life in America, like all the other hardworking Americans, and capable homeless who used to have jobs before our current system of government ran this country into the ground."

"What makes you think that Congress won't get into a deadlock, like it has with Obama's plans for improvement?"

"I think the American people will take care of that issue by removing some of the congressmen who haven't been willing to represent our democracy. *We* are a country of the people, by the people and for the people. And they have forgotten it is not about them. It is about *We the People.*"

August 29, 2012
Space Shuttle

The flight was ready for take-off. Mustafa and Abdul were aboard. More than a year had passed; it was time to relieve Omar and Arai of their post. They were suited up, on board, and in the middle of the countdown.

"We have a problem with the system check; repeat, we show a problem. Gas is leaking out. Shut down," one technical assistant at the monitor said.

"Countdown is on hold until further notice," the head flight coordinator said, "T-minus ten and holding."

"Get back to me with information. We'll need to scrub if we have a fuel leak."

The launch was scrubbed. The shuttle crew and WSL replacements were removed from the pad and brought in.

The problem took days to correct. By then, the weather prohibited a launch.

Two weeks later, they finally lifted off.

Nov 6, 2012
Election Night, Midnight

"All election precincts have closed. It is safe to say that Charles Smith has won the election. He was an unknown to most Americans before Occupy Wall Street. Now, he's won the people's hearts and votes."

"Well, it seems that he certainly has, since he's carried every state but Oklahoma."

"And he lost there by a very slim margin. When the count is fully in and counted, we may find that he actually has carried it as well. Now, let's listen to his acceptance speech."

The camera moved to Charles at the podium with his wife, Janice, and two sons, Chip and Jimmy. They had made a captivating picture of a decent family all through the campaign. As hard as the two major parties had tried, they couldn't dig up any skeletons in the Smith family closet.

GUILE tried and was unsuccessful as well. They even went far enough to start rumors. Every story was debunked by the press.

Dec. 19, 2012
WSL/Houston

"Abdul, can you create the hurricane like we discussed? I've run some models on the computers down here. I've sent you the data," Omar said, glad they were finally going to get somewhere. "*I want to return home. I'm tired of the American way of life and the Houston Texans. They make me sick with their Southern accent, hospitality, and evangelism.*"

"Omar, I've run the scenario over and over, but I can't cook one up out of thin air. We have to have a real tropical depression in order to make it strengthen and widen. You widened the one coming off of the coast of Africa. But it was summer."

Arai took over the console saying, "With all our global warming and the lengthened hurricane season, isn't there anything over Africa that you can use?"

"Arai, Abdul's trying his best. I've been watching him. If he could, he would. He isn't God, you know," Mustafa said.

Then they all laughed. They had been in the United States and speaking English for so long, that they spoke of God like any other America. They had gotten used to not speaking Allah's name aloud. Allah still existed in their heart of hearts, even if he wasn't on their lips.

Mustafa voiced what they all felt, "I can't wait to go home where I can worship again openly and freely."

They all answered that comment in their native tongues with the equivalent of a hardy evangelical 'Amen!'

Arai ended the conversation with, "I'll report that we can't do what they ask for December 21st. The Mayan calendar won't work for their plan. At the best, it'll be March or April next year."

December 25, 2012
Zurich, Switzerland

Claudia checked into a hotel in Zurich, using a very old identity that she had kept in case she ever had to back track. After showering, she lay on the bed, thinking through her past moves and where she would go next.

"*I guess I should thank Jack for showing up. I was just going to let it be. After all, I can never bring back all those lives. I just can't be a part of their overtly hurtful plans in order to remain rich and in control.*"

Placing on her new hooker costume, wig, and stilettos, she grabbed her large leather purse and sunglasses. Once outside on the street, she popped in several pieces of bubble gum. As she walked swaying her hips to and fro, she practiced blowing and popping bubbles, something she hadn't done in years. She laughed and turned the corner.

She went to her safe deposit box without a problem. Glancing at her last false identity passport, she noted it was due to expire in February. "*That should be enough time,*" she thought. She placed it in her bag with a credit card, linked to a central GUILE expense account. "*It'll never even be noticed.*"

They all had used the one account and wrote them off multiple times in each of their countries as business expenses. Lastly, she counted her cash, placing it in the bottom of her purse. She closed and locked the empty box, returning it to its place in the vault.

Nodding her head good bye, she left the bank and went to the hotel. She ate a fine European dinner, something she hadn't had in years. She sipped a glass of champagne and felt lightheaded. She wasn't used to such finery. She turned in early for a good night's rest.

January 1, 2013
French Riviera

"This has been a pleasant vacation, Paul. Thank you so much for inviting me for the holidays," the boss said.

"You never take a break, Philippe. You're so busy making the world go round I felt that you needed it. Your heart isn't what it used to be, you know," Paul Beorg said, sipping his champagne and watching the approaching boat glide across the clear Mediterranean water.

"Well, I did have the pacemaker put in back in 2000. I try to work out, but usually I can't find the time. This European Union will be the death of me yet. The doctor tells me all the French sauces on my meals are not good. But what good is life without enjoying it, hey?"

"Unfortunately, you either have money or time. We try to buy all our time so we can spend all our money," Paul joked.

Andre stepped aboard the yacht to join them after his night of work overseeing the casino.

"Hi, Philippe," Andre said, shaking his hand and kissing his cheek.

"Hi, Paul," he said, greeting him the same way.

"I'm glad you could find the time to drop by before retiring for the day, Andre," Philippe said. "I wanted you to hear the information that I've been sharing with Paul. In time, it will affect your business directly. You'll need to plan for it."

Because there was a new arrival aboard, the steward reappeared.

"Before we start, what host would I be without offering Andre some champagne?" Paul stated.

His steward brought each of them a fresh glass and slipped away again.

"To money," they toasted.

"Sorry, I forget sometimes," Philippe apologized.

"I was telling Paul, and we have already spoken with Juan by satellite link, about their mining companies supplying and minting our new world Euro."

Andre sipped and questioned, "I thought they had that contract already."

"Yes, we did. This is going to be the one for the world, not just Europe," Paul explained as they were brought the brunch entree.

"We're going to start minting what you may call Eartho. The coin doesn't need to have the name minted on it, just the symbols. We're placing an owl on the front side. O. W. L. will stand for One World Lira. The other side will have the denominations in numerals. No words needed. Any language can and will use them."

Andre nodded. He listened to the rest of the plan and how it would affect him in the casino. He asked, "Will they weigh the same as the Euros? If so I won't have to change the machines, like I did the last time."

Philippe relieved Andre's concerns, "Same weight for each denomination. Your machines should do fine. Don't most of your machines use credit cards anyway?"

"Yes, most do. But we still have those old die-hard gamblers. They have to feel the weight of the coin and the winnings. I don't think we can ever break them of that."

By the end of the breakfast, they had addressed the subject of world politics and whether they would be affected by the changes.

Paul voiced his concern, "Will this new president in the States be a bother? The people in the U. S. really seem to have incited the world's people into caring and feeling like they can make a difference. That Occupy Movement was a very contagious virus, not easily controlled."

"We need not control him for now; we have to let the contagion die out. Just like with Obama's Administration, it will die down with time. Have confidence gentlemen; we do rule the world," Philippe assured them with a smile.

CHAPTER 36

January 20, 2013
Capitol Steps

Director Haynes was seated on the platform not far from the Obamas. He watched Charles Smith and his wife take their positions next to the Chief Justice for the swearing in. Haynes invited Jack again, but he turned it down.

"Repeat after me: I, Charles David Smith, do solemnly swear," the Chief Justice began the oath. Janice held the Smith-Family Bible for her husband's auspicious occasion.

Charles repeated, ending the oath of office with, "and defend the Constitution of the United States."

There was a pause.

Charles added the not required phrase, "So help me, God."

A TV reporter said, "The swearing in has successfully been completed, unlike President Obama's that needed to be re-administered a second time the next day, due to the incorrect wording given by the Chief Justice at the time."

February 13, 2013
Brussels, Belgium

Claudia had been the only woman ever admitted to GUILE. Philippe had met her when recruiting Jack Jones in England that year. He had been instantly smitten with her beautiful Asian features, long black hair, and shrewd business sense. They had a two-day-one-night affair, but only after she had accepted the position. She had informed him the next day that she wasn't interested in attachments. Neither was Philippe. They were even on the score of independence and power, and had agreed to keep the whole thing between just them. At meetings, they cordially greeted each other. No one had known of their short-lived tryst.

Claudia slipped into the home of the Belgium Financier shortly after the maid left. She was now waiting for the mastermind of GUILE to arrive.

"Philippe may be seventy-five, and in good shape for someone his age, but he still has congenital heart damage."

Few in GUILE knew that about Philippe. The pacemaker was just a small piece of his health puzzle. Claudia had entered his personal life for only forty hours, but she had learned a lot about the boss during that space of time. She knew something about every member of GUILE. She recalled the details of the past as she waited quietly in the dark living room.

She hadn't slept with every one of the members of GUILE; but she had privately been to all of their homes. There, she had studied them closely. She never invited any of them to visit her private residence. She only entertained them out at the finest restaurants. She had never let anyone get too close to her, not even Jack. Of course, he thought differently. Her only mistake with him was that she had shared a picture of her parents with him.

Claudia heard something. She stood very still. She concentrated on her breathing.

Philippe stepped into the foyer. He locked the door before setting down his briefcase. He switched on the vestibule lamp; a soft light filled the small space.

Claudia knew he had already had his dinner on the way home. His preferred chef worked at his favorite restaurant. She recalled Philippe saying, "Why keep a chef on staff, if you can protect your privacy by eating out?"

Claudia, like Philippe, hadn't hired a chef. Unlike Philippe, she never had a maid either. Her apartment was a sacred secret space.

Philippe walked into the master bedroom to change. He was loosening his tie when she entered the room. He caught her image on the edge of his peripheral vision. He turned quickly. It was too late. Claudia landed a fisted punch to his heart.

He couldn't speak. The pain was excruciating. His dinner threatened to come up. He closed his eyes as his heart continued to spasm.

Claudia watched Philippe die as she talked to him.

"I thought you were going to let me live. But *no*, you had to send Jack in for the kill. It wasn't good enough to have a dead body in the rubble you caused in Yushu. Why do you have to kill so many to get your way?"

Philippe opened his eyes and whispered, "Not me; Jack wanted you dead."

Those were Philippe's last words. His eyes rolled up in his head. Claudia felt for a pulse. There was none.

Claudia checked his position on the floor. His hands were grasping his shirt.

"Perfect; I won't need to stage anything."

She opened her bag. She pulled out plastic gloves and a sixteen-gig flash drive. She had work to do before catching the next plane to New York City.

February 14, 2013
New York City

Ever since the new administration took office, Jack had been selling off a lot of stocks, derivatives, and insurance policies. He felt America's ship was going down. He wanted his monetary holdings to be in gold bullion.

"Soon, I'll turn this into the new One World Lira. At least, that's what Philippe promised me yesterday on the phone," Jack thought, as his driver pulled up to the restaurant for his regular lunch engagement.

Across town, Claudia rode the elevator to Jack's penthouse apartments. She held a large bouquet in front of her face. The fresh flowers smelled and looked fabulous. She knew Jack would be pleased with the red and white arrangement for his foyer table.

The door opened. The doorbell announced her presence as she stepped out of the lift. Chef Jean greeted her, wiping his hands on a towel. He was in the middle of preparing Jack's dinner.

"Thank you. Just place them there. Carry these back as usual," the chef waved his hand and directed, no longer paying attention to the delivery person. The door only partially closed as he returned to the kitchen.

Claudia removed the old arrangement and set the new one in place. She smelled the flowers again, side glancing to make sure the cook was still out of sight, even though the door sat ajar.

She entered Jack's favorite pass-code into the keypad. He used it for all his GUILE operations. The door lock clicked open.

"That was easy, maybe too easy. Is he expecting me?"

Claudia stepped inside and gently closed the door. She set the old flower arrangement on the computer desk. Glancing around, she noted that nothing had changed since she gave him the decorating tips years ago. His Eames chair still sat central in the room. A modern desk, state-of-the-art computer, and monitor had replaced the original one.

She spotted his newly acquired carpet. It filled a large floor space in a corner of the room. She walked over to get a better look.

"Yep, it's my design."

She shook her head thinking of how close he had come. She slipped out of the delivery uniform, revealing a slick ninja-like black outfit.

"*Actually, I'm surprised that you haven't moved, Jack; I'm so glad you're a creature of habit,*" she thought and began to work.

She only had a few hours before Jack got there. After he sent the chef home for the day, she'd finish what she came for.

Valentine's Day 2013
New Mexico

Mary had everything ready. The gang was invited. The table was set. She and John had a special surprise for the ones they loved the best. The spaceport authorities had given them a test-flight schedule. In a few days, their friends would be allowed to be test passengers.

They had already tested the G-force machine. All had gone well. Janie hadn't liked it much, but Mary could tell she didn't want to be left out of the experience, especially when her husband, Joe, was so keen on the idea. Now the go-ahead had come.

The doorbell rang. Mary opened it to find Jessie and John. "Hi, come on in," she greeted. *"I was hoping Ted would get here first. Oh well."*

"Here's the champagne, Mary," John said, handing her a bag holding two cold bottles of Dom Perignon.

"Wow! Thanks John. You even chilled it," Mary said, taking it to the refrigerator so it would stay that way.

Jessica followed her. "Is there anything you want me to do? You look lovely by the way. Your blonde hair looks good down. No wonder Ted's in love with you."

Mary smoothed her sexy little dress shyly. "You look great too. I like your red dress. It's striking with your dark hair. You usually wear pastels. The bold color looks good on you," Mary said honestly.

"Okay, you two, what are you up to?" John accused, joining them.

The doorbell rang again.

Mary welcomed Joe and Jane. "Hi. John and Jessica are in the kitchen."

"Here, we brought you some special chocolate decadence cake for dessert," Joe said proudly.

Mary voiced her concern as she led them into the kitchen, "I'm surprised Ted isn't here yet."

John knew Ted had left the port before he had. "He's probably just running behind. He'll be here soon," he replied, trying to ease Mary's mind.

"Let's get our drink of choice and head to the living room. I have stuffed mushroom caps waiting for us."

"It's a shame that Michael can't celebrate with us," Jessie said.

"He's with the people who love him most, his parents," Jane replied.

Joe added, "Michael's dad's in the hospital again. It doesn't sound like he'll make it this time. Michael might end up moving back with his mom."

Mary commented, "When you're an only child that often happens."

John answered, "And sometimes when you're not," thinking of his mother.

Joe nodded as if considering his familial responsibilities. He was the only one in the gang who had siblings; and he and Jane were the only ones married.

There was a quick rap on the door. Ted walked in apologizing for his lateness. Mary took that as a cue to redirect the topic of conversation to food preparation.

"Would you guys go fire up the grill? Holler when it's ready and I'll give you the steaks. We'll take care of the veggies and salad," she said, looking to Jessie and Jane.

When everyone reconvened at the table, John and Mary announced their surprise. "We're going to be allowed to take all of you with us on the ride of your life," Mary said. John added, "Free of charge."

Amazement was written all over their friends' faces.

"Clear your schedules," Mary added with a big smile, "We're flying in three days."

Everyone talked at once.

"I'll have to close the restaurant," Joe said.

"I'll have to put my New-Age Online Conference on hold," Jessie said.

Ted responded, "Great, I'd love it."

Jane had a worried look on her face.

"Let's toast," Mary said, not noticing Jane's discomfort.

Jane took a small sip and stood as Mary sat down. "I have good news."

Everyone stopped talking and looked her way.

"Joe and I are having our first baby."

Joe's face was blank until her words sunk in. He jumped up and became animated. "Great, cool, wonderful!" He gave her a hug and a kiss.

The gang spent the next hour discussing baby names as they ate. Finally, John and Mary realized that Jane's announcement meant that she wouldn't be going with them.

"I'm sorry you can't come with us," Mary said.

"That's okay," Jane said, "I hate to admit it, but I really didn't want to go anyway." She sheepishly looked around and added, "even if the G machine probably caused me to get pregnant."

Mary wrinkled her brow, tilting her head. "What?"

"That's what I think. I haven't used any birth control in years. My doctor told me I was infertile. The centrifugal force spun my eggs around, and now I'm pregnant."

John joked, "Or one of those aliens from Roswell abducted and impregnated you."

"If that happened, I'd know about it," Jessie added with a laugh.

Ted bused the table as Mary brought out the dessert.

Jessie leaned over to Jane and whispered, "Ted's going to ask Mary to marry him tonight."

Jessie was the only one who had heard her, but for some reason it had gotten quiet. Jane looked at Jessie with raised eyebrows, questioning if she knew it for a fact, or sensed it.

Jessie fingered her crystal in answer.

When they finished dessert, everyone departed to spend time together on Valentine's Day as couples.

When Ted and Mary were left alone, he helped her put the dishes in the dishwasher. As the machine noisily whirled and sloshed the water over the plates, they went to the quiet solitude of the living room.

"I'm really sorry I was late. The traffic was bad."

"This isn't the city. What kind of excuse is that?" Mary said laughingly, even though she thought what he said was lame.

"I had to pick up something my mother wanted me to have. So, when I got off work, I had to run down to Alamogordo and back."

"You couldn't have gotten there and back in the little time you had."

"That's why I said the traffic was *bad.* There wasn't any on the back road. I flew like the White Knight."

"So couldn't you get it some other night?" Mary asked, wondering if Ted was going to forever be a Mama's Boy.

"You'll understand in a minute."

"I'm waiting," Mary said, tapping her Navy watch that she had forgotten to take off. She couldn't believe she had forgotten; it didn't coordinate with her dress.

Ted stood; the special piece of jewelry was in his hand. He knelt beside her.

Now Mary realized what was happening. She quickly said, "Oh my God! Yes, is the answer; but say it anyway."

"Will you spend the rest of your life with me as my wife?"

"Only if you promise to spend yours with me as my husband."

They laughed.

Ted placed his grandmother's ring on her finger.

Mary swelled up with tears. The fit was perfect.

CHAPTER 37

Valentine's Night 2013
New York Time

Claudia placed the flash drive in Jack's machine. She downloaded any file that proved the past projects of GUILE. She found evidence of the current one in the works. She copied it as well.

An hour later, Claudia had what she needed. The monitor blinked off, indicating the complete shutdown of the computer. As she stood, she heard the elevator doorbell ring. Placing the drive on a chain around her neck, she dropped it inside her close-fitting black tee shirt. She moved to the door as quiet as any ninja warrior. In a short while, she heard the elevator swish open again. The doorbell rang, signaling Chef Jean's departure.

When it made its complete descent, Jack returned it to the penthouse floor. While he waited, he smelled the new arrangement. In front of the obvious floral scent, he smelled something else.

"*What's that?*"

In moments, it was gone.

"*Amber and sandalwood? Princess Borghese?! That's Claudia's perfume!*"

Jack cautiously glanced around without moving from his spot. He eyes were wide as he stared at the solid office door. He slipped back into his apartment without making a sound.

"*No doorbell. He must have locked it in place for the night. Smart move, Jack,*" Claudia thought.

Jack removed his nine millimeter Glock from the safe. He searched the house. No one was hiding there, or on the chilly patio. Satisfied he was alone, he quickly changed into comfortable clothes.

Jack arranged his dinner in the dining room with his back to the window, affording him a clear view of the living room. Gun in hand, he unlocked the apartment door. The trap was set for his mouse.

He enjoyed his dinner and sipped the paired wine, while listening to Verdi's Requiem. The gun rested ready on the table.

When Jack finished his meal, he took the dishes to the kitchen sink. He left the bottle of wine on the kitchen counter, deciding to finish it later. He took the gun to his room to wait.

"*What's going on?*" Claudia wondered. "*An hour's passed and Jack hasn't come to the office. He always does.*"

She patiently continued to wait. When another hour passed, Claudia knew that Jack knew she was there.

"*Okay; plan's changed.*"

She slipped out of the office and passed through the foyer. She tested the door handle. It turned.

Jack was sitting in the walk-in closet on his Louis XIV ottoman, listening for sounds. He wished he had shut off the music, but he didn't want to be caught in the open now. He thought he heard the front door quietly open and close.

Claudia slowly entered in a crouched position. No one was in view.

Jack stood with his feet wide. He locked his hands out in front of him, holding the gun steady.

She crept through the dark apartment. She approached each room cautiously. Jack wasn't in the kitchen, living room, or dining room. She entered his guestroom. She checked the bath and the closet. He wasn't hiding there.

Claudia entered the master suite. She saw a clear reflection of the open closet in the floor-to-ceiling window. It would've made a perfect mirror had Jack only left the light on in the walk-in. She tiptoed to the door frame. She could see his silhouette. He was standing ready, gun in hand. She was sure she could still startle him. She backed away.

Jack breathed slowly waiting for her to enter. The music was starting to annoy him. Between it and the plush carpeting, he couldn't hear her footsteps. He was unsure of her location.

Angrily he thought, "*What's taking her so long?*"

Claudia burst into the closet with a somersault.

Jack tried to get a shot off at the tumbling black mass.

Claudia landed at his feet with a well-placed kick. The automatic gun flew from Jack's hands. It landed somewhere under the hanging clothes.

Jack staggered backward, but not enough to miss her second jump and turn of leg.

Claudia delivered a deathblow to his trachea.

Jack made a cough sound as he dropped to the floor, holding his neck.

He gave her one last look of shock.

"That's for making it personal, Jack," Claudia said.

He coughed two times and died.

Claudia stood over his body expressionless, as if considering the life that lay before her. She felt nothing, no emotion for her supposed friend of so many years. She turned and closed the door behind her.

Now familiar with the apartment in the dark, she crossed the living room and checked the fridge for a sample of Chef Jean's cooking. The wait had made her hungry. She found warm Beef Wellington in a container.

"*Good, specialty de jour. I hope heating it in the microwave doesn't toughen it,*" she thought.

She poured a glass of wine from the bottle that sat on the counter. She swirled and sipped. The microwave dinged. She sat at the seldom-used kitchen table and enjoyed her meal, looking out at the lit cityscape minus the World Trade Buildings. The classical music quietly played and soothed her troubled mind.

"Enough for pleasure; I've got work to do."

She placed the dishes in the dishwasher and selected the pot-scrubber setting. Wiping the kitchen surfaces down, she continued through the apartment removing all fingerprints. She found the vacuum that the maid used and sucked up all traces of DNA. She removed the bag and wiped down the machine after placing it back in the entryway closet.

Claudia exited to the foyer and entered the office. She wiped it clean as well. She bundled the old flowers and vacuum bag into a kitchen garbage bag. After getting dressed in the generic uniform that she had arrived in, she took out the trash, leaving the biggest piece of garbage behind. The lobby guard ignored her, thinking that she was just someone's maid service.

February 15, 2013
Oval Office

"Sir, America is a complete mess," the chief advisor said to the President. "We need to convince the people to stand together. The big-four have now folded. They've closed their doors permanently. The people will find out from you in the morning. Here's the speech you'll need to deliver tomorrow."

Charles scratched his head and read: '*It will be a while before all of you will get your money back, but be assured the FDIC will back* <u>*all*</u> *of your insured accounts in time. Give our new government 'of the people, by the people, and for the people' time to get off the ground. We have only been in office for one month.*'

He lifted his head and said, "Not even a month. We didn't cause this mess."

He continued reading. *'We all need to band together. We will come out of this in time. We have some drastic economic ideas to bring this country out of the mess that we are in.'*

"Change this to 'we find ourselves in.'"

He glanced down again. "Don't you think this is too strong?" Charles pointed to the next line.

'All companies giving credit will no longer be allowed to operate. The only loans you can get will be on houses that you can afford, or on fuel-efficient cars made here in America.'

"We don't think so, Sir. I think they'll like the next statement. Continue on and you'll see."

'All current debt on credit cards is wiped clean, if you owed it to the big-four banks, which most of you did in one way or another. Only mortgages and car payments will exist as is. Those will be paid back, in this case, to the FDIC.'

"Those who never used credit cards won't benefit. How many is that? Less than one-percent I'd venture to say," the President answered his own question and read on.

'Nothing can be bought on time, unless a small business will agree to accept ninety-days-good-as-cash. Stores will be allowed to use lay-away plans at no extra charge, but it must be paid off in one year. If it isn't paid off by that time, the product goes back into the store's inventory, and all installments are returned to the customer.'

"That might work," Charles said under his breath, and kept reading.

'There will be further development of this plan. It will be forthcoming. This bill that I have explained to you is ready for vote in the House and Senate.

'Everyone currently on social security, welfare, and all government employees and retirees, including Congressmen, myself, and my staff, will receive the equivalent of one month less income this next year. We will pay out eleven-twelfths of the amount you received before each month. These funds will keep our government in Washington operating. Without a government in charge, there is no money; there is no FDIC; nothing is of value.'

"Boy, these are the hard facts," the President said. "Isn't there anything good we can say?"

"No, not really, Mr. President. That's why you were elected. The people want someone to take this crazy bull by the horns and tame it, Sir. And you're the man to do it," his aide said, giving him the confidence he needed to make the most unpopular speech in the history of America.

Charles put down the script and walked away shaking his head. He knew it was on him to save America. It was a heavy burden that he carried. He had said he was willing to take it on. Now he had to follow through.

February 16, 2013
JFK Airport

"Drive me past ground-zero please on the way to the airport," Claudia directed the taxi driver.

"That isn't exactly on the way, but I can do it as long as you are aware that there will be extra fare involved." He glanced in the mirror and saw her nod. "No problem," he said, pulling away from the hotel.

She walked over to the dedicated monument while the cab waited. "No matter what I do, I can't bring you back; but I will try to make the rest of the bunch pay," she vowed to the souls that died that day.

At the airport, Claudia was boarding a private plane for Dulles Airport. She was required to pass through TSA screening. She stepped into a booth that blew air around her. The force was so strong that her shoulder-length hair flew up over her head. They motioned for her to pass on.

"What's that for?" Claudia asked, smoothing her hair down in place.

"It monitors to see if you've been working around explosives lately, ma'am," the TSA agent said politely.

She hadn't gone through anything like that flying into the States. "*My, how everything has changed since 9/11,*" she thought, taking her seat gratis of GUILE.

The plane taxied as she watched the New York skyline. She wondered if she'd ever see it again. Her time was running out. It wouldn't be much longer before GUILE knew about the boss and Jack.

February 16, 2013
White House Lawn

The President left the portico. He stepped onto the temporary riser to give yet another speech to calm the public's fears about the country and the recession. The cameramen had several large cameras focused on the presidential seal that had just moments before been placed on the front of the podium. The microphones went live.

As the President was stepping up to the podium, a sudden and unexpected tremor caused him to stagger. He bumped into the Press Secretary. She glanced his way and asked, "Mr. President?"

The ground shook again. This time everyone felt it. Large klieg lights came crashing down upon the lawn.

Nearby Secret Service agents went into action. Two ran along side of the President. Grabbing him by each arm, they ushered him first into the hallway. Once there, they realized their mistake. Paintings were falling on the floor. Whipping him around, they headed back out to the center of the lawn.

The President noticed the tourists in the street, running this way and that, yelling and screaming.

"*Have we been attacked? A bomb must've exploded somewhere nearby?*" He knew he'd be told in a few more seconds.

The shaking continued. It seemed to go on forever, even though only twenty seconds had passed. The tremor finally stopped. But that was short lived. It was as if it had paused to gain power. When it came back with a burst of energy, it was twice as strong as before.

The agents ran Charles toward the Air Force One helicopter that was arriving from Andrew's Air Force Base. It practically landed right in front of them. During the first thirty seconds of shaking, the First Lady had been quickly escorted out of the White House to join the President.

They boarded the helicopter. Their belts were secured and the 'go ahead' sign was given to the pilots. Up they lifted above the city. They watched as the Washington Monument collapsed. It had survived the quake in 2011, even though it had never reopened to tourists. Now it was nothing but a pile of rubble.

The First Lady asked with her eyes, not speaking a word, "*Do you know what happened yet?*" She had learned quickly upon Charles being in office that disclosing information was forbidden. She wasn't allowed to know all that he knew. The President made a quick shake of his head.

He leaned and asked the man beside him, "Do we know what that was yet?"

"Yes, Sir, we're quite sure it was an earthquake. We're getting the data as we speak as to its size and which fault-line. We may not be setting down at Camp David. It may not be safe there. We're getting reports from the staff there that objects fell off the shelves. Excuse me, Sir," the agent said. He pushed on his earpiece in order to block out the sound of the helicopter blades. He turned aside.

The First Lady asked with motherly concern, "What about our boys?"

Another agent had that answer. "Ma'am we're landing in an open field up ahead. The boys will meet us there."

With the first tremor, the Secret Service agents who guarded the children at the middle school had jumped into action. They had been driven by limousine to a field outside Langley.

The helicopter set down. As the blades slowed their circular path, two agents jumped out. They were met by the agent escorting the boys from a black sedan.

The boys hadn't become used to the swish of the blades high above their heads. They ducked low as the air passed over their backs and tossed their hair.

The younger boy said excitedly as he buckled his belt, "Hey, Dad, wasn't that scary?"

His mother tugged it tight around his hips. She smoothed his tousled locks out of his eyes. "Did you feel it?"

"Yes, it was great," replied Chip, the older son, as he fastened his belt. His real name was Charles. He had been given the nickname at birth by his grandfather. The newborn had looked so much like his father that his grandfather had called him Chip, for 'chip off the old block.'

Two new agents boarded. They gave a 'thumbs-up' to the pilots. The blades whirled into action, lifting them again. When it reached its charted altitude, it turned and began a flight to a safe location.

"Reports have come in, Sir."

"Yes?"

"We had a 7.2 earthquake. It happened on the Appalachian fault-line below Camp David, Sir. Everyone in the line of succession has been moved out of Washington until we gather more information. We will be moving temporarily to Parris Island, Sir."

"Parris Island?! Isn't that a bit far away?"

"Yes, I understand, Sir. Air Force Two is currently located at Beaufort, South Carolina. We can't get Air Force One off the ground. The tarmac at Andrew's opened a fissure. Take off is impossible at the moment. Repairs have already begun to remedy the problem."

"I see."

"We will be landing at Dulles. We'll be taking a private plane. It's being swept clean. It will be ready upon our arrival."

The second agent added, "You will be briefed fully when we're on the jet, Sir. There will be cameras set up at Parris Island for you to address the country regarding the earthquake, Sir. The teleprompter will have your corrected speech ready for you." He handed the President a copy.

"Okay, carry-on," Charles Smith said. He could see that they were receiving information constantly through the ear monitors, and that his conversation with them interrupted the process.

"Dad, does that mean we won't be in school tomorrow?" The younger son asked with a large smile. Jimmy loved adventure and abhorred being in a traditional classroom. He thrived on practical experiential knowledge. That was his cup of tea.

"Yes, Jimmy, there will be no school for you tomorrow. But it doesn't mean you'll have no homework tonight," Charles Smith answered his son, knowing that Jimmy was trying to get out of all school work. "Your mom has your academic schedule on her at all times. She has a degree in education. We have multiple copies of your textbooks. We can teach you ourselves. You can't get away from education, Son. It's your family and your future."

Jimmy smirked. He shook his head.

His mother patted him on his back. "It's not all that bad, Jimmy".

Dulles Airport

Claudia's private plane landed on one runway as the President's plane took off on another, like ships passing in the night.

Once she debarked, she heard the news of the earthquake. Thinking they'd taken the President to Camp David, she altered her plans and rented a car to drive there.

"*I must see the President. No one else will do.*"

She looked over the map of the Metropolitan area before placing the Prius in drive.

"*I should be there in less than two hours.*"

CHAPTER 38

February 17, 2013
White Knight

Jane watched from the terminal. Ted and John had assured her that all would be fine. Somehow, she felt like it wouldn't. Something didn't feel right to her. She knew Jessie understand feelings like this.

"Jessie doesn't sense it, so everything must be okay. I guess I'm being a worry-wart; must be the hormones."

Mary taxied the plane into position. John, Jessica, Ted, and Joe were in Space Ship One. The White Knight shot down the runway and lifted off.

It wasn't long before Mary asked John, "We've reached altitude to release. Is everyone ready?"

John gave a 'thumbs-up' to everyone aboard his ship. Jessie, Ted, and Joe signaled their readiness.

"We're ready," John said with a smile of anticipation.

Mary released the ship.

John pushed the ignition switch. The thrust was jolting.

Ted thought, *"This seems tame compared to our lift-off."*

Jessie and Joe's faces were pulled back so much that they couldn't speak the only word that was on their minds, "*Whoa!*"

When the thrusters shut down, it was instantly quiet. They were now weightless.

"Okay everyone, you can get up and float around," John said, releasing his belt. He was anxious to feel it himself. He began to move awkwardly around in slow motion.

Ted unbuckled and right away began doing somersaults, showing off his space antics. Ted beamed with delight at the opportunity to do it again.

"Wow, Ted. You adapt like a fish to water. Are you an alien or something?" John asked. He was impressed and envious.

Jessie knew he wasn't an alien. She sensed, *"He's been here before."* Then she argued with herself, *"It isn't because he knows how to move either."*

Ted stopped short when he caught a glimpse out one of the portholes. He brought himself to a floating position in front of another porthole which gave a better view.

The WSL was shooting a laser beam at a storm in the Atlantic.

"What the heck!" Ted yelled as he watched the eye enlarge.

The laser fired again.

Joe had never seen Ted so upset. "What's up?"

"Can I swear all of you fellow-astronauts to secrecy?"

"Of course," Jessie said, anxious to know what was happening.

"I was on a top-secret space station for two years. This isn't my first time in space."

John and Joe wrinkled their brows, not sure whether to believe him or not. They knew he and Mary were jokesters.

Thinking it would make it easier on Ted, Joe confided, "Well, while we're into confessions, I wasn't always a chef. I was a Navy Seal at one point in my life. Like Ted, some things we've done can't be talked about."

"Gee, I don't think I have any confessions like that," Jessie said. "Would you believe I used to be a nun?"

"What?!" John said with a chuckle.

"See, I knew I couldn't fool you." She laughed, but found it a little difficult to do so.

Ted pointed out the window, "See that large craft over there? That was my station. Something isn't right," he said as another laser beam hit the hurricane below.

February 17, 2013
Spaceport, New Mexico

Mary landed the White Knight. She heard John say something like, "Ted thinks there are terrorists..."

"Repeat that Space Ship One."

But there was only static. She lost his transmission.

She pulled the plane into its parking place and shut down all the systems. She climbed out of the cockpit and gave a wave to Jane, who was staring down at her. Mary ran what she thought she heard through her head again and decided to say nothing. She was unsure of John's comment. It hadn't made sense.

She dismissed it thinking, *"He was probably attempting humor."* She walked into the building and chuckled. *"He never has been good at it."*

February 17, 2013
Camp David

"I need to see the President. It's urgent and involves national security," Claudia said to the guard.

"I'm sorry ma'am, but you cannot see the President. You must make an appointment through the appropriate channels," the Marine in uniform answered.

"Whom do I contact? This is urgent and needs immediate attention. It's about an agency that uses terrorists for subversive activity. I won't trust anyone with this information except the President. This organization has contacts in high positions in all the world governments."

"Wait here, ma'am," the Marine ordered. He stepped inside the booth to phone someone inside the Camp who was in charge.

February 17, 2013
WSL

"It looks like you're succeeding even if it's taking multiple firings of the laser. Let the laser cool off and recharge. Try again in three hours," Mustafa told Abdul, "We don't want to overheat it."

Space Ship One

"You were on that?" Jessie asked, watching as they orbited behind it unnoticed.

"Yes, my dad and I worked for a special weather agency. He was the head Meteorologist. I was the Astronautical Engineer."

Joe was trying to gather as much information in order to be of help. He had already set his mind in defense mode. He had sworn to protect America against *all* enemies. According to Ted, it sure seemed as if the people on the station were some of them.

"You worked for NOAA then?" Joe questioned.

"No, but the agency isn't the issue here. The use of that station is," Ted said in frustration. He needed to take action. He wasn't sure how they were going to go about it.

"John, can the thrusters on this ship move us over to board that station?" Ted asked.

"Yes. We were told that they have a contract to, in time, take payloads of supplies and personnel to the space station."

"So, this ship can actually dock with the International Space Station, just like the shuttle did with that station to take us off years ago?"

"Yes, but we haven't done it yet," John said. He was concerned. Ted was asking for him to do something that he hadn't practiced.

Jessica piped in, "Guys, I'm picking up their vibrations. There are two aboard. One is at the controls, using the laser. The other is like a technical assistant of something."

She held her crystal closer to her forehead. It glowed in the sunlight entering the porthole window.

"They mean harm. Someone powerful is controlling them. They're not working alone."

She fainted.

John pushed off. He was the closest to her and the most concerned.

Jessica didn't fall to the floor since she was weightless. Instead, she floated limply until John reached her.

He read her pulse meter. "She's okay," he diagnosed.

Jessie came around as John floated with her in his arms.

Assured that she was alright, Joe volunteered a plan of attack. Ted and Jessica had convinced him that the men on the station were indeed the enemy.

February 17, 2013
Camp David

Claudia was escorted to a building outside the main residence. She remained in the car until an obviously strong Secret Service agent approached her vehicle. He opened the door. She stepped out and was immediately frisked. Satisfied she was clean, he ordered, "Follow me."

Another agent came along Claudia's other side. They walked inside a disorderly room. Objects were on the floor. A chair was on its side.

"Excuse the mess. As you know, we had a very powerful earthquake. We haven't straightened this building yet. Please sit here," he said, as he righted the chair.

The one man remained at the door at-ease, watching and listening. Occasionally, he pressed his ear monitor tight to his ear.

Claudia knew he was being given some instructions. She glanced around the room. She saw a camera in the corner of the ceiling. She was being watched.

"Maybe you get hoaxes every day, but I know of a very serious threat that I found on a computer file. One piece of the plan was the earthquake that just occurred. I fear time is running out," she said, looking directly at the camera this time, and not the man standing near her. She now realized that he was just a muscle man to keep her subdued or in-line until they determined whether she was for real.

"I want to help, or I wouldn't be here. I can think of better things to do with my time. Soon the men, whom I'm going to tell you about, will be after me. Believe me; they can track you all over the world. I have spent the last eleven years of my life getting away from them to no avail.

"I'm not going to divulge what I know to a camera."

The agent by the door spoke into his hand microphone, "Yes, Sir." He nodded to the other agent.

He directed Claudia, "Come with me."

The agents escorted her out the door and across the lawn to the main house. Claudia noticed that it couldn't be seen from any parking lot or perimeter. It was secluded and well guarded by Secret Service agents.

Even so, she wasn't sure she was safe.

February 17, 2013
Parris Island

The President and First Family landed. They were escorted to a special residence that included an office space and small kitchen. It normally was reserved for priority guests of Parris Island. They never expected it to be temporarily used for the President of the United States.

An aide walked into the living space and announced, "The worst is over. There have been a few minor aftershock-tremors, Sir. The cameras have been set up for your original speech. Are you ready, Sir?"

The President nodded and followed the aide to the makeshift studio. Charles stood still while a person blotted his forehead again with foundation.

"Four, Three, Two, …" another man counted. The makeup person snatched the collar protector from around the President's collar and suit.

"I am sorry to report that Washington has yet again experienced an earthquake. We have lost one of our national icons. Many of you may have already seen the Washington Monument fall as I did when we lifted off from the White House lawn. All of our government officials were safely extracted to secure locations. We are in communication with each other even though we are miles apart.

"The earthquake was just an added piece of bad news I had to deliver to you today. As you may already know…"

The President continued with his previously planned speech. When he finished, the local news stations didn't return to normal broadcasting as they usually did. Instead, they used available anchorpersons to talk and debate the speech until the notable political commentators could reach the studios. The President's speech had hit like a bomb.

There seemed to be a silence over the nation. People all over the country turned on their televisions to hear it all explained to them over and over again by the networks. It was a devastating blow similar to 9/11, thankfully without the loss of so many lives.

February 17, 2013
Camp David

"Yes Sir. We have checked out the information regarding this person. We feel that she has given us enough information to believe that she is legitimate in her allegations. She refuses to talk with anyone but you, Mr. President.

"Normally, we would handle this at NSA headquarters, Sir, but quite a few of our staff were injured today in the earthquake. Transporting her to Fort Meade doesn't seem feasible."

"How about Langley?"

"They're deferring to you, Sir. I think your speech has affected their judgment in the matter. They have other issues that they feel are of more importance."

"Okay. Put her on the direct-line phone. I'll speak with her in fifteen minutes."

February 17, 2013
Space Ship One

Ted used the frequency that he and his dad had used to contact the WSL. "Weather Space Station, this is Space Ship One ready to link with a supply order," Ted lied.

Mustafa answered, "Hello, Space Ship One, we did not order any supplies. We brought our supplies with us when we changed commands a few months ago."

Mustafa didn't trust this communication since Arai hadn't said anything about it. Normally, he would've checked it out, but Arai and Omar weren't currently at their post in Houston. They only worked at night in order to further their covert operations.

"Whether you ordered it or not, I have to deliver the supplies. We will be coming," Ted said, and quickly switched off the microphone before Mustafa could protest more.

John turned on the thruster as soon as everyone was buckled into their seats. He counted down from three. They lunged forward, but not with as much force as when Mary had initially let them go.

"I haven't linked before. I haven't practiced such a thing. This might get dicey here," John apologized.

"Don't worry," Joe said, "Just do your best, man." Joe's pupils were large and fixed. He was ready for action.

John decided to pretend that he was playing one of his old video games from childhood, as he used the joystick to maneuver.

"When we link let me enter first," Ted said. "I know the lab space.

John and Joe, you subdue our crazed scientists. I will shut down the laser firing sequence. The hurricane is already reaching a Category One status, which is rare for this time of year. If it isn't encouraged to enlarge again, it might downsize. It's entering the cold winter waters of the Atlantic."

Jessie was shaking with fear. "What if you have problems over there? I can't get this ship back down."

"Don't worry," John assured her. You won't go home alone. Even worst-case-scenario, one of us will make it back."

"That's what I'm afraid of." Jessie worriedly thought, "*Joe needs to get back to be a dad for Jane's baby. Mary will want Ted back for her wedding. I might be able to read vibrations, but I'll never be able to bring this ship back to earth without crashing, especially if John doesn't make it, or if they're all injured.*"

Ted could hear Jessie hyperventilating. "Jessica, breathe deep and slow. Practice your meditative breathing. We can't be worrying about you fainting again. We need to know that you'll be here to communicate with us once we're over there. We need you to operate the door and limb."

That seemed to bring her back from the edge of hysteria. "*They're depending on me; I need to get a grip.*" She breathed in deeply through her nose and out slowly through her mouth.

They were now alongside the WSL.

"Linking arm is engaged," John said.

The collapsible tube extended. It suctioned to the side of the station's exterior opening.

"Keep your suits and helmets on, even after we enter the other side. Use this waist cord to latch onto a cord that should be in the arm. At least there was one in the shuttle connecting limb," Ted directed, familiar with making a transfer from the station to the shuttle.

"Airlock successful. Shall we open our door? Are you ready?" John asked with his hand hovering over the button.

They all took a deep breath.

Joe and Ted said, "Do it!"

John pushed the button. The door opened as they watched.

They unlatched their seatbelts and floated to the opening. Ted paused in the doorway, waiting to see the door to the station open to receive them.

WSL

"What are we going to do?" Abdul worriedly asked.

"Turn off the program. Make everything look normal. I've got the monitor over here on the NOAA satellite image. You set yours on NASA," Mustafa directed.

They felt the suction of the arm. The airlock bell rang. The strange ship had successfully linked.

Mustafa put on his helmet and locked it in place. Abdul reached for his. When he was ready, Mustafa said, “Act cool. The transfer of supplies won’t take that long. We only have so much space. Let me handle it.”

Abdul whispered, “Allah be praised.”

Mustafa repeated the phrase in response.

He pushed the button, opening the passage between the station and the unexpected ship.

CHAPTER 39

February 17, 2013
Camp David

"Mr. President, I'm Claudia Lei. I'm an American citizen who wants to be of aid to my country."

"Thank you, Claudia. Did you vote with the rest of America to be a part of our new dedication to a democracy of the people, by the people, and for the people?"

"Unfortunately, Sir, I wasn't living in America at the time of the election. I was on the run from an organization that works within the one-percent that you talked about during your campaign," Claudia said, getting down to business.

"I see."

"This organization controls the global governments. It has woven a web that reaches through, and within, all of our federal government as well. That's why, Mr. President, I couldn't trust anyone but you. You weren't a politician. You didn't hang with politicians or lobbyists. You came from the people.

"Some of your agents are unknowingly working for them in ways that they'll never understand," Claudia divulged.

Charles wanted to get to the particulars. "So, you said you know of an imminent plan."

"Yes, I read a file that spoke of the two earthquakes that have occurred in the Washington Appalachian Mountains' fault-lines. They were caused by this organization. Two of the members have mining companies in other countries. They know how to use detonation to create mines, and destruction if needed.

"I survived an earthquake in China in 2010 that was meant to kill me.

I only slipped through their fingers at the time because they thought I was dead."

"What are they trying to do?" Charles asked.

"They control banking through the world. They have made trillions of dollars on financial modules that they have put into place in this country and others. Your Occupy Wall Street touched on some of their schemes. They have many.

"The main leader and one of the members have been taken out of operation. I can testify that they are dead. But that won't stop the rest of their current scheme from happening.

"Do you know of an agency within the federal government that was started during the Truman Administration to monitor the fallout from atomic testing of bombs in New Mexico? It's called the American Weather Agency."

"Not as of yet; I'm learning about our different agencies, it would seem, on a need-to-know basis," Charles Smith said, glancing at his chief aide, who was listening in on an extension.

The aide spoke up. "Yes, we do know of the agency. It only deals with the weather. That doesn't really concern us right now. The economy of this nation is our priority at the moment. The too-big-to-fail banks have folded."

Surprised by the additional voice, Claudia raised her brows. She narrowed her eyes to slits, considering the lack of privacy.

"Who else is listening to this conversation, Mr. President? I thought it was just between you and me. I thought I could trust you."

"You can trust me. We, three, are the only ones on this line. Unfortunately, once you're the President of the United States there are no longer any private conversations, not even with my wife, Ms. Lei," Charles said, regretting the new lack of privacy himself.

"Do you trust your aide, Sir?" Claudia asked.

"Explicitly! He saved my life during Desert Storm."

"Okay, Sir. I'll continue. Understand one thing; as soon as these men get a hold of me, I'm dead. I've known this for some time. I can't continue to stand back and let them operate the way they have for the past century."

February 17, 2013
WSL

The door opened. Ted worked his way over to the station. He stood aside as the others made their way across. While they did, he looked over the monitors on the computers. Nothing looked strange.

Once everyone was in the station, Mustafa pushed the button to close the door. It slid shut before anyone spoke. Mustafa removed his helmet as soon as the air pressure returned to normal. The helmet made him feel claustrophobic. As he removed it, John recognized him from his years at VT.

"Hi, Mustafa. Wow, I never thought I'd see another Hokie in space," John said with a smile through his face shield.

Mustafa's expression changed. He didn't expect to be identified. "Well, you never know where a Hokie bird will fly off to," Mustafa joked back, trying to remain calm and act normal. "So where are the supplies?" He asked, throwing the ball back in John's court.

Ted interrupted, "Are you the meteorologist or the engineer? I guess if you know John, you're the engineer."

"The engineer; he's the weatherman up here," Mustafa said, pointing to Abdul.

"I noticed there's a little hurricane brewing down there. Kind of early isn't it?" Ted continued to make small talk, directing his attention on Abdul. Sitting down at the console where his dad used to work, Ted asked, "Do you monitor storms on this computer?"

Abdul nodded his head. He looked toward Mustafa for direction.

Joe saw that if they needed, the three of them could overpower the two men of obviously foreign descent. After 9/11 he didn't trust anyone from the Middle East. Jane had tried to convince him to get over it. She had told him he was just being prejudice without cause. But after what Ted had explained earlier about the purpose of the laser, and how it was actually being used incorrectly, he didn't need to know anything more.

"Mustafa, while he talks weather, come help me bring over the supplies," John urged with a motion of his hand. He wanted to separate the men.

"Okay," Mustafa said. *"Anything to get rid of these guys."* He locked on his helmet and advised Abdul to do the same. He pushed the button, opening the door to the airlock tube.

John clipped on his cord. Mustafa didn't; he was in a hurry to get the job done. Joe secured his cord and walked behind Mustafa.

Once they were clearly in the tube, Jessie retracted the limb. It unsteadied them just as they had planned it would.

When the tube pulled loose, Joe grabbed onto Mustafa, who interpreted it as an attack.

"You're one crazy dude, considering you're not attached," Joe thought. He used more force. He didn't want to lose him, just restrain him for transport back.

Ted's cord was attached to the console seat. Abdul wasn't attached to anything. The change in cabin pressure pulled him out of the station and into space. Ted saw that Abdul was already out of reach. His thrashing around made his distance too far to rescue. Since it was too late to catch him, Ted closed the door.

Mustafa fought with Joe, who out-powered him in strength. In the scuffle, Joe's cord broke loose and Mustafa's suit ripped.

John pounded hard on the door. Jessica tried reconnecting the limb. It moved toward the station, but it wouldn't connect with suction as it had before. Since she couldn't secure the limb in place, she pulled her strap tight and opened the door.

When John saw it opening, he moved in as soon as he cleared the space. He tried to reach Mustafa's unconscious body. Unfortunately, he and Joe where already out of John's reach. Joe remained calm and just floated still with Mustafa in his grip. He had seen what thrashing would do.

"Good thinking, Jessie. Let's retract the tube and then see what Ted thinks we should do," John said.

Ted saw through the window that Joe and Mustafa were free floating in space. He looked through the module for the space-walking kit. It was placed on board in case the Mechanical Engineer needed to go outside to work on the ship.

Ted attached the power-pack to his back. He opened the door after latching on the much longer tether cord. Ted depressed the gas and moved toward Joe.

"*I don't like this at all. I never even practiced this while Dad and I were up here.*"

Joe remained still. "*Come on, Ted. You can do it. That's it, Buddy.*"

Jessie and John watched from Space Ship One.

Ted reached Joe and pulled him and Mustafa back towards the WSL. Once inside the cabin, Ted closed the door. It took a while for the cabin pressure to readjust to normal.

"Jessie, try reattaching again," John said.

The limb successfully suctioned to the lab this time. Joe hooked Mustafa's cord and his own onto the line. He worked his way back to Space Ship One. Once inside, the door closed.

Joe removed Mustafa's helmet as soon as the pressure returned to normal. He felt for his pulse and found it was weak. "He's alive," Joe pronounced.

"Okay, what about that other guy? Can we get him?" Jessie asked, not wanting to kill anyone.

"I don't think we'll have enough fuel to do much more if we want to get home, Jessie." John knew how desperate they were for fuel.

Ted radioed, "Look guys, I can shut down the computer and stop the laser's use in case it can be controlled by some bad guy from the ground. Whatever they're up to, they weren't using the program that Dad used. How's your college buddy?"

John replied, "He's alive for now." John found it hard to believe that one of his alumni, who survived the massacre, was now the enemy.

Ted replied, "I can't leave this lab unmanned. It might still be able to be controlled from Houston. There's food and water on here for two. So it'll last me twice as long as it would have those guys. Leave me here. When you perform your next test flight, pick me up. I'll try reaching NASA in mission control instead of the weather agency. Maybe they can arrange new replacements for me that aren't terrorists."

It was the best and only option.

Accepting it, John said, "Let's put Mustafa in Ted's seat and get home."

Jessie helped Joe push Mustafa's limp body over to the chair. Joe strapped him in. Afterward, they got into their own seats.

"Okay, we're ready, John," Joe announced.

John double checked all systems. He used minimal side-thrust to widen their distance from the weather station. Once clear, he used his aft thrusters. Shooting forward, they began their descent.

John pushed the steering wheel forward and guided the craft. He was surprised at how easily it handled once they were falling back to earth. It self-righted on occasions, even though John's hands were on the wheel. Watching the latitudinal and longitudinal coordinates closely, John made sure they were going to return to the Spaceport, not some ocean, or foreign country.

"There's the California coastline!" Jessie shouted, anxious to be back on the ground.

John made one minor adjustment, causing them to descend even lower. They glided over the Mojave Desert and Arizona. They could spot notable locations on the ground through the crystal clear, dry atmosphere of New Mexico.

"There's White Sands. I can just make out the Spaceport," Joe said, watching the futuristic-looking terminal come into view. "Some alien would think the Earth rather advanced to have designed an airport like this," Joe replied with pride.

John could hear Mary on the radio. "I see you, John. Where have you been? I've been watching for hours. I sent Jane home. She was driving me crazy, worrying about Joe. Do you think you can land okay? Did you have difficulty? Answer me, John," Mary said worriedly.

John waited for her to stop talking so he could answer. It was obvious to him that she was nervous. She usually communicated by radio in short concise statements. "We did a little. We'll tell you over dinner," John said.

"Joe's isn't open, you know. Jane doesn't cook," Mary joked, relieved to hear John's voice.

"*That's more like her.*" "That's okay. I'm cooking."

"You're on!"

February 18, 2013
Camp David

Claudia was detained until the President could arrive. He wanted to read the files himself on a secure computer as Claudia had suggested. He didn't want it sent over any Internet channels no matter how safe. If all or any of it was true, nothing was safe.

"These accommodations aren't what I'd expect. I'd have thought those politicians had it better here in the mountains away from D.C.," Claudia thought, as she looked around her room for the umpteenth time as she waited.

She finally heard a helicopter land on the lawn. She looked out the window, but it was out of view. Within the next half-hour her door opened. Charles Smith introduced himself.

"Now come with me."

Claudia followed as the President talked and led her to another room. "I have a computer that doesn't link to the Internet and cannot be accessed by anyone per your suggestion. We brought it with us and have gotten it set up. I apologize for the delay in greeting you upon our arrival."

"Thank you, Mr. President."

Claudia stuck the flash drive into the USB port. Finding and pulling up information on the current project, she began explaining the earthquakes, the strengthening of hurricanes, how it had been orchestrated before, and why this time the quake was more intense.

"You referred to this before. While we were traveling here, I had my aide research the history of the AWA. The current director has been in office for some time now, spanning over several administrations. Are you saying you think he's part of this?"

"Maybe not directly, Sir, but I'm sure they're making him believe that if he listens to them, they'll fund his agency and keep it in operation. You know how so many government offices have had cutbacks and closures. He wouldn't want to lose a good job in Washington, and a brownstone in Georgetown would he?"

"You have a point there."

"He has hired the staff operating out of Houston from several of the operatives that were selected over ten years ago for this one project," Claudia disclosed. She brought up the list of operatives from the three Middle East countries. "You can see here the results of the training, and who actually made it through with university degrees as high as a doctorate."

Charles read over the names. He spotted the names of four of the staff with AWA. "Okay, what else?"

"These are working with the two mining members I told you about.

The pilot operatives fly their private jets."

"I see."

"The head of Belgium Finance, Philippe Peeters, was the mastermind during his reign and his father was before him. As I said, he's dead. He had no heirs. He didn't trust anyone enough to sire an offspring to take his place.

"He has been working closely with the European Union. I believe he was the one who thought up the Euro. I was selected years ago to join this organization. I made a terrible mistake to sell my soul to the devil named 'Capitalism'."

"Capitalism isn't really evil," Charles said.

"You're correct, Mr. President. Making a good income and paying back to your community and fellow man isn't evil. But when some worship at the feet of Money, the ultimate demon that drives them all to the point of only looking out for self and personal gain, exclusive of everything else, even family, it is a true adversary. That's the real meaning of the word 'satan' in the Christian Bible. In many world religions, caring about others, and being at peace and harmony with the world, is the goal."

"You're right. Many in America have lost sight of that. But things are different now, and it will be in the future in America. We're now awake. I believe we will return to our original principles, even though it'll take time."

February 18, 2013
Houston

"Hello, Houston Mission Control, this is Ted French on the Weather Space Lab. Come in please."

"Hello, this is Houston. Is there a problem on your station? We haven't been in control of it for several years." Confused by the transmission, the NASA assistant replied, "I thought Ted retired, who is this again?"

"This is Ted French, the Astronautical Engineer. My father was Ted French, Senior. He was the Meteorologist.

"I'm currently on the WSL. I wasn't scheduled to be here. It seems that terrorists have taken over the station. The personnel for AWA on the ground there in Houston, are not, repeat not, to be trusted either."

"How did you get there?"

"I flew up on a test flight from New Mexico. Contact John Germaine or Mary Matthews at the Spaceport. They'll verify my identity and how I got here." Ted watched the hurricane entering colder waters downgrade.

"It's urgent that you notify NASA command. Have them detain and question the personnel at the AWA Houston office," Ted said.

"Sit tight. We'll get back to you."

"I'm not going anywhere," Ted said with a grin.

February 18, 2013
Camp David

"It has come to the White House's attention that AWA in Houston may have terrorists operating the satellite. Please have them detained under presidential orders. We will have them questioned by agents from the CIA, who will arrive shortly," the chief aide said.

"Please forward us the order through the normal channels. We will execute as you request."

The orders were faxed and the original sent via the CIA agents. Marines were sent to the offices of AWA to detain Omar and Arai. When it came time to start their nightshift, they never arrived.

When the CIA agents arrived hours later in Houston for the questioning, original Executive Order in hand, they were apprised of the situation. Joining the two Marines, they searched for the operatives at their residence. They weren't found there either.

The agents traveled to New Mexico to question the suspected terrorist, who had been aboard the WSL. By the time they arrived, Mustafa had succumbed.

CHAPTER 40

April 2013
White House Dinner

All were dressed in tuxedos, gowns, and dress uniforms. They were standing around the State dining table as they waited for the playing of 'Hail to the Chief' to end. The President and First Lady made their way to the table. The cameras were flashing. They paused and then sat down.

Seated on one side of the President were Mary Matthews and her parents. To the other side of the First Lady were Ted French and his parents. Across the table were John and Emily Germaine and Jessica White Cloud, and Joe and Jane Lucca. Earlier in the afternoon, they had been given the Presidential Medal of Freedom for their service. Now was a time of celebration.

Ted French, the elder, said, "Thank you, Mr. President, for extending the invitations tonight to include the family members of your honorees."

"You're welcome, Mr. French. I was informed that you served our country on the Weather Space Lab with your son, Ted, several years ago. I appreciate your efforts in keeping our country safe, even from the weather," Charles said with a smile.

"It was a once in a lifetime opportunity, Sir. I was glad to be of service. I understand through the grapevine that the WSL was decommissioned from U. S. service."

"Yes, we have finally downscaled some of our older agencies, like AWA, in order to help bring the economy around."

"Will it be converted to a floating way-station and used by the Spaceport for customers who want a long stay in space?" Ted asked about the rest of the rumor he had heard.

"The owners of Spaceport were willing to buy the satellite and take it off our hands. I'm glad it can be of practical use."

The champagne had been served to all while they had chatted. The President stood and toasted, "To the young Americans, who so valiantly saved the East Coast from disaster this past February. You're a marvelous example of what the ninety-nine percent can do for the world and our country 'of the people, by the people, and for the people.'"

John and Emily toasted with Jessica.

"I don't usually drink," Emily admitted to Jessica, "but it's not every day you can sit at a White House dinner and be using the State china and crystal, either." She gulped some of the bubbly liquid, as Jessie and John laughed.

"Jessie and I thought this would be a good time to tell you that she has agreed to become my wife," John announced, looking handsome in his Army uniform.

Emily put down the fluted glass. She hugged her future daughter-in-law. "I know you'll be good for my son. Anyone who can make him happy can't be all bad."

"Thank you," Jessie replied and sipped her wine.

After passing her glass to Joe, Jane said, "I'm glad we got to see you again, Mrs. Germaine. Maybe you can move out to New Mexico after the wedding. You know you'll want to be near your grandchild, once you get one." Jane rubbed her now protruding stomach, thinking of her own baby.

Emily answered, "I don't want to rush them. When that time comes, I'll cross the bridge merrily. Who knows, maybe I'll be able to retire and make it an easy transition, if these two don't rush it."

Mary's father was talking with the First Lady about her projects and causes, while Mary talked with her mom about the wedding plans that she and Ted had been making. "No, I don't have my dress picked out, yet. I was thinking maybe I could shop with you while we're here."

An attractive woman, who had also received the Medal of Freedom that afternoon, leaned over. "I don't mean to be rude, but I've designed one-of-a-kind gowns in the past; maybe I can be of service to you."

Mary and Margaret Matthews looked at each other. Mary asked, "I'm sure that'll be far too expensive for me on my Navy salary. Where's your shop? I'd like to visit it just the same."

"Currently, I go to the customer," Claudia, alias Sarah Roberts, replied.

Margaret rolled her eyes at Mary, thinking it to be far too expensive. To confirm the thought she asked, "Did you do the First Lady's gown tonight? It's beautiful."

"Yes, I did her dress and mine. Here's my card," Sarah said, handing Margaret the business card that the protection agency had given her.

Sarah had several surgeries more before the protection agency would be through with her. Her strawberry blonde hair was cut in a striking style for the event. It complimented her lavender chiffon gown. The colored contacts and fat suit gave her a different silhouette from the Asian-looking Claudia Lei. She almost hadn't recognized her own self in the mirror when she took her last glance before the agent escorted to the dinner.

"Thank you, I'll give you a call tomorrow," Mary said. She placed the card in her dress-blues jacket. *"I'll be nice to wear a dress for my own wedding,"* she thought.

June 2013
Annapolis

Mary's dress was delivered to her a perfect fit. She didn't know how a designer could take measurements one time and have such success, but she was thrilled with the outcome.

Sarah Roberts wasn't that good of a seamstress; no one is. It just so happened, Claudia was Mary's size. Therefore, she fitted the dress to herself, knowing it would work on the wedding day.

Sarah received an invitation that she had to decline. She had facial bandages that couldn't come off. The government agency didn't want her seen again until they were finished. Five more surgeries were scheduled.

"What a perfect day for the wedding, dear," Mary's dad said, as he escorted her out the door of the house.

The Chesapeake Bay was glistening. The Columbian blue sky was dotted with small puffy clouds.

When they turned the corner of the house, the signal was given. Both mothers were seated. The music began at the sight of the bride and the guests stood. Mary saw Ted standing near the minister with his dad standing in as best man. Michael Matthews escorted his daughter down the aisle of white chairs leading to the lawn's edge.

Jessie and John were behind Margaret Matthews and Joe and Jane were behind Freda French. The other seats were filled with extended family and friends. They all watched as Mary took her position at the end of the aisle.

The Blue Angels roared overhead toward the ocean as they practiced for the graduation at the Academy. *"Perfect! A free flyover since it's the Sunday of June week,"* Mary thought. She beamed with pride.

EPILOGUE

2014

The Smith Administration had found it difficult getting America back on track. The federal government defaulted again. Social Security and Welfare checks weren't received for months. There was no Medicare or Medicaid available. Government pensions for retirees ceased as well.

The designer, Sarah Roberts, had no clients and no government-subsidized income, or protection for that matter. The Frenchs, Matthews, and Emily Germaine had no income. Luckily, they had no mortgages or debt. John, Ted, and Mary's incomes had been cut. They no longer could afford their mortgages. Jessie, Joe, and Jane had to close their businesses since no one could shop, buy, or afford to eat out. They had to foreclose and move in with their parents.

Working adult children all over the country were moving into parents' mortgage-free homes. The reduced incomes had to feed families of five or six. One after one, the smaller banks closed because of all the new foreclosures.

The NPR broadcasted:

> Federal Reserve goes bankrupt while World Leaders meet in Malta.
>
> It has been decided that the world economy can't hold with the United States in such dire straits. There will be one world currency. New World Banks will be opening for the citizens to trade in all money and receive the new One World Lire. Old money will be worthless in 2015.

Online News:

> Congress unanimously voted approval of the United States of America using the One-World Lire as its only currency. President Smith signed the bill and amendment into law along with all other leaders around world. All citizens will be issued the transition OWL credit card and given electronic credit as they turn in their outdated currency and coins. By 2015, the OWL will be minted for those who prefer to handle coins instead of electronically recorded currency.

"Yes, all CIA records of GUILE have been expunged from the computer files. All agents working on the case have been reassigned to other cases," the new boss, Chen Hui Long reported.

"Good. Paul and I are glad that the world leaders have agreed to use our mines for the metals for the new OWLs," Juan Perez confided. He glanced at Paul, who was nodding his head.

Andre complimented, "Even though we know Claudia took out Philippe and Jack, it's nice to know that our plans and hard work haven't gone to waste."

"You'll be glad to know that weeds are sprouting from the unmarked grave of Sarah Roberts, aka Claudia Lei, and from around the unused Spaceport terminal," Chen Hui Long reported, glad that he had finally buried a body that belonged to her.

With that statement, Sarah startled from another nightmare involving her prior self and the future of the world.

Discover Other Titles
Written by Joanne F. Lyons

Non-Fiction
Healing After Divorce, It's About Time
Healing After Divorce, Facilitator's Guide

Fiction
The Tower Apartments Series
The Tower Apartments: Andrew's Fury
The Tower Apartments: Drug Cartel

The Aging with Grace Series
Aging with Grace: The Formative Years
Aging with Grace: Growing Up in the Shadow of Camelot

Beguiled: The Tribulation Conspiracy

The Seventh Trilogy
The Seventh Time Portal
The Seventh Gate
The Seventh Gatekeeper

AFTERWORDS

This was originally written in 2011. The incidents of weird weather phenomena have continued. Hurricane Sandy, huge destructive tornadoes in many areas, not just tornado alley, and blizzards with accumulations of three feet and more have increased. Some blame it on global-warming, others say it is the End Times, and some say there's no such thing as either of these, while the polar caps continue to melt.

Many events in this book were historically correct. They were used to make this work of fiction seem fully real. I always feel that life can be as exciting as fictional tales, if told correctly. I hope that you have found that my historical research and the portrayal of real events in our recent history captured the time and solicited your emotions as you read it and remembered.

Of course, there is no organization like GUILE to beguile us all, but sometimes it would seem that someone is controlling the rest of our lives and not doing it for our benefit, but for their own gain. The saying was "I got mine, now go get yours." Today, it seems the one-percent are saying, "I got mine and I'm coming after yours too."

The 2012 election had not occurred at the time of the writing of this novel. Charles Smith was so fictional that no candidate could ever be like him. I never was a protestor. I didn't participate in any Occupy protest at Wall Street or any other city, but I am part of the ninety-nine percent. Many during this Great Recession, which I personally call Great Depression II, have lost homes, jobs, income, and a decent way of life. They have struggled since 2008 to survive, some from cars and shelters, finally gaining employment again that won't even pay for rent, food, and clothing. I can only hope and pray that these still too-big-to-fail institutions don't bring us all down with them, causing America, and in turn the world, to be in another Dark Ages. Gee, would we name it in history books Dark Ages II?

ABOUT THE AUTHOR

Joanne F. Lyons grew up in a Maryland suburb outside of Washington, D.C. After a career in education, involving teaching and guidance counseling in high schools, she retired. She currently lives in South Florida with her husband and writes fiction books for her and her reader's enjoyment. Her first published works of non-fiction are used as a ministry to help those recovering from a painful divorce. You can find more information at www.HealingAfterDivorce.com

Made in the USA
Middletown, DE
29 October 2023

41433915R00170